NASHVILLE GOLD

Dekker Malone

Copyright © 2001 Dekker Malone

All Rights Reserved

ISBN 1-931391-38-6

Published 2001

Published by
Dekker Malone Publishing
P.O. Box 93534
Lubbock, Texas 79493-3534
USA

© 2001 Dekker Malone
All rights reserved.

No part of this publication may be reproduced, stored in a retrieval system, or transmitted in any form or by any means, electronic, mechanical, recording or otherwise, without prior written permission of the author.

Manufactured in the United States of America

The characters and events in this book are fictitious. Any similarity to real persons, living or dead, is coincidental and not intended by the author.

Booklocker.com, Inc.
2001

NASHVILLE GOLD

Dekker Malone

Then it was time to dedicate this book and I thought of my wife,
as I should have ...
Thank you for your patience in guiding me from my world of lyric
to your world of prose, and for your encouragement,
and belief, and for sharing my dreams.
I will always love you.

For Rosanna

TO HEAR THE MUSIC CONTAINED IN THIS BOOK,

VISIT THE AUTHOR'S WEB SITE.

www.dekkermalone.com

Special thanks to the "staff"
who tediously and tirelessly tried to find all the goofs
I so cleverly hid within the manuscript.

PROLOGUE

The painted sign on the wood door was fading and cracked with age. Sure-Star Publishing was located in Nashville, three blocks off Music Row. Payne and Skeeter had tracked it down. It was in a disintegrating red brick building, on the second floor, up a narrow staircase that smelled musty from years of Tennessee humidity.

An obese receptionist sat behind a small desk, intently filing her nails. She looked over her reading glasses at the unlikely pair. They could've passed for brothers, had it not been for the extreme difference in height. Both were blonde, but Skeeter wore his hair short. Joyce smiled from amusement at Skeeter. "May I help you?"

But Payne spoke first. "Yes, ma'am. We're lookin for the man."

"What man would that be?" Looking up, she scowled at him.

"The man who stole my song *When Love Turns Out The Light*. That man." Payne looked over her shoulder, through a glass partition, eyeing a man in a white cowboy hat.

"You have the wrong publishing company. That doesn't ring any bells."

Skeeter took over. "We mailed the demo to *this* publishin company last year. We've been listenin to the song on the radio for a damn month. We've come for money."

"Names?"

"I'm Payne McCarty, and that's Stanley Doeppenschmidt."

"Ma'am." Skeeter tipped his cowboy hat. "I go by Skeeter."

She looked at him and laughed. "My goodness, your name's bigger than you are."

"Yes, ma'am. But it's not as big as your fat ass." After twenty-seven years of *short* jokes, Skeeter had a comeback for most anything.

The big lady was on her way over the desk when Roger Durwood appeared from his office door. He had seen the confrontation from behind his desk, through the wall of glass which separated his large office from the small reception area. The glass hadn't always been there. It was installed after he hired his first receptionist. In his business, he needed to keep an eye on the front door. But the work also demanded complete privacy.

Dressed like he had just walked off the stage at the Grande Ole Opry, Durwood wore a dark green western suit, complete with rhinestones. The white felt hat matched his tie and white boots. "What's the trouble here?"

"Are *you* the one who stole my song?" Payne asked.

"I don't have a clue as to what you're talkin about."

"*When Love Turns Out The Light*, ya know, Rusti King's top ten hit. The one we sent to ya last year. We sent it to ya off your advertisement in the back of one of those country music magazines."

"Joyce, I'll talk to these boys for a few minutes." He spoke with a phony southern drawl. "Have ya made that important phone call yet?"

"No, sir. Right away."

Durwood ushered them into his office, which reeked of cigar smoke, and shut the door. Joyce called the police.

"Now, what can I do for you boys?" Durwood's thin face wrinkled with a contorted smile. He looked at the two intruders blankly, behind dark squinty eyes.

"We came for money." Skeeter slammed his fist on the desk. "He wrote that damn song! We sent it to *you*, and *you* got it cut without botherin to pay him a penny. He wants what's due him."

Durwood walked to the tall metal filing cabinet in the corner of his office, next to the only window. He stalled, slowly peering and shuffling through the files in the drawers, waiting for the boys in blue. "We get a lotta demos in here from those ads. Most of em, we just throw in the trash. Maybe one in two hundred ever gets a song contract. Out of those, maybe one in fifty ever gets cut. If I had anything to do with *When Love Turns Out The Light* or Rusti King, Lord knows I'd remember that." Durwood let out a cynical laugh. "Seen the legs on that girl? She's as hot as her red hair. Too hot for a small-time publisher like me." Durwood took a seat in his worn leather chair. "Sounds like you boys need a good lawyer, if in fact, somebody really did steal your song."

"We're lookin at who stole my song," Payne said. "Don't try and give us no damn Nashville runaround. You're a thief and a liar!"

Timed perfectly with the arrival of the two cops in the front office, Durwood sprang from his chair. "Get the hell outta my office!" He waved his hands in the air for dramatics. Roger Durwood was as slick as a snake oil peddler.

Payne was lanky, but strong. Reaching across the desk, he grabbed Durwood by his white tie and pulled him over the piles of papers, just as the two cops crashed through the office door. Both rushed past Skeeter, tackling Payne.

"Run, Skeeter!" Payne managed to yell before the nightstick was pressed against his throat.

DEKKER MALONE

They didn't call Stanley Doeppenschmidt "Skeeter" for nothing. At just over five-foot tall, he was wiry and quick. The overweight cop that gave chase never had a chance.

CHAPTER ONE

The dimly lit Davidson County Jail stunk worse than a sweaty junior high gymnasium. The stench intensified during the heat of the day when the sweating went from trickle to torrent. It was a place where time rotted slowly and the days were numbered by the passage of sleepless nights.

Hearing the clinking of keys, Payne McCarty opened his eyes. He watched from his bunk as the jailer's hand moved toward his cell door. Closing his eyes, he listened to the lock clank and the squeaking of the old hinges. "Okay, cowboy, your time's up."

Escorted by one of Nashville's finest, he walked in the standard issue white jumpsuit and sneakers down the long hall. The passageway to freedom was lined with bars and nameless faces he would see again in his nightmares.

Standing with the toes of his white sneakers just outside a yellow line painted on the concrete floor, he stared at the window above the counter. A brown box, containing his clothes, boots, western belt, and a straw cowboy hat, was shoved through the opening.

Payne took the box. An envelope was opened and the contents poured onto the countertop. His timepiece, given to him by his grandfather, bounced and spun in a tight circle before coming to rest next to three quarters, two nickels, and four pennies. One unused prophylactic and two guitar picks landed next to the watch, followed by his billfold. It still contained eighty-seven dollars and a Texas driver's license. There were no pictures in the billfold; he never carried pictures. A ballpoint pen, clipped to a small pocket notebook, fell to the counter with the last shake of the envelope. It was all there.

Payne popped the small latch, opening the timepiece, and glanced at the clock on the wall. It was just past noon. He set his watch at 12:35 and wound the gold stem. The ten days in jail had felt like ten years, but it was still 1985 and he was still just twenty-seven years old.

A loud buzzer sounded in his ears, signaling the opening of the solid metal door. Payne was escorted out the portal and directed to a small dressing room. Having exchanged Davidson County's sneakers and jumpsuit for boots and jeans, he looked at himself in the dingy mirror. His bright blue eyes appeared tired and his golden tan had faded. He ran his fingers through his collar length blonde hair before feeling of the ten-day-old beard. The beard could stay, for now. The face, once voted Most Handsome in high school, appeared only distantly familiar in the mirror while he tucked in his wrinkled short-sleeved western shirt.

Putting on a cowboy hat had procedures to follow. Real cowboys always put their hats on from the front, then slid them to the back of their heads. He had learned that from his grandfather.

"Say, could ya point me to the bus station?" Payne spoke with his distinctive Texas drawl.

"What's the matter, cowboy? You don't like Nashville?" The jailer was fat and sweaty. He grinned at Payne, revealing stained crooked teeth.

Payne flashed his perfect smile, but said nothing.

"Take a left out the door. It's downtown. Now, you be sure and come back to see us the next time you're in town. Ya hear?"

Payne tipped his hat to the jailer and walked outside to a spring day in Tennessee. The bright sun caused him to pull his hat down while his sensitive eyes adjusted to the light. It was hot for early May. Heat was already rising from the sidewalk. Payne stretched and inhaled fresh air before traveling the streets of Nashville in search of a Greyhound back to New Braunfels, Texas.

The bus station was cold, causing a shiver to pass through his tall, muscular body. Air conditioning was one of the modern conveniences Payne had never grown to appreciate. He loved the outdoors, preferring the smells of fresh air and rain to comfort. Listening to the garbled public address system announcing the comings and goings, he walked with a long, confident stride toward the ticket window. The station was noisy. Tall ceilings and tile floors equaled bad acoustics, something only a musician would notice.

Payne pulled out his money. The bus ticket took fifty-eight bucks and some change. He had no baggage to check. Skeeter would've already taken everything else back to Texas, he hoped.

Second only to the county jail, the bus station was home to the destitute. Payne had even spotted a used syringe lying on the bathroom floor. Drugs were something he'd never had a use for, if you didn't count his weakness for a cold Budweiser. Armed with a Louis L'Amour paperback to fight the boredom, Payne boarded the bus home.

It was after midnight before the bus reached Texarkana. From there the trip was interrupted in Mt. Pleasant, Sulphur Springs, and Greenville. During the layover in Dallas, Payne counted his money before ordering breakfast. He devoured a plate of greasy bacon and fried eggs while watching people come and go from beneath the brim of his hat. From a distance, people fascinated him, but no one was allowed to get too close to Payne McCarty.

NASHVILLE GOLD

Pulling out his small notebook, he wrote down a few lines of lyrics for a song. He titled it *Late Night Bus*. The music would come later.

>*Riding on a late night bus,*
>*Damn sure a sign that you're out of luck*
>*Passing through those sleepy Texas towns,*
>*A bus shifting gears is the only sound.*
>*Yeah, a bus shifting gears is the only sound.*
>
>*Chorus*
>*Now I'm going back to where my baby stays,*
>*I can hole up there without no pay,*
>*My baby's going love me both night and day*
>*Hard to make a living when baby wants to play.*

Payne didn't have a *baby*. The closest thing to a steady woman in his life was Nova, the vivacious black-haired lead singer in their band. They'd had a brief fling in the beginning, but she'd been with most every cowboy in the Texas Hill Country. She was the only woman he'd ever known who had a standing prescription for penicillin.

Nova loved cowboys who could dance, especially if they had blue eyes. She also loved tequila. The combination was deadly. Nova Pearson looked and sounded great on stage, but her flaws became more apparent the closer you got to the real Nova.

Folding up the notebook, Payne jokingly declared the new song a *hit* and stuck it back in his pocket. It needed more work, but it had served to kill some time.

*

Skeeter was on the racetrack when Payne called the jockey shack from the bus station in New Braunfels. He knew better than to leave a message. If you wanted to talk to a jockey, you went to the track. At least he knew they had both made it home.

Nova answered her phone just after five o'clock and Payne considered his luck might be changing. The chances of catching her at home were usually slim to none.

"Payne!" Nova screamed over the phone. "Thank God you're home!"

"Almost. I'm needin a ride to the house. I'm at the bus station."

"Be there in a jiffy."

Nova pulled into the bus station an hour later without an excuse or an apology. Payne knew better than to ask where she'd been. She lied when the truth suited better. He was proud she had made it at all. After half-an-hour had passed, he figured there was a good chance he had already slipped her mind.

"Poor baby." Nova made a pouty face when Payne slid into the dirty front seat of the black TransAm. It had seen better days. She leaned over and gave him a kiss on the cheek, leaving her excess red lipstick for him to wipe off. "Nice beard. How's my favorite felon?"

"It was a misdemeanor." Payne took a quick glance at her bare shoulders and the tops of her breasts, which were spilling out of the blue tube-top.

"See something you like?" She smiled and seductively ran her tongue over her cherry red lips.

"Hell, after ten days in jail, you're even lookin good." Payne grinned. It was his first smile since Nashville. "Thanks for the ride."

"You'd better be nice," she said, and squealed the slick tires out of the bus station parking lot.

Nova had changed from conservative bank teller attire into tight fitting jeans, tucked into tall blue boots. Her tube-top *almost* matched the boots. Her short black hair blew carelessly with the wind. Payne held his hat as the black T-top Pontiac accelerated into the Hill Country.

Home for Payne was a ranch house that was almost as old as the three enormous oak trees that shaded it. North of New Braunfels, it was off Herblin Road, then a quarter mile west, up a hill on a gravel road. It was also home for Skeeter and Pardner, Payne's aging golden retriever.

Pardner greeted the TransAm with boisterous barking then shook his head, irritated with his own ado. He greeted all cars that way, when he was awake, except Payne's faded red Jeep.

Pardner didn't jump up on people any more. He was too fat. Now, his most annoying habits had been reduced to falling asleep in places he was most likely to be tripped over, and passing gas. Next to Payne's bed was his favorite place to fart, especially on those occasions when Payne was entertaining.

"I told you going to Nashville was a dumb idea." Nova followed Payne to the house. She watched him bend over to pet Pardner. "Payne McCarty, did I ever tell you I just love your ass?"

"Nova, ya love ever body's ass."

"Aren't you going to invite me in? You owe me something for the ride. I could use a cold beer."

"Me too. Wonder if Skeeter left me any?"

"I've got tequila in the car."

NASHVILLE GOLD

Payne shook his head at her and opened the back screen door, stepping into the dirty, dismal kitchen. He put his hat on top of the worn out fridge, safely out of Pardner's reach. Spotting a six-pack of Miller tallboys on the otherwise empty shelves, he handed the first one to Nova. That was Skeeter's beer. Payne's Budweiser always had a way of disappearing first.

Nova pressed the cold can to her forehead and glanced at the inadequate ceiling fan. The small rectangular ranch house had been rented, badly furnished. It had no air conditioning and only a wood burning stove for winter. But to its credit, the house had been built on top of a hill. If there was a breeze anywhere in the Hill Country, it generally rustled their dingy white curtains.

Plopping down on the living room couch, which turned a darker shade of brown every year, Payne propped his boots up on the scarred, cluttered coffee table. He let out a deep sigh and closed his eyes.

Nova picked up Payne's Martin six-string acoustic guitar and hit an "A Major" chord, followed by a "Cm#". She dramatically sang the last verse of his first and only Nashville hit.

If I ever get over the blow, I know my heart will break,
But now I'm just paralyzed ... Wondering why my hands still shake
And I don't know why my eyes won't cry,
God knows they've got the right...
It's amazing how far your heart can fall,
When love turns out the light.

Nova had a great voice, even in the living room without reverb. She put the guitar down and sat across from Payne in an antique rocking chair, which was possessed with an unfixable squeak. He still had his eyes closed. "Payne, you know your ex-wife will just sue you for half, if you ever do get paid for that song."

"How's that?" he spoke, without opening his eyes.

"Well, she *was* the inspiration."

Payne didn't respond. It had been five years, but he still wasn't over it. She had left him with a broken heart, his clothes and guitars, the old Jeep, including the payments, and Pardner. She hadn't even bothered to leave a note. Payne figured she'd already packed all the pencils.

CHAPTER TWO

The Texas Hill Country was nestled between Austin and San Antonio. It was spectacular country. The rocky hills, impregnated with rivers and tall trees, had originally been settled by the Germans. The thick guttural accent of their ancestors was still prevalent, making it easy to distinguish the natives from the transplants.

Nowhere was the beauty more evident than along the stretch of road known as the Devil's Backbone. It was a narrow back road north of New Braunfels, connecting Blanco and San Marcus. In the daylight the view was breathtaking, if you weren't the one driving. It snaked along the tallest hilltops. But negotiating the highway required both hands on the wheel and both eyes on the road. After dark, deer and fog descended, but even those additional hazards weren't as dangerous as the drunks.

Heidi's Roadhaus was near the middle of the dangerous stretch of road, perched atop one of the hills, just inside the Comel County line. Sonny Mayer had built the place in the early sixties and named it after his wife, who never darkened the door. It looked like a red two-story dairy barn with a steep pitched, tin roof. Huge Texas Flags had been painted on both sides of the corrugated roof. The colors had faded over the years, but the flags were still considered landmarks and could be seen for miles in either direction.

Sonny was added to the Devil's Backbone fatality statistics in 1978. A one-car rollover. A small marble monument was placed near the entrance of Heidi's, engraved to read:

SONNY MAYER
Paid his tab in full
April 27, 1978
R.I.P.

Heidi sold the place to Casey Bakker, who had come into money after divorcing an Austin banker. At thirty-nine and holding, Casey was showing some mileage around her eyes. She was tenderhearted, but had a mean streak, and the ability to turn into a bitch at the drop of a hat. She wasn't a natural blonde. But she had her own formula of diluted peroxide, which she applied monthly with an old horse brush to her shoulder length hair. It wasn't the perfect *do*, but it generally passed the neon lighting test behind the dark bar at Heidi's.

In 1981, Casey expanded the barn and added a small restaurant on the east side. It featured mesquite smoked Bar-B-Q. With the addition of gas pumps and a small convenience store on the west a year later, Heidi's Roadhaus had it all, including live country music on Friday and Saturday nights.

The local band, Nova-Scotia, had been playing at Heidi's for two months, packing the place. The honkey-tonk queens lusted after Payne, who played lead guitar and sang background vocals. And the cowboys all had a thing for Nova. She was very entertaining, especially after consuming her nightly dosage of tequila.

Nova could sing anything from Patsy Cline to Janice Joplin, and was fairly easy on the eyes. She delighted in resting her knockers on top of her rhythm guitar or doing a bump-and-grind routine behind the keyboard. She was loud and spontaneous. The band members had long ago stopped trying to guess what stunt Nova would pull next.

Skeeter played the drums beneath his pink jockey cap. His lucky number "8" appeared on each side, just above his ears. Ricky Hartman stoically played bass guitar without moving anything but his fingers. He was even taller than Payne, but skinny, with long thin brown hair and lazy hazel eyes.

With Payne's return from Nashville, the band was tight. Friday night at Heidi's Roadhaus, beneath the small row of red and green lights, their music was raising the tall dance hall roof. Drinks were flowing. The dance floor was packed in front of the small raised stage, and Casey was once again delighted.

After their first set, she caught up with Payne. He was leaning against the bar, nursing a Budweiser. "Put that on my tab," she ordered, before hugging his neck. "Sounds like you and Nashville had some problems getting along."

"Yep. Had more hell than a man on the wrong train."

Casey smiled at Payne's ability to say more, with fewer words, than anyone she had ever met. "Glad you're back, I've got news that might cheer you up."

"Do I look like I need cheerin up?"

"Maybe, or it could be the beard. I liked you better without it. You don't need to be hiding that handsome face of yours." Casey ran her hand over his beard then gave it a yank.

"Damn, girl. Take it easy."

"Your boss was in last night. He told me to tell you that you're fired, again." She hesitated before grinning at him. "He also told me to tell you to get your ass back to work on Monday. Said he was ready to start work on the Kraft house."

"Nice to know Jerry still appreciates me." He returned her smile and raised his bottle to her.

Casey leaned in close to Payne. "I was in Austin Monday. My attorney friend and I had lunch together. I told him about your band."

"It's not my band. It's Nova's."

"Whatever. Anyway, he knows the people producing Willie Nelson's Fourth of July Picnic. It's in Luckenbach this year. He gave me the name and number of the guy doing the bookings for the bands. Thought you might be interested."

"Ya oughta be tellin Nova."

"I didn't do it for Nova." Casey snuggled closer. "I did it for you."

"What's the catch?"

"Can't someone do you a favor without there being a catch?"

"Maybe."

"Do you want his name and number, or not?"

"Yeah, I'll give it to Nova."

"Will you let me shave your beard off?"

"What?" Payne leaned back and squinted at her. "I thought ya said there wasn't a catch."

"No I didn't. Anyway, it's not a catch, it's an invitation." Casey ran her hand over Payne's arm. "I know how to shave a man."

"Sure ya can handle a razor?"

"Honey, I can handle anything you got." Taking his arm, Casey pressed her breasts against him. "Hang around tonight. I'll make it worth your while," she whispered, and kissed him on the cheek.

Payne nodded and tipped his hat. "Yes, ma'am. Where's that number?"

"At the house."

Payne shoved off the bar. "Thanks for the beer."

*

The only thing more exciting than Casey in bed was the way she drove on the Devil's Backbone. She owned a little red Triumph and drove it like she stole it. It was just big enough for their butts and a couple of gallons of gas. By the time Payne was returned to the Roadhaus Saturday evening, his eyes were wide with fear and his ass had nearly eaten a hole in the leather seat from squirming.

Clean-shaven, Payne arrived in time to pick up his guitar for the first set. He waited till the break to give the name and phone number to Nova.

"Where'd you get this?"
"Casey."
"Really? What'd ... never mind, I don't think I want to know."
"Where ya been?" Skeeter asked.
"Out whoring," Nova answered.
"We've gotta chance to play at Willie's picnic. All Nova here's gotta do is convince the bookin agent to book us," Payne playfully hit Skeeter on the shoulder, "speakin of whorin."
"Not a problem." Nova winked at Payne.
"Well, I gotta problem with it." Skeeter said. "I've got races on the Fourth, remember?"
"Call in sick," Payne suggested.
"Man, that's my big money day."
"If we get to play, we'll probably be a breakfast band." Nova bent down and looked under Skeeter's cap. "Work it out. This could be our big break. And wipe your nose." She stood up and glared at Payne. "He's been snorting cocaine again."
"Hell, I ain't his mother."
Nova patted Skeeter on top of his cap before pulling the bill down over his eyes. She stuck the paper in her hip pocket. "Break's over, boys."

CHAPTER THREE

Jerry Boerne made his money the old fashioned way. He stole it.
After moving his parents off their two-section ranch which bordered the Guadeloupe River, Jerry sub-divided the land into five-acre tracts. They never saw a dime before decomposing in a nursing home.

From development and real estate, Jerry branched into the construction business. Payne had worked for Jerry, off and on, for most of five years. He worked as a carpenter, mainly. Jerry Boerne was a high roller who loved racehorses, wild women, and Jim Beam Kentucky Whiskey. He also had a soft spot for his only daughter, who had grown up in Houston with his ex-wife.

The first time Jerry fired Payne was over his daughter, Ragina. It was the summer after she graduated from high school, the summer of Payne's divorce. Ragina had been hired by Jerry to run errands and answer the phone. It wasn't as much a job as it was a scam to funnel tax-free money to her for college tuition.

Payne's dark tan and blonde hair had caught her eye the first day on the job. She had been lusting for weeks before she finally gave him the note with his paycheck.

Jerry had flown to Florida for the weekend to look at a stud horse. Payne had thought better of it at the time. He knew better. But that was before Ragina pulled up at the old ranch house in her daddy's gold Caddy. By Monday, word of the two of them seen out together honky-tonking had already gotten back to Jerry.

"Payne McCarty!" Jerry had yelled. "You're fired! Didn't anybody ever tell ya not to try screwin the boss's daughter?"

"Hell, Jerry, I didn't have to try," Payne answered safely from the roof.

Ragina's summer job of 1980 was terminated. She was sent back to Houston on Tuesday. Payne had been re-hired on Wednesday.

*

Jerry had a new stud horse just in time for the 1985 Texas Race season. He had summoned Skeeter late Sunday morning to the track for a time trial. The horse's name was Dial Sammy. Jerry had found him during a "fishing trip" in Old Mexico. After personally clocking the black stallion at just over sixty seconds in six furlongs, Jerry had bought him on the spot for twenty-five thousand U.S. dollars.

Payne drove Skeeter to the track in New Braunfels after lunch. The low clouds were clearing, but early morning fog had left the day dripping in humidity. With the exception of the few people Jerry had gathered at the track, the Comel County Fair Grounds were deserted. The Jeep traveled to the business side of the track. That's what Skeeter called the *backside*. They passed row after row of long, narrow white horse barns until they spotted Jerry.

The smell of freshly mucked stalls lingered in the thick air. Walking toward the barn Payne carefully stepped around the piles of round green horse apples, but Skeeter seemed to take pleasure in kicking them out of his way. "Damn, Skeeter, it's no wonder ever thing ya own smells like horseshit."

"Occupational hazard."

"Well, well, as I live and breathe." Jerry had already broken a sweat beneath his wide brimmed straw cowboy hat by just pacing in the heat. "How was the Nashville pokey?"

"Hot," Payne answered, and shook Jerry's hand. "Casey said ya fired me again."

"Yeah." Jerry grinned. "How many times is that?"

"Four."

"Start framin up the Kraft house in the mornin. That lady's been callin me ever other day. She's drivin me crazy." Jerry slapped Skeeter on the back and abruptly changed subjects. "This may be the fastest damn horse you've ever seen. He's half thoroughbred and half quarter horse." Payne hadn't seen his boss this excited about anything since he screwed the Simmons out of their river front property.

Jerry reminded Payne of Popeye, without the forearms and pipe. He was small in stature and his smile only went to one side of his mouth. His deep-set blue eyes had a tendency to roll up to the top of his head when he got excited. The first time Payne saw his eyes disappear, he thought the man was having a seizure. And Payne could always tell when he was lying. His eyelashes blinked like a yellow caution light.

"Skeeter, you and Payne listen up." Jerry's eyes were beginning to roll up. "This horse ain't nobody else's business. I know what he can do, but I don't want nobody else knowin nothin about him. Skeeter, we're gonna run him at 6 furlongs and don't let him get his tongue over the bit. You keep him around

1:25. And as far as you're concerned, that's as fast as this ol horse will ever go." Jerry's eyelashes were fluttering. "You boys help me out here and come Memorial Day, we'll all have a chance at some serious money."

Skeeter, dressed in his white racing silks and riding boots, sat atop Dial Sammy while Payne led them to the track, stopping at the six-furlong post. Payne waved his hat over his head to signal Jerry, causing the horse to rare up on his hind legs. "Easy, buddy," Skeeter cautioned, trying to calm the horse. "He's a little spooky."

"Sorry."

In the bleachers, on the other side of the track, Jerry leaned forward against the railing, anxiously holding a stopwatch in his hand. A small, carefully selected audience looked on when Jerry waved back with his hat. Payne dropped his arm to start the race.

Skeeter slapped the black horse on the ass with a riding crop and loose dirt flew from beneath the pounding hooves.

The horse had two speeds. On and off. Fighting to slow him down, Skeeter crossed the reins over Dial Sammy's neck in a *dead wrap* as they flew around the turn. Racing down the home stretch, Skeeter struggled to break the horse's thundering gait by discretely yanking the reigns back before crossing the finish line. Jerry clicked off the stopwatch. Outwardly disgusted, he marked the time at 1:29.

"Shit, Jerry," Skeeter yelled to him, as he galloped the snorting horse back by the stands. "Ya took a screwin on this one. Did ya pay that twenty-five thousand in dollars or pesos?" The small group erupted with laughter, with the exception of Red Phillips, the bookie. He had seen Skeeter dead wrap the horse around the turn.

Payne followed Skeeter into the jockey shack after the time trial. The place was as trashy as the centerfolds hanging on the dirty walls. The smell of spilled beer and a nasty crapper permeated the stale air of the small locker room. It was a suiting palace for the miniature band of pirates. With the possible exception of Skeeter, there wasn't a jockey in the Hill Country worth hanging. They were all known to lie, cheat, and steal. Especially on race day.

Studying Miss May's centerfold, Payne waited while Skeeter changed clothes by his locker. They had been friends since high school, when Payne stepped in to help Skeeter survive a fight in the school parking lot. In the beginning, it had been their love for music that had bonded the improbable pair. The bond no longer needed melody.

Skeeter had been Payne's best man the day he'd married Sylvia. But there hadn't been a straight face in the church when Skeeter escorted the towering maid of honor down the aisle. He had also been there for Payne the day Sylvia left him broken hearted.

Payne turned his attention back to Miss May when Skeeter leaned into his metal locker for a snort of nose candy. It was one of his few bad habits. The cocaine had begun as an easy way to keep his weight down. Skeeter tried to ride at 115 pounds. He had an ongoing battle with the scale, especially considering the number of calories he consumed drinking Miller tallboys. Skeeter wasn't alone. All the jockeys were cokeheads. Red saw to that with his endless supply of the white powder.

Nobody liked Red, but Payne politely tipped his hat to him when he entered the jockey shack. "Excuse us a minute," Red demanded. Payne thankfully left the smelly locker room. Red and Skeeter exchanged a small brown bottle of cocaine and a hundred-dollar bill. "That as fast as that horse will run?"

Sticking the small bottle in his jeans' pocket, Skeeter avoided eye contact. "That was about all of it."

"Ya know better than to shit me."

Skeeter stared up at him. "I said that was about it." Red whirled around and stormed out of the shack, almost running over Payne.

"Have a nice day," Payne muttered.

CHAPTER FOUR

After a hard day's work at the Kraft's house on Monday, Payne was looking forward to a cold Budweiser and a nice quiet evening. The oversized tires on his Jeep kicked up a trail of caliche dust as he turned up the hill for home. Skidding to a stop, he watched as Skeeter and Hartman unloaded the last of the band equipment from their pickups, until the trailing cloud of dust caught up to the Jeep and engulfed the group. Payne covered his eyes until the dust cloud settled. Brushing his hair back, he crawled out of the Jeep. Still hot and sweaty, he wore only a pair of faded cut-offs and tattered tennis shoes. Grabbing his once white T-shirt out of the Jeep, he looked questioningly at Nova. "What's goin on?"

Nova was ecstatic with news. "The booking agent from Austin is coming to Heidi's this Saturday night to hear us." She was rapidly slipping over the edge of excitement into melodramatics.

"Is that why ya moved the equipment outta Heidi's?"

"He wants to hear original material. Thirty-to-forty minutes worth. I told him that wasn't a problem."

"Liar, liar, pants on fire." Payne shook his head at her.

"Look, you've written enough songs for the whole Fourth of July Picnic. We just need to pick some out and do them. Okay?"

"We're gonna learn ten songs in a week?"

"Eight. We already do two of yours."

"Do I get royalties?" Payne asked on his way to the house. He stopped just long enough to ruffle the fur on Pardner's big head.

"You get the same deal here that you got in Nashville. A screwing." Nova cackled and followed him into the kitchen. "Come on, Payne. We can do this. We've got to do it. It's our big chance."

Payne grabbed a beer, without offering one to Nova, and sat at the ugly green kitchen table. The chrome plating on the legs of the table and chairs had cracked and were in the slow process of peeling, leaving the exposed metal to rust in the humid air. Gray duct-tape, used to cover the splits in the rotting green vinyl chair seats, stuck to his sweaty legs. He adjusted his position trying to find the small comfort zone. "Mind if I take a shower first?"

"Can I wash your back?" Nova teased, while helping herself to a beer.
"Beers are a buck a piece."
"Put it on my tab."
"Ya don't have a tab. Ya never paid the last one."
"What's wrong? I thought you'd be excited."
"I'm tired. It happens when ya work hard for a livin. I think I musta got outta shape while I was in jail."
"Well, your shape looks good to me. We'll get everything set up in the living room while you clean up. Where're your songs?"
"Just stay outta those. I'll look through em in a few minutes." Payne tossed the rest of his beer down and kicked off his dirty tennis shoes. He carefully peeled his legs from the chair before standing. "Excuse me," he said, brushing past Nova in the small kitchen. He grabbed another beer.
"Doesn't it ever cool off in this house?" Nova asked.
"January." Payne opened his second beer and took another long drink. "I've got two new songs we could do. They just need a little work."
"I've heard that before. Anything finished?"
"Hell, no. I didn't realize I was on a schedule."
"Nothing?"
"I've got some old stuff in there somewhere. Keep your shirt on."
"I'm planning on it, unless it gets any hotter in here." Nova grinned at him and teasingly started to unbutton her sleeveless red blouse. "Unless you prefer I just get naked."
"Take it off!" Skeeter yelled from the living room.
"I wouldn't want Hartman to get excited." Nova stuck her head in the doorway and winked at her bass player. He blushed.
"It'd take more than that to get Hartman excited," Payne said under his breath and disappeared through the door that led from the kitchen to the bathroom.
"I heard that!" Nova yelled after him.

*

Payne returned to the living room and plopped down on the couch dressed in a fresh pair of cut-offs. His hair was still wet, combed straight back. Pulling his worn briefcase out from under the coffee table, he placed it on his lap without opening it. "Most of this stuff is slow."
"We're not just a dance band anymore," Nova said, making a grab for the briefcase. Payne waved her off. "We're artists," she continued, "performing original tunes."

"Right. I forgot. Do I get to sing?"

"Sing what?"

"I don't know. Most of these songs were written from a male point of view."

"Payne, believe me, I know more about the male point of view than you do." Nova was getting testy. "Let's hear some, then we'll decide who sings what."

Most of the old songs were written about Sylvia. Payne was reluctant to share the memories he had set to music. The songs had been written as a self-prescribed therapy.

There were *love* songs, *love gone wrong* songs, and *love gone* songs. After two hours of culling and cussing, eight new songs were selected. And one by one, the band charted the new songs. In addition to *When Love Turns Out The Light* and Payne's other song, *Crankin Up The Country* that the band already knew, Payne would sing his favorite *Texas Rivera*. He had insisted. It was almost midnight when the songs were finally placed in order of performance.

1. *Rainy Lovin Night*
2. *Misloved Again*
3. *Talk About You*
4. *Walk Away* (a duet with Payne and Nova)
5. *Texas Rivera*
6. *Stalemate*
7. *Cowboy Rules*
8. *One More Warning*
9. *When Love Turns Out The Light*
10. *Crankin Up The Country*

The songs were practiced all week, late into the night under the oppressive heat of the ranch house. Friday night, Nova-Scotia debuted the new material in front of the regulars at Heidi's. Nova announced the diversion from their usual dance music before beginning their second set. The dancing stopped and the rowdy crowd cooperated, settling around their tables. The band played their ten-song set with just a couple of bobbles.

Payne's rendition of *Texas Rivera* had brought the house down with cheers. It was a funny song about a Colorado cowboy who got more than sunburned on the beaches of Corpus Christi. The duet *Walk Away* with Payne and Nova, was a real tearjerker, especially for Payne. Nova handled the rest of his songs with her usual flare. The set lasted thirty-five minutes, according to

Casey. She had helpfully timed it on the *Time For A Coors* clock behind the bar. "Almost," Nova said. "We'll practice again tomorrow afternoon."
"Boo!" Skeeter retorted from behind his drums.

CHAPTER FIVE

Ragina Boerne's marriage ended abruptly the day she walked unannounced into her husband's private law office. There, with his bare butt to the door, Jeffery had one of the firm's attractive legal clerks bent over his mahogany desk. At first, he had been too busy giving *free legal aid* to notice his wife standing in the doorway. But Ragina managed to get their attention when she sailed an expensive vase over his head, shattering it against the wall. "I hope you enjoyed yourself," Ragina screamed at him, "because that was one expensive piece-of-ass."

The marriage of the thirty-year-old Houston attorney and his twenty-two-year-old bride had lasted almost six months. Billing for *time spent* was negotiated out of court for a sum of five hundred thousand dollars, and a new red Porsche. Most of the money had been invested in oil. It was one of the few things increasing in value faster than her daddy's Hill Country real estate.

Since her divorce, Ragina religiously traveled once a month from Houston to see her daddy. Jerry Boerne owned a sprawling estate on Lake Dunlap, south of New Braunfels. Done in Spanish decor, the stucco compound stood in the middle of a large grove of ancient oak trees. Built less than fifty yards from the lake, the house had been furnished with collectibles and trinkets from his frequent trips to Old Mexico. Jerry also had a three-slip boat dock that held his bass boat, a ski boat, and a pontoon boat used for entertaining on the lake. A large in-ground pool, surrounded by lush green carpet grass, separated the house from the dock. Isolated at the end of a two-mile long private road, Jerry's lack of neighbors was due to his lack of common sense. The lake had a tendency to flood.

Ragina arrived just before noon on Saturday for her monthly parental checkup. The thought Jerry might not be home never crossed her mind. Things just had a way of working out in her little world of spontaneity. Everything except men.

Ragina's face wasn't particularly striking, but she did have big blue German eyes from her daddy's side of the family. Her light blonde hair fell to the middle of her back. It had been that color since high school. Tall and lean,

NASHVILLE GOLD

Ragina had never been particularly busty, until after her divorce. Money might not buy love, but it could sure buy a pair of *Double D's*.

The results of Ragina's overly successful surgery had changed more than her bust line. Her personality had transformed from quiet and moody to flirtatious and brazen. Now, everything she owned had been purchased with her new cleavage as the focal point. If it wasn't low cut or tight fitting, she didn't wear it.

Jerry wasn't pleased with the *new* Ragina. And he thought twice before suggesting that she accompany him to Heidi's Roadhaus that Saturday night. But Jerry had promised Casey. He had a thing for the tavern owner and her personal invitation clouded his better judgement.

Casey however, had made a lot of phones calls. Wanting a full house for Saturday night when Nova-Scotia played for the booking agent, she had called every regular customer in the triangle from San Marcus to New Braunfels to Blanco. There was never a cover charge at Heidi's Roadhaus, but Casey had stopped short of offering drink specials as an added enticement. The love of money was one of the few things she shared in common with Jerry Boerne.

Promising himself to keep a close eye on Payne, Jerry rode in his daughter's Porsche to Heidi's. Ragina was excited. A bit too excited for Jerry. She raced the German sports car over the Devil's Backbone like she was driving the Autobahn. Jerry's nerves were frayed by the time he bolted out of the small car and slammed the door. "Damn, baby. Do you drive like this all the time?"

"Like what?"

Jerry shook his head at his daughter and kicked a tire. "I need a drink."

*

Jimmy Earl Thompson looked more like a bookie than a booking agent. His black leather vest screened most of his beer belly. A thin beard covered his pitted face, and the cowboy hat topped his receding hairline. After the first set of dance music, Nova approached his table. "Jimmy Earl?"

"That's me."

"Nova took his business card and gazed into his eyes. "God, you've got the prettiest blue eyes I've ever seen."

Jimmy Earl gave her a wary smile. "Darlin, your bullshittin is almost as good as your singin. Ya said over the phone that y'all played original music. Was that more of your bullshit? I haven't heard any."

"The next set is just for you." Nova winked and leaned over his table. "No bullshit."

Jimmy Earl never had a chance. His eyes traveled to the third open snap on her western blouse where he caught just a glimpse of her red lace bra. "Girl, you've got my undivided attention."

Nova walked on stage with her back to the dance floor. She took two shots of tequila before strapping on her guitar, carefully arranging her boobs over the top. She exposed enough to show, but never enough to spill. Nova nodded at Skeeter. Raising his drumsticks above his pink jockey hat, he clicked off the set. The enthusiastic crowd cheered them on while Jimmy Earl listened to thirty-five minutes of flawless original music.

Casey sat with Jerry and Ragina at a table near the bar. "Payne wrote every one of those songs."

"I didn't realize he was that talented," Ragina commented, with her eyes glued to Payne.

"Honey," Casey smiled curtly at Ragina, "that isn't the only thing he's talented at."

"You're telling me," she replied, with her own smug smile.

"Shit! Not both of ya!" Jerry took another shot of Jim Beam. "Hell, we oughta just give him the damn mail to deliver while he's out about town."

Rolling down an old back road
Truckin just a fast as we can go.
We've got the windows down, letting it blow,
Crankin up the country on the radio.

Crankin up the country on the radio,
Sure beats today's Rock N Roll,
There ain't no gimmicks, just a lot of soul,
Crankin up the country on the radio.

Chorus
Sing about life, sing about love,
You won't catch Willie wearing no glove
Give me a fiddle, rosin up the bow.
There ain't no boy to the George I know.

Sing about heartache, sing about pain.
Blue eyes ain't crying in no Purple Rain.
When Jerry Lee starts talking on the telephone,
You can bet there's going be a lot a shaking going on.

Crankin up the Country on the radio ...

Payne's song *Crankin Up The Country* sold Jimmy Earl. At the close of the set, Nova rushed to his table and scooted her chair next to his. "What'd you think?"

"That last song hooked me. Damn, it's got Boy George, Prince's *Purple Rain* and Michael Jackson's silly little glove in there. Willie's gonna flip over that." He put his arm around her. "The only song that wasn't original was *When Love Turns Out The Light*. Why'd y'all throw that in?"

"Payne McCarty wrote every damn song we sang." Nova even surprised herself with the flash of anger.

"Nashville stole it from him. He wrote that song five years ago about his ex-wife."

"No shit? Wrote that whole set?"

"Every damn song," Nova leaned in. "Do we get the gig?"

"It'll be early in the day, but you're booked."

Nova jumped from her chair and screamed, "Yea-ha!" knocking off Jimmy Earl's hat. She kissed the bald spot on the top of his forehead and hugged his neck. Nova picked up his hat and put it on her head. She sat in his lap and wiggled her butt on his thigh. "Cowboy, you want to see what else I got?"

The good news spread quickly. Payne, Skeeter, and Hartman raised their beer bottles and toasted as they watched Nova working her magic on Jimmy Earl.

"Congratulations, boys!" Casey joined the circle and bent down to kiss Skeeter's cheek. Hartman politely shook her hand. Grinning at Payne, she held her arms out. "Well, come here." Payne graciously accepted her affectionate congratulations, but it was turning into more than he was comfortable with in public. Jerry cleared his throat.

"Remember me?" Ragina asked. Jerry stood next to her like an attack dog, glaring at Payne.

"Ragina?" Stepping back to look her over, Payne shook his head. "Mercy girl, you've sure filled out some." Payne's eyes lingered at her deep cleavage. "I swear I don't remember ... "

Ragina interrupted him. "You guys were great! Payne, I can't believe you wrote all those songs."

"Those and fifty more just as good," Skeeter added. Hartman stood motionless, staring at Ragina's marvels of modern medicine and grinning like a sixth grader who had just shot his first squirrel.

"Drinks are on the house," Casey told them. "Anything y'all want. Just make sure I get another set of music tonight."

*

The crowd had thinned by the 2 a.m. *last call*. And Nova was last seen leaving with a bottle of tequila in one hand and Jimmy Earl in the other. Payne, Skeeter, and Hartman sat at the table with Casey and the Boernes. After several awkward glances between Jerry and Casey; Ragina and Payne; Payne and Casey; and finally Jerry and Payne; Casey announced, "Well, I think its time to choose up and go home."

"Ain't no damn choosin to it." Jerry was still glaring at Payne. "Ragina, you need to drive your daddy home."

It was starting to sprinkle when Skeeter left the bar alone. He inhaled the scent of the approaching rain on his way to his pickup and pulled out his keys. The blow hit the back of his head like a bolt of lighting, sending him sprawling to the graveled parking lot. "This is a little reminder from Red. He wants ya to remember who ya work for, asshole." That was the last thing Skeeter heard before the kick to his head. Mercifully, Skeeter's lights went out before the vicious beating continued.

Payne left the bar with Casey. But his attention was focused on the approaching storm. The wind was whipping through the tall trees, rustling the leaves. Lightening streaked across the sky, followed by a deafening clap of thunder. "Skeeter!" Casey screamed over the storm.

Payne saw him with the next flash of lightening. He lay unconscious by his truck. Blood oozed from his nose and mouth. "Skeeter!" Payne tried to rouse him, but he lay motionless. Rolling him over, Payne spotted the keys to Skeeter's truck. "Let's take his pickup!"

Casey raced the Backbone beneath flashes of lightening while Payne held Skeeter like a mother would. They traveled south toward the hospital in New Braunfels, into the teeth of the vicious storm. The lights of New Braunfels appeared as they topped the last hill. Then the bottom fell out of the heavy clouds. Torrential sheets of rain blasted the windshield, rendering the wipers useless. Casey was forced to slow the truck to an agonizing crawl as the headlights searched for the road.

Skeeter's eyes were still closed and his breathing had become labored by the time they slid to a stop beneath the hospital's awning. Casey watched Payne carry Skeeter through the Emergency Room door before driving on to park the truck. She was soaked when she returned. Payne was pacing by the glass doors. "They took him inside."

Casey was shivering. "He'll be fine."

Payne didn't answer her. Instead, he went to the nurse's station. "Ma'am. Could ya give us a blanket? She's freezin in those wet clothes."

"Sure." The aging nurse looked at Casey. "It must be really pouring outside."

Nodding, Casey took the blanket. "Yeah." She wrapped it around herself before taking her seat next to Payne in one of the orange plastic chairs to wait for word.

It was after 4 a.m. when the doctor appeared. "He's still unconscious but stable. His vital signs are strong, but we've moved him to ICU. He obviously took quite a beating. The internal bleeding appears to have stopped. His blood pressure has stabilized. As for the head trauma, the next twenty-four hours will be the most critical. You can check with the charge nurse in the morning."

CHAPTER SIX

Casey woke up in Payne's bed to the sound of a pouring rain. It was just after noon on Sunday. A repulsive odor lingered in the thick damp air of the small bedroom. Opening her eyes, she clamped her nose between her finger and thumb and tried not to gag. "What the … " She sat up in bed, looking around the small bedroom. There was nothing hung on the dingy white walls except a tall mirror, mounted above a cluttered dresser. Water stained white curtains flapped gently with the intruding breeze from the storm. She glanced at Payne. He lay sleeping on top of the sheets with his lily-white ass aimed toward her side of the bed. "Payne," she said, shaking him, "Don't point that thing in my direction when you do that."

"What?" Taking in the smell, Payne groaned and buried his face into his pillow. "Damn, Pardner."

"Yeah, right. Just blame it on the dog."

Crawling out of bed, Payne led Pardner through the kitchen and opened the backdoor. "Get your stinky ass outside and take care of business." Pardner looked at the heavy rain then rolled his brown eyes up to look at Payne. "Go on. It's just water." But Pardner didn't move. "Get your ass outta here!" Payne yelled. Pardner moved slowly, entering the rain soaked day.

Payne put on a pot of coffee before returning to the bedroom. "I didn't do that."

"You put him out in the rain?"

"He needed a bath and I need a shower. I've gotta go see about Skeeter. That whole damn deal seems like a bad dream. Wonder how he's doin?"

"Who would have done that to him?" Casey asked, and rolled out of bed. "Skeeter never hurt anybody."

"He's gotta mouth on him. It wouldn't be the first time it got him in trouble," he muttered, on his way to the bathroom.

The water heater, stuck in the corner of the bathroom, roared to life when Payne turned on the hot water faucet. The house hadn't come with a shower, only a tub. The old white cast-iron tub sat on four small claws of iron, elevating it slightly from the wood floor. Payne had added the shower. A clear but water stained shower curtain hung from a makeshift shower rod. The rectangular shaped rods, made out of half-inch cast iron pipe, dangled precariously from the ceiling by small black chains. Casey followed him to the shower. "Can I wash your back?"

"Darlin, ya can wash anything you've gotta mind to."

*

McKenna Memorial Hospital had been built in stages and now appeared like a hand print in the sand. Five separate wings, from the oldest to the newest, connected to a long central hallway in the main building. ICU was at the end of the west wing. A big boned German nurse sat behind the counter, guarding it. Her white nurse's uniform was topped with a small white nurse's cap, attached with hairpins to her graying hair.

Payne leaned across the counter and whispered, "I wanna see how Skeeter's doin."

"Who's Skeeter?" She spoke with a native German accent.

"Stanley Doeppenschmidt."

"Are you family?"

"Hell, yeah, I'm family. How's he doin?"

"He regained consciousness earlier this morning." She glared at Payne. "He's sure got a vulgar mouth."

Payne let out a sigh of relief. "Sounds like he's back to his old self."

"Not quite. We're going to monitor him for another twenty-four hours in ICU. He suffered a severe concussion and internal injuries. If he's still improving, he'll be moved to a private room tomorrow."

"Can we see him?"

The nurse pointed to the sign above the counter. "Visiting hours are 10 a.m., 2 p.m., 6 p.m., and 9 p.m., ten minutes. Maximum of two people per patient."

Payne pulled out his timepiece. It was a quarter till three.

"We filed this incident with the sheriff's office." The nurse looked suspiciously at Payne. "It's required."

"Lot of good that'll do," Casey mumbled. "Payne, come on, I need to get back to Heidi's."

"Drive carefully," the nurse cautioned. "They've issued a flash flood warning. They say this rain is going to get worse. Storm's coming up from the coast."

*

Payne left Casey and Skeeter's army green Chevy truck at Heidi's. After pulling up the canvas top, he added the flimsy doors and wiped as much water as he could from the seat of his Jeep. He cussed himself for leaving the top off as he drove back through the torrential rain. He stopped only once for beer and food before reaching the house. After getting stuck at the house last year for three days during a flood, Payne had learned his lesson. One more day and he and Skeeter would've been fighting Pardner over the dog food.

Pardner followed Payne through the backdoor into the kitchen and shook the rain off onto the dirty tan linoleum floor. Payne made a second trip. Returning with a load of beer, he sat the two cases on the table and raced for the ringing telephone.

"Payne!" Jerry screamed over the phone. "I need help here. The lake's already over the boat dock, risin toward the house."

"Okay, I'm on my way." Payne cussed Jerry under his breath. Lake Dunlap was a stupid place to build a house. It was fed by the Comel River, which was fed by the Guadeloupe River. The dam at Canyon Lake had been built to control flooding on the Guadeloupe River, but that only worked if the rain fell north of the dam. This was the third time in five years he had been called to Jerry's to sandbag.

There were two water crossings on the two-mile stretch of road leading to Jerry's place. Instead of building bridges over the creeks, Jerry had placed a series of four-foot tall concrete culverts across the creek beds, then poured concrete over the tops to form a narrow trestle. The road dropped down from the banks of the creeks, crossed the makeshift bridges, and then sloped back up. That worked fine, most of the time. But water was already running over the concrete when Payne cautiously drove through the two crossings. His wide tires held the road against the current, but he could see the water was rising fast.

Jerry had been busy with his small tractor. The plush green grass in the back yard had been scooped up in his front-end loader and moved to form a dike between the lake and the house. When Payne arrived, Jerry had the tractor stuck in the mud. Payne passed the red Porsche parked in the drive. His Jeep left ruts in the manicured side yard on his way to the tractor. Taking the chain from Jerry, he hooked it to the Jeep. The tractor stubbornly rocked back and forth before the Jeep popped it free from the mud.

Standing in the pouring rain, Payne yelled over the noise of the tractor and storm, "Jerry, we've gotta get the hell outta here! Water's comin up fast on those crossins!"

"Get Ragina and that Porsche outta here," Jerry yelled back. "I'm gonna make another pass or two."

"Forget it Jerry! It ain't worth it!"

"Get her outta here!" Jerry gunned the tractor and took another scoop of his backyard to the makeshift dike.

Payne spotted Ragina throwing her suitcase into the Porsche, but waited for Jerry's return trip for more grass and mud. "Jerry! You've gotta get out!"

Jerry Boerne angrily waved him off. Reluctantly, Payne jogged through the rain toward the Porsche. Ragina lowered the electric window just enough to hear.

"Follow me out! Watch the Jeep! If the water gets over the bottom of my tires, don't follow me through the crossin. Got it?"

"Okay."

"If it's too high, just stay where ya are and I'll come back for ya. We may have to leave the Porsche!" Ragina nodded her head and rolled up the window.

The first water crossing had risen faster than Payne had expected. Water was well over the tires before the Jeep began climbing out the other side. But Ragina had already driven the Porsche onto the bridge. Payne turned the Jeep around. He watched in horror as the current floated the Porsche off the road. Jumping out of the Jeep, Payne ran along the bank screaming at Ragina. "Roll the window down and climb on top! Shit! Ragina! Get outta the damn car!"

Ragina panicked. Water was seeping inside and rising fast. The engine had died and the electric windows had shorted, trapping her. Releasing her seat belt, she climbed out of the small seat and stretched across the car, trying to wedge open the door with her feet and shoulders. It wouldn't budge. In desperation she violently kicked at the window. Nothing worked.

Abruptly the hood went under, dragging the Porsche down into the muddy water. Ragina took a deep breath before the car submerged. She found the door handle and pushed hard. It opened slowly. Swimming free, she fought the current. Her lungs were screaming, on the verge of exploding, when her head topped the water. She gasped for air before the current again drew her under.

Payne had already kicked his boots off and was frantically running along the bank, searching the water. He spotted her head and sprinted further down the creek before diving into the raging water.

Under water, Ragina's head snapped back. Payne had her by the hair when she broke free. Floating with the current, he managed to grab a limb from a willow tree.

Ragina's coughing and sputtering turned into frantic screaming when the air returned to her lungs. She clung desperately to Payne with her arms locked around his neck. She was choking him, screaming hysterically in his ear. The current wrestled with them, trying to pull them away from the tree. "Shut the hell up! Climb over me! Now grab the tree!" Payne yelled instructions at her. His head disappeared under the water as she climbed over him. He held to the tree with every ounce of his strength. Her weight finally eased and his head popped free of the water. She was on the bank. Payne pulled himself from the current and collapsed next to her in the mud. The rain beat on their faces while they lay exhausted. "Come on," Payne insisted and pulled her to her feet. "We've gotta get to the Jeep!"

Stopping just long enough to pick up his boots, Payne rushed her to the Jeep. The flimsy canvas doors closed out the storm. Soaked and muddy, only the sound of their labored breathing could be heard above the rain.

The storm beat against the canvas top and the wipers struggled to keep pace with the rain as Payne approached the next crossing. The heater in the Jeep was on high, but both were shivering. Neither spoke. Ragina closed her eyes and held her breath when the Jeep entered the second crossing. She exhaled only after she felt the Jeep begin to climb to safety. "Thank ya, Jesus!" Payne yelled, at the top of his lungs.

CHAPTER SEVEN

Payne battled the fierce rain during the drive home. Stopping the Jeep, he closely eyed the flood gauge at the bottom of his hill. "No problem," he assured Ragina before driving slowly through the last crossing. Water had begun seeping through the loose fitting doors of the Jeep before it climbed the gravel road to the old ranch house. There would be no more crossings.

Pardner greeted the shivering couple inside the back door with a bark and wagging tail. Payne glared at his dry dog, who appeared to be smiling at his drenched owner. "Ragina, this is Pardner," Payne said, setting his wet boots down.

Ragina embraced Payne. "Thank you. I thought I was going to die."

"Hell, I thought we were both dead. Guess the good Lord still looks after fools and children." Payne broke away from her embrace and pulled off his wet shirt. Draping it over the back of a kitchen chair, he began looking through the pale yellow cabinets.

"That was stupid of me to try that crossing. I just didn't want to lose my car. I'm sorry."

"We made it. That's all that counts."

"Payne, I'm worried about Daddy."

"Hell, Jerry's too ornery to let somethin like a little water ruin his day. He'll be fine. That's a stout house. I helped build it. Anyway, there's no way the water will get to the second floor. He'll be fine." Payne stopped looking through the cabinets long enough to glance at his shivering guest. "We need to get ya outta those wet clothes. I'll find somethin for ya to wear in a minute. The shower's in there. That'll warm ya up."

"Payne, I don't know how to thank you."

"Forget it." Payne was still frantically opening and closing cabinets.

"What are you looking for?"

"There's a bottle of Nova's tequila around here somewhere. I'm gonna have a shot ... or two. Want some?"

"Definitely."

Payne finally found the bottle behind a sack of flour. He remembered hiding it from Nova last week, but that seemed like a lifetime ago. It was nearly full. He took a shot before handing it to Ragina. "Whoa!"

"Do you have salt and lime?"

"Salt."

Payne watched her pour a little salt on her hand. She licked it before taking a shot. "Mercy!" Her body trembled from the burn.

In the bedroom, Payne rummaged through his clothes before deciding to give up his last pair of clean cut-offs for Ragina. Changing into his cleanest dirty pair of jeans, he pulled out a white T-shirt and smiled to himself. Anticipating the view, he returned to the kitchen. "Here ya go."

Ragina held up the thin T-shirt. "This was the best you could come up with?"

He shrugged his shoulders and grinned. "Hey, it's clean."

"Well, I guess beggars can't be choosers."

Payne watched her disappear into the bathroom. He took another shot of tequila before moving to the living room. Turning on the TV, he slumped down on the couch. The flood was all over the news. A wall of water had risen on the Guadeloupe. Everything remotely close to the rivers, from New Braunfels south to Seguin, was being evacuated.

"All done," Ragina announced from the kitchen doorway. "Your turn. I hope I left you some hot water. That felt really good."

Payne left the couch and turned off the TV. He suspected flood news wasn't something Ragina needed to hear. His eyes became riveted to her white T-shirt. "Mercy, girl. I swear I don't remember ... "

"What?"

Ignoring her rhetorical question, Payne pressed by her in the doorway on his way for a shower. "Tequila's on the kitchen table."

Feeling like an inquisitive ten-year-old, Payne examined Ragina's enormous bra, which dangled majestically from the towel rack. He had expected to find some padding. The hot shower felt good, but his mind was troubled. He worried about Jerry, then about Skeeter. His thoughts had returned to Ragina when the lights went out and the shower slowed to a trickle.

With the sun setting, the shadowy ranch house was getting darker by the minute. Payne went to the kitchen for candles. Placing one on the kitchen table, he took another shot of tequila before entering the living room. Ragina was sitting on the couch with her knees tucked beneath her chin. Payne lit the candle on the coffee table and sat next to her. "Better?"

"Much. Payne, thanks again." She laid her hand on his leg. "What happened to the lights?"

"Could be Skeeter didn't pay the bill."
"Seriously?"
"Naw, out here in the country, they come and go. Especially when it storms. I'm gonna have a beer. Want one?"
"Another round of tequila sounds better."
Payne returned with the bottles and salt shaker. "Hear about Skeeter?"
"No, what happened?"
"Got the hell beat outta him last night at Heidi's. He's in ICU." Payne turned up his Budweiser, chugging most of it.
"Is he going to be okay?"
"Think so. I'd sure like to get my hands on whoever did it. It's not like he's big enough to fight back."
"You two have been friends a long time, haven't you?"
"Since high school." He took another big drink. The effect of the alcohol was beginning to settle his nerves.
"Is there a woman in Payne McCarty's life?"
"Nothin regular. Not since my divorce."
"I went through that last year. My ex is an attorney. I caught him with his pants down, giving "dictation" to his secretary. What happened with you?"
"Came home one day and ever thing was gone. No note, no nothin. Just an empty house."
"Why'd she leave?"
"Ran off with her boss. I'd been suspectin, but I just didn't wanna admit it to myself. He was rich and I wasn't."
"Money's not everything."
"Never thought it was."
Ragina poured salt on her hand, licked it, and chased it with another shot, straight from the bottle. "How about Casey?"
"What about her?"
"She mentioned you were talented in other areas, besides your songwriting." Ragina gave him a knowing smile. "I saw the way she congratulated you last night."
"She helped us out, gettin that bookin agent there last night."
"And you did her a favor in return?"
"Hey, we're just friends. Somethin wrong with that?"
"No, just jealous."
"You? Just what would *you* be jealous about?"
"Did you know you were my first lover?" Ragina took his hand.
"Ya sure didn't act like a beginner."
"You never forget your first time."

Payne squirmed on the couch. "Ya hungry?" he asked, jumping to his feet. "Are you trying to change the subject?"
"I need another beer."
Ragina followed Payne into the small kitchen, stepping over Pardner, who was sprawled out on the dirty kitchen floor. She caught him as he closed the refrigerator door and kissed him. But Payne didn't respond. "What's the matter? Afraid my daddy will fire you again?"
"Maybe."
Laying her arms over his broad shoulders, she pressed her breasts against him. "I won't tell." She kissed him. "I promise."
Pulling her to him, Payne returned her kiss, passionately. His hands roamed over her borrowed cut-offs before finding her soft skin beneath the T-shirt. She moaned He slowly pulled it up from both sides. Ragina raised her arms and stepped back to help him pull the T-shirt over her head, but tripped over Pardner. Payne caught her by the arm before she fell. "He's gotta real bad habit of that."

*

Sometime Monday night, the rain stopped. Tuesday morning, Payne, Ragina and Parder strolled down the hill to check the water crossing. Payne looked at the flood gauge and shook his head. He figured it'd be another twenty-four hours before the Jeep would be able to make the crossing.
"Too bad," Ragina said. "Gosh, I guess you're stuck with me another day."
"I was about to say the same thing." Payne took her hand as they walked back up the hill. Pardner saw a rabbit cross the road and took a few steps in its direction, before thinking better of it. Payne did his Elvis impersonation, singing a few lines from *Hound Dog*.
Ragina laughed and pulled his hand back, stopping him in the road. "I can't remember having a better time in my entire life. I'll never forget this. Not ever."
Payne squeezed her hand. "Yeah ya will."

*

The lights and phone began working again late Tuesday afternoon. Up till then, Payne had managed to keep Ragina's mind off Jerry. He had taken great pleasure in showing off his survival skills. "Most impressive," she had bragged, as they shared a much needed bath. He had managed to catch rainwater and had heated it on the gas stove. That had been Monday night, under the soft glow of candles. Payne figured if he was going to be stranded, it didn't get any better than this. Part of him hated to see the lights come back on.

Ragina was distant Tuesday night after watching the news. The footage of uprooted trees and washed away homes was troubling; five fatalities, seven missing, and over a hundred injured. The wall of water, which had descended from the Guadeloupe, had demolished most of the houses on Lake Dunlap. With that bit of news, the party was over.

The phone was still dead at Jerry's place, but Skeeter answered from his room in the hospital Tuesday evening. "Ya still alive?" Payne asked.

"Yeah, and I'm ready to get the hell outta here. You've gotta come get me. Ya wouldn't believe some of the things they've done to me."

"Can't. Water's still too high to cross. Maybe by mornin."

"Well, shit. Hey! Did ya see Jerry's place on the news?"

"No, we just got the power back on awhile ago. Ya know we're always the last back up."

"Who's with ya?"

"Ragina."

"Oh, shit," Skeeter paused, "Jerry's dead."

"What?"

"Heard it from a nurse here at the hospital this mornin. They figure ol Jerry tried to get out in that pontoon boat of his. Heard that wall of water crushed that boat like tin foil. They found him floatin, still wearin his life jacket. Wasn't a damn thing left of his house, either. Not a stick. That wall of water took out ever thing."

"Damn." Payne glanced at Ragina.

"Ya gonna tell her?"

"Look, Skeeter. I'll be there as soon as I can get out, sometime tomorrow."

"Ya better come get my ass outta here. I ... "

Payne hung up the phone.

"How's Skeeter?" Ragina asked.

"Fine. Ready to come home." Payne took her hand. "Skeeter said he heard at the hospital that ... Jerry's dead." It hadn't come out the way he wanted it. He held her in his arms and closed his eyes. But the horrified look on her face was branded in his mind as he listened to her cry. "Babe, I tried to get him to leave with us. I did. I told him it wasn't worth it. That the water was comin. I'm so sorry. I kinda liked Jerry."

"God knows it wasn't your fault." She looked up at him with tears in her eyes. "You barely got me out alive. I've got to call Mother."

CHAPTER EIGHT

Elizabeth Courtney's last name had changed twice since it had been Boerne. The only link remaining to Jerry was Ragina, who she had raised alone. "Liz" called Kelsheimer's Funeral Home from Houston and made the arrangements before flying into San Antonio Wednesday morning. She appropriately rented a black Lincoln and drove the thirty miles to New Braunfels.

Payne made the water crossing just after noon on Wednesday and delivered Ragina to Kelsheimer's. It was one of the older buildings in New Braunfels. The brown brick structure resembled a church, complete with a steeple. Plans were on the drawing table for a new funeral home. One more flood and they'd be able to pay cash.

Dressed in her clothes from Sunday, Ragina held Payne's hand as they approached the tall oak doors. "Will you sing something at Daddy's funeral?"

"I'd be proud to," he promised, opening the door for her.

"My baby!" Liz spotted Ragina from her seat in the lobby and rushed to embrace her daughter.

"Mother, this is Payne McCarty. He's the one I told you about over the phone."

Liz looked Payne over while shaking his hand. But her eyes were filled with suspicion, rather than gratitude. She was tall, a lean woman with short, dark brown hair. Her expensive clothes gave her a sophisticated demeanor. "Payne, I don't know how to thank you. Ragina means everything in the world to me."

"No need," Payne said, holding his hat in his hand. "Ma'am, I worked for Jerry. If there's anything I can do for either of ya, just give me a call. I'm in the book."

"That's it!" Liz backed up and wagged her finger at Payne. "You're the one that caused all that trouble the summer Ragina came to work for Jerry. I knew that name sounded familiar."

"Yes, ma'am."

"Mother, that wasn't Payne's fault."

"Y'all give me a call if ya need anything." Payne turned to escape, then stopped. "Ma'am, when's the funeral?"

"Friday afternoon, at two," Liz snapped at him. Whirling around, she protectively took Ragina's hand.

"Thanks again for everything," Ragina said, before she was led away. She mouthed over her shoulder. *I'll call.*

Payne tipped his hat to the ladies and disappeared through the door.

*

Skeeter didn't bother checking out of McKenna Memorial Hospital. Using Payne to shield him from view, he passed the nurse's station without notice. Skeeter was still "stove-up," as he called it. With the exception of a few cuts and bruises on his face, Payne didn't think he looked too worse for the wear. "Hell, ya don't even look hurt," Payne teased as he removed the canvas doors and top from the Jeep. "I've been worried for nothin." But to Payne, Skeeter and the clear blue skies were both welcome sights.

"Payne, just shut the hell up and get me outta here."

"So, who did this?" Payne asked, as they pulled up to the first red light.

"Didn't see em."

"You're tellin me ya don't have a clue?"

"Didn't say that. I said, I didn't see em. Just leave it alone. I'll live."

"They didn't take anything. Ya still had money on ya."

"Leave it alone."

Payne left New Braunfels and headed for Heidi's to get Skeeter's truck. "Jerry's funeral is Friday, at two," he yelled to Skeeter, over the wind whipping through the open Jeep.

"So. I never liked him anyway," Skeeter yelled back.

"Nobody liked him, but I'm goin. Ragina asked me to sing."

"Sing what?"

"Hell, I don't know."

"Maybe you could come up with a new song. Call it *After Screwing Ever Body He Knew, He Got It In The End.*" Skeeter laughed and grabbed his ribs. "Whoa, it still hurts when I laugh."

Payne resumed his interrogation along the Devil's Backbone. "Ya gonna tell me who did this to ya or not?"

"What the hell difference is it to ya?"

"I'm gonna kick somebody's ass, that's the difference."

"Ya don't need to get mixed up in this. I'll handle it."

Payne pulled the Jeep over to the side of the road. The big tires slid to an abrupt stop in the loose gravel. "Skeeter, how would ya like to walk the rest of the way to Heidi's?" Payne looked his friend square in the eye. "Tell me what-in-the-hell's goin on."

"Ya need to stay outta this."

"Get out."

"I ain't gettin out."

"Tell me or get the hell out. I'm serious."

"If I tell ya, you've gotta promise me ya won't go doin somethin stupid. I don't want ya gettin mixed up with Red."

"Red did it? That son-of-a-bitch!" Payne slammed his hands on the steering wheel.

"No. He just had it done."

"Why? What'd ya do to piss him off?"

"It was a reminder that I work for him. All the jockeys work for him. It's the system. Red runs the races and gives us a split of the juice at the end of the day. Most of the time, ever body just trades it out with him for coke."

"What *juice*? What are ya talkin about?"

"His winnins at the track." Skeeter looked off into the trees. "Red tells us which horses are to win and lose. That's the way he makes all that money. Hell, ya knew it was crooked."

"Yeah, but what'd ya do to get beat up?"

"He probably saw me tryin to slow Jerry's horse in that time trial. Not much gets by him. I magine he figured me and Jerry was tryin to do a deal without him. It was just a reminder he still runs the tracks around the Hill Country. That's it."

Loose gravel flew as Payne accelerated onto the highway. Nothing else was said until they stopped at Heidi's. "How ya gonna handle Red?" Payne asked.

"I've been thinkin on it in the hospital. I was gonna set him up, usin Jerry's horse, but that ain't gonna work since Jerry ain't around to run him. I'm gonna have to come up with another horse. I don't know yet, but I'm workin on it."

"If he had ya mugged over a time trial, what'll he do if he figures ya set him up in a real race?"

"I wasn't plannin on bein around long enough to find out."

"What?"

"I'm thinkin on goin to Kentucky or Florida. I'm sicka this place. I wanna be a real jockey in a real horse race. I'm good enough to ride anywhere. Hell, who knows, I just might make a run for the roses at the Kentucky Derby. Stranger things have happened."

"Get him busted over the coke. That would send his ass away for a long time."

"He's connected. Ya don't wanna mess with those people."

"What if his connections thought Red was messin with em?"

"They'd kill him. They're that serious. They'd kill *us* if it didn't work. I asked ya not to get mixed up in this."

"I can think about it, can't I?"

"Leave it alone. You'll get us both killed if ya start screwin around with the wrong people."

"I said I was thinkin, not doin. What if we figured a way to do both? What if we could figure a way to take his money at the track and get him side ways with his coke connection? Or just get him busted? We could use his money for travelin and both haul ass somewhere. I been thinkin about goin back to Nashville."

"Ya don't know who you're messin with. These people kill folks. I'm tellin ya one more time. Just leave it alone. I'll work this out in my own way, in my own time."

"I said I'm just thinkin."

"Hey. When'd ya start thinkin about Nashville?"

"Ever since I heard my song on the radio. I figure we're both good enough to make it somewhere besides here. I think it's time for us to get the hell outta Dodge."

*

Payne would have guessed Jerry would be lucky to have a two car funeral procession. But he would've guessed wrong. Dressed in his best boots and jeans, Payne stood in front of a decent crowd gathered in Kelsheimer's chapel and sang *Amazing Grace*. He counted over thirty people in the small chapel, most of whom would be intending to spit on Jerry's grave.

Payne nodded to Ragina after the song. She and Jerry's brother, Tommy, were the only ones crying. Tommy Boerne hadn't seen his brother in three years. And he had shown up at the funeral, drunk.

Reverend Mooty had a contract with Kelsheimer's. When there wasn't a preacher of choice, Mooty stepped in for a quick twenty-five bucks. Friday afternoon, the short bald-headed preacher earned his money trying to come up with nice things to say about the deceased. "Jerry Don Boerne loved country music. He loved races horses and he loved his only daughter, Ragina." His voice boomed through the small chapel until he flipped his note over. There was nothing else. He smiled nervously as an awkward silence filled the chapel. Recovering, he continued, "I think we should all just take a moment and remember Jerry in our own way." He could have mentioned Jerry's love for money, wild women, and Jim Beam, but the pause allowed the audience to fill in their own blanks.

From his seat on the first pew, Tommy Boerne wailed like a lost coyote pup throughout the condensed funeral. The service was concluded by playing Jerry's favorite country song. Reverend Mooty announced Hank Williams, and his classic *I'm So Lonesome I Could Cry* with the flair of a morning disk jockey. The "mourners" sat quietly while the scratchy record played. Tommy wailed along.

Liz held Ragina around the shoulder as they filed by the open casket. Tommy staggered along behind them. Stumbling into the casket, he dislodged it from the stand. Someone in the crowd yelled "Oh, shit!" just as the casket and ol Jerry spilled on the chapel carpet. The boys from Kelsheimer's rushed in and quickly escorted the horrified assembly outside.

Tommy passed out in the limousine during the short ride to the cemetery and the graveside ceremony was concluded without anyone bothering to wake him up. After the Lord's prayer, Liz rushed Ragina to the black limo. "Get us the hell out of here!" she yelled at the driver, causing Tommy to stir.

"Mother, please." Ragina held a finger to her lips. "You're going to wake the son-of-a-bitch up."

*

The majority of the cemetery crowd consisted of regulars from Heidi's. Having arranged for the rest of the day off, they reconvened at the Roadhaus. Skeeter was already at Heidi's by the time the funeral crowd arrived. He and Casey had decided to declare a wake in Jerry's memory. She even went so far as to hang a sign behind the bar.
It read:
IN MEMORY OF JERRY BOERNE,
ALL DRINKS WILL COST DOUBLE!

CHAPTER NINE

Nova arrived at Heidi's half-an-hour early for Friday night's show. Crossing the dance floor, she watched the regulars raise their glasses and toss back the last round of Jim Beam. Jerry Boerne's "wake" was officially over. As the group dispersed, Nova rounded up the band for a business meeting. Beneath the glow of a neon Lone Star Beer light, Nova enthusiastically broke the news. "I signed a contract with Jimmy Earl. He's going to be our agent!" She clapped her hands. "He's getting us some bigger gigs in San Antonio and Austin. He wants us to be better known before we play at Willie's Picnic. Boys, we're on our way!"

"Where?" Hartman asked, when she paused for a breath.

"To the big time. It's the break we've been waiting for. Hartman, where'd you think we were going, Disneyland?" Nova laughed and leaned back in her chair.

"Disneyland sounds better to me," Skeeter said.

"Skeeter, what the hell happened to your face?" Nova sprang from her chair for a closer look. High-stepping it around the table, she peeled off his jockey cap to examine his wounds.

"Cut myself shavin."

"Ya shoulda seen the other guy," Payne added, but without his usual smile. He waited until Nova had stopped doting over Skeeter to ask, "What are ya talkin about, Jimmy Earl is our agent?"

"I'm talking about the band getting five hundred bucks a night instead of the hundred we're pulling down here, less Jimmy Earl's commission. He's putting us on the Texas Bar Circuit."

"What's he gettin?" Skeeter asked.

"Twenty percent," Nova answered, and replaced Skeeter's jockey cap. "That's still $400 a night, split four ways."

"I'm in the wrong end of this business," Skeeter grumbled.

Nova held her hands up in surrender. "Look guys. The money's not the most important thing. We've got a chance to make it big and get exposure."

"Ya shoulda talked to us first," Payne said.

"I'm sorry. I didn't have time. And I've already signed the contract. We start next weekend in San Antonio. He's got us booked at the Crystal Stallion." Nova's enthusiasm returned. "Come on guys. This is great! Trust me on this."

Payne took a sip of his Bud. "Okay. But, I wanna see ya tell Casey how great it is."

"She'll just have to get over it. We're done here after tomorrow night."

"That's not much notice," Payne pointed out.

"That's all the notice we got. That's all the notice she gets. What do you guys think?" Nova asked, on her way back to her chair. "Ain't it great?"

"Well, Hartman don't look too excited," Skeeter said. "Anyway, sounds to me like you've already done all the thinkin for us."

"I thought you guys would be happy. What's the problem?"

"Casey's done a lot for us," Payne argued. "It don't seem right just walkin out on her like this."

"Yeah, well that's because you're getting fringe benefits from Casey." Nova leaned across the table. "You guys in or out?"

"I'm in," Hartman said. "I'm with ya."

"Payne?"

"I'll give it a shot. I'm in through Willie's Picnic. After that, I'm not sure."

"What're you talking about?"

"Nashville."

"You've already been to Nashville. Got thrown in jail. Remember? Why go back there?"

"I've got unfinished business in Nashville. Thinkin on stayin awhile next time."

"Skeeter, you in or out?"

"I'm with Payne. I'll give it till the Fourth, then we'll see."

"Good. Then it's settled, at least through the Fourth."

"Not yet. Ya still haven't told Casey," Payne reminded her.

"You tell her. You're her boy."

"I ain't nobody's boy and this ain't my band." Payne shoved his chair back and headed for the bar.

"Payne, I'm sorry. I didn't mean it that way," Nova called after him. She followed him to the bar. "I can't do this without you."

"Sure ya can. Hell, guitar players are a dime a dozen." He took a seat on the tall stool. "I said I'd give it till the Fourth."

"Songwriters aren't a dime a dozen." Nova sat next to him.

"No shit. That's cause they don't get paid nothin at all."

"My, my." Casey's words were slurring while she struggled with the barstool next to Payne. "If it's not Payne McCarty, the hero of Comel County. I just heard about you saving Jerry's little girl from drowning."

"Ragina?" Nova asked. "I wouldn't have thought she could drown with those big inflated tits to hold her up." Nova laughed and winked at Casey behind Payne's back.

"Tell us Payne. How do those fake ones feel?" Casey asked. "Good as real ones?"

"Wouldn't know. I pulled her out by her hair."

"Don't try to shit an old shitter. I heard you two were stranded together for three days at your house. You going to try and tell us y'all just played Monopoly the whole time?" Casey let out a loud cackle. "Bullshit!"

"Skeeter's gotta big mouth."

"I'm getting jealous just thinking about that," Nova said, and ran her hand through the back of Payne's hair.

"Jealous about what?" Payne asked, with his best poker face. "Playin Monopoly with me?"

"I do believe he's blushing!" Nova laughed, and tried to pinch his cheek.

But Payne knocked her hand away. "I was just bein neighborly. Why don't we change the subject? Nova here's got some news for ya," he said to Casey, and crawled off his stool.

"Uh, yeah. Casey, we signed a contract with Jimmy Earl," Nova announced. "He's booked us in San Antonio, starting next weekend."

"Well, that's just too damn bad." Casey slid off her stool, but had to grab it for balance. "Y'all are playing right here."

"Not after tomorrow night."

Casey looked at Payne. "That right?"

"Just heard about it myself." He shrugged his shoulders. "I told ya before. It ain't my band."

"After all I've done for you!" Casey screamed at Nova. "After getting you booked at Willie's Picnic! You ungrateful little slut!"

Nova's nose flared. "Who're *you* to be calling *me* a slut?" She leaned across Payne's empty barstool. "You old bar whore!"

Casey took a hand full of Nova's short black hair and yanked her away from the bar. Nova fought back. Grabbing Casey's blouse, she pulled, ripping the buttons off. Grinning, Payne stepped out of the way. He watched Casey let go of Nova's hair just long enough to score a hard slap to her face, stunning the dark-haired singer. Grabbing the sleeve of Nova's blouse with one hand, Casey shoved her backward with the other, ripping the sleeve loose at the shoulder. "Come on bitch!" Casey taunted. "Let's see what you've got!"

"Look at my blouse!" Nova screamed. "You ... " With renewed fire in her eyes Nova charged, both hands swinging. Retreating from the onslaught, Casey staggered backwards toward the dance floor until she tripped over a chair leg. Nova pounced on her while she was down and both rolled on the wooden floor.

The crowd hooted and hollered for their favorite while the "ladies" struggled to gain an advantage. Grappling on the dance floor, they slapped, ripped, and cussed until Payne finally stepped in to break it up. "That's enough! Come on ladies, break it up!"

It took the help of a couple of regulars, but the brawlers were finally separated. Payne restrained the furious bleached-blonde tavern owner. "You're fired!" Casey screamed at Nova, her chest heaving for breath. "Get the hell out of my bar!"

Hartman was holding on to Nova. "No problem bitch!" she screamed back. "We're out of here!"

Casey jerked free from Payne and stormed off, shoving her way through the crowd. Hartman released Nova. "Ya okay?"

"Shit!" Nova screamed at no one in particular. Sitting down at the closest table, she examined her ripped sleeve. She ran her hands through her hair and felt of her face. "I can't believe that bitch!"

Skeeter was still laughing, holding on to his sore ribs. "Well, she took it better than I thought she would."

"Yep. Now it's settled," Payne said, and patted Nova on the head. "Let's pack it up, boys. Like she said, we're outta here."

CHAPTER TEN

Payne woke up Saturday morning to the smell of coffee and bacon frying. He scratched Pardner's ears, waking his friend. "Somethin's smellin good." Pardner followed Payne to the kitchen. Skeeter, dressed in his white Fruit of the Looms, was busy stirring a pan of scrambled eggs and sipping coffee. "Ya made breakfast?"

"Yeah. Hungry?"

"Starvin." Payne poured a cup of coffee from the plastic, harvest gold coffeepot and grabbed a piece of bacon. "Where're the races this weekend?"

"Junction."

Payne took his coffee to the green kitchen table. "Wanna go?"

"Not really. Why are *you* suddenly so interested in the races?"

"Thought I might case out Red."

"Shit. Not that again. I told ya to leave it alone."

"Ya comin with me or not?"

"What're ya gonna learn that I can't tell ya?"

"Don't know. I just wanna watch him work, now that I know what's goin on."

"You're startin to scare me again." Skeeter sat at the table with his huge plate of bacon and eggs.

"Damn, Skeeter. Did ya leave me any breakfast?"

"Oh." Skeeter grinned at him over his pile of eggs. "Did ya want some?"

Payne left the table. He scraped out the last of the eggs from the pan and took a bite from the last piece of bacon. "There's gotta be a way to pull this off. How much money does he hold?"

"I ain't sayin nothin else," Skeeter said, with a mouthful. "Leave it alone."

"Comin with me?" Payne peppered his small portion of eggs almost black and ate them while leaning back against the kitchen counter.

"Hell no. I'm takin the weekend off. I'm still recoverin, in case ya haven't noticed. Anyway I need to rest. I've gotta get well for next weekend. With Memorial Day comin, I'll have three days of racin right here at the Comel County Fair Grounds. It's a big money weekend. And one of us needs a job. Rent's comin due."

Payne finished his eggs. He looked at the pile of eggs on Skeeter's plate and shook his head. "Here ya go, Pardner." Payne handed his dog the last bite of bacon and put the plate on the floor for Pardner to wash. "Ya know, I sure hate not playin at Casey's. I feel bad we crapped out on her."

"We didn't crap out on her. Nova did. Why'd ya break that fight up anyway? Two more minutes and they'd both been rollin around in the floor naked." Skeeter laughed and grabbed his ribs. "Damn, that was funny."

"Just seemed like the thing to do."

"Well, some of us don't get to see as many naked women as *you* do. Hey, Ragina's ain't real, are they?"

"Not hardly."

"Well, they look damn good on her. Hell, they'd look good on any girl." Skeeter crammed a whole piece of bacon into his mouth. "Wonder what a pair like that would run?"

"Why? Ya in the market?"

"Just wonderin."

"I think I kinda like her." Payne sat across from Skeeter with his coffee. "She's got more class than most girls around here."

"Well, I wouldn't get love struck. She's too rich for a poor country boy like you. Ya ain't got enough money to keep her happy for ten minutes."

"Well, she was happy enough for three days. Didn't get one complaint." Payne smirked at Skeeter. "Ya comin to the races with me or not?"

"I told ya, no." Skeeter shoved his plate forward.

"Ya done with that?" Payne pulled Skeeter's plate to him.

"Yeah. Help yourself."

Payne scraped up the last bite of egg between his fingers and the last piece of bacon. "Anyway, what else ya gotta do?"

"Stay alive."

"Suit yourself." Payne put Skeeter's plate on the floor for Pardner and warmed his coffee before heading for the shower.

"Okay, I'll go. But ya gotta take my turn washin the dishes."

*

Junction lay between two hills, along the banks of the South Llano River. The afternoon heat had turned the gulch into a melting pot, with not so much as a whisper of a breeze. Dust, kicked up by Payne's Jeep, settled straight down to the fair ground's parking lot. The small bleachers, in need of a fresh coat of white paint, were already crowded with racing fans. There was no shade from the bright sunny day except beneath the brims of the cowboy hats that dotted the crowd.

The racetrack at Junction looked like most other small tracks on the Texas Racing Circuit. A mile long oval of dirt, guarded inside and out by white railing, separated the bleachers from the horse barns on the backside of the track. And they all smelled the same on race day; a peculiar blend of mesquite smoked Bar-B-Q and stockyards.

The first race had already posted when Payne and Skeeter entered the bleachers. Red stood at the bottom of the stands with a wad of money in his hand. A Sheriff's deputy was on guard next to him. Climbing the steps, they sat as far away from Red as possible.

"Quarter-mile races are the easiest to pull." Skeeter began his lesson in horserace fixing.

"What?" Payne looked blankly at his little friend.

"Ya just slow em half a step comin outta the gate. They get boxed in and it's over. Simple as that. It's the longer races where you've gotta be sneaky. Sometimes ya hold em back just a little too long before ya let em run or take the bend too wide, or get boxed in. That's my favorite, gettin boxed. But there's lotsa tricks. Main thing is, ya try not to make it look too obvious. Horse owners and trainers have a tendency to get real pissed off, if they catch ya." Skeeter slapped Payne on the leg and stuck his feet out. "But when all else fails, ya just stick your feet out like this and rare back on em with ever thing ya got." Skeeter pretended to pull back on the reigns. "Those horses are bred to win. It's damn hard to hold em back."

"I've seen horse races before. I don't care who they pull, I wanna know how to tell which ones they're gonna let run. How do ya know who's gonna win?"

"Hard to tell. Most folks like to bet a particular horse. Some like to bet the favorites. Don't win much, but they win some. Some folks bet on the color of the horse or the last horse to take a shit on the track. Sometimes they just have a favorite number. Somebody always bets on the bay colored horse, just like the song *Camp Town Races*." Skeeter laughed at his own wit. "See that?" He pointed excitedly to the track. "Number *five* just took a shit in front of the stands. He's gonna win for sure."

"Enjoyin yourself?"

Skeeter chuckled. "Hell, yeah. Thanks for invitin me."

Payne surrendered a grin. "Please continue, Dr. Doeppenschmidt."

"There's no odds when ya bet with Red. Only the winner gets paid. Red holds the bet money and he keeps it, unless there's a winner. If ya bet a hundred, ya win a hundred. Ya bet ten grand, ya win ten grand. Bet twenty grand ... "

"Shit," Payne cut him off, "Skeeter, I don't need a lesson on how to bet with Red. How do ya tell which horse is gonna win?"

"See there? You're thinkin like ever body else here in these stands. I'm tryin to tell ya how Red makes his money. It's not 'which horse wins'. That ain't the right question. It's, 'which horse is gonna lose'. That's the real question. Got it?"

Payne took off his hat and wiped the sweat from his brow. "Go on."

"Sometimes folks get drunk or they're just born plain stupid by nature. They'll bet five or ten grand on a horse. Hell, I've heard up to fifty. Sometimes ya get somebody that's new to the tracks that'll bet a wad. But most the time it's somebody who just bought a new horse they're real proud of, like ol Jerry. That's the one that gets pulled. Don't really matter who wins. He can pay nickels and dimes out all day. What's important is who loses. Sometimes he'll pull two or three horses in one race. Sometimes he won't pull any. That's why the cheatin is so hard to spot. It's really simple, if ya think about it. Easier to make a fast horse lose than a slow horse win. It's bass-ack-wards."

"So, if we ... "

"Don't even think about it."

"How do ya know when to pull a horse?"

"Red, or one of his goons, tells ya."

"When?"

"Sometimes it's as late as gettin to the gate. But once the horses are in the gate, there's too much goin on to be talkin."

"How do the goons know which race and what horse, or horses?"

"They get a signal. Ya know, like baseball. But most of the time Red knows before the races. We have a little "prayer meetin" before the races even start. That's when Red usually gives us the word."

"Who signals the goons?"

"Could be anybody. Personally, I think it's the deputy. He's the only one close enough to Red for him to talk to. It's gotta happen fast."

"So if we could set Red up with a big bet ... "

"Payne, shut the hell up. We'll talk about it later. Let's watch Red and his deputy buddy. See if we can spot em signalin. First clue is a heavy bet. Hey, ain't ya glad I came with ya?"

"Delighted. What's a heavy bet to Red?"

"I don't know. Depends on how he's doin that day. Twenty-five hundred and up would get his attention. Just depends."

Payne eyed Red from his seat. The bookie was sharply dressed with expensive boots and a wide-brimmed straw hat. His dark red beard was trimmed short. He was leaning against the railing, facing the bleachers. Payne noticed the only time he turned around to face the track was after the race had started.

The deputy moved around, looking in all directions. There didn't appear to be a pattern to his movement. "Does he use the same deputy all the time?"

"I think so, but I don't normally see things from this side."

"Wonder if he's from Comel County?"

"Go ask him."

"Sure."

"Go walk by em. The name of the county oughta be on a patch or somethin. Look on the sleeve. He does look familiar. Could be from Comel County."

"Need a beer?" Payne asked, standing to stretch.

"I could use one. Ya buyin?"

"Yeah." Payne walked by the deputy and Red on his way for the beer. As suspected, he was from Comel County. Red had brought him along. From the beer stand, he watched Red and the deputy closely for a few minutes before returning to the bleachers. "Comel County," Payne announced, returning with the beer.

"Figures."

"I think I'm gonna sit a little closer and get a better view."

"Don't forget to yell for your favorite horse," Skeeter called after him.

Payne moved closer to Red and watched them from beneath the brim of his hat. Before each race, a small crowd formed around Red to place their bets. Red recorded the wagers on the racing form. It was the fifth race before a heavy bet was placed. Red handed the roll of bills to the deputy. "Ten thousand on number *four*," he announced to the deputy.

The roll of money disappeared into the deputy's pocket as he turned his back to the crowd. He took his hat off and wiped his head with a white handkerchief. Replacing his hat, he continued to peer across the track. Payne couldn't see the signal or the goon receiving it, but he was sure it had been given.

The quarter-mile race was over in seconds. The number *four* horse had been slow out of the gate, got boxed, then took to the outside. He was closing fast when the horses thundered across the finish line, followed closely by a cloud of dust that slowly drifted back to the track. The number *four* horse finished third.

Payne returned to his seat next to Skeeter. "It's the deputy."

"So."

"So, that's how they signal."

"Feel better, Sherlock?"

Payne nodded. "Say, wanna go to San Antonio? I wanna get somethin good to eat then go hear the band playin at the Crystal Stallion. Let's see how we stack up before we show up next week."

"Sure." Payne stood to leave but Skeeter didn't move. "Hell, I didn't know ya meant right this damn second. Mind if I watch the rest of the races first? I mean, as long as ya drug me all the way to Junction, we might as well watch the rest of the races."

"No problem." Payne started to sit down.

"Wait." Skeeter handed him a five-dollar bill. "As long as you're up, why don't ya go get us a couple of more beers? And some Bar-B-Q."

"That's not enough money."

"Hell, I ain't buyin yours."

CHAPTER ELEVEN

The Jeep accelerated out of Junction, merging into the Interstate traffic, east bound to San Antonio. "Tell me about the cocaine," Payne yelled at Skeeter, over the hot wind whipping through the open Jeep.
"I'm not a coke-head," Skeeter yelled back.
"I never said ya were. That's your business. I'm not talkin about you. Where does Red get it?"
"There's a place between San Marcus and Austin. I've never been there, but I hear it's tighter than Ft. Knox. They've got lotsa guns and I hear they turn guard dogs out at night. They supply Austin to San Antonio. These people are big-time. Don't even think about that."
"Why would they sell to Red? He's small time if all he's doin is supplyin the jockeys."
"Did I say that was all he was doin?"
"Skeeter, why don't ya just tell me what the hell ya know. I'm gettin tired of diggin all this outta ya."
"Red's not small time. He's got his goons sellin dope for him. They cover San Marcus and New Braunfels, for sure. And I think pretty much ever body in between Austin and San Antonio. He ain't big time, but he ain't small time either."
"Where does he keep it?"
"Don't have a clue. I'd be surprised if he keeps much on him. Red's no dumb-ass. He's got an organization. I'm tellin ya he's dangerous. Is there anything else ya wanna know, Sherlock?"
"Yeah. Why'd Red have ya beat up?"
"I told ya. He musta seen me dead-wrap Jerry's horse."
"I don't see what that would matter to Red. He coulda just had Jerry's horse pulled, if he put a big bet down. There's gotta be more to it than that."
"Nope, that's it."
"Don't make sense."
"Look Sherlock Red runs the track. Anybody gets outta line ... they get the hell beat outta em, or worse."

"Dead wrappin Jerry's horse was outta line?"

"Not so much that, but when he came around to the jockey shack, after ya left that day, he caught me lyin to him. If I'd known he'd seen the whole thing, I'd told him the truth. That Dial Sammy's the best horse at six furlongs I've ever been on. The lyin's what crossed the line. That's somethin ya don't do to Red. I'm livin proof."

"Why'd ya lie? I know ya didn't do it for Jerry."

"Cause I want outta here." Skeeter leaned closer to Payne. "I figured Jerry and that horse just might be my ticket. I need money to leave. The way I saw it, Jerry was gonna run Dial Sammy a couple of times and keep his track speed slow, then put some big money down on him. Jerry said as much at the track that Sunday ya went with me. Only knowin Jerry, he was the only one gonna get any big money off that deal. I figured I'd work a side deal with him. Get a cut of his winnins."

"Well, now I'm back to Red. Wouldn't he just order Dial Sammy pulled if Jerry put a big bet down?"

"Might. But I figure Red woulda looked at the track speed and figured Jerry was just being Jerry. It wouldn't be the first time he's blown a wad on one of his new horses. I'd have told Jerry to bet late. Even if Red ordered him pulled, it'd probably be too late to signal. I was plannin to get that horse to the gate early."

"Hell, Skeeter. Jerry woulda just screwed ya outta your money, even if ya did pull it off."

"Jerry was a crook, not a killer. I coulda handled Jerry."

"Were ya gonna tell me bye, or just haul ass outta town?"

"I'm tellin ya bye right now, cause the first chance I get, I'm gonna screw Red in his pocket book and get the hell outta here. I'll catch back up with ya one of these days. Send ya a postcard or somethin." Skeeter laughed and tapped Payne on the leg. "I'm serious about goin to Kentucky. I oughta have enough money saved up by the end of racin season."

"So ... how ya plannin on payin Red back before ya leave?"

"Same way. Only now I'll have to wait till the last race of the season. It's in Fredericksburg, on the Fourth of July. I figure I'll get told to pull a horse sometime durin the day. I'm just gonna let that horse run and cost Red some big bucks. Then I'll get the hell off the track and outta town. Hit him where it hurts the worst."

"There's gotta be a better way. If we had a big bet on the right horse and ya didn't pull it, we could win money and screw Red too. Both leave town. I could use some travelin money myself."

"We don't have that kinda money and even if I let the horse run, there's no guarantees I'd win. Things happen on the track ya can't control. I wouldn't even bet on a fair horserace with my own money."

"I got faith in ya."

"Well, you'd better have faith in Jesus. This ain't no damn James Bond movie. Payne, these guys play for keeps. You're gonna get us both killed if ya don't stay outta this. Just let me handle it. Ya don't need to get involved."

"I'm just tryin to help."

"Appreciate it, but I'm bigger than I look."

*

It had once been a roller skating rink, before the expansion in 1983. Now, hundreds of light bulbs spelled *Crystal Stallion* across the top of the sprawling building. The glow, reflecting off the windshields in the packed parking lot, glimmered invitingly as Payne and Skeeter approached one of San Antonio's favorite honkey-tonks.

"Well, this ain't no Gillies, but it's damn sure a step up from Heidi's," Skeeter observed during the long walk. "Looky there!" Skeeter pointed. "I told ya we could find a parkin space closer if ya just tried."

"Walkin ain't gonna kill ya."

"Ya seem to keep forgettin I'm injured."

Payne opened the door for Skeeter. "Two dollar cover charge," said a muscular bouncer, dressed in black.

"Damn," Payne muttered. He handed him a five for both of them.

"Enjoy." He dangled the dollar bill in change in the air.

"Hope to," Skeeter answered for them, and grabbed the dollar out of the bouncer's hand.

The dancehall was dark and crowded. Neon beer signs littering the walls provided most of the lighting. To the left, the band played beneath a row of colored track lights on a raised stage. The dance floor, once roller-rink, stretched in front of the bandstand. Over the dancers, spotlights reflected off a rotating saddle made of crystal. Payne went right, circling the big club. Skeeter followed. Payne counted six bars before finding a table near the dance floor.

The waitresses all wore the same black short-shorts, low cut red tops, with white boots and matching cowboy hats. They also wore gun hostlers that held a bottle of peppermint schnapps on one hip and cinnamon schnapps on the other. "Handsome, shots of schnapps are a dollar." Their waitress smiled at Payne and deliberately bent over the table to empty the ashtray.

"No thanks," Skeeter answered. "If I wanted to kill myself, I'd use a real gun. It'd be less painful. Give me a Miller."

"Bud," Payne said.

"Hon, you just let me know if there's anything else I can get you."

"It must be tough being you," Skeeter commented. "Ya draw women like shit draws flies. I thought she was gonna sit in your lap."

"What do ya think about the band?"

"What I've heard sounds good. They're better than us. I hope the crowd don't throw beer bottles at us."

"Hell, they're not that much better. Anyway, Nova'll keep their minds off the music."

"Yeah, but we need to practice before we show up here." Skeeter leaned closer to Payne. "Ya know, if ya went to Nashville and I went to Kentucky, we'd still almost be neighbors."

"I'm goin'," Payne vowed, as their waitress set their beers on the table. Again, she bent over in Payne's direction, making change out of his ten. "Thanks. Keep a dollar." He smiled politely at her before picking up where he had left off with Skeeter. "I think I could make it there in a year or two. I hear ya gotta be livin there or nobody will give ya the time of day. I've mailed my last song to Music Row. Next time, I'm gonna hand deliver it."

"You'll make it. We both will. I'm a damn good jockey."

"No doubt about that." Payne raised his Bud in the air for a toast. "Here's to Kentucky roses, and Nashville gold."

"And good friends," Skeeter added.

"Keep our table. I'm gonna wander around a bit."

Skeeter winked at him. "Well, find one for me, too."

Payne found his way to the bar closest to the restrooms. He figured that was the best place to spot women. They all went and went often. Leaning against the bar, he sipped on his beer and watched the cowgirls come and go. He had started to order another beer when he spotted her, all five feet of her. She had shoulder length brown hair with matching dark brown eyes. Dressed in Wrangler jeans and a pink western blouse, she was shapely and cute as a button. She caught him looking and smiled before turning away. Payne left his empty bottle on the bar and tapped her on the shoulder. "Excuse me. Name's Payne McCarty. Could I interest ya in a dance?"

"Lisa." She extended her hand and giggled. "I'd love to dance," she answered in a high pitched voice. Looking up, her eyes twinkled at Payne.

Payne took her hand and led his little lady through the crowd to the dance floor. Two-stepping to *Amarillo By Morning* Payne asked, "Are ya a regular here?"

"Every weekend." She smiled up at him.

"I'm part of the band that's gonna be playin here. Startin next weekend. Me and the drummer came tonight to check it out."

"Really?" she squealed. "What's the name of your band?"

"Nova-Scotia. It's not my band, its Nova's, the lead singer. I'm just a guitar player. My buddy, Skeeter, is the drummer."

"Skeeter? What kind of name is that?" She giggled again.

"Nickname. He's also a racehorse jockey. To be honest, I was hopin to introduce y'all."

"Because I'm short?"

"No, because you're pretty. Nothin wrong with short." Payne pulled her closer to him as they danced. "Skeeter's short, but not too bad on the eyes."

"Handsome as you?"

"People say we look an awful lot alike."

"Do you always pick up women for Skeeter?"

"No, but he's kinda shy tonight. He had a little run-in, involvin a racehorse. His face is still a little scratched up. Would ya care to meet him?"

"Does he dance?"

"I imagine. Skeeter's a good dancer."

"Okay." But she sounded disappointed. "I thought this was too good to be true."

"Why's that?"

"Cause you're about the best looking thing to walk in here since I've been coming to the Stallion. I couldn't believe you asked me to dance."

"Tell ya what. If ya don't like Skeeter, we'll dance some more. Deal?"

"Deal."

Payne led Lisa by the hand to their table. "Skeeter, I want ya to meet Lisa."

"Pleased to meet ya." Skeeter sprang out of his chair like a jack-in-the-box and tipped his hat.

"Lisa here is a real fine dancer. I told her you were too, but just a little shy tonight because that racehorse accident messed your face up. I told her ya weren't usually this ugly." Payne winked and motioned to Skeeter with his head toward the dance floor.

"Hell, I ain't that shy."

Payne smiled to himself watching the two disappear onto the crowded dance floor. He settled in with his beer and listened to the music until they returned to the table. "How many times did he step on your toes?" Payne asked Lisa, with a straight face.

Lisa giggled and put her arm around Skeeter. "Not once. He's a real good dancer."

"Damn good. She is, too." Skeeter was beaming.

"Well, if y'all will excuse me, I think I spotted an old friend over there by the bar. I'll be back after while." He tipped his hat to Lisa before leaving the table.

Payne sat alone at the bar, with his beer and his thoughts. Red was still on his mind. He flashed on Nashville, and Roger Durwood. But he refused to entertain the memories of the Davidson County jail. Payne ordered another Bud and smiled to himself recalling the three days with Ragina. Half-an-hour had passed before Sylvia crossed his mind. The thought of his ex-wife caused him to shove off the bar.

"Payne!" Lisa was all smiles. "You're just in time. Skeeter and I were fixing to take off and find something to eat, after I tell my friends goodnight. Want to go with us?"

"No, thanks. Y'all go right ahead." Payne dug into his pocket for the key to the Jeep. "Skeeter, don't ya forget to come back and pick me up."

"I've got my car," Lisa said.

"Payne, don't worry about me. Lisa lives in Universal City. Hell, we're almost neighbors."

"I can get him home." Lisa blushed.

"Does this mean I don't get to dance with ya again?" Payne winked at her.

"Not tonight." Lisa giggled before being led away.

Payne sat at the table just long enough to finish his beer. "Well, Pardner, looks like it's just you and me tonight."

CHAPTER TWELVE

Pardner broke into a barking fit just before noon on Sunday.
Crawling out of bed, Payne looked out the bedroom window and watched a dark blue Lincoln approaching the house. He studied it closely until he recognized Ragina's blonde hair. Rushing to the bathroom, he brushed his teeth and decided on a quick shower and a shave.
 "Payne? Anybody home?" she called, walking through the back door.
 "Well hello, Pardner." Ragina bent down and petted the big golden dog. "Where's your big buddy?"
 "Hang on," Payne yelled from the bathroom. "I'll be out in a few minutes. Make yourself at home."
 When he entered the kitchen his hair was still wet. He wore a white T-shirt and cut-offs. "Mornin. Ya caught me sleepin in."
 "Good morning to you." She smiled. "Hope you don't mind that I barged in. I just got into town. Hey, I think I recognize that T-shirt."
 Payne glanced at his shirt before his eyes traveled up and down Ragina's lanky frame. She was dressed in designer jeans and an expensive light blue blouse, with matching heels. But it was the plunging neckline that had Payne's attention. "It looked much better on you," he said, and grinned at her.
 "Oh, really?"
 Payne placed his hands on her face and kissed her. "I'm glad ya came back."
 Ragina let out a sigh. "Couldn't stay away." Reaching up with both hands, she drew his face to her and kissed him passionately. "Your kiss is just a good as I remembered it," she whispered, before taking a step back to look into his eyes. "I took an early flight to San Antonio and drove out. I was hoping I could stay with you. I have an appointment in the morning to discuss Daddy's will with his attorney. I hear everything in town has been booked since the flood."
 "Ya don't need an excuse to stay at this Hilton." Payne ran his hands up and down her sides. "Are ya hungry?"
 "No, thanks. Coffee would be nice, if it's made."

"Only take a minute. I was needin some myself." Payne took her hands and kissed them before going to make coffee.

"Payne, I was hoping your offer to help is still good." Ragina took a seat at the ugly green table and watched him wash out two old coffee mugs.

"Sure. What's on your mind?"

"Daddy left everything he owned to me. I was wondering if you would drive me around and show me his properties. I also want to go back to Lake Dunlap."

"I'll show ya ever thing I know about, but Jerry always had a lotta deals goin on. I'm not sure I know ever thing." Payne sat across the table from her and took her hand. "Ya sure ya wanna go to the lake? I hear there's nothin left." He held her hands looking at her long fake nails. They were painted bright red and matched her lipstick.

"I need to see it. Can we go there first? I'd like to get it over with."

"Today?"

"If you're not too busy."

"I've got time. "Did ya bring anything cooler to wear? It's gonna get hot in the Jeep."

"We could take the rent car. It has air conditioning."

"That Lincoln ain't gonna make it where we're goin."

"I'll change."

*

The water had receded below the concrete culverts, but the last half-mile of road to Jerry's house had been washed out. Payne put the Jeep into 4-wheel drive. There was no sign of the Porsche. Jerry's house was gone. Only the foundation and a few plumbing pipes protruding through the concrete remained as a landmark. Payne parked the muddy Jeep on the driveway and watched Ragina walk with her head down to the overturned tractor. She had tied her hair back in a ponytail and swapped her designer jeans for yellow short-shorts that showed off her long tanned legs.

Sitting on one of the tractor tires, Ragina buried her head in her hands. Payne left her to herself and looked around what was once the showplace of Lake Dunlap. He gave her some time before walking to the tractor and putting his hand on the back of her neck. "Ya okay?"

Ragina looked at him with tears running down her cheeks. "I know a lot of people didn't like Daddy. But he was never anything but good to me."

"Jerry had a good side," Payne said, in an effort to console her. "Babe, come on. It's time to move on." He helped her up by the hand and held her without another word until she stopped crying. "We've gotta lotta ground to cover. We best get goin."

Payne drove to the Kraft house that had been under construction. It was Guadeloupe River front property. The river was back within its banks, but a week's worth of work and lumber had been washed away. "This was the last house I worked on. Ya oughta have your attorney contact the Krafts. I guess they're gonna be needin a new contractor if they wanna start over."

Payne took her hand and walked to the river. "I never understood why people would pay ten times what a piece of property was worth to live next to a river. This is the third bad flood since I've been here. You'd think people would learn." Payne squatted down and stared at the flowing river. Picking up a twig, he snapped it into small pieces before dropping them to the water. "The Kraft's house was closest to the river. There're nine more tracts on this property for sale runnin back up the road we came in on. Jerry was askin twenty-five grand a piece. Might wanna call a realtor. Get someone to sell em for ya."

"What else did Daddy have going on?"

"He was fixin to subdivide thirty acres up on Canyon Lake."

"Can I see it?"

"I'm all yours."

"I'd like to think so."

Payne smiled and walked her back to the Jeep with his arm around her shoulders. Nearing the Jeep, Ragina turned into him and kissed him. "I've missed you. I haven't been able to get you off my mind."

Payne returned her kiss. "Come on. I wanna show ya this place at the lake."

They stopped for sandwiches and beer during the drive to Canyon Lake. The day was turning hot. Payne iced down the beer in a small ice chest before driving the rest of the way to the lake. He slowed the Jeep and pulled off the highway, stopping at a cattle guard. The Jeep traveled through the property, dodging trees until they reached a small clearing. "This is where I'd build a house," he said, bringing the Jeep to a stop. "If it was mine, I sure wouldn't sub-divide this place. Stand up in the seat and ya can see the lake from here."

"It's beautiful."

"I'd build me a two-story house with a balcony and watch the sun set over the lake ever evenin. Come on, I'll show ya the cliffs." Taking a couple of beers from the cooler, he led her through the trees until they stood overlooking Canyon Lake. The rocky cliffs dropped sharply to a small cove in the lake. Payne took her hand as they sat on the edge, dangling their feet. "Don't get much better than this," he said. "Don't have to worry about floodin up here, either."

"It's so peaceful here." She said, and drew a deep breath. "Listen to all the birds."

"Jerry just got this a month or so back. It hasn't even been surveyed for the sub-division yet. I came out here with him a couple of times to mark off the road. It's not my business, but if I were you, I'd just hold on to this place. One of these days it'll bring a fortune."

"Is this everything?"

"Far as I know. The riverfront we looked at is the only thing platted. I wouldn't try to mess with the Kraft's house. They're still livin in town. She's a real bitch. And they're not hurtin. With all the rebuildin that's goin on around here, it's gonna be tough gettin material and labor for awhile. I'd steer clear of that little project."

"How many people did Daddy have working for him?"

"There was just three of us workin on the Kraft's place."

"Well, I guess y'all work for me now. Do I owe you wages?"

"We've all got a week's worth comin." Payne tossed a small rock down to the lake. "Ragina, I'm not gonna work for ya."

"Payne! You're not just going to quit on me, are you?"

"I'm not quittin. The way I see it, ya don't have any work for us. You've gotta have work before we have work. You're not seriously thinkin about gettin into the house buildin business are ya?"

"I might be. You could work for me. We could do it together."

"Forget it. Ya don't owe me any favors. Week's pay is all we got comin. End of discussion."

"What are you going to do?"

"There's plenty of work around here for a carpenter. I'll find somethin this week. I'm not worried about it."

Ragina shot him a pouty look then carefully crawled away from the cliff before standing to her feet and dusting off the seat of her shorts. Payne followed her back to the trees and broke out the sandwiches. They ate in the shade of an oak grove. "It's a hot one," Payne said, finishing off his second beer. "Wanna take a dip in the lake? There's a path from the cliff down to the water."

"I didn't bring a swimming suit."

"Don't need one around here."

"Skinny dipping in broad daylight?" She giggled. "I don't think so."

"Suit yourself. I'm goin in."

"You're crazy!" she called after him. "Hey, wait up!" Following him down, she watched Payne peel his clothes off and dive into the water. "I can't believe you just did that!"

"Come on in. It's the only way to swim."

Ragina looked around the secluded cove. "Turn around."

"Hell, no. I wanna watch ya take it off."

"Payne McCarty!"

"Go on. Take em off and get in," Payne ordered, treading water. "Come on. No need to be bashful. Don't play shy around me. I've already seen it all, remember?"

"What if someone comes along?"

"Ya gonna talk or strip?"

"I can't believe I'm doing this," she said, unbuttoning her blouse. "I swear you bring out the absolute worst in me."

"Or the best. Come on. Keep goin."

Removing her lacy white bra, Ragina struck a poise. "See anything you like?"

"Hell, yeah. But don't stop now."

"Well, here goes everything." Ragina slid out of her shorts and panties and eased into the cold lake water. She swam with her head above the water to Payne. Pressing her body to his, she gave him a quick kiss. "There, I did it. Happy?"

"More than happy." Payne tried to kiss her, but she splashed him in the face and swam away. Swimming after her, he playfully dunked her head under the water.

But she came up screaming, "Don't! Don't do that!" Ragina swam frantically to the rocky shoreline.

"I'm sorry. What's wrong?" Payne swam after her.

Reaching the rocks, she held to the shore with both hands, her chest heaving in the water with each panicked breath. "I'm sorry, I guess I'm not over almost drowning."

Payne swam to her side. "Ya know what they say. If ya get thrown off a horse, ya just gotta get right back on it."

"I don't want my head under water."

"Look, just hold on to me. I want ya to take a deep breath and we'll go under the water together."

"No."

"Come on. You've gotta get over this." Payne held to a rock with one hand. "Look, just turn loose and wrap your arms around my neck."

Ragina obeyed, tightly wrapping her arms around his neck. The water surrounded them as they sank into the lake. Ragina broke free and surfaced first. Payne's head popped out of the water. "How was it?"

She smiled at him. "Can we do it again?" She stayed with him longer the second time before they surfaced. "Payne, I love you. I've never been this happy in my life."

"Once more, just for fun?" Payne asked, ignoring her declaration of love. Surfacing, they kissed until Ragina broke away and crawled out of the lake. Payne watched the little beads of water dripping from her skin as she climbed out. They sat in the silence of the spring day, drying under the hot sun. He waited until she had closed her eyes before gathering all the clothes. "Race ya to the Jeep!" Grabbing their clothes, he started up the cliff butt-naked.

"Payne! Bring my clothes back! Payne!"

"Come get em!" he called down to her.

Topping the cliff Ragina chased Payne around the trees and bushes back to the Jeep. He slowed, allowing her to jump on his back. Laughing, they playfully wrestled before he gently laid her down on the soft carpet of grass.

*

It was late afternoon when the Jeep turned up the gravel road to the old ranch house. Payne parked in the shade and Ragina took his hand. "Payne, I meant what I said at the lake. I love you. I've never been happier in my life than when I'm with you."

Settling back into his seat, Payne closed his eyes.

"You don't have to say anything back. I ... "

"Look," he took a deep breath after interrupting her, "I'm happy that you're happy. And I've really enjoyed bein with ya. But love's somethin I'm not any good at." He patted her hand. "Ragina, you've just been through a lot. I mean, I appreciate what ya said. I really do. It's just that ... "

"Payne, it's okay. I just wanted to tell you how I feel."

Leaning over, he kissed her softly. "Okay, but I want ya to understand how I feel, up front. We can have all the fun together two people can have, but love's not somethin I'm interested in. At all. Period. And I'm just bein honest with ya."

"I understand. Can I still stay at your Hilton for the night or have I spoiled everything?"

Payne kissed her. "I'd love for ya to stay. I just can't love ya."

CHAPTER THIRTEEN

After freshening up, Payne and Ragina escaped the suffocating house. They created a slight breeze under the shade of the front porch by lazily swinging back and forth in an antique swing. Beneath them, the wooden porch had settled in places over the years. And roots from oak trees had managed to push it up in others. Now, the only consistent thing about the planking was that it creaked and moaned under every step.

Pardner avoided the squeaky porch at all cost, unless it was raining. He lay contentedly in the grass until he spied a car coming up the road. His deep growl turned into an irritating salvo of barks as the brown Pinto kicked up a trail of dust.

"Skeeter's got him a new girlfriend," Payne said.

"Oh, really?"

"Name's Lisa. They met last night in San Antonio, at the Crystal Stallion." Payne left the swing and walked to the steps to wave at them. "We're gonna be playin there startin next weekend."

"Well that certainly sounds like a step up from Casey's place. How'd she take the news you were leaving Heidi's?"

"Not too good." Payne smiled. "Nova signed the band up with Jimmy Earl, outta Austin. He's gonna be our agent. He's the one that booked us for Willie's Picnic. I guess it's a step in the right direction. He's puttin us on the Texas Bar Circuit. So she said."

"I remember him. The guy with the beard and black vest?"

"Yeah."

"Payne!" Skeeter yelled from the car. "Hey, Ragina!" Approaching, Skeeter towered over his new friend by a full two inches. "This is Lisa. Lisa ya remember Payne. That's Ragina Boerne."

"Skeeter, how are you feeling?" Ragina asked.

"Better. I guess Payne musta told ya about that horse throwin me."

"What? I thought ... "

"Remember?" Payne interrupted her. "I told ya that horse threw him at the track and tried to kick him to death."

70

"Oh, that horse."

"We're gonna cook some steaks out tonight." Skeeter cut off the horse conversation. "Y'all wanna join us?"

"Great," Payne answered. "Did ya bring some extras?"

"Didn't bring any."

"Ya goin back after em?"

"Nope. *You* are. You're buyin, too." Skeeter latched his thumb in Lisa's back pocket, dangling his hand over her butt. He grinned at Payne.

"Flip ya," Payne challenged.

"We'll go." Ragina laughed at the two compadres.

"We'll need charcoal, and somethin to go with the meat. And bring back some Miller tall boys," Skeeter ordered.

"Skeeter, did ya bring anything besides a good idea?"

"Nope. Not a damn thing."

Payne held his hand out to Skeeter. "Money? I ain't buyin all that."

"I've got it," Ragina said. "Let's take the Lincoln. It's got air conditioning."

*

"I'm plannin on movin to Nashville, after the Fourth of July," Payne announced on the way back from the grocery store. He stared out the window of the Lincoln, at nothing in particular.

"Payne! Are you serious?"

"Yeah. I thought ya oughta know."

"Why Nashville?"

"I got some unfinished business there. And I wanna see if I can make it as a songwriter."

"I don't want you to go."

"Why not?"

"Because, I'll miss you. I've already told you how I feel about you."

Payne turned from the window. "Ragina, look. *You* live in Houston. I live in the country. *You're* rich and I'm not. *You* went to college. I barely finished high school. I drive a Jeep and *you* drive a Porsche. I live in an old house ... "

"And *I* live in a condo."

"There's no way this is goin anywhere, besides havin a good time together."

"Do I have till the Fourth of July to change your mind or are you trying to tell me it's already over?"

"I'm tellin ya, I'm plannin on movin to Nashville. That's all."

Ragina drove in silence for an uncomfortable two miles before speaking. Payne had resumed staring out the window. "What are you looking for in a woman?"

"I'm not lookin for a woman."

"If you were?"

"I said, I'm not lookin." He turned and ran his hand over the back of her hair. "Ragina, I like ya, a lot. I like bein around ya, but don't ... "

"But what? But don't try to tie you down? You're not the marrying kind?"

"Let's say that's right. Still wanna be with me?"

Ragina didn't answer until she parked the Lincoln next to the Jeep. "Yes."

"Yes?"

"Yes. I still want to be with you."

"Hell, I'd already forgot the question."

"Well, I've been thinking about it. And yes, I still want to be with you."

"No commitments?" Payne searched her eyes.

"None," she answered, tossing her hair back. "I'm just here for a good time."

"Long as it lasts?"

"Long as it lasts." Ragina turned away. She started to open the door, but stopped. "Payne, she must have hurt you real bad. I'm sorry. But not all women are out to break your heart."

"It's not my heart I'm worried about." Payne left the Lincoln. "It's yours."

*

The steaks were eaten on the picnic table under one of the towering oak trees, beneath the glow of an oil torch. The smell of the cookout lingered in the thick air as the coals turned to ashes. Pardner lay under the table crunching on a pile of T-bones. A light breeze occasionally rustled the leaves, offering some relief from the humidity. Payne had even played his guitar and everyone had sung along.

"This has been a wonderful evening," Lisa said. "Payne, I'm sure glad you asked me to dance last night."

"Yeah, Payne. Thanks." Skeeter's eyes left Lisa long enough to ask, "Ragina, what're ya gonna do with Dial Sammy?"

"Who?"

"Jerry's race horse."

"Payne, you didn't tell me Daddy had a race horse."
"Slipped my mind. I musta got sidetracked out at the lake."
"I figure Jerry has him paid up through the end of May for stablin and trainin," Skeeter said.
"I don't know." She turned to Payne. "What do you think?"
"I think I'd ask Skeeter."
"Okay, Skeeter. What should I do with Dial Sammy?"
"Ya could sell him, but he wouldn't bring nothin. He don't have a good track record yet." Skeeter gently pushed Lisa off his shoulder. He stood behind her playing with her hair. "If it was me, I'd run him this weekend. I'd get his track speed up before I tried to sell him."
"Is he slow?"
"Hell no, he ain't slow!" Skeeter's hands left Lisa's hair. "That may be the fastest damn horse I've ever been on. Hell ... "
"Hey, Skeeter," Payne interrupted. "You're inspirin me for a new song." Payne picked up his guitar and hit an "A Major" chord. He sang,

> *We had us a racehorse, named Dial Sammy.*
> *Swear that horse was just part of the family.*
> *Black as midnight, and twice as mean.*
> *That's the fastest damn horse you've ever seen.*

Payne put his guitar down. "Well, it's a start."
"I love it!" Ragina was clapping. "You're so talented!"
"Is that the horse that threw you?" Lisa asked. The two cohorts and Ragina erupted with laughter. "You said he was mean. What's so funny?"
"It's a long story." Skeeter hugged her from behind. "Yeah, that was the horse that threw me, but it wasn't his fault. I was bein stupid."
"Skeeter, can we run him in the races this weekend?" Ragina asked.
You got the money, honey. I got the time Skeeter sang and danced like a little leprechaun, clicking his heels together in the air. "Fact is, if it was me, I'd put a big ol bet on that horse winnin this weekend."
"Skeeter, I thought ya said you'd never bet on a horserace," Payne cautioned.
"I said, not with my money. Not around here. I can't afford to lose. But she can." Skeeter winked at Payne and changed the subject. "I'll tell ya what. If they ever get pari-mutuel bettin in Texas, I could be a rich man. Till then, all we've got is the Texas Race Circuit blues."
"Pari-mutuel blues is more like it," Payne corrected him.

"My daddy told me pari-mutuel betting is coming to Texas," Ragina said. "It might be another year, or two, but the State Legislature is going to pass it. He was sure of it."

"Believe that when I see it." Skeeter mumbled.

"Let's do it. Let's race Dial Sammy," Ragina said. "How much would it cost?"

"I usually charge ten bucks a race to ride, plus ten percent of the purse if I win. Entry fee is fifty bucks. We could run him Saturday and Monday in the Six-Furlongs races."

"What would we win?"

"The purse is the total of the entry fees for that race. If they had eight horses, that's four hundred. The track usually matches that, so that's eight hundred for the purse. Winner gets sixty percent and second gets forty percent. Nothin gets paid after second."

"Will you do it?"

"Consider it done."

"What would it cost me if I wanted to keep him?"

"Sam Blackburn is the trainer. He charges ten bucks a day to train, but that includes feed. He's as good as they come. That'd be about it."

"I want to see Dial Sammy. Payne, will you take me tomorrow?"

"Tomorrow evenin. I plan on findin work tomorrow."

"Skeeter, can I watch you race next weekend?" Lisa asked.

"Hell, yeah! We'll all meet up at the Crystal Stallion and make a *memorial* weekend of it."

CHAPTER FOURTEEN

Payne turned off his Monday morning alarm and left the bed.
Ragina had barely stirred. Alarm clocks were one of the things in her life she rarely had to answer to. Payne returned to the bedroom after a shower with two cups of coffee. "Good mornin, sleepyhead."

Ragina stirred and took the coffee. "Thanks." She took a sip and smiled. "I could get used to you bringing me coffee in bed every morning."

"I wouldn't get too used to it." He slipped out of his jeans and crawled in bed.

"Payne, last night I was thinking. Why don't you come back to Houston with me for a few days?"

"What for?"

"So we could spend some more time together. We could just party for a few days. Maybe go to the beach. It would be my way of thanking you for all you've done for me."

"Thanks, but I need to find work and the band needs to rehearse some this week."

"I'll have you back by Thursday afternoon. A few days isn't going to make that much difference."

"That's easy for *you* to say. I need the money."

"You could consider it an all expense paid vacation for saving my life and helping me with Daddy's business."

"I don't think so."

"Please? It'll be fun. We could leave after lunch. Fly to Houston and just enjoy ourselves for a few days. I want to spoil you. Please?"

"I don't know."

Ragina put her coffee cup on the floor. She rolled over to her side and ran her hand over his chest. "Please?"

"Maybe."

"I'll make it worth your while. I promise. It'll be fun." Her hand slid lower. "Pretty please?"

"You're makin it hard to say no."

"I'll drive you back in my new Porsche. I'm going to pick it up as soon as we get to Houston."

"Okay. But I've gotta be back by Thursday."

Ragina rolled on top of him. "You know, since you don't have to go looking for work this morning, we've got some time before my appointment."

*

William Gotzen Jr. had joined his father's law firm after a messy divorce. The rift had resulted from him spending three years of long hours and little pay in the Criminal District Attorney's office in Austin. As he approached thirty, he still thought about those years. But the jury was still out on which had been worse, his marriage or the D.A.'s office. Family law in New Braunfels was comfortable. So was his big house. The young attorney had it all, except that special woman to share it with.

"Billy" Gotzen, Esquire, was handsome. Tall, with wavy black hair, he was sharply dressed on Monday morning and had started the week with his usual confident air. But the sight of Ragina Boerne had him on the verge of hyperventilating. She strolled into his office wearing heels, a tight short skirt and low cut silk blouse. Billy managed not to stutter through his rehearsed greeting, "Ragina, it is a pleasure to meet you. I wish it was under different circumstances."

"Thank you." Ragina took her seat, crossed her tanned legs, and drummed her long red fingernails on the armrests of the plush chair.

Billy opened Jerry Boerne's file. "Let me get right to this. As I discussed with your mother, Jerry left everything to you." Turning the itemized list of fixed assets around, he slid it across the desk. "I'm afraid there was no insurance on his house at the lake. The property will be yours, however it won't be worth much after the flood. Jerry had several horses on the property. We haven't been able to locate them." Ragina leaned forward and studied the list, searching for dollar signs. Billy's brown eyes searched her cleavage until she looked up. "Also listed is a sub-division on the Guadeloupe River, which Jerry was holding for sale. That is yours. I could suggest a good realtor, if you're interested."

"Thank you." Ragina nodded without looking up. "That would be helpful."

"There is a property at Canyon Lake. You might consider selling that through the same realtor."

"I've seen both properties." She looked up from the list. "I think I may hold on to the Canyon Lake property, for now." Ragina shoved the file back to him and leaned back in her chair.

"From what we can tell, Jerry had a safety deposit box at the New Braunfels State Bank. He also had Certificates of Deposit there for a total of close to half a million dollars. The liquid assets are itemized on this list." Billy handed her a paper out of the file folder. "This is your copy. He also had two accounts in the same bank, listed beneath the CD's. One has a balance of just over twenty thousand. The second, just under sixty thousand. I couldn't find any life insurance, unless it's in the safety deposit box."

"Daddy didn't believe in insurance." Ragina took the paper. Her breath caught in her throat when she finally spied all the dollar signs.

"I've arranged an appointment this morning with Mr. Keller, to have the lock drilled. You can review the contents. If you find anything in the box that requires my help, just let me know."

"Thank you."

"If you'd like, I'll drive you to the bank and introduce you to Mr. Keller."

"Thank you." She smiled. "That would be nice."

Billy quizzed Ragina like a game show host on the short drive. He proudly escorted her into the bank and, as he expected, she turned every head in the old downtown building, including Mr. Keller's. He was way past his prime, but still appreciated a good-looking woman. Kneeling on the floor, he held the drill up with two shaky hands. But his attention was on the shapely pair of long legs standing next to him.

The spinning drill bit finally connected with the brass lock on the third try and the high pitched sound of the drill echoed off the thick depository walls. Keller opened the door and retrieved the heavy box. Mission accomplished, he struggled to lay the metal box on the tall hardwood table. It landed with a thud. "We'll leave you alone. Just call if you need anything."

Ragina took a deep breath before opening the box. She stared in disbelief at the neatly arranged pile of cash. Each stack was held together by an aging red rubber band. "Oh, Daddy," she said out loud. Thumbing through the money, she determined each stack contained twenty-five, one hundred-dollar bills. She counted forty stacks. Behind the money was an envelope. Beneath the envelope lay a pistol and a box of shells. She had hoped for something personal when she opened the envelope, but discovered only registration papers for his horses.

Closing the box, Ragina called Mr. Keller and rented a new safety deposit box. She dropped four stacks of hundreds, the pistol, and shells into her purse before transferring the balance to the new box. Ragina left the depository trying her best not to smile.

NASHVILLE GOLD

*

Billy Gotzen pulled his Mercedes into the parking lot of The Berlin Wall Restaurant without asking Ragina's permission. "I hope you like German food."

"Actually, I have plans for lunch. I'm meeting some people at the racetrack to look at Daddy's racehorse."

"It's only eleven-thirty. Let's grab lunch, then I'll drive you to the track."

"I really should go on."

"Ragina, I'm not taking no for an answer." Billy left the car and jogged around the back of the Mercedes to open Ragina's door. His gentlemanly efforts were rewarded with the sight of her long legs and deep cleavage as she left the car. The downtown streets of New Braunfels were already warming for the day. But it was Ragina, not the heat that had Billy sweating. He pulled out his pressed handkerchief and mopped his perspiring brow as they traveled the sidewalk. "Looks like another hot one," he said, and politely opened the door for her.

"Thank you." She intentionally brushed against his arm as she passed.

Seated in a secluded corner, polka music blared from a scratchy record. Billy ordered two glasses of Zoeller Schwartz Katz. "Could I recommend the schnitzel?"

"That sounds real good. It's hard to find good schnitzel in Houston. I was raised on that stuff." Ragina smiled flirtatiously at her doting admirer, enjoying his attention.

"It's not often I get to buy lunch for such an attractive client. In fact, I must tell you, my heart was racing when you walked into my office this morning. Actually," he let out a nervous laugh, "it's still racing."

"That's sweet."

"Was there anything of interest in the safety deposit box?"

"Not really. Some horse papers."

"Ragina, I know I'm prying, but is there anyone special in your life?"

"Yes there is. And yes, you are prying." Ragina took a sip of white wine.

"Sorry. It's the attorney in me."

"I understand. I was married to one. I'm trying not to hold that against you." She smiled curtly.

"I'm divorced also. Ragina, I'd like to see you again. I realize you live in Houston, but that's only a couple of hours away."

"Do you ask all of your clients out, or just the ones with money?"

"Fair question, but I only ask the ones who are beautiful. I'd love to see you again. I'm afraid I'm smitten."
"I'm involved at the moment."
"Is it serious?"
"You're prying again."
"I'm sorry. It's just ... "
"The attorney in you?"
"Actually, I was going to say, it's just that I don't want to miss a chance with you. A woman like you doesn't walk into my life everyday ... " The waitress placed their steaming plates of schnitzel on the table, interrupting his closing argument.
"Billy, I want you to know, I do appreciate it when a handsome man asks me out. But right now is just a bad time for me." She took another sip of wine. "I've got your business card and I'm not shy. I'm not telling you no. Just ... well, I'll let you know."

*

Payne and Skeeter watched Ragina and Billy exit the Mercedes. The sharply dressed couple approached the barn, tiptoeing around the horseshit as if the dark green piles were landmines.
"Lover boy, looks like you've got some stiff competition," Skeeter said.
"Payne, this is Billy Gotzen, Daddy's attorney. And this is Skeeter."
"And this is Dial Sammy." Skeeter held the black stallion by a lead rope without offering to shake Billy's hand.
"Skeeter, he's beautiful!" Ragina ran her hands along his neck, causing the horse to jerk the rope in Skeeter's hand.
"Nice looking animal," Billy commented. "Ragina, are you planning to keep him? Are you going to race him?"
"What the hell business is that of yours?" Skeeter demanded.
"I was Jerry's attorney."
"That ain't much of a reference," Skeeter said. Payne turned his head to keep from laughing at the confused look on Billy's face.
"You'll have to excuse my over-protective friend," Ragina said, trying not to laugh.
"Payne," Billy asked, "do you work here at the track?"
"No."
"What kind of work do you do?"
"I worked for Jerry."

"Payne is the one who saved my life during the flood," Ragina said. She took Payne's arm in both hands.

"I see." Billy placed his hands on his hips, assessing Payne like an opposing attorney. "I heard about that. Hard to compete with a hero."

"You'd done the same."

"Yes, I would've. Given the opportunity."

"Shit," Skeeter muttered under his breath, just loud enough to be heard.

Billy shot Skeeter a look before returning his attention to Ragina. "If you're ready? It's time for me to get back to the office."

Ragina handed Skeeter two one-hundred-dollar bills. "This should do it for the weekend. Keep the change."

"Yes, ma'am, boss lady."

"Okay, well, I guess we're off. Payne, I'll see you at the house?"

Payne nodded and tipped his hat.

"It was nice meeting you." Billy politely shook Payne's hand. "Skeeter, it was a real treat. Next time I need my ego deflated, I'll look you up."

"Anytime," Skeeter called after him. "Hell, I'll be here all afternoon."

CHAPTER FIFTEEN

The taxi dropped Payne and Ragina at the Houston Porsche dealership Monday afternoon. A middle aged, sharply dressed salesman greeted her by name. Without waiting on the insurance money for the Porsche she'd drowned, Ragina had simply written a check for a new one. That had been Saturday, before her trip to New Braunfels.

Payne watched Ragina complete the paperwork and eyed the service attendant pulling the shiny red sports car in front of the showroom windows. The "new car" smell, mingling with the strong scent of leather escaped from the Porsche when Payne opened the door for Ragina. "Smells good," Payne said, folding himself into the front seat.

"Hang on to your hat!" Ragina flashed a smile then stomped it, burning some of the new rubber off the tires.

"Runs good, too." Payne laughed, and gripped the brim of his hat.

Ragina raced the Porsche in and out of Houston's five o'clock traffic while trying to set the stations on the radio. Leaving Interstate 45, she turned on San Jacinto Street before making a sharp left, in front of an oncoming delivery truck, to enter her parking garage. The Porsche screeched to a stop in her reserved parking space. Payne's head popped forward, then back, from the sudden stop. "Damn, girl. Ya drive like a drunk Indian goin after more whiskey."

"Let's get freshened up and go out on the town."

"This is as fresh as I get."

"You haven't seen my bath tub yet."

"I might could use a bath."

They rode the elevator from the parking garage to the tenth floor of the exclusive apartment tower. Her elegantly furnished condominium was done in white with black accents to match the black grand piano. It was anchored in the center of the large living room like a yacht in a fishpond.

"I didn't know ya played the piano."

"I don't. It was my ex-husband's. It's a trophy from my divorce. It was the one thing he really wanted from the house."

"That was nasty."

"So was screwing his secretary."

NASHVILLE GOLD

Ragina opened a wall of curtains to reveal the unusually clear afternoon framing the Houston skyline. Payne walked to the wall of glass and looked down. "Nice view. How do ya open the windows?"

"They don't open. Believe me, you don't want to breathe the air." She walked up behind him and ran her hands through his hair. "Come on." She took him by the hand. "You can put your bag in my bedroom."

Payne followed her down the hall, past the guestroom and bath. He entered the master bedroom and tossed his bag on the king sized polished brass bed. Walking into the elegant master bath, he glanced at the Jacuzzi for two before opening the glass door to an oversized marble shower. "Why've ya got two shower nozzles?"

"Like they say, save water. Shower with a friend." Ragina came up from behind. She ran her hands over Payne's chest and began to unsnap his western shirt. "Will you be my friend?"

"You bet."

"Shower or bath?"

"Shower. I don't like to wash my face and my ass in the same water."

*

Lying naked on the brass bed, Payne was beginning to recover from the long, steamy shower. Having found the remote control, he was checking out the endless cable channels when Ragina returned from the kitchen with two Coors, and a smile.

"Sorry, I didn't have a Budweiser, but I do have a surprise for you this evening."

"I'm listenin."

"Rusti King is playing at Gillie's tonight. I thought we could go out to dinner, then catch her show. Do a little dancing." Ragina raised her arms in the air and shook her big boobs at him.

"Hell, yeah!" Payne took a drink of Coors. He held the can out and looked at it suspiciously. "I'd like to see her do my song," he said to the gold can.

"How do you get a song to someone like Rusti King?"

"Beats the hell outta me."

"Well, how'd she get *When Love Turns Out The Light*?"

"Stole it."

"What?"

"Me and Skeeter sent the song off to Sure-Star Publishin about a year ago. Never heard a word from em. Then one day I'm drivin along and hear it on the radio."

"You never got paid for it?"

"Not a penny. Me and Skeeter went to Nashville and tracked down the publishin company. I ended up in the Nashville jail for assault. Never even got to hit the guy. I'm goin back after the Fourth of July for round two with that son-of-a-bitch."

"Why don't you just sue him?"

"I might, but I'll do it there, not from Texas. I wanna be there. I wanna piece of Roger Durwood's ass. Stealin my song was bad enough, but he added insult to injury gettin me thrown in jail. I've gotta score to settle in Nashville."

"I had no idea. When you said you were going to Nashville, I didn't realize you had a good reason to go."

"Well, I've done a lotta things for no reason. This just ain't one of em."

*

Just after nine, Ragina parked the Porsche in front of Gillie's. The mammoth club was packed for Monday night. Payne escorted her through the dark, crowded honky-tonk, proud to have her on his arm, even if she was wearing designer jeans instead of Wranglers. She wore a fitted white satin Western shirt, with the top three snaps undone. The sleeves were blue with white fringe hanging from the arms.

"Darlin, you're sure turnin a lotta cowboy hats."

"Why, thank you." She gave him a quick kiss for the compliment. "I've definitely got the best looking cowboy in Texas."

"There ain't no reason for anybody to go thirsty around here. How many bars they got in this place?" Payne asked, searching for a table near the raised stage.

"I don't know. But they've got three and a half acres under roof and it holds 7,000 people. Even has a mechanical bull ride, if you're interested."

"No thanks. I've been on a real bull. Think I'll just hold on to my balls a little while longer."

Ragina stopped and turned into him. Her hand found his crotch. "Well, just let me know if you need any help," she whispered in his ear. "I'd be more than happy to volunteer."

The warm up band was still playing when Payne finally found a table in front of the stage, but it was thirty yards away. After their second round of drinks, he led Ragina to the dance floor.

"I do believe ya dance almost as good as ya look," Payne complimented her, after twirling her around the floor.

"Why, thank you. Flattery will get you everywhere."

"Already been there, but I'm ready to go back."

"You're insatiable."

"I'm what?"

"Never mind. It's a good thing. Believe me." Ragina laughed as Payne spun her under his arm, out, then back close. "Is there anything you're not great at?"

"Won't hear it from me if there is." Payne smiled and held her close when the song ended.

"Thank y'all very much!" The warm up band was closing it out. "Please stick around for one of Country Music's brightest new stars ... Rusti King!"

It was just after ten when Payne watched Rusti King take the stage. Dressed in white leather from her hat to her boots, she was stunning, even from thirty yards away. Payne squinted for a better look. Her tight, white leather pants and vest contrasted against her long wavy red hair, which fell below her shoulders. He followed her every move.

"Payne, I think I'm getting jealous. You haven't taken your eyes off her."

"Care to dance?"

"If you'll look at me instead of her."

Payne led Ragina to the floor. They danced to three songs with Ragina's back to the stage. But Payne's eyes never left Rusti. Giving up all pretenses, he moved Ragina into a small but growing crowd gathering in front of the stage.

Rusti was a pro. Payne watched her move smoothly back and forth across the stage, working the crowd with every step, with every note. She was genuine country. And her magnificent voice was second only to her natural beauty. Toward the end of the show, all dancing had stopped. Rusti King had seven thousand people on their feet, cheering and applauding after every song.

"She didn't sing your song," Ragina yelled, when Rusti waved goodnight.

"She will. Savin it for her encore. You watch. She'll be back."

Payne was whistling and yelling in the darkness with everyone else when the stage lights flashed. They came back up. The crowd roared even louder when Rusti again took the stage. "Thank y'all so very much," Rusti screamed into the microphone. "Thank you! And thanks to y'all, this next song just climbed to number three!"

DEKKER MALONE

The crowd was still roaring when the lights went out in Gillie's. Sounds of a single acoustic guitar played the opening riff of Payne's song. Timed perfectly with a lingering guitar chord, a single red spotlight exposed Rusti. Then Payne heard his words.

> *If I hadn't had a lump in my throat,*
> *You know I'd have said good-bye.*
> *But you, you just walked away*
> *Thinking I'd be okay.*
> *You never slowed down long enough*
> *To see my face drain white ...*
> *It's amazing how far your heart can fall*
> *When love turns out the light.*
>
> *I guess you've got the right*
> *To live as you see fit.*
> *But I, I just realized*
> *My whole world now lies in pieces.*
> *I know I should have seen it coming*
> *But I guess my love was blind ...*
> *It's amazing how far your heart can fall*
> *When love turns out the light.*
>
> *If I ever get over the blow*
> *I know my heart will break.*
> *But now, I'm just paralyzed*
> *Wondering why my hands still shake.*
> *And I don't know why my eyes won't cry*
> *God knows they've got the right ...*
> *It's amazing how far your heart can fall*
> *When love turns out the light.*
>
> *And I don't know why my eyes won't cry*
> *God knows they've got the right...*
> *It's amazing how far your heart can fall*
> *When love turns out the light...*

The spotlight went black. Her voice faded into the darkness, leaving only the soft sound of the acoustic guitar playing its final riff. Payne McCarty was the only one in Gillie's who didn't cheer and applaud after the guitarist's final

NASHVILLE GOLD

note. When the spotlight came up, Rusti King took a final bow and waved goodnight to her appreciative audience.

Ragina tried to pull Payne close, but he resisted. When the lights came on he gave her a forced smiled. "Damn fine song. If I do say so myself."

Payne's mood had turned sullen on the drive back to the condo. He rode in silence until Ragina tapped him on his leg. "Payne? Hello, in there. Is anybody home?"

"Sorry. I was just thinkin."

"Well, it's time to think about me. Tomorrow I'm taking us to the beach for a couple of days. We'll stay at a beachfront hotel."

"Sounds good."

"You're not going to believe the string bikini I'm going to wear for you. I promise it'll take your mind off Nashville, and Rusti King."

"Sounds even better."

*

Skeeter had followed Red from the track Monday and Tuesday afternoon, keeping a safe distance. Both days, the black Corvette disappeared mysteriously in the small town of Gruene, near New Braunfels. On Wednesday, Skeeter left the track early and drove through Gruene. He parked behind a row of trees near Highway 306. It was just after one in the afternoon when Red passed by. The Vette turned north toward Canyon Lake. Skeeter followed until Red took a dirt road. Pulling over to the shoulder of the highway, he glanced at his watch. He waited exactly five minutes before taking the dirt road.

The decaying mobile home sat inside a fenced property, well off the road, behind a row of trees. The black Corvette looked out of place parked next to a rusting pickup and two-dozen years of accumulated junk.

Skeeter drove over the next hill before turning his pickup around and parking. He traveled by foot through the trees until he reached a safe vantage point.

Red appeared at the front door and looked both ways before walking to his car. He held a briefcase. Skeeter watched the Corvette drive through the gate. Red got out of the car and locked the gate behind him. He drove out the way he had come in.

Checking his watch, Skeeter waited fifteen minutes before approaching the trailer from the rear. He listened patiently for any sound before trying the backdoor. It was locked. Pulling out his pocketknife, Skeeter jimmied a feeble window lock and crawled through a bedroom window.

86

Working room to room, Skeeter carefully searched the trailer for Red's stash of cocaine. The house was cluttered and dirty. The kitchen cabinets were empty, but the oven contained two shoeboxes filled with small brown bottles. They rested on the rack, next to a pair of scales. Skeeter licked his finger and touched the white residue on the scale. He licked it off his finger and smiled at the familiar bitter taste.

Certain Red's stash was in the trailer, he continued the search. He gagged when he opened the bathroom door. "Jeez, Red, that smells worse than three kinds of shit in a gas station toilet!" Staggering backwards, he slammed the door. "Damn!"

Having thoroughly searched the house for the second time, Skeeter returned to the small living room and sat on the filthy couch. The heat inside the closed trailer was suffocating. He wiped the sweat from his eyes. *Think. Damn it. Where is it?*

His eyes traveled around the living room. There was nothing hanging on the walls, only the small wires that dangled from a missing thermostat. "Shit!" Skeeter yelled. He rushed down the narrow hall to the heater. Sliding the cover off, he smiled. "Gotcha!"

There were four kilos of cocaine wrapped in plastic, a stack of cash and a pistol. Without disturbing a thing, Skeeter replaced the cover, locked the window, and left through the backdoor, locking it behind him. "Catcha later."

*

Payne loaded their luggage early Thursday afternoon. Ragina slid behind the wheel. Leaning over in front of Payne, she placed the pistol and shells into the small glove box of the Porsche.

"Expectin trouble?"

"A girl can't be too careful these days."

"Remind me not to piss ya off."

Ragina laughed. "Silly." She hit him playfully on the leg. "It was Daddy's. I found it in his safety deposit box Monday."

She punched the Porsche, popping Payne's head back. The tires squealed as they left the parking garage, entering the Houston traffic. "Payne, thanks for coming. I had a marvelous time."

"Thank you. I swear, I'm gonna have to go back to work to get some rest. Ya liked ta wore me out."

"Has a woman ever worn you out?"

"Nope, but I've had to quit on a couple."

"Payne, I'm trying very hard not to fall in love with you."

"Hey, this is just a good time. For as long as it lasts. Remember?"

"I remember." Ragina's turned serious. "Payne, I'm not sure how much longer I can go on like this. I want us to be more than just good in bed together. I want someone to share my whole life, not just my bed."

"There's always Billy Gotzen. I saw the way he was lookin at ya. Anyway, he's more your kind."

"What *kind* am I?"

"Rich."

"He asked me out. Are you jealous?"

"No."

"So you wouldn't mind if I went out with him?"

"Didn't say that."

"I'm going to get an apartment in New Braunfels. I want to stay there for awhile. I need to finish up Daddy's business."

"You're welcome to stay at the house."

"Your house is too hot. And I feel like I'm crowding you and Skeeter." She glanced at Payne. But he was looking out the window. "If you're not going to love me ... I'm going to need some space."

"So you can go out with Billy?"

"It's really ironic. Billy's chasing after me and I'm chasing after you."

Payne looked at her. "You can stop runnin anytime ya want to. Just turn around and ol Billy boy will be fallin all over ya, simple as that."

"It's not quite that simple. I care about you, not Billy."

"And I care about you. I care enough that I don't wanna see ya get hurt. Not by anybody. Especially not me."

"I'm a big girl. I can take care of myself."

"No doubt about that."

"I'd like to stay with you through the weekend. I'll look for an apartment next week. We'll just take it a day at a time from there. If that's alright."

"Okay by me." Payne ran his hand down a strand of hair that had fallen in front of her shoulder. He grazed her breast with the back of his hand. "Are we through talkin serious?"

"Definitely."

"Good." Payne's hand fell to her leg. He lightly ran a finger up and down the inside of her tanned thigh. She squirmed. From the bottom, he began to unbutton her cotton blouse.

"Just what do you think you're doing?" she asked, looking around to check the traffic.

"Tryin to get your mind off Billy Gotzen."

"Who's Billy Gotzen?" She took a deep breath when he released the front snap of her lacy bra. "Payne! What if somebody sees me?"

"Hell, it never seemed to bother ya before." Payne lightly ran his hand over her soft skin while she drove.

"Payne McCarty, I can't believe I'm letting you do this to me in the car. You're driving me crazy."

"Just keep your eyes on the road and both hands on the wheel."

*

Pardner was asleep when the new red Porsche pulled in next to the old Jeep. Payne got out of the car and whistled. Pardner appeared from around the house with his tail wagging. "There's my good watch dog. Howdy Pardner."

Pardner barked, sat, then held his paw up for Payne to shake.

"Good boy! I missed ya, too." Payne squatted down and rubbed his old friend's ears with both hands.

"Howdy Pardner," Ragina said.

Pardner stuck his wet nose on her bare thigh before licking her leg. "Payne, I swear that dog's starting to act just like you." She followed him into the stuffy house.

"You're right about one thing. This house sure is hot. Are ya gonna let me come see ya when ya get your new apartment?"

"I'll give you a key."

Payne picked up a note from the kitchen table. "Nova's got a rehearsal scheduled here for this evenin. Looks like we've gotta little time to kill." Grabbing two beers from the refrigerator, he headed toward his bedroom. "Wanna finish what we started in the car?"

CHAPTER SIXTEEN

Payne glanced nervously at his timepiece for the third time in ten minutes before sticking it back into his pocket. Nova was late. It was almost nine, time for Nova-Scotia to begin their first set at the Crystal Stallion. The band was pacing nervously when she finally stumbled around to backstage.

"Howdy boys!" Her eyes were red and her words were slurring.

"Did your Friday night AA meetin run late again?" Payne asked.

"I'm fine. Just point me to the stage."

"Don't expect to find me behind ya when they start throwin shit at ya," Skeeter said.

"I told you, I'm fine!"

"Let's go." Payne stepped onto the raised bandstand and looked over the smoky dance hall. The Crystal Stallion was packed. He spotted Lisa and Ragina seated at their table before returning his attention to Nova. She was near the drums, strapping on her guitar and adjusting her boobs. With her back to the crowd, Payne watched her remove a bottle of tequila from her large purse. "Skeeter!" he yelled, and pointed to Nova. She took a shot.

Skeeter clicked his drumsticks at her. "Hey, Nova. Sometime tonight would be nice."

"I'm ready. Click it off."

Nova was dragging. Their timing was off during the first song, but the crowd didn't seem to notice. Nova slowly began snapping out of her stupor, spurred on by the whistles and catcalls coming from the cowboys. She picked up the pace during the second song. During the third song Payne began to relax as the band found their groove.

After the first set, Payne caught Hartman by the arm. "Try to keep Nova outta the tequila. Me and Skeeter will be back in a few minutes. Hide it if she turns her back."

"Gotcha."

Ragina and Lisa had their men's favorite beers already sitting on the table when they arrived. "Sounding good!" Ragina bragged. Payne gave her a quick kiss.

"Skeeter, you're great!" Lisa patted him on the arm in between clapping her hands. "I'm impressed."

"We're not at our best," Payne said. "Hartman's gonna try to keep Nova off the bottle durin the break."

"Wouldn't count on that," Skeeter said. "She's liable to slap him up side the head with his bass guitar if she sees him make a move for her bottle."

Payne heard his named called from behind him. It was a familiar voice, but he didn't place it. He set his beer down. "Yeah?" He turned in his chair.

"I thought that was you." Sylvia was still stunning. She hadn't changed a thing, except last names.

"Sylvia?" Payne's eyes blinked in disbelief. He watched his ex-wife toss her long black hair behind her shoulders. It was one of her nervous habits. Her thick mane still fell to her lower back. "I saw you on stage. I just wanted to say hello." She was smiling at Payne like he was a long lost friend at their high school reunion. "How've you been?" she asked, placing her hand on his shoulder.

"What's it to ya?" Payne jerked away from her touch, turning back to the table.

"Hi, Skeeter."

"Well, if it ain't my favorite bitch."

"Nice to see you, too." She forced a smile in the direction of the table. Ragina and Lisa were staring at her. "I'm sorry to interrupt. I guess it was a mistake."

Payne rose to his feet and stared into her dark brown eyes. "Ya coulda left me a damn note." It was the first thing that popped into his mind.

"I tried. I didn't know what to say."

"Good-bye woulda worked."

"Payne, I'm sorry I hurt you. I've wanted to say that to you for a long time."

"Feel better?" Payne turned away from her and sat down, leaving her standing behind his chair.

Sylvia again placed her hand on his shoulder. "I'd like to visit with you sometime. I'm back in San Antonio, listed under my old name."

"Would that be under "B" for bitch?" Skeeter asked.

"Real cute. You haven't changed a bit." Sylvia spun around and stormed off, disappearing into the crowd.

"So that's Miss Heartbreak?" Ragina asked.

"Shit! I ain't believin that!" Payne slammed a fist down on the table and bolted from his chair, knocking it over.

"Excuse me, ladies." Skeeter tipped his hat and followed Payne to the stage. "Payne! Wait up!"

"Nova, I don't want us doin any of my songs tonight."

"Why?"

"His ex-wife's here," Skeeter answered, from behind him.

"Damn it, Skeeter, I know how to talk."

"Afraid she'll want royalties?" Nova cackled.

"I'm serious."

"Payne, we can't screw with our sets. It'll run us short."

"Put somethin else in."

"Nope. The show must go on," she said, and threw her arms in the air for dramatics. But Nova's sudden movement caused her to stagger backwards.

"Shit!" Payne stormed onto the stage in search of Nova's tequila bottle. "Hartman, what'd ya do with the tequila?"

"Ya told me to hide it."

"I know that. Where'd ya hide it?"

"Behind your amp."

"You hid my tequila!" Nova jumped on stage. The lights flashed, signaling the band to begin their next set. Payne managed to take a shot before Nova snatched the bottle out of his hand. "Payne, just calm down!" She took a swig then handed it back to him. He took another shot. His body shook involuntarily from the fiery spirit.

"Mind if I hold on to this?" Payne asked.

"Hell yes, I mind. My throat gets dry."

"Let's go boys and girls!" Skeeter yelled.

Payne handed the bottle back to Nova.

"Damn, Payne. I've never seen you like this. Settle down. Just concentrate on your music." She tried to hug him, but he pushed her away. Skeeter clicked off their second set.

During the set, Payne searched the sea of faces for Sylvia. But she had disappeared as quickly as she had popped back into his life. To Payne, the second set seemed to go on forever. When it was over, he followed Skeeter back to their table.

"Payne, are you alright?" Ragina asked.

"Fine."

"Well, I don't think she'll be back. I sure wouldn't. Not with Skeeter at the table." Ragina winked at Skeeter. "Hey, Skeeter, you ready to ride tomorrow?"

"I was born ready! Ya ready to win some money on that ol horse of yours?"

"Can't wait."

"I'm ready to watch," Lisa said. "I've never known anybody that did so many exciting things."

"Yeah, he's a real excitin guy," Payne muttered.

Ragina took Payne's hand. "Are you mad at Skeeter for calling your ex-wife a bitch?"

"No. I'm pissed at him for not givin me the chance to say it myself."

"Ya weren't sayin nothin."

"I don't have to say nothin with *you* around. *You* do all the talkin for me. You're always doin that."

"Well, excuse the hell outta me. I think someone didn't get his nap out."

*

Nova was sailing three sheets to the wind by the end of their final set. With slurred speech, she closed out the evening by dedicating *When Love Turns Out The Light* to Sylvia.

CHAPTER SEVENTEEN

Payne walked into the kitchen Saturday morning in time to catch Skeeter bent over the kitchen table snorting two lines of cocaine. "Little early in the day for that, ain't it?"

"Breakfast of champions. Gotta thin up some for the races."

"Think Red will pull Dial Sammy if Ragina bets on him?"

"Doubt it." Skeeter rubbed his nose and sniffed. "If he pulls him early, I'll take my cap off and adjust it in front of ya durin the Post Parade. Otherwise, keep the bet around a couple of grand and bet late."

"Think Dial Sammy can win?"

"No doubt in my mind he's the best horse, but if I get told to pull him, I will. I'm savin my revenge for the Fourth of July." Skeeter licked his finger and wiped the residue of coke off the table. He licked the small trace off his finger and put the short straw in his pocket. "I've got my own fireworks that I'm gonna set off on the Fourth of July." He grinned. "Yes, sir. Big time."

"Lisa still in bed?"

"Sleepin like a baby. Man, that was weird last night. I still can't believe Sylvia popped outta thin air. You're not gonna call her, are ya?"

"What do ya think?"

"I wouldn't be askin if I knew. Ya went a little crazy last night."

"I'll just let *you* call her."

"Yeah, she'd like that." Skeeter laughed and headed out the door. "I'll catch up with y'all back here after the races. Be sure and brag on me to Lisa," Skeeter yelled. The screen door slammed behind him.

*

The day had already turned hot by the time Payne and the ladies reached the fair grounds. All three were appropriately dressed in boots and jeans. Payne and Lisa wore western shirts. But Ragina was wearing a low cut blouse with ruffles along the plunging neckline. A large diamond hanging from a thick gold chain accented her cleavage, as if the area needed help drawing attention. Payne adjusted his cowboy hat as he walked up the ramp to the bleachers. The small grandstand at the Comel County racetrack was almost filled by the time they took their seats. He checked through the racing program. Dial Sammy was the number *five* horse in the seventh race. Skeeter was riding in all nine races.

"Why are they plowing the track?" Lisa asked.

"So they can get dust on ever body in the stands," Payne answered, watching a cloud of dust engulf the bottom rows of the bleachers.

"Why?"

"I was just kiddin. They're just softenin it up some for the horses, so they don't slip and fall on top of Skeeter." Payne patted her leg.

"Being a jockey is dangerous, isn't it?"

"Can be. Lotsa things can happen when ya get that many horses runnin. Don't worry about Skeeter. He's too damn ornery to get hurt."

"Why are they wetting the track with that truck?"

"Settlin the dust they just stirred up."

Payne rubbed Ragina's back. "Darlin, did ya bring us a little bettin money along?"

"Of course."

"How much ya gonna wager?"

"I don't know. What do you think?"

"I think it's your money."

"How about five-hundred?"

"Chicken."

"A thousand?"

"Loan me a thousand and we'll bet two."

"You going to pay me back if we lose, big boy?"

"Losin never crossed my mind."

"Where do you gamble?" Lisa asked.

"See that ol boy in the wide brimmed hat? His name's Red. He's the bookie."

"Is that legal?"

"Must be. The law's standin next to him." Payne chuckled. "The Hill Country has different laws than the rest of the State when it comes to horse racin."

Payne watched Red and the deputy closely the first six races. He saw them pull a horse in the second and fifth races. Both times, the bet was made early and Red had handed the roll of money to the deputy, who in turn, had removed his hat and wiped his forehead with his white handkerchief. But Payne never spotted the signal.

Before the seventh race, Ragina pulled a wad of money from her purse and peeled off two grand. Payne held the money and watched closely for Skeeter to signal. His hat never came off.

"Okay, we're in the race."

"What?" Ragina asked.

"Nothin."

"When are you going to bet?"

"In a minute. Hang tight."

Payne waited until the horses neared the starting gate before walking up to Red. He was last in line. "Two thousand on number *five*."

"Name?" Red asked, without looking up.

"Payne."

"You're Skeeter's friend." Red eyed him suspiciously. "That's a lotta money for a cowboy."

"Jerry's daughter wanted to bet on her new horse."

Red squinted, looking into the stands. "Next time, tell her to come down herself. I wanna get a better look at that." Red took the money. He held it in his hand while writing Payne's name down on the racing guide, next to Dial Sammy's. "Hell, I hope her luck's not as big as her tits are. Shit, I'd give two thousand just to see that pair." Payne tipped his hat and let the comment slide.

"Are y'all ready to win?" Payne asked, taking his seat between the two ladies.

"I'm nervous," Ragina said. She took Payne's hand.

"This is so exciting!" Lisa squealed. The bell rang. The horses were off and the fans sprang to their feet. Lisa stood on the seat for a better view.

Skeeter wore green. But he wasn't immediately visible in the throng of horses that had bunched together out of the gate. Then the horses began to thin, stringing along the backstretch before entering the turn.

"There he is!" Ragina screamed and pointed. She jumped up and down, clapping her hands.

"He's runnin a tight second," Payne yelled.

"Go baby! Go baby!" Lisa screamed over and over in Payne's right ear. She was pounding her fists on his shoulder, getting louder and harder with each *go baby*!

Skeeter rode with ease in second place around the turn before letting Dial Sammy have the reins. The black horse passed the leader, thundering down the home stretch.

Payne jumped in the air. "Skeeter's passin that horse like he's tied!"

Dial Sammy moved into first. The horse he passed began slowing and falling back. Skeeter quit whipping and tucked his crop as Dial Sammy continued to pull further away from the field of horses. Crossing the finish line, Skeeter stood in the stirrups and waved his cap. There wasn't another horse in the picture.

Ragina was jumping up and down. She threw her arms around Payne. "Hell, yeah! He did it! He really did it! I wish Daddy could've seen this."

"Come on, let's go," Payne said.

"Where?"

"To get your picture made with Dial Sammy. You too, Lisa. This is gonna be a family portrait."

The three stopped in front of Red who quickly counted out the money and handed it to Ragina. "Nice race. But your daddy would've bet ten times that wager. The less ya bet, the more ya lose when ya win."

"What?"

"He said, ya shoulda bet more. Ya woulda won more," Payne interpreted.

"Next time I will. A lot more."

Payne escorted the ecstatic ladies across the dusty track. Sam Blackburn was holding Dial Sammy by the bridle in the winner's circle. "Helluva horse ya got here, ma'am. Congratulations. Ol Jerry would be proud."

"Thank you." Ragina shook his strong, callused hand. "Skeeter said you were the best trainer around."

Sam grinned at the compliment. "That horse don't need trainin. Just needs a little exercisin to keep his wind up."

"Told ya this son-of-bitch could run!" Skeeter bragged, trying to keep control of the sweating, boisterous black steed.

Ragina reached for the horse. "I swear he knows he won. Skeeter you're great!"

"Oh my God!" Lisa said, gazing up at Skeeter. "This is so exciting!"

"Okay girls, line up for the camera," Payne directed. "Skeeter needs to get back to work." The moment was frozen in time with a snap of the camera. Payne stood beneath Skeeter with one arm around Ragina and the other around Lisa. They were all smiles.

Returning to their seats, Payne pulled his pen out and began writing in his little pocket notebook. "What are you doing?" Ragina asked.

"Writin down some ideas for that song I started last weekend."

"Always the songwriter."

"Can't help it. Sometimes stuff just pops out unexpected." Payne put his pen and notebook in his shirt pocket and patted his pocket. "That's why I always carry paper and pen."

"What'd you write down?"

NASHVILLE GOLD

"Just a couple of thoughts. I'm gonna call that song I started *Pari-mutuel Blues*."

CHAPTER EIGHTEEN

The spring flood had displaced hundreds of people from their homes all along the rivers. After hearing the same story for the third time, Ragina gave up on finding an apartment anywhere near New Braunfels.
　"I told ya, you can stay at the house," Payne volunteered on the drive home. "Skeeter won't care."
　"If I'm going to stay at your house, you have to get me an air conditioner. I'll even buy it," Ragina pleaded. "How would that be?"
　"Nothin's open around here on Sunday. Specially on Memorial Day weekend."
　"Then let's take the Jeep to San Antonio. Something will be open there."
　"I'd rather get some beer and float the river. Did ya bring that string bikini?"
　"Yes, as-a-matter-of-fact, I did." But Ragina was pouting. "I was hoping to work on my tan around the pool at my new apartment."
　"City girl."
　"I'm not letting you off the hook. You've got to get me an air conditioner."
　"Maybe Tuesday. Wanna float the river, or not? That'll cool ya off."
　Ragina slammed the Porsche into forth gear and hit the gas. "Fine."

*

　Payne drove the Jeep along River Road. He appeared more interested in the uprooted and mangled trees than the busty blonde in the skimpy blue bikini. "This ol river's gonna be scarred for years from that damn flood. Water's still high."
　"Is high water bad for floating?"
　"No. Really, I like it better when it's high. Ya don't get your ass scraped on the rocks."
　"I haven't done this since I was a kid," Ragina said, her mood brightening.

Payne parked beneath a tree. Jack's River Rides consisted of a small wooden shack surrounded by one stack after another of inner tubes, inflated rafts, and canoes. It was packed with people, all hot and looking to the river for relief.

Payne surveyed the crowd. "Better slip your T-shirt on. Ya go walkin around all these people in that little thing, somebody's liable to have a stroke."

"Is that a compliment?"

"That's a fact."

But even with the T-shirt, Ragina was turning every male head around the small yellow shack. A rowdy crowd of leering young bucks had indiscreetly followed them to the riverbank. "Girl, you're causin quite a stir around here," Payne said. He handed her the ice chest. A collective moan came from the bank when Ragina deliberately bent over from the waist to set the ice chest down.

Kneeling in the raft, Ragina rewarded her admirers by peeling off her T-shirt, eliciting more moans and a splattering of applause. "Do you mind?"

"Not as long as they don't try to get in the boat with us."

Payne shoved the rubber raft off just as the moaning on the bank began to turn into crass suggestions. He shook his head at her and opened a couple of beers. Handing the first one to Ragina, he reclined in the raft and relaxed with the motion of the water.

"This is the life. Hot day, water, cold beer, and the most beautiful girl on the river."

"Payne, that's two compliments in a row. What's come over you?"

"I don't know."

"Well, whatever it is, I think I like it."

Floating downstream, Ragina's curiosity got the better of her. "Tell me about Sylvia."

"I already told ya what happened."

"Do you still love her?"

"Do ya still love your ex?"

"No. I'm not sure I ever did. Not really. I was still in college when I fell for his good looks and Corvette."

Payne didn't answer. She watched him lean over the side and push the raft away from an approaching rock protruding from the water. He leaned back and closed his eyes.

"You didn't answer my question."

"I loved her. She was my whole world. I'm not sure ya can just quit lovin someone."

"So, you still love her?"

"Maybe. I don't know."

Ragina sipped on her beer and silently watched a mile of countryside pass by before she spoke again. "I think you must still love her."

"Why's that?"

"Because you've never fallen in love again since your divorce."

"Really?"

"Really."

"Well, maybe I just haven't met the right woman yet."

"Damn you, Payne."

"What?"

"What you just said is, that I'm not the right woman either."

"Hell, I didn't think that was a news flash. I've already told ya why this ain't gonna work between us. There's too many differences."

"Love doesn't rise and fall on difference. Love can overcome differences. I'm not buying that any more. Payne, if you'd give it a chance, this might work between us."

"Maybe that's true, but I'm still goin to Nashville. That's a lotta distance between us."

"I'd wait for you."

"What if I don't wanna come back?"

"Then I'd come after you."

Payne opened his eyes. "I'm not playin a game with ya. I've been honest from the start. I'm not the marryin kind, remember?"

"Yeah, I remember. But I was hoping to change your mind."

"Are we through talkin serious yet?"

"Yeah." Ragina turned away from him. "We're *through*," she said, ending the conversation.

After a silent ride to the house, Payne parked the Jeep next to the Porsche. "Do ya know how to shoot that pistol?"

"Not really."

"Ever shot a gun at all?"

"No."

"Get it out. If you're gonna carry a gun around, ya need to know how to use it. I wouldn't want ya to shoot yourself."

Payne lined up a row of Skeeter's tall boy beer cans on a log before handing the .38 to Ragina. "Okay, lock your right elbow and point the gun toward the beer cans. Take your left hand and wrap it around the back of your right hand." She followed his orders. "Look down the barrel and aim it at a can. Inhale slowly. Now *squeeze* the trigger. Don't jerk it."

Ragina fired the pistol. She jumped back and screamed.

"Try it again." Payne stepped behind her and helped her aim. Now just *squeeze*."

The beer can flew into the air. "I did it!"

"No, we did it. Try it again without me helpin ya."

Half a box of shells later Ragina was hitting almost as many as she was missing. Payne stood behind her as she aimed and ran his hands up and down her sides.

"You're distracting me."

"I know. If ya ever have to use this, you're gonna be distracted. Ya need to concentrate on shootin the gun regardless of what's goin on around ya."

"I think I like this part of the lesson."

"Concentrate."

After another round, Payne took the gun from her. "You've got the hang of it. Come on. I'm gonna clean it and reload it for ya. Then I want ya to promise me ya won't ever use it on me."

Ragina laughed. "I promise."

Payne grabbed a couple of beers and sat at the kitchen table. Ragina watched him clean the .38.

"Payne, I'm hot. I want an air conditioner."

"People in hell want ice water, but they don't get it."

Ragina stormed out of the kitchen in a huff. Returning with her suitcases, she glared at Payne. She had tears in her eyes. "I'll always be grateful to you, but you're never going to change. Call me if you ever fall out of love with your ex-wife. I give up."

Payne laid the cleaned, loaded gun on the table. "Where're ya goin?"

"Back to Houston."

"I thought ya had business to take care of."

"Billy makes house calls."

"Ragina?" Payne scooted his chair back, but didn't get up.

"What?" she screamed at him.

"Don't forget your gun."

*

The speeding Porsche passed Skeeter's pickup along the narrow road to the house. Ragina didn't bother waving.

Payne was still seated at the table when the little lovers came through the back door. He had finished his beer and was working on Ragina's.

"Where's Ragina goin?" Skeeter asked.

"Houston."

"What about the race tomorrow?"

"What about it?" Payne spoke without looking at them.

"Is she comin back for the race?"

"Doubt it. I wouldn't expect her back."

"Shit, Payne. We needed that horse."

"Skeeter," Lisa interrupted. "I think Payne's got more on his mind than that horse."

"Hell, this ain't the first time Payne's sent a woman packin." Skeeter turned his attention back to Payne. "What're we gonna do without Dial Sammy?"

"I'll split the stable bill with ya for June. Just keep him at the track. We can still run him, can't we?"

"I suppose. Long as she don't sell him. He's worth some money after yesterday."

"She don't need the money."

"What about the race tomorrow?"

"Scratch him."

"Red's gonna be disappointed. I figure he's already plannin on pullin him." Skeeter crossed his arms and grinned at Payne. "Sure hate to disappoint Red."

Reaching into the refrigerator, Skeeter pulled out three beers. He handed a Budweiser to Payne. "Why'd she leave?"

"Wouldn't buy her an air conditioner."

CHAPTER NINETEEN

Payne rolled over in bed on Memorial Day and draped his arm over Pardner. He rubbed his old dog's ear between his thumb and fingers causing a deep moan to escape from his new bedfellow. He thought about Ragina.

"Just as well she's gone," Payne said to his dog.

Pardner didn't move when Payne left the bed and went for coffee. Skeeter and Lisa were seated at the table. Both were dressed in running shorts, T-shirts, and tennis shoes. Skeeter, covered with sweat, was drinking a Miller tall boy. Lisa set her glass of water down and gave Payne a little wave. "Good morning," she said.

"Mornin, Lisa." But Payne was looking at Skeeter. "That looks like sweat. I didn't know ya knew how to do that." Payne rinsed out a coffee cup and glanced over his shoulder at Skeeter.

"Been joggin."

Stumped, Payne shook his head and poured his coffee. He didn't bother responding.

"Aren't ya gonna ask me why?"

"Skeeter, I've known ya long enough to know you're gonna tell me whether I ask or not."

Lisa giggled.

"Tryin to keep the weight off."

"Orange juice instead of beer for breakfast might work just as good."

"I swore off cocaine. Promised Lisa, never again."

Payne sat at the table. He blew on his coffee before taking a sip. "That kinda sounded like a commitment. I didn't know ya knew how to do that either."

"Yeah, well I'm an amazin guy."

"Sweatin and committin? Skeeter, you're startin to worry me." Payne grinned at them. "Kinda sounds like love."

Lisa let out another giggle.

"Maybe." Skeeter wrapped his small, strong arm around Lisa's shoulder. "Payne, ya know what I like about Lisa?"

Payne didn't bother to answer.

"She looks just as good in the mornin as she does when she goes to bed."

"That's a fact," Payne said. He took a sip.

"Thank you. You guys are sweet."

"Goin to the races today?" Skeeter asked Payne.

"Doubt it. Unless ya want me to take Lisa."

"Hell, I wouldn't trust ya with my woman. No way. She's goin with me. She's bringin me luck. Won four races yesterday. Got close to five hundred bucks. Countin Saturday, I'm already over a thousand with a day to go."

"I won a thousand on ya Saturday."

"Ya bet on a horse race? Where'd ya get a thousand?"

"Borrowed it from Ragina."

"What if I'd lost?"

"Didn't."

Skeeter shoved his chair back. "I'm gonna take a shower and change. Then we're off to the races."

Payne waited until he had left the room before asking Lisa, "What've ya done with my little friend, Skeeter?"

Lisa giggled, but her face had blushed red. "He said he loves me."

"What's not to love?"

"Oh, Payne."

"He told ya?"

"Yes."

"Well, I can see that." Payne leaned over the table. "He's got the easy end of that deal. Lovin the little shit back would be the hard part."

"No it's not. It's the easiest thing I've ever done. You love him too. I know that's a fact."

"I reckon, but don't ya ever tell him I admitted it." Payne leaned back in his chair. "Y'all makin any long term plans?"

"Not yet."

"Well, before ya do, you'll have to learn how to spell Doeppenschmidt."

Lisa laughed and got up from the table. "I need to get ready." But she turned back at the door. Leaning over Payne's shoulder, she whispered in his ear, "D-O-E-P-P-E-N-S-C-H-M-I-D-T."

*

Payne waited until he heard them drive off before going to the phone and dialing San Antonio information. "Need a listin for Sylvia Taylor." Payne wrote the number down. He stared at it for a moment, then wadded it up. "Nope," he said out loud, and went for a shower. "Ain't gonna do it."

Payne worked on *Pari-mutuel Blues* until he got bored and left the house for a drive with Pardner. Loading into the Jeep by himself was another thing Pardner didn't do anymore. Payne had to lift him into the front seat. "I swear you're gettin fatter than the town dog," he said, then petted him on the head. Pardner barked in agreement.

With no particular direction in mind, Payne drove out the Devil's Backbone to Heidi's Roadhaus. It was almost two in the afternoon when he sat down with his Budweiser and a brisket sandwich.

Casey spotted him while passing through the small restaurant and stopped in her tracks. She watched him eat for a moment before strolling over and pulling up a chair.

"How's the food?"

"Good." Payne chased down a bite with his Bud. "How's Casey?"

"Good. You know that." Payne grinned at her and took another bite.

"What brings you out this way? Lost?"

"Bored. Just went out for a drive with Pardner and got hungry. Thought I'd drop in and say hello."

"You must be between women."

"Yeah." Payne grinned at her. "I needed a break."

"What happened to Jerry's little girl? The last I heard she had moved in."

"She got hot and went back to Houston."

"How's my favorite little drummer boy?"

"In love." Payne stuck the last of his sandwich in his mouth.

"No shit?"

Payne nodded his head while he chewed then chased down the last bite with his beer. "Met her in San Antonio, at the Crystal Stallion. She's a cute little thing. Looks just like Charly McClain. So far, she thinks Skeeter hung the moon."

"And you haven't told her any different?"

"Far be it from me."

"How's the band?"

"Nova's bein her usual. We did all right last weekend. But I ran into my ex-wife there Friday night. She's divorced and livin back in San Antonio."

"What'd you say to her?"

"Not much. Skeeter ran her off. She wants me to call her."

"Do I look like Ann Landers? Why are you telling me all this?"

Payne finished off his beer. "I didn't ask ya anything. I was just makin conversation. Now you're caught up."

"Where're you working?"

"Haven't started back yet. Been in Houston for awhile."

"With the Silicone Queen?"

"Yeah. Hey, I saw Rusti King at Gillie's. Stood right there and listened to her do *When Love Turns Out The Light*. I think I'm in love."

"With Rusti King?"

"Definitely. We even have somethin in common."

"What's that?"

"My song."

"Well, somebody better warn her." Casey drummed her nails on the table. "I've got some work for you, if you're interested."

"What's that?"

"I'd been talking to Jerry about building a big redwood deck around a hot tub. I want it covered, like a gazebo. You know he was sweet on me."

"Hell, Jerry was sweet on ever body he was tryin to screw. Ya got the tub picked out?"

"It's sitting in the crate, in my backyard. Interested?"

"What's it pay?"

"I'll treat you right." Casey leaned back and crossed her arms. "I always have, haven't I? Need another Bud?"

"Ya buyin?"

"You broke?"

"No."

"Then you buy it. I'll get it." Casey returned with his beer. "Want to come see my project? Take a look at it and tell me what you'd charge me."

"I don't need to look at it. Ten bucks an hour and I'm yours. I'll be there in the mornin, about eight."

"Make it ten, unless you want to come home with me and spend the night."

"Ten it is. No offense, but I'm swearin off women." Payne left the table and reached for his billfold. "For a week or so anyway."

"I thought you were bored."

"That was before I found a job. Now, I've got some things to take care of before mornin. Anyway, Pardner's probably gettin hot. I'll see ya in the mornin."

"Keep your money. Lunch is on me."

"Really? Well, thanks. Beer, too?"

"Beer, too."

"Hey, ya got any rib bones back there?"

"Sara!" Casey yelled toward the back. "Payne needs some bones for his old dog!" Standing next to him, she rubbed on his back while they waited for Pardner's to-go order.

"Here you go, sweet thing." Sara appeared from the kitchen and handed him the bag of rib bones.

"Thank ya, darlin." Payne gave the plump German woman a hug and his best smile. "Thanks again for lunch." He hugged Casey before heading for the door.

"Thanks for stopping by." Casey called after him, "One more thing. Speaking from experience, I'd leave well enough alone with your ex-wife. Life goes on. It's too short to start backing up."

"Thanks Ms. Landers." He waved to her from the door. "I'll see ya tomorrow."

CHAPTER TWENTY

Sylvia Taylor had grown up poor on the south side of San Antonio, the product of an interracial marriage. She had been blessed with her mother's Mexican black hair and dark brown eyes. The light skin had come from her father. As a child, both sides of her heritage had cruelly labeled her a half-breed. But the combination had blossomed during adolescence into a striking, exotic look. The ridicule had stopped.

In high school, Payne had been the first. The first to treat Sylvia with respect. The first to tell her she was beautiful. The first to love her. He had swept her off her feet with his good looks and guitar.

Entering the Crystal Stallion on Friday night, Sylvia sat alone at the end of the bar closest to the band, and thought about Payne. She wasn't certain she had ever stopped loving him. But she had given up on his dream and moved on. She lit a cigarette before ordering a gin and tonic. Without turning to look, she listened to the familiar guitar. It was a sound that took her back through the years.

In the beginning, Sylvia had shared Payne's music dream, certain of his imminent stardom. But she hadn't bargained for the long bumpy road to Nashville. The route from Texas to Tennessee wound its way through smoky, dirty bars, surrounded by disgusting drunks. Sylvia had begun searching the highway for an exit sign while Payne contentedly honed his skills.

The last year, Sylvia had stopped going to the bars. Payne had understood. But with the nights apart, she had been vulnerable to Richard. Five years later, she again glanced over her shoulder at the lead guitar player. Now, just as then, she waited for the first set to end.

At the break, Skeeter bolted from the stage to take his seat with Lisa. Leaving Hartman and Nova, Payne strolled over to the closest bar in search of a cold Budweiser. But there was Sylvia. He watched her run her fingers through her long black hair then toss her head before turning to face him.

"Payne, I've already bought you a Budweiser." Her pouty lips, covered in bright pink lipstick, struggled to form a smile. "I'd like to talk to you, without your pit bulldog attacking me. Where'd Skeeter go?"

Payne motioned with his head toward Skeeter's table. He approached the bar and felt her hand on his back as he reached for the beer. "I'm listenin," he said.

"I know you don't owe me the time of day, but I'd really like a chance to explain things to you."

"I'm still listenin."

"Not here. I'd like to go somewhere quiet. Some place we can talk."

"I'm kinda busy, if ya haven't noticed."

"Tomorrow?"

"I'm busy tomorrow."

"Payne, please?"

He hesitated before answering. "I'd like to hear your side. Will ya leave here, if I agree?"

"Why?"

"It's just the deal. Take it or leave it."

"I'll leave." Sylvia lowered her eyes and removed her hand from his back. "How about lunch tomorrow?" She ran a long pink fingernail along the back of his left hand that was griping the edge of the rustic bar. "I'll meet ya at the La Fiesta Restaurant on I-35, at noon."

Payne set his beer on the bar and nodded.

Her eyes searched his. "Promise?"

"I'll be there. Promise to leave?"

Sylvia tossed back the gin and tonic. "See you tomorrow." She slid off her stool and was gone.

"Payne, tell me I didn't just see ya with Sylvia," Skeeter said, stepping on stage.

"She's gone."

"What'd she want?"

"She wanted to talk. I told her I was busy."

"Payne, do yourself a favor and stay away from the bitch."

"I said, she's gone." Payne turned his back on him and picked up his guitar.

"Okay boys." Nova clapped her hands at them. "Back to work. By the way, Jimmy Earl has us booked in Austin starting next Friday."

"Where?" Skeeter asked.

"At Stetson's."

"Like the hat?"

"Yeah, like the hat."

"Never heard of it."

"It's somewhere around 6th Street, near the campus. Lots of college girls for you boys to gawk at."
"Good. Maybe one of em will get Payne's mind off his ex-wife."

*

Payne rolled the Jeep to a stop in front of the white stucco restaurant on Saturday. It was exactly high noon. Thick low clouds blocked the sun, but not the heat. The muggy day had caused his short-sleeved western shirt to stick to the seat of his Jeep. Looking at himself in the rearview mirror, he ran his hands through his hair before putting on his hat. He took a deep breath and headed toward the restaurant's thick wooden doors.

A blast of cold air from La Fiesta's air conditioning penetrated his damp shirt, causing his body to shiver. Sylvia was already there, standing in the foyer.

"I wasn't sure you'd come."

"I'm not the one who breaks promises."

Sylvia's smile disappeared. Her head dropped just long enough for Payne to study her without notice. She wore a short, straight skirt, exposing her tanned legs and sandals. Her cotton blouse was tucked in, accentuating her shapely figure. A Mexican woman, in a flowing, colorful dress, ended the awkward moment. "Table for two?"

Payne nodded and followed Sylvia through the restaurant, remembering her body and her touch. The rich scent of her perfume trailed behind her.

Seated across from him in the booth, Sylvia ordered a frozen margarita. Payne looked out the window at the passing cars on the Interstate. He ordered a Budweiser without looking at the waitress.

"Payne, you're looking handsome as always. Who was the busty blonde you were with last weekend?"

"A friend from Houston."

"Are you involved with her?"

"No."

Sylvia leaned back and fumbled through her purse. "Mind if I smoke?"

"Help yourself. When'd ya start that?"

Sylvia nervously lit her cigarette. "It was one of Richard's bad habits I picked up."

"So what happened to good ol Richard?"

Exhaling the smoke above Payne's head, she tossed the spent match into the ashtray. "We divorced about six months ago. It's a long story."

The waitress sat their drinks on the table and Payne snatched his beer. He took a long drink and looked to Sylvia. "Are ya ready to order?"

"I'm not really hungry."

"Me either." He looked up at the waitress. "We're good for now."

"Payne, this isn't easy for me. I'd like to start with ... I'm sorry. What I did to you was so very wrong. I didn't mean for things to happen the way they did." Sylvia searched Payne's expressionless face. "Richard and I had an affair."

"No shit."

Sylvia looked down and continued. "Toward the end ... the nights you were away playing in the bars ... he would take me to expensive restaurants. He bought things for me. Payne, he gave me things I'd never had. Promised me things. I'm so sorry I hurt you." She shook her head and wiped tears from the corners of her eyes. "I got tired of sitting alone at the bars watching you play."

"Okay. I've got it so far. Ya got bored. And decided to start screwin Richard."

"I felt like you loved your music more than you loved me."

"Bullshit," Payne said. "If I'd known ya felt that way, I woulda quit. All ya had to do was ask. I'd have done anything in the world for ya. Are ya gonna sit there and try to blame me, for what *you* did? Ya said ya were all for the music. It was our one ticket out. Remember?" Payne started to leave the booth.

"Wait! I'm not trying to blame you. Please ... sit down." She reached for him and took his hand. "I'm just trying to tell you how it happened. I couldn't ask you to quit your music. It meant too much to you. Right or wrong, I justified everything that way."

"Whatever." Payne pulled his hand away from her. He watched his own finger trace the grout around the blue and yellow ceramic tiles that formed the tabletop. But he was listening, intently, to her every word.

"Richard rented an apartment for me. He hired the movers. I wrote you a letter, explaining things." She paused. Payne looked up. "It never got mailed."

"Damn, for a minute there, I thought ya were gonna blame it all on the mailman."

Sylvia smiled. "I've missed your sense of humor."

"I wasn't tryin to be funny."

Sylvia stirred the slushy drink and changed the subject. "So, how's Pardner?"

"Old and lazy."

"Where are you living?"

"Out in the country with Skeeter. North of New Braunfels."

"Skeeter hasn't changed any. He never did like me."

"Skeeter's always been a good judge of character. I shoulda listened to him."

"Maybe this was a bad idea." Sylvia looked out the window trying to collect her thoughts.

"Probably."

"Payne," Sylvia reached across the table and took his hand, "can you ever forgive me?"

"Are ya askin me to?" Payne withdrew his hand and reached for his beer. "Is that what this is all about. Ya want me to forgive ya?"

"It would be a nice place to start."

"Then you're forgiven. But that doesn't mean I've forgotten a damn thing." Payne saw their waitress and waved her over. "I'll have another beer." He looked at Sylvia. "Ready?"

"Please." Sylvia lit another cigarette. "Your band sounds good. You're moving up in the world, playing at the Crystal Stallion. That's a long way up from where you and Skeeter started in high school."

"It's not my band. It's Nova's. I'm just a guitar player."

"Still writing songs?"

"A few. I'm plannin on movin to Nashville after the Fourth of July. We're gonna play at Willie Nelson's Picnic. Then I'm leavin. I'm gonna try to push some songs up there. Figure I can do carpenter work up there just as easy as I can do it around here." Payne leaned back from the table. "I've been needin a change of scenery."

"Still following your music dream, I take it?"

"Same dream, different day." Payne removed the round cork coaster from under his beer and spun it on the table. "So, what's Sylvia *Taylor* doin these days?"

"I'm a receptionist at Glenn-Brook Ford. I got a nice settlement from Richard. It was a mutual thing. The job doesn't pay much, but I don't need a lot to live on. A bunch of us from work went out for drinks the night I ran into you at the Crystal Stallion. I couldn't believe that was you. I didn't think I'd ever see you again."

"Small world."

"Payne, when I saw you up there in the band, I was so happy for you. I still care for you. I know that may be hard for you to believe, but I do." She took his strong hands in hers. "I don't think I ever stopped loving you."

"You've gotta funny way of showin it."

"Payne, please don't make this any harder on me than it already is. I'm trying to tell you ... I'd like to see you again."

The waitress set their drinks down and took the empties. "Are you going to want to order any food?"

"No, thanks," Payne answered. "You can bring the check next time ya come around."

"Does that mean my time's up?"

"I told ya I was busy today."

"I know this sounds crazy, but I was hoping that we might start over. Just back up a few years and start it all over again."

"Just like nothin happened?"

"Exactly. I'd like to try and make things up to you. Just give me a chance. No promises. No commitments. Let's just see where it goes."

Payne withdrew his hands. "I already know where things are goin. I'm goin to Nashville and you're not." Payne leaned into the table. "Look Sylvia, I'm not gonna lie to ya. There hasn't been a day gone by that I haven't thought about ya. I've had so many questions in my head. I've wondered what ya were doin. Wondered if ya ever thought about me. Wondered how I could hate ya one minute and still feel like I loved ya the next. Mostly, I wondered what I did to cause ya to start screwin your boss."

"Payne, I'm so sorry."

"No. Let me say my piece. I kept thinkin it musta been somethin I did or didn't do. But ya know? It wasn't me. It was just you. Just Sylvia."

"I've already said I'm sorry. I can't change what happened."

"And I wondered why ya didn't even bother tellin me good-bye. I've had a real hard time with that one. That wasn't even common damn courtesy."

"Payne, I'm so sorry."

Sylvia's eyes were tearing again. The waitress laid the check on the table without a word and quickly escaped the obvious lover's quarrel.

Leaning back, Payne folded his arms. "Ya know, I've wondered for years what I'd say, if I ever saw ya again. But ya know what?"

"No, I don't know what." Sylvia wiped more tears from her eyes.

"I'm through wonderin about ya." Payne looked at the check and pulled out his billfold. Laying down the money for the tab, he looked back to Sylvia. "I don't know about *you*, but *I* feel a helluva lot better. We've been needin to clear the air. Thanks for the invite. Help yourself to my Budweiser. I'm gone."

"That's it?" Her eyes widened watching Payne slide out of the booth. She watched him put on his hat and slide it to the back, just so.

"Nope, there's one more thing." Payne stuffed his billfold back in his pocket. "I've always wanted the chance to tell ya good-bye, just so I could get on with my life." Payne tipped his hat to her. "Adios, darlin."

DEKKER MALONE

*

Payne stayed around the house on Sunday, determined to work on his music. He finished *Pari-mutuel Blues* and charted it before he allowed himself to think about Sylvia. He replayed their visit in his mind. But this time, when she crossed his mind, the familiar pain was gone. For the first time in five years, he felt good about himself. Picking up his six-string, he took a deep breath and smiled. He found a waltz in three simple country chords. The lyrics came as fast as he could write them down.

>   Well it's sure good to see you
>   It must have been almost a year.
>   The last time I saw you
>   I was looking at you through my tears.
>   You left me here crying
>   Didn't have a dang thing left to say.
>   So imagine my surprise
>   When I saw you walk in here today.
>
>   You say things are rough,
>   But you know that the world turns that way.
>   Yeah I hear what you're saying,
>   But I just never saw it your way.
>   Now you're askin me darlin
>   Can we back up and start it again?
>   Let me help you out darlin,
>   Do you remember the way you came in?
>
>   Chorus
>   Do you remember the way you came in?
>   Askin me darlin please love me again.
>   You say we'll be much more than friends ...
>   So I'll help you out darlin
>   Do you remember the way you came in?
>
>   You can cry all you want to,
>   But don't talk to me about tears.
>   Cause I know a heartache
>   And that's not what you're having here.

NASHVILLE GOLD

> *So don't paint me a picture*
> *Of the way our love might have been,*
> *Let me help you out darlin*
> *Do you remember the way you came in?*
>
> *Repeat Chorus*
> *Tag: Yeah, I'll help you out darlin*
> *Exit the way you came in.*

Payne looked at his old golden retriever who lay sleeping next to him on the couch. "Pardner, Skeeter's gonna love this one."

CHAPTER TWENTY-ONE

Skeeter and Lisa came bouncing through the backdoor while Payne was still charting *Let Me Help You Out Darlin.* "Payne!" Skeeter yelled from the kitchen. "Ya in here?"
"Last I looked," Payne yelled back from the couch.
"Payne, we're gonna get married!" Ushering Lisa into the living room, Skeeter held her hand. Both were glowing.
"I'll be damn."
"That's it?" Skeeter asked. "That's all ya gotta say?"
Payne put his guitar down and crossed the room without a word. First, he shook their hands then hugged the happy couple. Stepping back, Payne looked them over. "I'll be damn. When's the big day?"
"Not sure yet. Pretty quick though. I don't wanna give her a chance to change her mind."
"It's going to be a really small wedding," Lisa was beginning to talk faster with each word, "since both of our parents are old ... did you know both of our parents retired in Florida? We'll be able to see all of them in one trip. Isn't it a small world? Anyway, I'm going to ask my sister to be my maid of honor. She's bigger than I am. We're going to have just a few friends and ... "
Skeeter cut her off and changed the pace to his slow Texas drawl. "We're thinkin since the Fourth of July is on a Monday, and that's the big racin weekend in Fredericksburg, maybe the weekend before that one. The races are in Brady. That'd be a good weekend to skip em. That's a long way to travel."
"That would be three weeks," Payne said. "Lisa, I really need to talk to ya about Skeeter before then. There's some things ya oughta know."
"Like what?" She looked at Skeeter and back to Payne.
"Like he's a little shit with a big mouth. He can't cook worth a flip and he rarely does the dishes. I can't honestly recommend him as a roommate."
"Oh, Payne, I thought you were being serious. I already knew that." Lisa giggled. She gave Skeeter a quick kiss and giggled again, for no apparent reason.
"Payne, I want ya to be my best man."

117

"You'd hurt my feelins if I wasn't. It'd be an honor." Payne shook his head at the little lovers. "I'll be damn."

"Will you sing at our wedding?" Lisa asked.

"Anything ya want. Skeeter, what are y'all gonna do after ya get married? What about the Kentucky Derby?"

"I'm still gonna make my run for the roses. She's goin with me, that's all. We're gonna postpone our honeymoon till after the Fourth of July. Spend it in Kentucky while we're gettin settled in. Then we're gonna go to Florida and surprise the hell outta our folks."

"We want to get married outside. Under some trees." Lisa was getting wound up again. "I know that may sound funny. Some people might not like it, but ... "

Payne cut her off. "I got the perfect place. Jerry's got some property up at Canyon Lake."

"Don't ya mean Ragina's got some property?" Skeeter corrected. "We wanted to invite her anyway."

"I've got her number if ya wanna call her. I'd give her some notice. She stays awful busy in Houston. She might have to cancel a trip to the mall or somethin." Payne continued to shake his head from amazement. "I'll be damn. This calls for a toast."

Payne caught the phone on the way for beer.

"Payne!" Nova screamed over the phone. "I've got news. Y'all there?"

"Yeah, we're both here."

"I'll be there in twenty minutes."

"Nova's coming over," Payne said. "She's got her panties in a bunch over somethin." Returning with the beers, Payne raised his Budweiser. "Here's to my best friend in the world and the woman who loves him, despite him."

They toasted and drank. Skeeter raised his Miller tallboy to Payne. He turned serious. "Here's to true love, and to the day she walks into your life."

"Hell, I'll drink to that."

*

The three were sitting at the kitchen table when Nova came through the back door. She tripped over Pardner. "Shit! Payne, does that damn dog of yours ever do anything besides try to trip people?"

"Yeah, he farts a lot," Skeeter answered for Payne.

"Where's Hartman?"

Skeeter looked under the table. "I don't see him."

"He's supposed to be here."

"Give him a few minutes," Payne said. "You know Hartman. He don't get in a big rush. Hey, guess who's gettin married?"

"You?" Nova cackled.

"Nope. Skeeter and Lisa"

"Well, I'll be damn."

"I wish someone would say somethin besides, I'll be damn," Skeeter said. "Congratulations is the word most people use."

"Excuse the hell out of me. Well, congratulations then." Nova took a seat at the table. "Does this mean I'm going to have to find a new drummer?"

"Yep. We're outta here after Willie's Picnic."

"Me too," Payne added.

"Shit! I can't believe this!"

"What?" Hartman asked, opening the screen door.

"Watch out for Pardner," Payne warned.

"Oh, nothing." Nova turned in her chair toward Hartman. "We just got the break we've been looking for and I don't have a damn band. Jimmy Earl called. He's got us booked as one of the two warm-up bands for the Rusti King concert. It's in the Joe Freeman Coliseum this Thursday, in San Antonio. Somebody cancelled. It's two thousand bucks!"

"Less his commission," Skeeter added.

"That's still four hundred bucks a piece. More important, it's a chance to showcase our stuff. If we do good, somebody important might see us and pick us up. We could go national. I can't believe you guys!"

"We only agreed to stay through the Fourth," Skeeter said.

"No, you said you would give it a chance through the Fourth and see where it goes. It's going great!"

"No we didn't," Payne argued. "We both said we'd *give* it till the Fourth. Period."

"Maybe you should just concentrate on the Rusti King concert," Lisa suggested. "Just take one thing at a time."

"I need a drink." Nova left the table to retrieve her tequila from the car.

"Hartman," Skeeter said, "me and Lisa are gonna get married ... and don't say I'll be damn."

"Congratulations."

"Thank you." Skeeter smiled at Lisa.

"When's the big day?"

"Three weeks."

"I'll be damn."

"Hartman!" Skeeter yelled. "I told ya not to say that."

"Nova," Payne said, when she came through the door, "I've got two new songs ready."

Nova pulled out a glass from the cabinet and examined it. "Do you guys ever wash your dishes or just put them back in the cabinet when you clean up once a month?" She washed the glass out and poured a shot. "So? Tell me about your new songs."

"One's about a racehorse. I called it *Pari-mutuel Blues*. The other one's about my ex-wife. It's called *Let Me Help You Out Darlin*."

"Payne, have ya been seein Sylvia again?" Skeeter asked.

"Just once."

"Damn. She's no good for ya. Don't do that to yourself again."

"We just had a nice conversation. She begged me to take her back and I told her adios. I've never felt better."

"Look out girls. Hide your hearts." Nova took a shot. "Payne McCarty's on the loose. I hope that means you're in the market place again."

"Why? Ya interested?"

"Hell, yeah! We could just have a double-wedding with Skeeter and Lisa."

"Yeah, right." Payne left the kitchen and returned with his guitar and music. Strumming an "A" Major chord, he played *Pari-mutuel Blues* seated in the crowded kitchen. "So? What do ya think?"

"I think I hear a great keyboard part for me. Kind of a gettie-up beat. It's worth working on. Let's hear the next one."

Payne played *Let Me Help You Out Darlin*.

"I love it! Maybe ya really are healed." Skeeter sprang from his chair and danced a jig around the kitchen. He sang t*he wicked witch is dead! The wicked witch is dead! Ding damn dong! The wicked witch is dead.*

"Jeez, Skeeter!" Nova shook her head at him. "Have you lost your damn mind? Payne, it's perfect. We've been needing a waltz. Okay, let's get the equipment out and go to work. We can get this done in couple of hours."

"Heard that one before," Skeeter mumbled.

"Payne, can I talk to you outside a minute?" Nova asked.

"Sure."

Nova and Payne stepped over Pardner and sat on the back porch. "Payne, if you could get contracts on your songs without moving to Nashville, would you consider staying on? I can find another drummer, but I can't replace you. I'd be willing to let you do more solos. Let you take a bigger piece of the show. What do you think?"

"How ya plannin on gettin my songs contracted?"

"If we make it big, we can do your songs. I'm talking about an album."

"Doubt it. Even if we went national, somebody would be tellin us what songs we're gonna do and where we're gonna be doin em. Ya can't control that."

"Look, Jimmy Earl knows people. He could get it done, even if we didn't do them. The man's connected. He knows people in Nashville, publishers, producers, agents. I'm telling you, he's got connections."

"Tell ya what. You get Jimmy Earl to get me paid for *When Loves Turns Out the Light* and I'll consider it. Fact, if he can get that done, and get me connected with a good publisher, I'll agree to stay on." Payne nodded his head. "And I like the part about doin a few more songs."

"I'm on it."

"One more thing up front. If we have to hit the road, Pardner goes with me."

"You and that damn dog. Okay then, let's get started tonight. You sing your two new songs on Thursday, along with *Texas Rivera*. That's not a bad way to start is it?"

Payne got to his feet. "I'm happy."

"Jimmy Earl said we couldn't do *When Love Turns Out The Light* Thursday night."

"I can see that."

"So why don't you close the show with *Follow Your Dream*."

"That's a rocker. Ya sure?"

"Yeah. Let's leave the house rocking instead of crying. That's four out of ten songs you'll be doing."

Payne stretched. "Nova, I'm serious about gettin paid for that song. If I have to go to Nashville, I will. That's my deal. He's got till the Fourth to get somethin done."

"I'm on it, darlin. And Jimmy Earl's gonna be on it before he gets on me again. That's a fact." Nova stood up and extended her hand. "Deal?"

"Deal."

Payne followed her into the house. She stopped just long enough to pour more tequila. "Payne, why won't you get a damn air conditioner?"

CHAPTER TWENTY-TWO

Jimmy Earl had known Dennis Couch since 1971, from the early days of the Austin music boom. They had been around for Willie Nelson's first Fourth of July Picnic in Dripping Springs. At the time, both were booking agents in Austin. But that was before Dennis had rolled the dice and followed one of his bands to Nashville. The band had crashed and burned upon arrival, but Dennis had stayed on in Music City after finding a job with Golden Star Entertainment.

It had been Dennis who had spotted Rusti King's talent in a small honkey-tonk in Ft. Worth. He had brought her to Nashville in 1982, just after her twenty-first birthday. From there, James Houlette and his company, Golden Star Entertainment, had aimed the girl with the golden voice and wavy red hair toward the pinnacle of stardom.

Jimmy Earl arrived in San Antonio early afternoon on Thursday. He had two things on his mind: his love life with Nova and his newest project, Nova-Scotia. Heat was something Jimmy Earl usually tried to avoid. It didn't mix well with his black leather vest and black felt hat. But Jimmy Earl was on a mission. He roamed around Joe Freeman Coliseum for over an hour before *accidentally* running into Dennis Couch.

Rusti King's overweight, balding road manager listened patiently while Jimmy Earl bitched about the heat. He listened politely as he bragged about his new band. But when Jimmy Earl eventually got around to the subject of copyright infringement on Rusti's current hit, Dennis Couch hung on his every word. "Assuming this Payne fellow really did write the song, what's it gonna take to get this matter cleared up?" Dennis asked. "The last thing anybody needs is a law suit."

"Standard writer's royalties." Jimmy Earl went for the jugular.

"Get real! We've got a contract on that song with Branch Publishing Company in Nashville. Sounds like T.R. Branch has a problem, not us." Dennis shook his head. "I can't believe T.R. had anything to do with this. He's good as gold. This whole damn thing is hard for me to believe."

"Look, here's the way I see it." Jimmy Earl knew just enough to be dangerous. "Branch Publishin is gettin fifty percent of all the royalties. Charlie Keith's name's on the song as the writer."

"He's a staff writer for Branch."

"Well, he's gettin fifty percent of Branch's fifty percent. My guy sent the song to Sure-Star Publishin. So they've got to be gettin a piece of the pie somehow."

"That's Roger Durwood. He's a snake." Dennis folded his arms and shook his head in disgust. "Damn."

"Damn's right. Look, we're not after Branch's split. We'd be content with the money goin to Sure-Star and Charlie Keith. That's the standard writer's royalty we're after. And we don't have much time. Those royalty checks are fixin to start flowin. Once that money goes to the wrong people, all hell's gonna break loose."

"Jimmy Earl, this isn't our fault. We've got a legal contract for that song. All I can do is advise Houlette to contact Branch. It's their problem unless your guy want's a quick deal. I could probably get that done."

"I'm listenin."

"Five grand and he signs a release."

"Twenty-five."

"No way. We can settle it with our attorneys for less than that. Ten. That's it. We might get that much money back from Branch. And you've got to get us some evidence he wrote the song before anybody signs anything."

"Twenty thousand. That's ten grand from y'all and ten from Branch." Jimmy Earl removed his hat and ran his fingers through his thinning, sweaty black hair. "Payne might take that, less my commission. That'd be sixteen to him."

"I can't believe you'd try to take commission off something like this."

"Hell, I'm his agent. Is it a deal?"

"I can get this end done. What about Payne? Can you handle him?"

"Maybe." Jimmy Earl scratched his chin. "Dennis, what's the chance of Rusti talkin to him about it? Give him a little personal touch. Make him feel important."

"What? Why should she?"

"I got a feelin that if Rusti got involved ... maybe apologized about the mix up and bragged on his song, he might take the offer on the spot. I damn sure would if she batted those big green eyes at me."

"She doesn't get *involved* in business. She sings. Things run a lot better that way. You know that." Dennis took a deep breath. He closed his eyes and exhaled. "Let me think about it."

"Think hard. This could go away real quick or it could get real nasty. He's got his stinger out over it. Dennis, if I can't get him paid he's leavin the band and goin to Nashville. He's got a lawsuit on his mind. Besides that, without him and his music, my band's dead in the water. I wouldn't be askin if it wasn't important to me."

"I'll talk to her, but I'm not making any promises."

"They're scheduled for a sound test at five this afternoon. Talk to her. Let's see if we can get this behind both of us." Jimmy Earl shook hands with Dennis. "You're gonna like this band. I'm telling ya. The lead singer's a pistol. She's hot."

"Jimmy Earl, if I didn't know you better, I'd say there's more to this than you're letting on."

Jimmy Earl tried to hide his smile. "Hey. I'll owe ya a big one."

"Yeah. You damn sure will."

Dennis was out of breath and red in the face when he reached Rusti King's tour bus. He recounted his conversation with Jimmy Earl, concluding with his own sales pitch, "So, all you have to do is agree to meet with him. I'll do the rest."

"I can't believe you're asking me to be a part of this. It doesn't seem right. If he wrote it, he ought to get paid for it."

"We're going to offer him money. That's not the issue. The issue is avoiding a lawsuit and getting the royalties tied up in court for who knows how long. It could take years to settle something like this. Believe me, we don't need that."

"I'll meet him. But I don't like it."

"That's all I'm asking. Just be your charming self. I'll handle it from there."

"Should I change into something more seductive? Maybe a negligee?" She sneered at Dennis. "I mean that is what you're asking me to do, isn't it?"

Dennis looked at her baggy Houston Oilers football jersey and jeans. "No, you're fine."

*

Jimmy Earl spotted Rusti and Dennis walking through the backstage area shortly before five. Leading Nova by the arm, he greeted them at the top of the stage stairs. "Nova, this is Dennis Couch." Dennis shook her hand and flashed Jimmy Earl a grin before introducing them to Rusti.

"So, which one's the songwriter?" Rusti asked.

Nova pointed at Payne. "He's the blonde-haired hunk over there with his shirt off, helping with the drums."

"Mercy."

"Yeah. He's a real heartbreaker."
"Payne!" Jimmy Earl yelled at him. "Come here. I want ya to meet some folks." Rusti watched him pull his T-shirt on over his tanned, muscular back before her eyes traveled to his tight butt. Grabbing his hat, Payne strolled over to the back of the stage. "Payne, I want ya to meet Rusti King."
"It's a real pleasure." He smiled confidently at her and shook her hand. "Payne McCarty."
Rusti studied his blue eyes and handsome face. "It's very nice to meet you."
"And this is Dennis Couch, Rusti's manager," Jimmy Earl continued, interrupting the lingering eye contact between Payne and Rusti. "We've been discussin your song. They're ... "
Dennis interrupted Jimmy Earl. "Payne, we'd like to discuss the song with you. When you're done with your sound check, why don't you come out back to the bus? It's the blue and yellow one. We'll be expecting you."
"Yes, sir. Thank you."
Payne tipped his hat to Rusti and watched her descend the stairs. Nova jabbed him with her elbow. "Hey. Down boy."

*

The bus was parked in the afternoon shade of the Coliseum. Payne had changed from his plain T-shirt to his western shirt, the one he had planned to save for the concert. He introduced himself to the beefy bodyguard, who, without a word, pressed a concealed button on the bus. The door swung open with a *hiss* and he entered the cool luxury of stardom. It *hissed* behind him. He inhaled the scent of new leather, reminding him of Ragina's Porsche.
"Payne, thanks for coming. Have a seat." Dennis shook his hand and pointed to a plush brown leather couch beneath the tinted side window. "Can I get you something to drink?"
"What do ya have?"
"Anything you want."
"Budweiser."
Dennis knocked on the door separating the lounge from Rusti's quarters before getting the beer out of the refrigerator. Rusti had changed out of her football jersey into a fitted blouse. It was tucked into her jeans, defining her tall, shapely figure. Payne could smell her fresh perfume when she walked out the door.
She smiled. "Payne, thanks for coming by."

"Hey, thanks for invitin me." He shook her hand. Rusti sat next to him on the couch. Dennis sat on the other couch, across the narrow aisle. "I caught your show in Houston last week. Enjoyed it. I especially liked the way ya did my song. Best I've ever heard, or seen it done." He gave her a nod of approval while continuing to gaze into her green eyes.

"It's a wonderful song. But we were all surprised to learn it's your song. When did you write it?"

"Five years ago. Right after my ex-wife left me."

"I'm sorry." Rusti searched his eyes for any sign of deceit.

"No. It's okay now. It took awhile, but I'm over it."

"When I heard the song for the first time, I fell in love with it. It's got so much emotion. It's a powerful song."

"Thank you." Payne grinned at her and took a sip from his beer. "I couldn't even sing it after I wrote it. Just put it away with several others on the same subject. Nova found it a year or so ago. You met Nova."

"Yeah," Dennis answered. "Jimmy Earl looks like he's got more than just a professional interest in Nova."

"Yes, sir. And I think Nova's got her hook set pretty deep her own self. Anyway, I agreed to let her do it. Then Skeeter and I taped it and sent it to Nashville."

"Who's Skeeter?" Rusti asked.

"He's our drummer. Fact, Skeeter went with me to Nashville after we heard it on the radio. We tracked down Sure-Star Publishin, but we didn't get anywhere with him."

"That would be Roger Durwood." Dennis explained.

"Yes, sir. I spent ten days in the Nashville jail after our little visit."

"For what?" Dennis asked.

"They called it assault, but I never laid a finger on him." Payne grinned at Rusti. "Well, I did get a hold of his tie. Drug him over his desk, just as the cops came bustin in." He shook his head. "I swear it was a setup."

"It sure sounds like it," Rusti said. Her eyes were sparkling, listening to Payne's tall tale. "You wouldn't have any more songs like that laying around, would you?" She laughed, but was dead serious.

"I've got lotsa songs. We're doin several of em tonight." Payne took a sip. "I'll tell ya, I'm nervous. We've never played in front of this many people before."

Rusti patted him on the leg. "You'll get used to it."

"I'd like to think so. We're still playin mostly dance halls. Jimmy Earl's got us some better gigs, but we're still pretty much small time. Except for tonight."

"Things can change in a hurry. One day I was singing in a little club in Ft. Worth and the next thing I knew, Dennis had me in Nashville."

"Payne," Dennis interrupted them. "I talked to Jimmy Earl about the song. The long and short of it is this. We've got a contract on that song with Branch Publishing in Nashville. Your fight is going be with T.R. Branch. He's got a lot of money and the most powerful attorneys in Nashville. I'm not saying you can't eventually win, but I am saying it could take years."

"Yes, sir."

Dennis left the couch and began to pace in the aisle. "Frankly, we don't need any bad publicity on the song. People are funny about things like that. It's already number three. I see it hitting number one in another week or two and staying there for awhile. Hell, we even named the album after that song title."

"It's even starting to cross over to the pop charts," Rusti added. "It's a huge hit."

"The whole thing's amazin to me." Payne looked at Rusti, ignoring Dennis.

"Our company, Golden Star Entertainment, has a reputation to maintain. It would be worth something for us to see this whole thing go away, without any adverse publicity."

"What'd ya have in mind?"

"Five thousand and you sign a release. You're name would never be associated with the song, but it sounds like you've got a lot more where that came from. People in Nashville don't forget things like this. In addition to the money, we would be in a position to help you get more of your songs contracted, with reputable publishers. Point you in the right direction, so to speak. Maybe even Branch Publishing. T.R. Branch will be grateful to you. He'd be a good guy to have in your corner. But I wouldn't want to get in the ring with him, if you know what I mean."

"Dennis, that's nothing!" Rusti blurted. She glanced at Payne.

"Look. Thanks for the offer, but I don't think so. And thanks for the beer." He leaned forward to get up, but Rusti put her hand on his shoulder. "Hold on." She looked at Dennis. "You can do better than that."

"Ten thousand. That's all I can do."

Payne leaned back. "You and me both know that song's worth a helluva lot more than ten thousand dollars." Payne and Rusti's eyes met. She nodded.

"Twenty and that's it. Take it or leave it."

"That'd be a screwin." Payne glanced at Rusti. "Sorry."

She laughed. "Don't apologize. It would be a *screwin*." Dennis glared at her when Payne turned to look out the window, stalling, trying to think. She stuck her tongue out at Dennis before her eyes traveled back to Payne.

"Tell ya what. I'll make ya a deal." Payne stood and looked Dennis in the eye. "I won't sell it for that, but I'll give it to Rusti for nothin."

"What?" Dennis stopped pacing.

"I'll take your twenty grand. That'd be two thousand a day for ever day I spent in your Nashville jail. That'd help my pride some. But you've gotta keep your word about givin me those pointers toward the right publishers, like this Branch fella."

"Payne," Rusti stood next to him, "are you sure?"

"I've never heard anybody sing it better than you. It's your song." He smiled at her. "It'd be my pleasure to give it to ya. What goes around, comes around. I can live with this deal."

"I'll have the paper work done and a check cut," Dennis said, trying to contain his excitement. "I'll also call Houlette and have him have a little talk with T.R. Branch. I'll let everybody know what's going on here."

"James Houlette is the president of Golden Star Entertainment," Rusti explained. "You also have my word that T.R. Branch is going to hear your music. I promise you."

"Where can I get a hold of you?" Dennis asked.

Payne looked at Rusti ignoring Dennis. "I heard you're playin at Willie's Picnic."

"Yes, we are."

"We're gonna be a breakfast band. Why don't we just hook up again at Luckenbach? Get it done there." He looked at Dennis. "You bring the check and I'll bring ya some songs to send to Branch Publishin."

"It's a deal. And you bring me a copy of your original song. Just the way you wrote it." Dennis slapped Payne on the back, like he was his new best friend. "I'll see you there. But I still need your address for the paperwork."

Payne pulled his billfold out of his hip pocket. He took out a deposit slip and handed it to Dennis. "There ya go."

Payne shook hands with Rusti. "It was a real pleasure meetin ya. If ya don't mind me sayin so, you're just as pretty as your music is."

"I don't mind you saying so." She smiled, almost blushing. "A girl can never get too many compliments. Especially from handsome songwriters." She glanced at Dennis. "Would you excuse us?"

"What?"

"I said, would you excuse us ... please?"

Dennis shook his head at Rusti and hit the door button. It hissed. Looking back over his shoulder he called to Payne, "I'll see you at Luckenbach."

"Can I get you another beer?" Rusti asked.

"Sure." Payne sat back down and watched her walk to the refrigerator, admiring her rearview. "Nice bus."

"It's nice, but it gets old. It almost feels like a prison sometimes." Returning with two beers, she sat back on the couch, closer to Payne. "Thank you for the song. I hate the business end of music. It's so cutthroat."

"Well, seems most things get that way when there's money involved. How much ya figure I left on the table?"

"All said and done, couple of hundred."

"Thousand?" Payne almost choked on his beer.

"Want to change your mind?"

"No. A deal's a deal. I got more where that came from."

"Sounds like you just need the right connections. We'll get T.R. to listen to anything you send him. I gave you my word on that."

"Well, I'm not mailin nothin else to Nashville. I've learned my lesson."

"T.R.'s not that way. You can trust him."

"If ya say so."

"I promise." Rusti raised her beer bottle. "Well, here's a toast to your first in a long line of hit songs." She smiled at Payne and they clanked beer bottles. "What are you driving?"

"A Jeep."

"Would you consider taking me for a drive? I could stand to get out of here for awhile. I need some fresh air."

"I've got just the place. Ever been to the River Walk?"

"Yes, but it's been a long time. That's perfect. Sure you don't mind?"

Payne bolted from the couch. "I'll get the Jeep and drive around for ya. Better pull that red hair back. You're gonna get lotsa fresh air in that Jeep."

*

Payne didn't have to honk. She was outside having words with her bodyguard. Rusti King's green eyes were hidden behind sunglasses and her red hair was pulled back into a thick ponytail. A black baseball cap, perched on top, completed her guise. "Sorry to keep you waiting," she apologized, and slid into the Jeep. "I had to check out of jail."

"Not a problem." Payne shoved the stick in gear and hit the gas.

CHAPTER TWENTY-THREE

By six, rush-hour traffic had cleared from the streets of downtown San Antonio. The Jeep traveled through the shadows of downtown before parking near the historic River Walk. Descending aged brick steps, Payne led Rusti into the cool oasis. Wide sidewalks, with colorful flowers shaded by tall palm trees, paralleled the remarkable canals. "This is fantastic," Rusti said, watching a tour boat cruise by. She inhaled the strong scent of the murky river.

"Care for somethin to drink?" Payne asked. He pointed down the winding sidewalk to the closest outdoor café.

"You're reading my mind."

Payne laid his hand on Rusti's lower back and guided her to a round table that sat beneath the shade of a Corona Beer umbrella. She smiled when he politely handled her heavy wooden chair and sat next to her.

"Name your poison," Payne said, and laid his worn hat upside down on the table.

"I think I'll stick with your Budweiser." Rusti glanced at her surroundings before removing her sunglasses. "Thank you for getting me out of there. This is wonderful."

"Well, just pinch me. I can't believe I'm sittin here with Rusti King. Wouldn't have figured on that this mornin."

Rusti playfully pinched him on the arm.

"Ouch!" Payne grinned at her before waving at the waiter. "Two Budweisers."

"So, you wrote that song about your ex-wife leaving you, five years ago?"

Payne nodded. "That's a fact."

"Tell me about it."

"Well, it ends up I actually wrote the third verse first. That's what it felt like at the time. A few days later, I wrote the second verse. Then I just put it away. I worked on it off and on for awhile, but couldn't come up with the last verse."

The waiter returned and placed their beers on the table. "Do you want to run a tab?"

"Yeah, thanks." Payne returned his attention to Rusti.

"Do you have a credit card?" He was young, tall, with an attitude.

"No. Don't ya take real money?"

"I need a credit card to run a tab."

"I've got a card," Rusti volunteered.

"I got it." Payne gave the waiter a twenty. "Buddy, that's not the way we run tabs in Texas. Bring my change."

Rusti was grinning at him when he looked back.

"City boy, I guess." He returned her smile. "Where was I?"

"You were telling me how you wrote the song."

"Well, anyway, so I moved the first verse to the third and wrote a whole new first verse. Sometimes when ya think you've said it all, it's best to back up. Add to the beginnin instead of the end of a song. It's an old songwriter's trick."

"Fascinating." Rusti laid her hand on his arm. "But I was trying to be nosier than that. Why'd your ex-wife leave you? I can't believe any woman in their right mind would leave Payne McCarty, without a good reason."

"Ya are bein nosey, aren't ya?"

"Yes." Her laugh was disarming. "So, she broke your heart. I mean, that's the way the song goes."

"Yeah." Payne looked down at her soft hand resting on his tanned forearm. Her olive-toned skin was unique for a redhead. "Ya ever been married?"

"No. Not yet. I'm way too busy for a relationship. I'm on the road six to eight months out of the year." Rusti let out a sigh. "It can sure get old. I mean, I love performing, but the traveling is hard. There's a lot of time with nothing to do and nobody to even do that with."

"I'd bet that's right." Payne took a drink. "I told Nova, if we ever hit the road, I'm takin my dog with me. That's my deal. I go, he goes."

Rusti removed her hand from his arm and took a drink. "You didn't really answer my question."

"No, I guess I didn't." Payne leaned back in his chair. "She got bored with me workin all day and playin music at night. Ends up havin an affair with her boss. They ran off together and got married. That's it in a nutshell."

"That's another reason I don't want to get married. People don't understand the sacrifices the music business demands."

"Think it's worth it?"

"Right now I do. I'm really enjoying what I'm doing. It's all I've ever dreamed about. I guess there've been times when I've wondered if it was really all worth it. But I'm determined to make it. It's been a long road ... most of it uphill."

"Looks to me like you've already made it."

"Not yet." Rusti watched Payne peeling the label off his beer bottle. "What'd you do after she left?"

"I moved in with my best friend, Skeeter. Then the band broke up right after that. Me and Skeeter decided to get outta San Antonio. Get a fresh start on things. We found a place out in the country, north of New Braunfels. It's an old ranch house. Not much to look at, but it's peaceful. Back then, I just worked durin the day and worked on my songs at night."

"What kind of work do you do?"

"Carpenter work."

Rusti nodded. "When did you meet Nova?"

"About three years ago. Skeeter saw her playin in a little joint outside of New Braunfels. He walks up to her at the break and says … " Payne paused and grinned at Rusti. "You'd have to know Skeeter to appreciate this. We kinda look alike, but he's real little. Actually, he's makes a livin as a racehorse jockey. And he's gotta smart mouth on him. Anyway, so he says to Nova, ya sound pretty good, but your band sure sucks."

Payne laughed at the memory and Rusti laughed along. "Go on."

"So, Skeeter tells her if she was smart, she'd fire those guys and give him a call. Told her he was the best damn drummer in Texas and I was the best guitar player he'd ever heard." Payne took a drink and winked at her before continuing. "Skeeter has a tendency to exaggerate. Anyway, he gives her our phone number on a napkin. She called him a couple of weeks later. The next thing I know, she shows up with Hartman, he's our bass player, and we're back in the band business."

"Nova said you were a heartbreaker. Did you break her heart?"

"Hell, no." Payne finished his beer. "She's always sayin stuff like that. Ya can't believe half of what Nova tells ya. We're real good friends, but there's nothin more to it than that." Payne waved at the waiter and stuck two fingers in the air.

"Still, I'd bet you've broken your fair share of hearts." Rusti smiled at him and replaced her hand on his forearm.

"Nope." Payne shook his head. "I'm real careful about that. I don't let things get that far."

"Just love them and leave them?"

"Didn't say that either. I just try real hard not to hurt anybody. I know how it feels. Anyway, things are simpler by myself."

"So, you're not involved with anyone?"

"There ya go again."

"What?"

"Bein nosey."

"Well, are you?"

"No." Payne put his hand on top of hers and looked her in the eye. "Ya interested?"

"Well, you're sure not shy." Rusti laughed. Surprising herself, she leaned into the table. "I don't know yet." She placed her other hand on top of his, making a pile. "Maybe. Does that surprise you?"

The waiter sat the two beers on the table. "That will be four-fifty."

Payne removed his hand from between Rusti's and handed the waiter a five. "Keep the change." Looking back to Rusti, he asked, "Where were we?"

"You were holding my hand."

Payne took both of her hands in his and stared at them before looking up. "I'm not usually at a loss for words."

She smiled at his sudden awkwardness. "If I wasn't Rusti King ... just someone you'd met, would you still be at a loss for words?"

"Yeah."

"Really?" Rusti sounded surprised. She peered deeper into his piercing blue eyes. "I find that hard to believe." She squeezed his hand. "A songwriter lost for words? And why is that?"

"Because it's not who ya are. It's how I'm feelin toward ya."

Rusti drew a slight breath. She let it out slowly. "And, just how *are* you feeling toward me?"

Payne pulled her left hand to his lips and kissed it. "Like I don't ever wanna stop holdin your hand."

Her eyes closed when Payne pulled her other hand to him and kissed it. His lips moved hesitantly closer to hers. A soft moan escaped her when he lightly kissed her full lips. Again his lips brushed against hers, lingering. She opened her eyes when the soft kiss ended. He was only inches away. Moving to him, she returned his tender kiss.

Rusti's eyes remained closed after the kiss ended. Payne waited until her eyes opened. "Sometimes even a songwriter can't say what he's really feelin."

Her eyes left his. She stared at their hands locked together, afraid he could hear her heart pounding. She cleared her throat. "Well ... I think you phrased that quite nicely."

*

"I'll be damn," Skeeter said, spying Payne walking into the backstage area holding hands with Rusti King. It was past seven-thirty and the coliseum was already beginning to fill. "Glad ya could make it tonight."

"Rusti, this is my friend, Skeeter."

She extended her hand to him. "Nice to meet you, Skeeter. Payne's told me all about you."

"Don't believe anything he said," Skeeter grinned up at her and placed his hands on his hips, "except the good parts."

Rusti laughed. "It was all good. And good luck tonight."

"This is Hartman, our bass player." Hartman smiled and shook her hand without a word. "And ya met Nova this afternoon."

Nova squinted at Payne. Her mouth opened, but nothing came out.

"Nova, looks like we got our deal done on the song," Payne said. "I ended up givin it to Rusti."

"What?"

"Ya heard me. They've agreed to reimburse me for my jail time in Nashville. It's a done deal."

"What?"

"Well, I'll let you guys at it," Rusti said. "Payne, I'll catch your show from over there." She pointed stage left. "I'll see you after the show." She smiled and gave him a soft kiss. "Good luck."

"I'll be damn," Skeeter said.

"Me too," Hartman added.

"Can't somebody say somethin besides *I'll be damn*?" Payne laughed.

"Yeah, I can," Nova said. "Let's go over our set again." She pulled a flask out of her purse. "I need a drink. Damn, Payne. Can't leave you alone for a damn minute."

*

Nova-Scotia took the stage in darkness. Payne had butterflies the size of eagles. He noticed his hands shaking as he was strapping on his guitar. The disk jockey, from one of the local country stations, walked to center stage. "Let's do it!" he yelled behind him to the band. The bright spotlight silhouetted the DJ and the crowd roared to life. "Thank y'all for coming out this evening. I'm Gary Manning from WRGN, 97.5 on your country radio." The crowd cheered louder. "Please help me welcome ... Nova ... Scotia!"

Skeeter clicked off the time as the lights came up. Nova was on the keyboards and played her gettie-up beat to *Pari-mutuel Blues*. She stuck her butt out and began moving it up and down, like she was riding a horse. Payne swallowed hard before singing.

*We had us a racehorse, named Dial Sammy,
Swear that ol horse was just part of the family.
Black as midnight and twice as mean,
That's the fastest damn horse you've ever seen.*

*Part Thoroughbred, Part Quarter,
Ran that horse just south of the border,
Blistered those Mexican tracks,
Now it don't pay to take him back.
No, it don't pay to take him back.*

*Chorus
It's got us singing, got us singing,
Got us singing those Pari-mutuel Blues
Got us singing, got us singing
Got us singing those Pari-mutuel Blues.
Pari-mutuel Blues.*

*So we took him back to Texas
To those Hill Country tracks,
Bettin ain't legal, so the bookies run the tracks.
But you can't cheat a cheater,
No, you can't fool a fool,
Somewhere I guess we just forgot that rule.
Well we lost our ass on those Hill Country tracks,
The sheriff came to get him, now we can't get him back.
Now he runs for the bookies most every day,
I swear that damn horse never fails to pay.*

*It's got us singing, got us singing,
Got us singing those Pari-mutuel Blues ...*

    The applause following Payne's song was louder than anything Nova-Scotia had ever heard from the stage. The butterflies were gone. Nova had already strapped on her guitar and was standing center stage by the time Skeeter clicked off the second song. The upbeat song *Crankin Up The Country* got Nova bumping and grinding. She shook and strutted her stuff, flirting with the cowboys in the front row. As usual, she was inspired by their rowdy attention and the crowd came to life, one row at a time. One song after another, Nova-

NASHVILLE GOLD

Scotia went through their set of songs. The audience cheered and applauded, rewarding each song. Their confidence was growing.

"Thank y'all! Nova screamed before the final song. "Ladies, I want to introduce y'all to Payne McCarty!" She waved Payne up to the center stage. As he approached, she took his hat from his head and put it on. Payne glanced nervously at Nova and waved to the crowd. She slid behind him, reached around, and ripped open the snaps of his western shirt, exposing his tanned chest. The female members of the audience whistled and screamed while his face flushed red.

The lights went out. A single spot hit Nova, who slowly, soulfully played the first four measures of *Follow Your Dream* alone on her acoustic guitar. She stopped abruptly and screamed, "Y'all ready to rock?" The band came to life on the fifth measure and the lights came up. The tempo accelerated and Payne took off on his Les Paul Gibson electric guitar.

When storm clouds hide your rainbows
And your dreams, well they die so hard ...
It's time to remember,
It was your dream that got you this far...

Rainbows are the promise of tomorrow,
Blue skies will always come again.
And when the wind blows ...
Those old storm clouds will go ...
Follow your dreams to the end, my friend.
Follow your dreams to the end.

Ride out the storm on the wings of your dream,
Sunshine and rainbows will come again.
Ride out the storm on the wings of your dream
Follow your dream to the end, my friend,
Follow your dream to the end.
Follow your dream to the end ...

The stage went black leaving only Nova in the spotlight. She again slowly soloed the last four measures on her acoustic guitar. Timed perfectly, the band hit the final chord together, hard and loud. The stage went black before the lights came up. Nova-Scotia waved goodnight to the spirited crowd.

Stepping off the backstage stairs, Nova threw her arms around Jimmy Earl while the guys did a high five over Skeeter's head. "Great job!" Jimmy Earl yelled to them. "Payne, you were great!"

"Thanks. And thanks for the help on my song. We gotta deal done."

"That's what agents are for. Thank me by staying in the band."

"That was the deal."

Nova turned her flask up.

Skeeter looked at Payne. "You're stayin'?"

"I made a deal. If Jimmy Earl got me paid for the song, I promised to stay awhile longer. I got twenty grand for it. Two thousand a day for my jail time."

"Ya got screwed, is what ya got."

"Maybe, but it just seemed like the thing to do at the time."

Lisa had tears in her eyes when she embraced Skeeter. "I'm so proud of you." She looked at Payne. "I'm proud of all of you!"

Payne watched the little couple lock together. "Hartman, I do believe Nova just might be right. We really could be on our way."

"That was intense," Hartman answered. "Man, I'm excited."

Payne eyed him carefully. "I'm glad ya told me. Now I know what ya look like when ya get excited."

"How do I look?"

"Regular." Payne laughed and slapped him on the back. "Let's pack it up."

Rusti appeared, with her bodyguard. "Payne, you guys were great!" Rusti clapped as she approached. She hugged him. "I especially liked the part where Nova ripped your shirt open." She looked down at his bare chest and nodded. "Very impressive."

"Ya never know what she's gonna do next."

"It wasn't planned?"

"Hell, no." Payne shook his head. "She's always fulla surprises."

Rusti ran a finger over his chest. It was hot and damp. "Well, it sure got me squealing. Would you walk me out to the bus? I need to change and get ready."

"I'd love to, but I need to help get our equipment outta here first."

"Randall," she looked at her bodyguard, "could you get someone to help them, please?"

"Yes, ma'am." Randall whistled and pointed.

"Coming?" She smiled and crooked her finger at Payne.

"Yes, ma'am."

Music from the second band drifted away in the distance as they walked arm in arm through the warm night air. Randall followed closely until Rusti waved him on to the bus. "Payne, I feel like I've known you forever. I feel so comfortable around you."

"I guess I'm feelin like I need another pinch."

Rusti stopped and slid into him arms. "Maybe a few more kisses will do instead." She pulled his head down and kissed him.

"Might take a lot more," Payne whispered, and returned her passionate kiss.

"Definitely. But not here." She took Payne's hand and led him into the bus. "Have a seat. I'll be out in a few minutes. Help yourself to the beer."

"Are ya gonna wear that white leather outfit ya wore in Houston?"

"Would you like me to?"

Payne nodded his head. "Yeah."

"Then don't go away."

Payne waited until she had closed her door before walking to the refrigerator. He grabbed two Buds. After chugging the first one, he took the second one back to the couch. He was on his way for one more when her door opened.

"Still like it?"

Payne's eyes fell to her white boots and worked their way up. They lingered at her vest. She hadn't bothered to tie the leather tethers in the usual square knots. Instead, they had been loosely wrapped. "Looks good."

The tethers separated as easily as the snaps on Payne's western shirt during their burning kiss. The touch of their warm bodies pressing together ignited their passions. Breaking the kiss, Rusti pulled Payne through her door and kicked it shut with her boot. Wrapping her hands around his neck, she walked backwards, pulling him along while peppering his lips with kisses.

"You're going to have to take me home with you," she whispered, pulling Payne down to her bed.

"I'd love to, but I'm afraid it's not much of a place. I don't even have air conditionin."

"I don't care. I want to be with you." She moaned beneath his touch and kisses. "I want to get away from all this for awhile. We could leave after the show."

"I'm all yours."

"Promise?"

He answered with another kiss.

*

Closing her show, the crowd stomped and clamored for more in the darkness of the coliseum before Rusti King returned to the stage for her encore. She sang two more songs before clasping the microphone in both hands. "Thank you! Thank you!" She looked down at Payne while the crowd quieted. He stood on the floor, right of the stage. "San Antonio, I'd like to introduce to you ... one of country music's up and coming songwriters. From right here in San Antonio, Texas ... put your hands together for Payne McCarty." The crowd roared when the spotlight hit him. Surprised, Payne waved his hat in the air then bowed to Rusti. "Thank you, Payne!" Smiling, she spoke softly into the microphone, "You're just as special as your song."

Then the lights went out. An acoustic guitar played the introduction to *When Love Turns Out The Light* in the darkness. As in Houston, a soft red spotlight shone on Rusti as she sang Payne's song. He hung on every word until the spotlight went black with her last note. He listened to the soft acoustic guitar finish the song in darkness and looked at the small flickers of lights, from thousands of lighters raised in the air, throughout the packed coliseum. With the last guitar note still ringing in their ears, the crowd erupted with cheers and applause. The stage lights were raised just long enough for Rusti King to wave goodnight. "Thank you, San Antonio!"

*

Rusti reappeared from her quarters dressed comfortably in shorts and a cotton blouse that matched her eyes. Payne's eyes traveled her body, from her long shapely legs, upward. "What are you staring at?"

"You're beautiful. I'm starin at you."

"You're a real charmer." Rusti tossed her overnight bag to him. "Can I drive?"

"Do ya know where you're goin?"

"Yeah. I'm going to finish what we started before the concert."

"Can ya drive a stick?"

"Maybe," she said, skipping down the steps of the bus. "I think I can handle it."

The bodyguard watched them closely as they left the bus. "Randall, tell Dennis I'll be back when I'm back."

"I don't think so. You need to clear it with him yourself."

"He's not here and I'm leaving."

"Rusti, please don't. He'll be around in a few minutes." But Rusti ignored him. She took Payne's hand and ran toward the Jeep. "Rusti, please! He's gonna be really pissed at both of us."

Rusti waved to him from behind the wheel. She started the Jeep, but popped the clutch. It died. Payne grinned as she started it again. The Jeep lurched and jerked as she struggled with the gears, leaving the parking lot. Payne directed her to the Interstate and pointed north. The warm night air blew through their hair as they accelerated into the light, late night traffic. She drove intently, with both hands on the wheel.

"Thank ya for what ya said tonight, before your last song."

"I meant every word of it," Rusti yelled to him over the sound of the wind. "Thank you for writing it. And giving it to me."

"Well, I appreciated what ya said. This has been a red-letter day for me."

Rusti glanced at him and smiled. "It's not over yet."

Payne leaned over and kissed her shoulder. He lightly ran his hand up and down her arm. "If I'm dreamin, I hope I die in my sleep."

*

Turning in, the Jeep climbed the hill and came to a stop in front of the old ranch house. Pardner, out of habit, went to the driver's side of the Jeep.

"That's Pardner," Payne said, as Rusti reached down to pet him. "I gotta warn ya. He's got a tendency to pass gas."

"You're a big pretty dog," Rusty baby talked him. "Yes, you are."

Payne jumped out of the Jeep with Rusti's bag. "Well, this is it. I told ya it wasn't much."

"It's perfect." She took his hand in front of the Jeep and kissed him. Pressing her body to him, she moaned as his light kisses turned passionate. Payne's hands slowly explored her body as they pressed together. Their soft sounds of passion drifted into the still Hill Country night until Rusti broke off the kiss. "Where's Skeeter?"

"I figure they'll stay at Lisa's place. It's closer to San Antonio."

Rusti rested her head on his chest and listened to the sounds of the crickets singing their own love songs. "This is so peaceful." She took his hands in hers. "I need a bath. That leather gets hot under those lights."

"Look, I wasn't expectin company. I'm afraid the house is a mess."

"Payne, stop worrying about your house. I was raised in the country and I was raised poor. It doesn't take a lot to make me happy. What I'd really like is a cold beer and a nice bath. You've got a bathtub, don't you?"

"Yeah, I gotta tub." Payne reached down and petted Pardner before picking up her bag. He gave her a soft kiss and took her by the hand. "I've got cold beer, too."

Payne opened the creaking screen door for her. Handing her a beer from the refrigerator, he said, "I'll be right back." After washing out the tub, he ran her bath and returned to the kitchen. "Take your time." He kissed her. "Need another beer while ya soak?"

"Please."

Payne watched her disappear into the bathroom, then rushed to the bedroom and put fresh sheets on the bed. He frantically began picking up around the house before Rusti reappeared from the bathroom. She wore only a towel. Tucked together on top, it exposed most of her breasts and barely covered the rest. "I guess I forgot my pajamas."

"Don't look to me." He grinned and took her hand. "I don't own any."

CHAPTER TWENTY-FOUR

The phone woke Payne Friday morning. Leaving Rusti asleep in bed, he walked to the living room to answer it.
"Payne?"
"Yeah."
"This is Dennis Couch. Is Rusti with you?"
"Yeah. How'd ya get my number?"
"Off your deposit slip."
"Oh, yeah." He yawned into the phone.
"Payne, are you going to let me speak to her?"
"Ya didn't ask to."
"May I speak with Rusti, please?"
"She's asleep. Can she call ya back?"
"I'm awake," she yelled.
"Hang on a minute."
Rusti left the bed with the top sheet wrapped around her, but immediately tripped over Pardner. Recovering her balance, she readjusted the sheet and paraded into the living room with the sheet trailing behind her. With her hand over the phone, she whispered, "Do you always walk around the house naked?"
"Not always. How bout you?" Payne tugged at her sheet.
"Quit that!" Laughing, Rusti slapped his hand. She popped him on his white butt when he turned toward the kitchen to make coffee. "Hi, Dennis."
"Well, it sounds like you're having a good time."
"You can't imagine."
"Rusti, what in the hell are you doing over there? I've been worried sick."
"Do you want details?" She smiled watching Payne wash out the coffeepot.
"I mean, this just isn't like you to just run off."
"I needed some time away. I didn't realize I needed a permission slip."
"We're leaving for Austin in an hour."
"Fine, I'll meet you there."
"When?"

Glancing at Payne, she whispered into the phone, "Sunday."

"Sunday!" Dennis yelled over the phone then lowered his voice. "Rusti, look. I know you've had an occasional fling, but never with a complete stranger. And you've never just disappeared. Sunday is three days from now!"

"Look, Dennis," Rusti said, watching Pardner meandering toward the kitchen. "I've been on the road for almost three months. Give me some room, okay? I'll see you then."

"Sound check is at three o'clock. You'd better be there."

"I'll be there." Rusti hung up the phone and walked to the kitchen dragging her sheet.

Payne was holding the screen door open. "Good boy. That's it. Come on. Time to go outside." But Pardner sat. Still holding the door open with one hand, Payne bent over and tugged on Pardner's collar with the other. "Damn it, Pardner. Please go on. You're lettin the flies in." Pardner turned his head to look at Rusti, ignoring Payne. Payne followed his eyes. "She's not gonna save ya. He's really gotten an attitude this last year." Using his foot, Payne pushed Pardner out the door. "Do ya have to get back?" he asked, turning from the door.

"Are you trying to get rid of me?" Rusti said, trying to maintain eye contact.

"Not hardly. I just figured ya were on a schedule or somethin."

"I'm free till Sunday, if that's okay with you? I don't want to intrude if you have plans, or someone else to ... "

"No plans. And there's nobody else," Payne interrupted. He placed his hands on her bare shoulders and ran them up and down her arms. "We're playin in Austin tonight and Saturday night. Wanna come along?" Payne leaned in and laid a series of light, soft kisses down her neck to her shoulder and back up along her neck.

Rusti moaned. "I'd like that."

"Last night was incredible," he whispered into her ear.

"Yes. You were." Rusti took a deep breath and closed her eyes. "I need a shower."

"Me too. I'll wash your back, if you'll wash mine," he said, continuing his kisses along her neck.

"Can we have coffee first?"

"Yeah, but it'll take a few more minutes to make." Payne straightened up and hooked a finger in the top of her sheet. He slowly ran his finger back and forth between the top of the sheet and her soft skin, gently tugging at it until the white sheet fell in a heap on floor. He pressed himself to her, eliciting a moan from her.

"Payne, what are you doing?" Rusti tried to retreat across the small kitchen, but he followed her step for step. "What if Skeeter were to come home?" she asked, bumping against the kitchen table.

Payne lifted her up and deposited her bare butt on the edge of the table. "Don't worry about Skeeter. He don't get embarrassed too easy."

*

Payne brought Rusti another cup of coffee while she combed out her long red hair in the bathroom. "Anything special ya wanna do today?"

"I thought we just did." She smiled at his reflection in the mirror. "But some fresh country air would be nice."

"There's lotsa that around here. We could float the river or go to the lake."

"Do you have fishing poles?"

"Yeah. Ya wanna go fishin?"

"Kind of. It's been a long time. But I used to go with my daddy around Lake Worth."

"You got it. I'll get the stuff loaded up while you're finishin up. We can stop and get somethin to eat on the way. We'll need some bait."

*

Payne drove the Jeep through the gate at Jerry's Canyon Lake property. Shutting it behind him, he drove on, stopping at the cliff. He carried the ice chest. Rusti followed him down the steep path to the rocky shoreline with the fishing gear. Payne smiled watching Rusti bait the hook with a worm, like a seasoned angler. She cast her hook into the water and sat on the ice chest. Payne cast his line and sat next to her.

"You have no idea how much fun this is for me. Thank you for bringing me out here." Payne watched the two red and white floats bobbing in the water from beneath his hat without answering. She glanced at him. "Is something wrong?"

"Not unless ya can get too happy."

She laughed. "I'm happy, too. What's going on here between us?"

"What do ya mean?"

"I mean, one minute I'm on tour. The next thing I know, I'm sharing your bed and your shower. Now I'm fishing without a care in the world. Having the time of my life."

"Don't forget the kitchen table."

"Oh ... I'll never forget the kitchen table."

Payne took his hat off and placed it on her head. "Wouldn't want ya to get sunburned."

"You didn't answer my question."

"I'm thinkin on it."

"Don't hurt yourself." She playfully nudged him with her elbow. "I mean, we barely know each other, but ... "

"I feel the same. Hard to explain. Maybe we're just both lookin for the same thing, at the same time."

"And just what would we be looking for?"

"Catfish."

They laughed together. "I don't think that's it," she said.

"Love."

"Are you looking for love?"

"I think most people are."

"Have you ever been in love?"

"Yeah. I was in love with my ex-wife. How bout you?"

"Not really. I've had a few relationships. I thought I was in love once, in high school. Wanted to call it love. I guess I've been too busy with my career to take time to fall in love."

"How long do ya think it takes to fall in love?"

"I don't know." The float disappeared beneath the water. "I've got one!" Rusti sprang to her feet and set the hook with a yank. The catfish jerked and struggled on the other end of her line.

"That's a keeper," Payne declared, as she reeled it in to the shore.

"I don't want to keep it. Throw him back."

"Okay. It's your fish."

Payne expertly grabbed the catfish and removed the hook. He eased it back into the water and watched it disappear. Rusti baited her hook again and cast it back into the lake before sitting down.

"It doesn't take that long to fall in love," Payne continued the conversation. "It's the fallin outta love that takes awhile."

"Are you still in love with your ex-wife?"

"No." Payne shook his head. "Not anymore. I was for a long time. But I finally got over it."

"How?"

Payne shrugged his shoulders. "Just finally got to see things for the way they are, not the way they were."

"Payne, how long is ... not that long?"

He thought before answering. "A moment." Standing, he peeled his shirt off. "It's gonna be another hot one today. This really isn't the best time to fish."

"Payne, you've got a way of changing the subject on me. I'm not letting you off the hook, so to speak." Rusti smiled at him from beneath the brim of the oversized cowboy hat. "How long is a moment?"

Payne snapped his fingers. "That fast. If it takes any longer than that, it's not love."

"My, that is fast."

"It's admittin to it that takes longer."

"So, you can fall in love," Rusti snapped her fingers and grinned at him, "that fast. But it just takes longer to admit it. I like that. I've never heard it put quite that way before."

"Kinda sounds like a country song in the makin, don't it?" Payne lifted the brim of the hat and kissed her. He sang ... are ya ready ... to admit to love?

"Is that a question or the *hook* in your new song?"

"You can take it either way."

"I'd like to hear the rest of the song before I commit."

"Admit," Payne corrected her. "Commit is a whole different subject."

Rusti laughed. "Okay, let me see if I've got it. First, you fall in love in a ..." she snapped her fingers, "moment. Then you admit it. Then you commit to it?"

"I do believe you've got it." Payne tugged on the brim of the hat. "It's a good thing for you I came along when I did. Did I answer your question?"

"What question?"

"About what's goin on here between us."

Rusti moved the hat to the back of her head. She stared into his blue eyes. "Yes." She nodded. "I believe you did."

"Hey, you've got another one!"

Rusti clapped her hands like a little girl and reeled in the fish.

"Ya gonna keep this one?"

"No."

Payne shrugged and released the fish. "Just as well. It was the same one."

"Now how would you know that?"

Still squatting by the lake, Payne looked up at her and grinned. "He admitted it to me."

CHAPTER TWENTY-FIVE

The stalwart two-story brick building near the Texas Capitol had once held the largest seed house south of Ft. Worth. But in 1983, the old warehouse had been gutted. Leaving only the crimson brick walls and plank-wood flooring, Stetson's Western World now boasted a dozen bars and the best dance floor in Austin.

Nashville recording artist, Rusti King, watched Nova-Scotia take the raised stage at Stetson's. She was seated with Lisa and Jimmy Earl. Her red hair was pulled back discretely into a ponytail beneath a baseball cap. The sunglasses, once used for her stealthy entrance, were stuck on top of the cap; their usefulness replaced by the darkness in the bar.

"Payne," Skeeter said, as they took the stage, "I take it back."

"What's that?"

"Ya didn't get screwed on that song."

"How so?"

"I don't believe ya really need me to answer that. I see the way she's been lookin at ya."

"Yeah."

"Buddy, I also see the way you're lookin at her. Ya'd better hide your heart or it's gonna get broke. That's for damn sure."

"Too late for that. She's already holdin it in her hand."

"Well, let's hope she don't drop the damn thing."

"Okay boys," Nova's speech was already slurred, "Jimmy Earl said we're open the next two weekends. Next gig is Willie's on the Fourth, unless he comes up with something between now and then."

"We could go back to Heidi's," Payne suggested.

"I'm not asking that bitch for nothing."

"Not a problem. I'll ask her," Payne volunteered. "We need to stay tight for Willie's Picnic."

"See if you can get us two hundred a night."

"Yeah, right."

"Payne," Nova leaned into his ear and held on to him for balance, "I can't believe you're screwing Rusti King. Is she a natural redhead?"

"Who said I was?"

"Look, you've had a shit-eatin grin on your face since Thursday. Don't try to shit me. I know how you are."

"It's not like that."

"Shit!" Nova yelled, stumbling backwards. "Payne McCarty is in love! Well, somebody bite my butt on Broadway. I never thought I'd see the day."

The stage lights came up and Skeeter clicked off *Pari-mutuel Blues* to begin the set. Rusti's eyes never left Payne. Throughout the evening she savored the frequent grins he flashed to her from the stage and cherished the brief time during the breaks when he held her hand and petted on her.

Jimmy Earl had wandered off by midnight leaving Lisa and Rusti alone at the table. Rusti scooted her chair closer to Lisa. "Payne said you and Skeeter were getting married. Congratulations."

"Thank you. Payne's going to be Skeeter's best man."

"I know. He told me. How long have you known Payne?"

"Almost a month. Payne introduced me to Skeeter."

"You've only known Skeeter a month!"

"Yeah. But it was love at first sight. We both knew it. Skeeter said we'd wasted enough time apart. It was past time we got on with our new life together."

Rusti snapped her fingers. "Happened that fast?"

Lisa nodded her head and giggled. She looked back at the band. Rusti glanced at Payne, then back to Lisa. "So, you don't know much about Payne?"

"I know everything about Payne. Skeeter's told me everything. They've known each other since high school." Lisa laid her hand on Rusti's arm. "What do you want to know?"

"Is there a woman in his life?"

"To hear Skeeter tell it, that ranch house has a revolving door. They come in, stay awhile then leave. Skeeter says Payne got hurt real bad when his ex-wife left him. He swore Sylvia, that's her name, was going to be the last woman to ever hurt him. Anybody tries to get too close, and Payne sends them packing."

"Yeah, he mentioned his ex-wife."

"I saw her in San Antonio a week or so ago. She was at the Crystal Stallion, where the guys were playing. Came to our table during the break."

"What's she look like?"

"Real pretty. Real long, straight black hair. Look, I wouldn't worry about his ex-wife. Skeeter says Payne's finally over her. He hadn't seen her in five years till last week. She was divorced again and asked Payne to take her back. Can you believe that?"

"Payne said no?"

"Hell no, is more like it."

Rusti watched Payne on the stage. She clapped when the song ended then tapped Lisa on the arm. "So there's really no one special in his life?"

"Besides you?"

"Me?"

Lisa leaned into Rusti's ear. "Skeeter told me, while ago, that he's never seen Payne look at a woman like he looks at you."

"Really? I'll take that as a compliment."

Lisa nodded her head. "You should."

*

After the "last call for alcohol" Lisa patted Rusti's arm. "You know, I like you. I always figured stars would be stuck up. But you seem regular."

"Well, thank you. I'll take that as another compliment."

"You should."

*

When Payne woke up Saturday morning, Rusti was gone. Panicking, he jumped out of bed and slid into his cut-offs. Rushing from the bedroom, he tripped over Pardner, inducing a moan from deep inside the dog.

"Shit, Pardner."

"He followed me out." Rusti was grinning at him from the kitchen. "He's bad about that, isn't he? He got me again this morning."

"Yeah. Among other things."

"I made you coffee." Walking into the kitchen, Payne held her in his arms. "Payne, are you going to let me go long enough to get your coffee?"

"I thought ya were gone there for a minute."

"Sorry, but I woke up early. I lay there for the longest time just watching you sleep. Would you like some coffee?"

Payne looked at the kitchen. "Ya did the dishes?"

"And I would have cooked you breakfast, but there wasn't anything in the refrigerator that I recognized, except beer."

Payne took a sip of his coffee. "Let's run up to the store and get some food. I'll grab a shirt and be right back." Payne returned pulling a T-shirt over his head. "Come on Pardner. Let's go for a ride."

Walking outside, Rusti inhaled the country morning. "I can't get over how fresh the air smells. I love it out here. Reminds me of home."

"Nothin like it." Payne loaded Pardner in Rusti's seat. "Get in the back," Payne ordered. The old golden looked at Rusti like Payne was talking to her. "Pardner, get in the back!"

Rusti laughed as Pardner slowly moved between the seats and sat in the back of the Jeep. "You two make quite a pair."

*

When Payne left the Jeep at the convenience store, Pardner immediately took his seat. Rusti petted on him, but his eyes remained fixed on the store until he saw Payne returning. Without being told, he moved slowly to the backseat. "That dog only has eyes for you," Rusti said, as he climbed into the Jeep.

Payne leaned over and gave her a quick kiss. "He loves me, but he's too ornery to admit to it."

"Maybe so, but he's definitely committed to you." She smiled at him. "See, I remember how it works."

Payne reached to start the Jeep, but Rusti caught his hand. "I can't commit to you."

"I know that." Her face was sullen. He reached out and ran his finger along her soft lips. "Hey. Where's that smile?"

"Payne, you know this has to end. Right?"

"If ya say so. Do ya want me to take ya back to your bus?"

"No." She squeezed his hand.

"Things get confusin when ya get em outta order. Committin comes last, not first. See, ya already forgot that." Payne started the Jeep and backed out. He forced a smile toward her. "I guess our clock's tickin."

"Let's not think about that right now." Rusti patted him on the leg. "Take me home. I want to cook my man some breakfast."

*

Watching her pull the bacon apart, Payne draped his arm over her shoulder. "When's the last time ya cooked breakfast for someone?"

"I don't remember."

Payne poured them more coffee. He sat at the table, watching her putter about the kitchen.

"Good morning, guys," Lisa said, taking a seat across from Payne.
"Coffee?" Rusti asked.
"Make it two," Skeeter answered from the door. "Hell, I'm gonna have to write home and tell ever body I spent the night with Rusti King."
"Skeeter!" Lisa scolded. "You behave yourself."
"Y'all are up and at-em early," Rusti commented.
"Gotta get to the races. Goin to Seguin. What're y'all gonna do today?"
"No plans yet," Payne answered.
"Why don't y'all come down and watch me race Dial Sammy?"
"I didn't know ya were runnin him."
"Believe it or not, I don't tell ya ever thing I know." Skeeter slapped him on the back, a bit too hard, and took his seat next to Lisa. "Talked to Ragina this week. Invited her to the weddin. I kinda suggested she needed to run him this week. Need to keep him ready for Fredericksburg."
"She's coming to the wedding," Lisa added.
"How about it?" Payne asked Rusti. "Wanna go to the horse races?"
"I'd love to go!" She turned from the stove. "Dial Sammy? That's a real horse in your song?"
"Black as midnight and twice as mean," Skeeter added. "He belonged to Payne's old boss, before he got killed. We're kinda borrowin him." Skeeter grinned. He spotted the clean sink and counter. "Damn! Payne, did ya do the dishes?"
"No, Rusti did em. She got up early."
"Thanks, Rusti. It was my turn."
"Skeeter, it's always your turn," Payne said. "Ya never do em."
"Yeah, well now it's your turn again. Thanks, Rusti. I owe ya one."
"Who's Ragina?"
The three of them exchanged glances before Payne answered. "She's my old boss's daughter. She owns the horse now."
"Lives in Houston," Skeeter added.
"Houston? Payne, she wouldn't have anything to do with why you were in Houston, the night you caught my show. Would she?"
"Payne saved her life durin the flood that killed her daddy." Skeeter tried to change the subject. "Jumped in a floodin creek and pulled her out by her long blonde hair. Both of em nearly drowned. Ol Payne here was the hero of Comel County."
Rusti turned around with a plate in her hand. "I'm impressed. Tell me more."
Payne glanced at Lisa and Skeeter. Both were grinning.
"Not much more to tell," Payne answered.

Skeeter laughed out loud. "Sorry."

"Oh? Maybe I should ask Skeeter?"

"I ain't sayin shit."

"Payne, I'm listening. Are you going to tell me about Ragina or do I have to get it out of Skeeter?"

"It'd be easier to get it outta Pardner," Skeeter said. "Payne, ya know if that ol dog ever learns to talk you'll have to shoot him."

"He can talk." Payne left his chair and took a piece of bacon from the plate. "Pardner, say *howdy*." Pardner rose slowly to his feet and walked to Payne, wagging his tail. He sat, then raised his paw to shake. "Other hand," Payne instructed. Pardner changed paws. "Say *howdy*." Pardner barked and was rewarded with the bacon.

"Very good!" Rusti clapped then dangled another piece of bacon in the air. "Okay, Pardner. Tell me about Ragina."

Payne looked at Pardner and pointed his finger at him, like a gun. Aiming at his dog, Payne said, "Bang. You're dead." Pardner slid his front paws out and dropped his nose between his outstretched legs.

Rusti laughed and tossed the bacon to Pardner. "Okay, boys. I give up."

"We're off to the races," Skeeter said.

"Don't you want some breakfast?" Rusti asked.

"No thanks. We gotta go. Ya gonna bet on Dial-Sammy?"

"We might."

"Watch for my hat before the race. Same thing goes. Bet late," Skeeter advised, heading for the door. "I figure Red will pull him if he sees Ragina there."

Rusti waited until after the screen door slammed behind them to ask, "What'd he mean?"

"I'll explain it later." Payne watched her scrambling the eggs with his head resting on her shoulder. Moving her hair behind her shoulder, he began kissing her neck while his hands gently roamed over her body.

Rusti turned off the blue gas flame. She turned around and slid into his arms. "The eggs are going to get cold if you don't stop that."

CHAPTER TWENTY-SIX

Concerned with her appearance for the races, Rusti insisted Payne stop at Buster's Western Wear in Seguin. It was just off the main highway. Rusti had laughed at the billboard's advertisement. *If we ain't got it, you don't need it.* Buster's did have everything ... everything but a lot of customers. Payne escorted her through the small store to the jeans and watched her flip through the sizes before selecting two pair. The young male clerk, sharply dressed in new western attire, eyed Rusti as she walked by him on her way to the dressing room. "You know, your girlfriend sure looks a lot like Rusti King. I saw her concert in San Antonio. She was great."

"Yeah, I saw it, too." Payne said, with a straight face.

Rusti appeared from the dressing room in a new pair of Wranglers. "What do you think?"

"Girl, I think you've got legs all the way up to your ... " Payne stopped short and grinned.

"My what?"

"Elbows."

After selecting three blouses, Rusti returned in a green one, sleeveless with white stripes. "I need a belt and some boots. Do you have socks?"

"Yes, ma'am."

Payne watched her carefully select a pair of brown dress boots and matching belt. "Cowgirl, ya need a hat." Payne placed his worn straw hat on her head. "There ya go."

"It's a little big. Do you have something more my size?"

"Yes, ma'am. Hats are over here."

As the kid shaped her straw Stetson, Payne fondled the seat of her new Wranglers until she playfully slapped his hand away. "Stop that."

"Just workin on the tags."

Outfit complete, she headed to the register. "Do you have something to cut the tags off? I feel like Minnie Pearl."

"Yes ma'am, just as soon as you pay for it all."

Rusti pulled out her American Express and placed it on the counter. The young clerk looked at the card, then at Rusti, then at the card again. "Do you have some I.D.?"

"How about she just sings a few bars for ya?"

"Good Lord! Buster! Come here a minute!"

The gray-haired cowboy appeared from behind the curtains. "Is there a problem?" He peered at them over the top of his reading glasses.

"No sir. I just thought you might want to shake hands with Rusti King."

Rusti removed her new hat and smiled. "Nice to meet you, Buster."

"Well, I'll be a monkey's uncle. The pleasure's all mine. What brings ya to Seguin?"

"We're going to the races this afternoon. It was short notice. I needed a little something more appropriate to wear." She glanced at Payne then back to Buster. "You have a lovely store."

"Can I have your autograph?" the clerk asked.

"Certainly."

"My name's Don," he said, reaching beneath the counter. He pulled out a stack of *ON SALE* posters.

Rusti turned one over and wrote on the back *Don, Thanks for everything* and signed it. "Buster, here's a little something for you." Rusti wrote in large letters *When I shop in Seguin, I shop at Buster's*. She signed it and handed it to him.

"Give her a discount," Buster ordered.

"How much?"

"Twenty percent." Buster grinned at Rusti. "Hell, I'd give it to ya if I could afford it." He peered at Payne. "Son, what's your name?"

"Payne McCarty."

"Don't recognize it. Are ya somebody special?"

"No, sir."

"He's a songwriter. He wrote my song *When Love Turns Out The Light*." Rusti proudly took Payne's arm in her hands and gave it a squeeze.

Buster extended his hand to Payne. "Pleasure meetin ya, son. That's a real fine song. Reminds me of ... well, hell, y'all don't wanna hear about that."

Rusti signed the receipt while Payne pulled out his pocketknife and went to work on the tags. "Thank you, Don." She looked at Buster. "It was very nice meeting you both."

"Y'all come back!" Buster called after them. "Miss King, I'm gonna tell ever body I know that you're just as nice as ya are pretty."

Rusti turned at the door. "Why, thank you, Buster."

"Ya sure made their day," Payne said, walking her to the Jeep. "I guess ya get that a lot."

"All the time."

"You're liable to stop the races when ya walk into the stands, Miss King."

Rusti grabbed his rearview mirror and turned it to her. She rummaged through her purse before pulling out a brush and a rubber band. Holding the rubber band in her teeth, she brushed her red hair back into a ponytail and slipped it around her thick mane. Replacing her hat, she added sunglasses and turned to Payne. "There. What do you think?"

Payne nodded. "Ya look like you're gonna be the prettiest girl at the races. What's your name?"

"Betty ... Betty Green."

"Around here you'd have to spell that G-R-U-E-N-E. That's the German way to spell it." Payne gave her a quick kiss and started the Jeep. "Well, Betty Gruene, hold on to your new hat. We're off to the races."

*

By early afternoon the overcast sky was surrendering to patches of blue, exposing another hot, muggy South Texas day. Payne stopped just long enough to buy two German Sausages on sticks and a couple of Budweisers before escorting Rusti up the narrow ramp.

Red was leaning against the railing. The bookie glanced at Rusti and gave Payne a nod. Ragina was seated with Billy Gotzen, close to the aisle. Payne tipped his hat to them.

"Payne!" Ragina called after him. She stood from her seat. Her sleeveless blouse was low cut, even by Ragina's standards. "Don't you just tip your hat to me. I want a hug." Reluctantly, Payne surrendered a hug, trying not to spill his beer down her back, while she smashed her Double D's into his chest.

Billy stood and extended his hand. "Payne, nice to see you again."

"Yeah, you too."

"Aren't you going to introduce us to your friend?" Ragina demanded, glaring at Rusti.

"Sure. Excuse my manners. Betty, this is Billy Gotzen and Ragina Boerne. This is Betty Gruene, from ... uh, Austin."

Rusti smiled. "Pleasure to meet both of you."

"Good luck today," Payne said, trying to keep a straight face. Starting up the stairs, Payne led Rusti to an open area near the top of the bleachers.

"So that's Ragina," Rusti quipped. "You failed to mention she had boobs the size of Dolly Parton's."
"I don't recall mentionin anything about her at all. Anyway, they're not natural."
"You've got to be kidding me. Next you'll be telling me she's not a natural blonde."
"Wouldn't know."
"Payne McCarty, don't you start lying to me."
Payne readjusted his hat and appeared to study the racing program. "Looks like Dial Sammy is runnin in the fourth race."
Rusti spotted Ragina bouncing up the steps toward them. She leaned over, took Payne's hat off, and kissed him on the cheek. "Looks like Dolly's not finished with you," she whispered, and replaced his hat.
Ragina slid into the seat next to Payne. "Skeeter is racing Dial Sammy in the fourth race."
Payne nodded. "Yep, that's what it says."
"I'm going to bet big on him today."
"What's big?"
"Ten thousand."
"Whoa." Payne shook his head. "Well, I hope you've got it to lose."
"He won't lose. He's the best horse in the race."
"Best don't always get it on these tracks."
Ragina leaned forward and looked at Rusti. "Betty, you sure resemble Rusti King. Payne and I watched her show together in Houston, at Gillie's. I bet you hear that all the time."
"Yes, as a matter-of-fact, I do." Rusti answered, managing to keep a poker face. "How was she?" she asked. Payne lowered his head and put his hand on top of his hat, fighting back his laughter.
"It was a very nice show. Wasn't it, Payne?"
Payne looked at Rusti and nodded. "Sure was."
"Payne, I'm coming to Skeeter and Lisa's wedding." Ragina put her hand on his leg.
Payne nodded and covered his mouth with his hand, trying hard to stifle a laugh. But his shoulders were beginning to shake. Rusti looked away trying not to catch Payne's contagious laughter.
"Payne, what's wrong with you?" Ragina asked. "What's so funny?"
"Yeah, Payne. What's so funny?" Rusti repeated and nudged him with her elbow.
Payne coughed, "Sorry."
Rusti leaned forward and removed her sunglasses. "Ragina, we're not

being fair. My name is Rusti, not Betty. I'm sorry. We aren't laughing at you. Payne was just trying to keep me from being recognized. We'd ... "

"We'd appreciate it if you'd keep it to yourself." Payne managed to stop laughing long enough to finish her sentence. Ragina's jaw dropped. She leaned forward and stared at Rusti, but was speechless.

Defending her territory, Rusti laid her hand on Payne's other leg and leaned across him. "He kind of rescued me, too."

"Payne, you son-of-a bitch!" Glaring at Rusti, Ragina stood and placed her hands on her hips. "Well, good luck with Payne. Believe me, you'll need it." Ragina tossed her blonde mane over her shoulders and stormed down the steps.

"I'm surprised you let that one get away."

"Why's that?"

"She's very attractive and obviously crazy about you."

"Rich, too."

"Looks like a keeper to me."

"Yeah, well, I fish like you do. The excitin part's catchin em."

"Then you just throw them back out after you've had your fun?" Rusti's smile was gone. "Is that why she wished me luck?"

"I was just kiddin. I didn't mean it like that."

"Are you going to throw me back, too?"

"Not hardly. You're definitely a keeper." Payne put his arm around her shoulder and gave her a hug. "Anyway, ya don't need luck with me."

"Oh? Is that right?"

"That's right."

"Why's that?"

Payne snapped his fingers in front of her face. "Because ... I'm in love with ya." He placed his finger across her lips. "Ya don't have to say anything. I'm just admittin it to ya."

Rusti shook her head. She started to speak. But the crowd, reacting to a close finish in the second race, drowned out her response.

"What?" Payne yelled.

Rusti looked away. He tried to pull her close, but she resisted. She was still shaking her head. Removing his arm from her shoulder, Payne waited until the crowd had settled down to speak. "I know we're goin our own separate ways right now. I just didn't want our time to end without ya knowin how I feel about ya."

"Payne, I can't love you. And I can't let you love me." She shook her head again. "I don't know what else to say."

"Ya don't have to say anything." Payne's heart was pounding, his mind desperately searching for the right words.

Rusti replaced her sunglasses. "I'd like to watch Skeeter race Dial-Sammy." She looked down, then to Payne. "I'll need to go after that. I'm sorry."

Payne nodded. He pretended to check the racing program, but it was a blur. "There's another race before he runs. I could use a beer. Want one?"

"Please."

Payne lingered around the concession stand, his mind searching for the right words to say. But nothing came. He felt foolish. Returning to his seat, he watched Skeeter parade Dial Sammy in front of the stands. "There he is. The black one." He pointed.

"He's beautiful. Do you think he'll win?"

"No."

"Why not?"

"Skeeter just told me he wasn't. He adjusted his hat. That means he's gonna pull him."

"What?"

"Just like my song. The bookie runs the track and the jockeys. When there's too much money bet on a horse, the horse gets held back. That's Red, the bookie." He pointed. "I'm guessin he spotted Ragina early on and figured she was gonna put a big bet down on Dial Sammy."

"Well, she's certainly hard to miss. Shouldn't you warn her?"

"I tried. Ten grand ain't gonna hurt nothin but her feelins. She was already rich, before Jerry left ever thing to her. I'd guess she's got a million or better. Ten grand's nothin to her."

Payne and Rusti stood with the crowd when the horses left the gate. Skeeter ran Dial Sammy in the middle of the pack along the backstretch, then took the black horse wide around the turn. He stayed wide, losing ground, until breaking for the home stretch. Then Skeeter let him run. Passing the field of horses, Dial Sammy began closing on the leaders. He was running neck and neck for the lead as they approached the finish line. Payne laughed out loud when he saw Skeeter throw his legs forward and rare back on the reigns. Dial Sammy finished a close second.

Payne was still laughing when he turned to Rusti. "Damn he's good. He finished second so he still gets part of the purse. The track pays two places to the horse owners. Jockeys get ten percent of the purse. But if ya bet, Red only pays the winner."

"That's crooked."

"Yeah, I'd say ol Ragina just got a bad case of the Pari-mutuel Blues." Rusti turned away. Payne's smile disappeared when she picked up her purse.

"I'm ready."

*

It was a silent trip home. Payne sat at the kitchen table petting Pardner, while Rusti packed her overnight bag. "All set?" he asked, when she appeared in the kitchen doorway.

Rusti didn't answer. She set her bag down and walked to the refrigerator. Returning with two beers, she sat across the kitchen table from Payne. Taking the beers from her, he opened them and shoved one back to her.

"What's on your mind?"

Rusti watched him intently peeling the Budweiser label off his bottle. "Payne, I told you this morning I couldn't commit."

"I remember." He looked up to see tears filling her eyes.

"What good does it do to admit, when you can't commit?"

"You're confusin things again." Payne lowered his head. "I just wanted ya to know how I felt. I guess that was stupid. I'm sorry. I ruined the weekend."

"No, it wasn't stupid. I'm sure that wasn't easy for you to say. Payne ... look at me." She waited until she saw his eyes. "You didn't ruin the weekend. I'll never forget this weekend. Never."

Payne nodded. He looked down and finished peeling the label off in one piece.

"I'm committed to my career," she said, and wiped her eyes. "That's it. That's the only thing I'm committed to. Just my career."

"I understand."

"I'm not sure that you do. I've worked my whole life to get where I am now. I've struggled, starved, and sung at every damn dive from Texas to Tennessee. Do you know how many times I've had my ass grabbed in a bar? Can you imagine the sickening things drunks have said to me? Do you have a clue how hard it is for a woman to make it in this business without having to fuck her way to the top? Do you? Do you really think you understand?" Rusti fought back her tears.

"No."

"I can't give up now! I'm almost there. I'm right on the verge of making it big. I don't need any distractions!"

"Fine." Payne took a drink to wash down the lump in his throat. He leaned back in his chair. "Don't make this so hard on yourself."

"Damn you, Payne. It is hard!" She bolted from her chair, the fire in her eyes mingling with tears. Turning away from him she held onto the kitchen counter. Her shoulders shook as she sobbed.

Payne was on his feet in an instant. Taking her by her shoulders, he turned her toward him and held her. Stepping back, he gently wiped the tears away. He placed a soft kiss on her forehead. "I don't wanna get in your way. And I don't wanna see ya hurt like this. I was bein selfish. I'm sorry."

Rusti pushed him away and sat back down, placing her head in her hands. But she had stopped sobbing.

Payne stood behind her. He rubbed her shoulders and tried to comfort her. "Look, I understand ya have to go. Whether it's today or tomorrow, I understand that. Understood it when I said what I said at the track. But that doesn't mean we can't see each other again. It doesn't have to end with this weekend. Not unless ya want it to."

She shook her head. "I'm sorry."

Payne swallowed hard. "Let me ask ya one thing." He squatted by her side and turned her face to him. "Do I need to turn out the light? Cause, I'd leave it on for ya ... forever. If ya asked me to."

Rusti closed her eyes, but she could still see his face. "No." The word was barely audible. She looked at him "Don't give up on me."

"Ya don't have to go till tomorrow."

"I'm afraid of the way I'm feeling toward you. This was just supposed to be a little fling. Just for the weekend." She closed her eyes again. "This wasn't supposed to happen. Not to me. Not now."

Payne wrapped his arm around her and squeezed her shoulder. "Please stay. Don't run away from me."

"I'm sorry. I have to go. I need some time to think. This is scaring me."

"Okay. I've got plenty of time." Payne stood to his feet. "I'll wait forever." Releasing her, he reached down and picked up her bag. "Ready?"

"No."

"Stayin?"

"I don't know."

Payne put down the bag and folded his arms across his chest. "It's your call. Ya know I want ya to stay."

Rusti tried to slump in the old kitchen chair, but the frayed duct tape was sticking to her new jeans. "Damn you, Payne McCarty," she muttered. Peeling her legs from the chair, she stood and faced him. "Staying."

CHAPTER TWENTY-SEVEN

Stetson's Western World was packed Saturday night. Nova had shown up drunk and was getting worse with every song. With three songs left in their final set, Payne watched her stagger back to her bottle. Turning it up, she tilted her head back to get the last drop and just kept going, falling like a fence post. She was out before her head bounced off the stage.

The gasps heard from the crowded dance floor quickly turned to boos while Payne and Hartman tried to revive her. Jimmy Earl rushed to the stage and helped them carry her off. Her butt was bouncing up and down off the floor as Jimmy Earl and Hartman dragged her by the arms and Payne held her feet. They sat her up, leaning her against the cool brick wall. "I got her," Jimmy Earl said. "Payne, you and Hartman get back up there and finish the set with somethin."

Payne turned around and almost stumbled over Lisa and Rusti who had rushed to the scene. "Is she okay? Lisa asked.

"She'll be fine," Payne answered. He turned to Rusti. "Jimmy Earl wants us to finish out the set with somethin. Just stay here. I'll be right back."

"Would you do your song, for me?" Rusti asked. She took his hand. "I've been wanting to hear you do it."

"This might not be the right time. The crowd's restless."

"Please."

Payne nodded. "Sure."

The crowd was still booing when Payne took Nova's microphone. "We apologize for the delay." He waited until the booing had started to wind down before again trying to speak. "We've got one more song for y'all tonight. This is our version of Rusti King's hit *When Love Turns Out The Light*. Dance with someone ya love, or at least dance with someone ya'd love to love on." Payne strapped on Nova's black guitar. He played the intro over the crowd noise, then sang.

If I hadn't had a lump in my throat
You know, I'd have said good-bye,

NASHVILLE GOLD

Rusti had already removed her baseball cap and fluffed her long red hair. Taking the stage, she winked at Skeeter before leaning over Payne's shoulder. She sang along.

> *But you, you just walked away*
> *Thinkin I'd be okay.*
> *You never slowed down long enough*
> *To see my face drain white.*
> *It's amazing how far your heart can fall,*
> *When love turns out the light.*

The crowd roared to life when they realized Rusti King was on stage. The dancing stopped. The mob pressed the stage, listening to the duet. As the last note faded from the borrowed guitar, Rusti leaned over and kissed Payne. The thrilled audience erupted with cheers.

It happened fast. A drunk cowboy jumped on the stage, yelling, "I love you, Rusti!" He lunged for her. Payne's kick caught him square between the legs, sending him reeling backward into the crowd. "Get her outta here!" Payne yelled at Skeeter, who was already on his way to his friend's side.

Payne unsnapped the guitar strap as two more cowboys charged the stage. He swung Nova's guitar like a baseball bat. It shattered against the big one's chest, causing him to stagger backwards. But the second cowboy caught him. Regaining their balance, they both charged Payne.

Hartman appeared from nowhere. Flying through the air, he tackled the smaller of the two, rolling with him off the stage. Payne landed a right hook to the jaw of the big man. It staggered him long enough for Payne to score another shot to his body. But Payne was pulled off the stage, into the brawl that had erupted on the dance floor.

Payne grimaced with the paralyzing punch to his kidney. His knees buckled. He helplessly took the next blow to the side of his head on the way down. Struggling to all fours, he was kicked in his ribs. The blow laid him out flat on the dance floor, wheezing. He saw the boot coming and closed his eyes. His world went black with the impact.

After tucking Lisa and Rusti securely away in his pickup, Skeeter rushed back into Stetson's. The dance floor was still in the process of being cleared by the bouncers when Skeeter spotted Payne lying in a pool of blood on the old plank-wood floor. Hartman was kneeling over him holding his own bleeding, broken nose in one hand, and a bar rag on Payne's head with the other.

"He ain't moved," Hartman managed to say. "They're callin an ambulance."

"Payne!" Skeeter yelled at him, and shook him by the shoulders. "Wake up, we've gotta get ya outta here."

"He's gonna need stitches," Hartman said, removing the rag from Payne's head. The gash was next to his left eye. It was deep, stretching from just outside his eyebrow, to his hairline. The blood ran freely until Hartman replaced the rag. "Got him in the temple. He's out cold."

Skeeter took Payne's feet and raised his long legs in the air. "This is an ol jockey trick." The blood from Payne's legs rushed to his head. His lanky body began to twitch and his eyes began to flutter.

Groaning, Payne opened his eyes and reached for his head. "Damn."

"Sit him up," Skeeter ordered.

Hartman raised Payne by the shoulders and steadied him. "Payne, ya okay?" Hartman asked.

"Shit," Payne grumbled.

"Let's get him outta here." Skeeter helped Hartman get Payne to his feet.

"Payne!" Rusti screamed, when she saw his blood stained shirt and bolted from Skeeter's pickup.

"He's gonna need some stitches," Skeeter said. "Hartman needs his nose set. You girls follow us in the Jeep."

"Payne, oh baby, I'm so sorry." Rusti lifted his chin. Removing the bloody bar rag, she looked at the bleeding gash. "Oh, shit!"

"It's a long way from my heart." Payne managed a small grin, but was wobbling on his feet.

"It was all my fault. I knew better than that." Rusti kissed his forehead as Skeeter opened the door of his pickup.

"Get his keys," Skeeter ordered.

Rusti dug in Payne's left front pocket.

"Further down and to the right," Payne directed.

"That's not funny," she said, retrieving his keys.

Payne started to laugh, but grabbed his side. "Shit! I think my ribs are broke."

*

The nurse behind the Emergency Room counter raised her eyebrows when she saw the five of them walk through the door. Skeeter went to the tall counter and stood on his tiptoes. "We need a doctor. One needs stitches and the other one needs his nose set."

"Accident?"

NASHVILLE GOLD

"What the hell do ya think?"
"Insurance?"
"Look lady, why don't ya get off your fat ass and get us some help."
"I'm going to call security if you don't watch your mouth!"
Rusti put her hand on Skeeter's shoulder. "I'll take care of the charges."
"Cash, check, or credit card?"
"Shit!" Skeeter yelled. "Charge it to Stetson's Western World."
"Skeeter, let me handle this."
The nurse took Rusti's American Express and looked at the name. "Rusti King! Mother Mary, I'm a big fan. What are you doing mixed up in this?"
"Could you please help us?"
The overweight nurse pulled out two clipboards. Fill these out. I'll get a doctor."

*

Hartman reappeared first, still holding his nose. Removing his hand he asked, "How's it look?"
"Better than it did." Skeeter winked at him. "I swear, ya look better with a fat nose."
"They want to keep Payne overnight."
"Bullshit. Where is he?"
"Three curtains back, on the right. They've got his head stitched up. X-rays showed two cracked ribs. They're worried about a concussion."
"Oh, my goodness," Lisa said.
"Oh, no," Rusti moaned.
"Hell, that ain't no big deal," Skeeter reassured them. "I'll handle this."
Payne was alone, lying on the table, when Skeeter tore open the curtains. "Dr. Doeppenschmidt reportin." He grinned. "So, I understand ya think you're sufferin from hemorrhoids?"
Payne laughed and grabbed his side. "Shit. Skeeter, don't make me laugh."
"Hemorrhoids can sometimes be confused with a good ol fashioned ass-kickin." Skeeter kept a straight face. "Ya sure it feels like hemorrhoids?" He folded his arms and scratched his chin. "Hmm ... looks more like an ass-kickin to me."
"Skeeter, get the hell outta here."
"Not without my patient. Get your sissy ass off that table and let's go before they decide to keep ya." Skeeter helped Payne stand to his feet.

Entering the waiting room with his arm around Payne's waist, Skeeter handed him off to Rusti. "Here, *you* take him. He's more your size. We're outta here."

"Hold it right there!" yelled the hefty nurse, from behind the counter. "You can't leave until I've got the paper work completed."

"Lady," Skeeter yelled. "Why don't ya wipe your fat ... " Lisa put her hand over his mouth as the automatic door opened. Prying her hand from his mouth, Skeeter continued giving orders. "We'll take Hartman back to Stetson's for his truck."

"I can get our stuff tomorrow," Hartman volunteered.

"Look around for my hat while you're at it," Payne called after them.

Rusti helped Payne into the Jeep and slid behind the wheel. He buckled up and held his ribs. "Try not to pop the clutch."

CHAPTER TWENTY-EIGHT

Skeeter banged on Payne's bedroom door Sunday morning.
"Rusti, telephone."
Rusti watched Payne stirring as she dressed. "How do you feel this morning?"
"Lonesome. Ya comin back?"
"I'll make coffee first."
Rusti didn't bother saying hello. "Good morning, Dennis."
"Have you seen the Austin paper this morning?" he screamed.
"No, Dennis, I haven't seen the Austin paper."
"Rusti King's Surprise Performance Sparks Brawl at Stetson's! What in the hell is going on with you?"
"I'll explain when I see you this afternoon."
"Three o'clock, Rusti. And I'm going to want some answers! We could be looking at a lawsuit."
"Don't push me, Dennis. You'll get what I give you." Rusti hung up the phone and went to the kitchen to put on the coffee.
Returning to the bedroom, she leaned over and stroked Payne's forehead. "How's the head? Do you need anything?"
"I'm fine." Payne took her hand. "I got ever thing I need right here."
"Sounds like someone's feeling a little better. You moaned all night." Rusti pulled the sheet down and looked at the deep purple bruise on his ribs. Bending over, she lightly ran her fingers through his hair, while examining his stitches. "Payne, I'm so sorry. It was stupid of me to get on a stage that close to the dance floor."
"Yeah, well, I thought we sounded pretty good together."
"We're perfect together." She sat on the edge of the bed and ran her hand over his chest. "Do you still love me this morning?"
"Yeah. Is that still a problem?"
Rusti smiled. "Sure you didn't change your mind over night?"
"That'll never change."
"Will you stop loving me when you don't see me? When we're apart?"

"No. I'll never stop lovin ya." Payne reached up and twirled a strand of her hair around his finger. "I'll see your face ever time I close my eyes."

She took a deep breath. "Payne, about yesterday. I'm sorry I blew up at you. It wasn't you. It was me. I've never felt this way about anyone before. It scared me."

"Hey, don't worry bout that. I'm just proud ya decided to stay."

"I don't want you to stop loving me. Not ever." Rusti's eyes were welling up.

Payne wiped her first tear away. "Hey, what's wrong?"

"Promise you won't stop loving me?"

"I promise."

"Last night, I was so afraid for you ... it's crazy. But I realized in that hospital waiting room ... that suddenly nothing else in the world mattered to me, but you." She took his hand and closed her eyes. "I love you, too." Rusti bent down, her thick red hair covered their faces as she kissed him softly. "I love you," she repeated. "I do. I really love you." They held each other until Payne moaned. She sat up. "Oh baby, I'm sorry. Did I hurt you?"

Payne shook his head. "Naw." He smiled at her. "I love ya, too." He stroked her arm. "Thank ya for sayin it."

"Admitting it," she corrected.

His blue eyes were sparkling. He took her hand and kissed it over and over. "I thought ya felt the same when I said what I did at the track."

"Oh, really?" Rusti looked surprised. "And just when did you know?"

"At the lake. When ya asked me what was goin on between us. I think we both knew it by then."

Rusti gently stroked his face. "I always thought love at first sight was just in fairy tales and romance novels."

"Like I said," Payne snapped his fingers, "if it takes any longer than that, it ain't love. Love's not somethin ya can just make happen, or stop it when it does. It's gotta mind of it's own. When it happens, then it's up to the two people not to let it get away from em. Not ever."

"You certainly seem to know a lot about it."

"I'm a songwriter." He smiled at her. "I'm supposed to know about stuff like that."

"I love you." She pulled his hand to her lips and kissed it. "This is the craziest, most wonderful, happiest feeling in the whole world."

"I feel the same way. Ya know ... I wasn't exactly plannin on this either. All I know is, I love ya more ever time I look at ya. I can't help myself."

"Now what? Where do we go from here?"

Payne shrugged his shoulders. "I guess the next step is committin to each other."

Rusti managed to turn away from him before her face fell. She left the bed and walked toward the door. "Coffee's probably ready. I'll be right back."

Payne was sitting up in bed when she returned. She handed him both cups and fluffed her pillow before slipping out of her clothes and crawling back under the sheets. She took her coffee.

"Payne, nothing has changed. As much as I want to, I can't commit to you. I mean, I can't just get off the bus in New Braunfels and stay with you."

"I know that. Didn't expect ya to."

"Then where does that leave us?"

"In love. Ya don't have to get off the bus to commit. That bus is gonna stop one of these days and I'll be waitin there when ya get off. We could just commit to that."

"I'm not talking about the future. I'm talking about today." She took his hand in hers and squeezed it. "I want us to be together. I don't want to say goodbye today." Rusti sat up and looked at him. "What would you think about finishing the tour with me? We're done after Willie's Picnic, until September. You could just go with me the next couple of weeks. Then we could still be together."

"I'm sure Dennis will love that."

"Dennis doesn't count."

"I'd be a distraction to ya. I'll promise ya that."

"You're already a distraction to me. I'd be real disappointed if that changed."

Payne ran his hand over her bare back, feeling her soft skin. "Am I distractin ya now?" he asked, as his hand disappeared under the sheet.

"Don't start something you can't finish. And from the looks of you, I have my doubts."

"Looks can be deceivin."

Payne tried to pull her sheet down. "Stop that." She gently slapped his hand away. "Anyway, I'm not comfortable with Skeeter and Lisa in the next room. You might scream if I hurt you." Payne continued his light touch until she grabbed his hand and held it. "Are they going to the races today?"

"Yeah."

"Then just hold your horses. Besides, you didn't answer my question. Will you finish the tour with me?"

"I don't know if I can. Willie's Picnic's in two weeks. Assumin Jimmy Earl still let's us play, we'll need to practice. Man, Nova blew it big time last night." Payne thought about it. He shook his head. "And I can't miss Skeeter's weddin."

Rusti was silent. When she spoke, she tried to hide her disappointment. "I understand. No. You can't miss their wedding." She leaned back against her pillow. "Would you consider coming back to Nashville with me? Like you said. When the bus stops, after the tour? After the Fourth of July?"

"Hell, yeah. I've been wantin to go back there anyway." He took a sip of coffee then shook his head. "But I promised Nova I'd stay on with the band if Jimmy Earl got me paid for my song."

"Payne! You can't be serious. Baby, you can't sacrifice us being together for a promise you made to Nova and Jimmy Earl!"

"I can't break my word to em." He thought about it while she fumed. "But if I didn't get paid for the song, I wouldn't be breakin my word. Not exactly anyway." He took another sip of coffee. "I'll just forget about the money."

"So, you'd turn down twenty thousand dollars not to break your word to Nova and Jimmy Earl."

"If it meant we could be together, I would. Dennis and Jimmy Earl were screwin me anyway. I got the right to change my mind before I sign anything." Payne grimaced as he adjusted his position. "I'll just tell em no deal."

"You could sue that Durwood guy when we get to Nashville. I could help you when we get there."

"Maybe, but I don't wanna make any trouble for y'all over it. That song's already got me somethin no amount of money could buy."

Rusti took his hand and kissed it. "Payne, I want your name on that song. I want people to know who wrote it. It's going to be a classic."

Payne finished his coffee and changed the subject. "Did I tell ya Skeeter and Lisa are movin to Kentucky?"

"No." Rusti took his cup and leaned over the bed, placing the coffee cups on the floor.

"He wants to race in the Kentucky Derby."

"Really?" Rusti smiled. "I'm not sure Kentucky is ready for Skeeter."

Payne laughed and grabbed his ribs in pain. "Damn. I've hurt worse than this, but I sure can't remember when. Don't make me laugh."

"You promise to come back with me? After the Fourth?"

"Committed to it, unless ya wanna live here. I'd even buy ya an air conditioner."

"No, thanks. It's nice, but ..." Rusti carefully snuggled next to him. She ran her hand over his chest. "Then what? I mean after the Fourth."

"We've got time to think." Payne kissed the top of her head. "All I know is, I wanna spend the rest of my life with ya. I figure we'll know what to do when it's time to do it. Let's just take it a step at a time."

Rusti grew quiet. Payne felt a tear drop on his shoulder. "What's wrong, babe?"

"I don't want to say goodbye today."

"Let's not think about that now." Payne held her closer. Neither spoke as he played with her hair.

"I've got it!" she said, and sat up in bed. The sudden movement caused Payne to flinch. "You could go with me for awhile. After we shoot Austin City Limits tonight, we go to Ft. Worth next, then Oklahoma City on Thursday. You could fly back from there on Friday and be back in time for Skeeter's wedding!"

"Damn, girl. You're smart, too."

"We could leave your Jeep at the Austin Airport. Take a cab from there. Then you'd have a ride when you got back."

"Hell of a deal." Payne smiled at Rusti's excitement.

"What are you grinning at?"

"You. I don't believe I've ever seen ya look this happy. I like it. Love looks good on ya." Payne took her hand and kissed it. "I want ya to look like this ever day, for the rest of your life."

CHAPTER TWENTY-NINE

"You're sure all smiles for someone who got their ass kicked last night." Lured to the kitchen by the blended aroma of coffee and bacon, Skeeter started in on Payne. "Looks like somebody gotcha on the other side of your head, too. Was there anybody there who didn't get a shot in on ya?"

"Yeah, the guy I hit with Nova's guitar," Payne said, from his seat at the table.

"You broke Nova's guitar? Shit, she's gonna be really pissed."

"Not unless ya tell her I did it. As far as I'm concerned, it was just a casualty of war."

Rusti pulled the stopper on the dishwater and wiped her hands. "Skeeter, you could be a little more sympathetic."

"Not really." He winked at her. "Ya don't get sympathy around here for losin a fight."

"It wasn't a fight," Payne said. "It was a brawl."

"Okay, it was a brawl. Ya still got your ass kicked."

"Well, I guess there's a first time for ever thing."

"That ain't the first time. Remember ... "

"Okay, boys," Rusti interrupted. "Let's change the subject. Skeeter, we've already eaten, but there's bacon and toast left, if you're interested."

Skeeter poured a cup of coffee and grabbed a piece of bacon. "Thanks for doin the dishes again."

"No problem. But I took Payne's turn this time. Now it's yours again."

"Fat chance," Payne mumbled.

"Good morning," Lisa said, entering the kitchen. "Payne, how are you feeling?"

"Fine. Thanks for askin."

Lisa walked over and touched him carefully on the shoulder. "Are you sure? You don't look too good."

"I'm sure." He smiled at her. "Skeeter, at least Lisa cared enough to ask how I was feelin."

"What the hell would ya expect from someone who works in a doctor's office. I didn't have to ask. Ya look like you've been through hell with your hat off."

"Thanks."

"Well, ya do."

"Are you a nurse?" Rusti asked Lisa.

"No," she giggled, "I work in the back. I'm a bookkeeper. Skeeter was just being funny."

"Yeah, he's real damn funny this mornin," Payne mumbled. "Skeeter, I need to ask ya for a couple of favors?"

"Well, ask me."

"Would ya look after Pardner for a few days? I'm goin with Rusti when she leaves from Austin tonight."

"Rusti," Skeeter looked up at her from the table, "if you're lookin for a bodyguard, I'd keep lookin. Payne couldn't fight his way outta a paper sack."

Rusti threw the wet dishcloth at Skeeter.

"Where y'all goin?"

"Ft. Worth and Oklahoma City."

"Gotta reason or just leavin?"

Payne glanced at Rusti before answering. "Gotta reason."

Skeeter studied Rusti who was grinning at Payne. "And that would be?"

"None of your damn business. That's what that would be."

"Aw, come on, Payne. Tell me."

Payne shook his head. "None of your business."

"Payne, are ya blushin?"

"No."

"Hell, he's blushin!" Skeeter laughed.

"I think you're right," Rusti said, joining in Skeeter's fun. "Payne, you're not ashamed to admit it to Skeeter, are you?"

"No. It's just none of his damn business."

"Admit what?" Skeeter pressed him, thoroughly enjoying himself. "Come on Payne. Is there somethin ya need to tell me?"

"We fell in love. There, damn it. Are ya happy?"

"We?" Skeeter looked at Rusti and raised his eyebrows.

"We," Rusti answered. "*We're* in love."

"Oh, my God!" Lisa squealed. "It must be contagious!"

"Must be," Payne muttered.

"Will you be back for our wedding?" Lisa asked.

"Wouldn't miss it. I'll be back Friday."

Payne looked at Skeeter. "What the hell are *you* still grinnin at?"

"Nothin. I was just tryin to remember the last time I saw ya blush."

"Well, I hope you'll try that damn hard to remember to feed Pardner while I'm gone."

"Damn, Payne. Are we a little grumpy this mornin?"

"Hell, no."

"Sure?"

"Damn it, Skeeter ... " Payne shook his head at him, "never mind."

"Was there somethin else?"

"Yeah, there was. Run out to Heidi's and ask Casey if we can play there the next two weekends. Nova said to ask for two hundred a night."

"Shit. After the cat-fight they had ... we'll probably have to pay her."

"Get what ya can. Also, tell her I'll finish her deck next week after my ribs quit hurtin. It'll only take two or three days to finish it."

"Who's Casey?" Rusti asked.

"She owns Heidi's Roadhaus," Payne answered, and shot a look at Skeeter. "It's a bar we used to play at. Before Jimmy Earl signed us up."

"And?"

"And, I've been doin some carpenter work at her house."

"And?"

"Well, she ain't bad, but she ain't no Ragina." Skeeter answered for Payne. He grinned at Rusti. "Nothin to worry about."

"I'm not worried." Rusti left the sink and placed a kiss on top of Payne's head.

"Speakin of Ragina," Skeeter said, "man, did I get an ear full from her after the races yesterday." He looked at Payne. "She ever rip into ya?"

"She called me a son-of-a bitch yesterday. Does that count?"

"She chewed my ass up one side and down the other for not winnin that race. Said she lost a lotta money."

"Poor thing," Rusti said, while rubbing Payne's shoulders.

"How'd ya explain that one?" Payne asked.

"Didn't. I told her to double up next time and she'd get her money back and then some. I told her there was no way Dial Sammy was gonna lose at Fredericksburg." Skeeter winked at Payne. "I personally guaranteed it."

"Will ya talk to Casey?"

"Anything else?"

"That'll do it."

"Okay then, Lisa and me are off to the races." He hugged Rusti, his head lingering on her breast. "Ya know, there're some advantages of bein short."

"Skeeter!" Lisa scolded.

Skeeter flashed a big grin up at Rusti. "Congratulations you two. I'm proud for both of ya. Rusti, I guess that means we'll be seein more of ya."

"Definitely. The Fourth of July for sure."

"Well, try to keep Payne outta trouble. I'd hate to see him get his ass kicked twice in one week."

"Good-bye, Skeeter," Payne said.

Lisa gave Rusti a quick hug. "It was very nice meeting you. It sure has been an exciting few days."

"Yes it has." Rusti laughed. "Best wishes on your wedding. I know you two are going to be happy together. I wish I could be there."

"Match made in heaven," Skeeter added, and opened the screen door for Lisa. "Y'all take care."

Rusti ran her fingers through Payne's hair. "Well, I think you're my hero. I don't care if you did get your ass kicked in a fight."

"It was a brawl."

Rusti laughed. "How would my hero like a nice hot bath, some aspirins, and a cold beer to help ease the pain?"

"Great. Will ya join me?"

"You need to stretch out and soak. But I'll sit with you."

Payne took her hand and kissed it. "Remember Thursday night? A hot bath and a beer is what ya wanted when ya first got here."

"Yeah, I remember. Baby, I'll remember every moment of this weekend." She sighed. "I hate to leave, but at least you're coming with me. I couldn't stand it if you weren't."

"What was your favorite part?"

"Fishing."

"Fishin?"

"Yeah, when you were explaining what was happening between us. That was my favorite part. That moment at the lake." Rusti snapped her fingers.

*

The gloomy Austin sky had stopped sputtering rain by early Sunday afternoon. Dennis Couch bolted off the bus when he spotted the Yellow Cab pulling into the parking lot. "Rusti, thank God you're back! I was beginning to wonder ... "

"You remember Payne," she interrupted.

Payne extended his hand, but Dennis ignored him. "What's *he* doing here?"

"*He's* coming with me for a few days."
"The hell he is!" Dennis turned to Payne. "Just who do you think you are?"
"I'm fixin to be your worst nightmare if ya don't calm down."
"Dennis, let's go inside." Rusti stepped between them. "It's starting to rain again."
Plopping down on the couch, Dennis studied Payne as he came up the steps. But it was Rusti who threw the first punch. "Dennis, Payne and I are in love."
Dennis laughed. "Yeah right. Rusti, he's just chasing your money, or looking for a shirttail to ride into Nashville on. What's wrong with you?"
"Get the hell off my bus!"
"Okay. Okay. Just calm down."
Payne wrapped his arm around Rusti. "Look Dennis, what's she's tryin to say is *get the hell off her bus*. Got it?"
Dennis was the first to blink. He broke eye contact with Payne and glanced at his watch. "Sound check's in five minutes."
Payne waited until the bus door hissed to speak, "I'd say he took that pretty good, considerin." He forced a grin.
"He didn't mean that."
"Sure he did. He's just tryin to look after ya."
"He's just trying to get fired, is what he's doing." Rusti walked to the refrigerator and pulled a beer out for Payne. "Why don't you just relax here for awhile. I won't be gone long." She opened the door to her bedroom and motioned with her head to Payne. "You can put your things in here." Catching him as he passed through the door, she stole a quick kiss. "You okay?"
"I'm fine."
Rusti lifted his chin. "You sure?"
"Yeah. As long as *you* know I'm here because I wanna be with ya. That's the only reason. Money don't mean shit to me."
"I know why you're here." She held him gently in her arms. "I'll talk to Dennis after he's had a chance to settle down. He's just upset. I'll be back in a flash."

*

Dennis took Rusti by the arm when she left the stage. "Tell me about last night, at Stetson's."

NASHVILLE GOLD

"It was my fault. Nova, their lead singer, passed out drunk toward the end of their last set. The crowd was restless and Jimmy Earl sent Payne up to finish out the set. I asked Payne to sing his song. I waited until he had already started the song, then walked up behind him. We did a duet. I wasn't thinking. By the time I saw the crowd pressing against the stage it was too late. Just as the song ended, some drunk cowboy jumped on the stage and headed for me. Payne kicked the guy in the balls and yelled for Skeeter to get me out of there."

"Who's Skeeter?"

"He's their drummer. Payne's roommate." She held her hand out breast high. "He's about this tall. A racehorse jockey. Anyway, Skeeter managed to get me and his girlfriend out the backdoor. He went back in and found Payne on the floor. Payne has two cracked ribs, a concussion, and half-a-dozen stitches. Dennis, don't blame him for what happened. It was my fault. He saved my butt."

"Well, according to the paper, it must have been quite a fight."

"It was a brawl," Rusti argued. "Payne broke a guitar over somebody before he got dragged to the dance floor. Their bass player, Hartman, got his nose broken. It was awful."

Dennis sat down in a folding chair and motioned for Rusti to take a seat. "Tell me about you and Payne."

"I can't explain it. Dennis, we just clicked." She snapped her fingers. "Just like that. I wasn't looking to fall in love. You know that. And neither was he. It just happened. I've never felt like this about anyone before."

"Plans?"

"We're taking it slow. He's going with us as far as Oklahoma City. I want my parents to meet him when we get to Ft. Worth."

"That serious? Already?"

"He hasn't asked me to marry him, but I'll say yes when he gets around to it. Dennis, he makes me happier than I've ever been in my life."

Leaning back, Dennis closed his eyes. "Rusti, you're on the brink of becoming a superstar. I hate to see you throw it all away."

"Look. The way I see it, we could have us a good-looking guitar player on stage and a songwriter off stage. Nothing's changed as far as my goals are concerned. I still want it. I'm just in love. Even superstars fall in love."

Dennis leaned forward in his chair. "I'm just trying to look out for you. That's part of my job."

"Payne and I both know that." Rusti took his hand. "Dennis, you and I have been through a lot together. I appreciate everything you've ever done for me. You're one of the best friends I have, but you're going to have to get along with Payne."

"Or?"

Rusti withdrew her hand, eyes flashing. "Or, we'll get along without you." "I'm not going to take orders from him." Dennis flared. "We have a contract with over a year left on it. I'm still in charge of your career."

"Fine. Just don't forget whose life it is. You can make this easy on yourself, or hard on yourself. That's your choice. But it's my life and I intend to spend the rest of it with Payne."

Dennis shoved off his chair and paced in front of her. "Okay." He threw his hands up in surrender. "Sounds like I need to start over with him."

"You can start over by getting his name on that song. Gold records don't come easy. I want his name on it when it goes gold."

"We've already got a deal with him on that song."

"Dennis," Rusti stood and faced him, "I'm not going to stand by and watch you and Jimmy Earl screw him out of his song. As of right now, there is no deal. Right's right and wrong's wrong. I want his name on the song and that's that!" Rusti whirled away from him, heading for the exit.

"Rusti!" Dennis went after her. "I can't get his name on that song without turning Nashville upside down. Do you realize what you're asking me to do? Heads are going to roll! Lawsuits. Bad press ... "

Rusti stopped and spun around. "Fine. Then I'll do it!"

CHAPTER THIRTY

The sun rose behind a thin layer of clouds, casting a brilliant mixture of gold and red on the new day. Approaching Ft. Worth, the blue and yellow bus left the caravan of buses and trucks, exiting from the north bound lane of Interstate-35. Making a circle in the entry ramp, Randall squinted briefly into the morning sun before joining the westbound Ft. Worth traffic. All four lanes of Loop 820 West were filling as the Monday morning motorists rushed to begin their new workweek.

Picking up the microphone, Randall announced their arrival. "Good morning, Rusti. We're in Ft. Worth. I'm going to need directions from the Jacksboro Highway to your parent's house." He paused. "Oh yeah, good morning, Payne."

Rusti flicked on the soft light above the bed and watched Payne yawn. "I love you this morning," she said with a smile, and lightly ran a finger over his lips.

"I love ya more." He took her hand and kissed it.

"No you don't"

"Yes I do. I love ya the most."

"You can be wrong if you want to." She kissed him and left the bed. "How's the head?"

Payne watched her walk naked to the small sink to brush her teeth. "It's better today."

"Ribs"

"I'm fine."

"We're almost to my parents' house." Rusti stared at her reflection in the small mirror and tried to fluff up her wavy red hair.

Payne watched her dress, then pull her hair back into a thick ponytail. He stretched in bed. "That was a short trip."

"For us it was. Time flies when you're having fun." She blew him a kiss. "I need to show Randall how to get there. Come on up when you get dressed."

Rusti patted Randall's thick shoulder. "Thank you, Randall. I don't know how you drive all night."

"It's the best time to drive. Not a problem."

"Turn west on Highway 199, toward Jacksboro."

Payne joined Rusti on the couch and looked out the window. "Lake Worth. So, that's where ya learned to fish?"

"That's it. Want to go fishing again?"

"Are ya gonna make me throw em back?"

"Probably."

Payne grinned. "Are ya excited about seein your parents?"

"I'm always glad to get there, but I'm usually just as glad to leave. Payne, we can't sleep together at my daddy's house."

"Can we sneak out?"

"Maybe." Rusti pointed over Randall's shoulder. "See that Circle K store on the left? You need to turn left there."

"Got it."

"It's pretty country," Payne observed. "Looks a lot like the Hill Country, without all the hills. Looks like mostly oak and cedar trees."

"See that little white house ... right there?" She pointed excitedly. "That's where I grew up. Rode the bus to school. I told you I was raised poor. Hey, did you know Roger Miller is from Azle?"

Payne sang a few lines from *Dang Me*.

Rusti took over when he stumbled over the lyrics. Then she changed keys and sang *King Of The Road*. Payne joined in until Rusti laughed and waved him off. She tapped Randall on the shoulder. "Turn left just past that red feed store." The big bus slowed for the turn. "It'll be on up the road. Third house on your right."

"What are your parent's names?" Payne asked, with just a hint of panic in his voice.

"Leon and Dot, short for Dorothy." Rusti patted him on the leg. "Don't be nervous."

As the road dust settled around the tour bus, Randall sounded the horn and opened the door. "Come in with us," Rusti insisted. "Stretch your legs."

"Yes, ma'am." Randall stood from the driver's seat and left the bus first. His long black hair was pulled into a tight ponytail, falling just below his neck.

Stepping off the bus, Payne looked at the muscular bodyguard. "Man, we coulda used ya at Stetson's the other night."

"Yeah." He nodded in agreement. "I'd say so. Judging from your face."

Leon and Dot King appeared on the front porch of the newly constructed brick house. Dot began waving her hand above her head as the three walked up the driveway.

"Hi, Honey!" she yelled. Her hair was freshly dyed red. Once long and red, like Rusti's, it had thinned and grayed over the years. She now wore it shorter. Both parents were tall and lean, dressed in boots and jeans. Dot wore a blue and white broad striped western blouse and, with her red hair, she resembled a Texas flag.

Rusti had gotten her dark complexion from Leon. He hadn't bothered to put a shirt on over his undershirt. Gray chest hair protruded out the top. His thin shoulders stooped some, but he held his head proudly beneath his *Texas Rangers* baseball cap. It covered the small amount of gray hair left on his balding head.

"Mom, Dad, I want you to meet Payne McCarty."

Payne looked Leon in the eye. "It's a pleasure," he said, while firmly shaking hands. Turning to Dot he shook her hand. "Ma'am."

"This is Randall Reynolds. He drives the bus and looks out for me."

"Nice to meet both of you. Anyone want coffee?" Dot asked, looking at Payne.

"Yes, ma'am."

"What in the world happened to you?" She stared at his bruised, battered face.

"It's a long story," Rusti answered.

Leon put his long arm around Rusti and led her into the house. Payne and Randall followed the family. "Nice house," Payne said.

"Thank you. Rusti bought it for us." Dot smiled at her daughter. "Payne, what do you do?"

"I'm a carpenter, by trade."

"He's also a songwriter. He wrote *When Love Turns Out The Light*," Rusti added.

"And?" Dot took Rusti's hand and looked into her daughter's sparkling eyes.

"And, we're in love." Rusti was beaming.

Payne's right boot tapped nervously on the kitchen floor. "Yes, ma'am."

Dot took Payne's hand with her other hand and looked at him, then back at Rusti. "I do believe I can see it in your eyes."

Leon poured the coffee without a word. He handed a cup to Randall, while looking Payne over. "Songwriter, huh?"

"Yes, sir. I play guitar and sing a little, too."

"I've been known to do a little pickin myself."

"Daddy played back in the days of Western Swing."

"Played every joint around here. All up and down the Jacksboro Highway," he boasted. Leon wrapped his arm around his daughter again and squeezed her shoulder. "Taught her ever thing she knows." He winked at Payne.

"He actually knew Bob Wills," Rusti added.

"Texas Swing music was born right here on the Jacksboro Highway," Leon said. A thin smile crossed his face. "Don't let nobody ever tell ya no different."

"Y'all take a seat at the kitchen table," Dot ordered.

Payne sat next to Rusti, across the solid oak table from Leon. But the old man's dark, deep-set eyes were focused on his daughter. Randall stood behind Rusti, out of habit.

"Randy, take a seat and join us," Dot ordered.

"Thank you, but I'm still stretching my legs."

"What kinda work do ya do?" Payne directed his question to Leon.

"Retired."

"Daddy had a garage on the Jacksboro Highway."

"Forty-five years of grease under my fingernails. Been retired two years and they're just now comin clean." Leon stuck his large, strong hands in the air as proof.

"Mrs. King," Randall interrupted. "Thank you for the coffee, but I need to get on down the road."

"There's a "T" up the road about a quarter mile," Leon said. "You can turn that thing around up there."

Rusti and Payne followed Randall to the bus and walked back with their luggage. "I think Daddy likes you."

"How can ya tell?"

"You'd already known it if he didn't. He's not shy when it comes to his girls. I have three older sisters. And Daddy's caused his share of grief for all of us. One night, he caught my oldest sister parked out front with someone he'd told her not to see. He kicked in the door of the poor guy's brand new Chevy. I'm surprised any of us ever had any dates after that."

"Ya coulda warned me."

"I didn't want to scare you off." She laughed. "He's harmless. Just a little rough around the edges."

Payne could smell the sausage frying when they returned to the kitchen. He poured Rusti another cup of coffee, folded his arms, and leaned against the wall. Looking around the big kitchen, he watched Rusti helping her mother with breakfast. The kitchen was flawlessly clean, as were the stark white cabinets. He eyed Leon, who remained seated at the table. Leon finished his coffee and caught Payne looking at him. Shoving his wood chair back from the table, he motioned to Payne. "Son, I wanna show ya somethin." Payne followed him into the living room. Leon opened a closet door and pulled out a guitar case. "Take a look."

Opening the case, Payne looked in awe at the old mahogany Martin Guitar. Leon reached down and removed the guitar. He handed it to Payne.

"It's beautiful." Payne inspected the old man's treasure.

"1951. Bet she's older than you are."

"This must be worth a fortune. It's in excellent condition."

"I won her in a pool game in 1957. Ever heard a thirty year old Martin?"

"No sir." Payne picked at the "B" string.

"They sound better with age. Play it."

Payne took the classic guitar to the couch and sat with it on his lap. He did a series of scales up and down the neck. "Nice. Soft action, for a Martin. They're usually a lot tighter. Got one myself, but it's nothin like this."

"Bet you'd thought twice about using that one in a bar fight," Rusti said. She was leaning against the wall, watching her two favorite men.

"That what happened to your head?" Leon grinned, exposing his nicotine stained teeth.

"Yes, sir. We were playin Saturday night in Austin, when a fight broke out. It got kinda ugly."

Leon let out a loud belly laugh, startling Payne. "We used to say we'd play from nine till fist fights or closin, which ever came first. That way, we always got paid. Been in a few scrapes myself."

"Come on boys. Breakfast is ready," Dot called from the kitchen.

Payne was almost done with his eggs when Dot started in. "Payne, where are you from?"

"I live just north of New Braunfels."

"Were you raised there?"

"No ma'am. Mostly in San Antonio. My dad was in the Air Force. We moved around a bunch."

"Air Force brat, huh?" Leon eyed him.

"Yes, sir."

"Are your parents still in San Antonio?" Dot continued the interrogation.

"No, ma'am." Payne glanced at Rusti. "My dad was shot down over Vietnam in 1967. I was nine. My mom remarried. They moved to San Diego as soon as I graduated from high school. But I stayed in San Antonio."

Rusti's eyes were wide. "Payne, you never told me that!"

"It hadn't come up yet. Ya didn't tell me your dad knew Bob Wills, either."

"That's too bad," Leon said. "Pilot?"

"Yes, sir. He flew an F-4. It was a fighter jet."

"Damn shame," Leon muttered, and took another bite of toast.

"It seems to me," Dot said, "you two need to spend a little more time talking. How long have you known each other?"
"Almost a week." Rusti blushed.
"Well, I guess that would explain that." Leon grinned at Payne. "At this rate, I reckon y'all will still have lots to talk about when ya get to be our age. Ain't that right, son?" Leon let out another loud laugh.
"Yes sir," he looked at Rusti and winked, "I reckon we will."

*

Tuesday morning, Payne pulled out his grandfather's old timepiece for the third time. But it was still before noon. He wound his watch, then listened to hear if it was still ticking. The bus arrived at twelve-thirty, exactly on time.
Leon and Dot walked them to the end of the driveway and hugged them both goodbye. Randall expertly turned the big bus around at the "T" in the road. He blew the horn as they passed back by her parents. They were still waving when the dust from the passing bus caused them to turn their heads. "I hope that wasn't too painful for you," Rusti said, and patted Payne on the leg.
"Hey, the food was great. And I really enjoyed swappin songs with your dad. He can do a mean Bob Wills."
"Yeah, well you can do a mean George Strait."
"Really, it wasn't bad at all." Payne squeezed her leg. "I loved our little walk in the county. But I'll tell ya one thing. I don't ever wanna see another domino."
Rusti laughed. "Babe, I hope you didn't mind me volunteering you to sit with them tonight. I know it will mean a lot to them."
"No problem. Your dad's a real hoot."
"Well, don't let him sucker you in at the pool table. He still shoots a mean game of pool. He'll take your money if he gets half a chance." Rusti kissed his cheek. "Still love me after meeting my parents?"
"Ya can't run me off that easy." Payne gave her a quick kiss. "It needed doin."

CHAPTER THIRTY-ONE

On Wednesday When Love Turns Out The Light reached number one on Billboard's Country Music Chart. Payne and Rusti celebrated her third number one hit, and his first, in the privacy of their hotel suite with two bottles of champagne. Payne used the second bottle as a squirt gun, chasing Rusti around the room.

On Thursday, Oklahoma City announced a sellout for the Rusti King Concert. Despite all the good news, Rusti's mood had darkened with the thought of their impending goodbye. The crowd, which had been enthusiastic all evening, was brought to the verge of tears during her finale. Her voice had cracked and the tears that fell from her eyes during the last line of Payne's song had been real. The coliseum exploded with her emotion. Her audience clapped and cheered insistently from the darkness. Their voices chanted her name in unison, screaming for another encore beneath the flickering flames of their lighters.

Emotionally exhausted, Rusti rushed backstage and threw her arms around Payne. Dennis was clapping with his hands above his head. "That was it!" he screamed, over the crowd noise. "That was your best performance, ever! Listen to that crowd!" Prying Rusti from Payne's arm, Dennis demanded she return for another song. But while he corralled the band, Rusti pulled Payne to center stage with her. The spotlight hit them instantly and the crowd erupted, chanting, Rusti! Rusti! Rusti!

She bowed graciously then screamed into the microphone, "Thank you, Oklahoma!" The crowd continued to chant her name. "Thank you!" she tried to speak over the noise then became quiet. The crowd slowly hushed. "Thank you for helping make *When Love Turns Out The Light* reach number one!" The audience again exploded with cheers. They calmed when she held up her hands. "So many times songwriters go unnoticed, but tonight, please help me say thank you to the man who wrote this wonderful song ... Payne McCarty!" She bowed to Payne. He waved his hat in the air while the fans in the sold out coliseum cheered. "Want to hear it again?" Rusti yelled.

The crowd roared as the lights dimmed. The spotlight illuminated the two lovers holding hands, sharing a microphone. Their voices joined together in a singular, impermeable harmony of love as they sang their song.

After the final notes had sounded and their voices faded, the lights went out as the lone guitar played on. "I love you," Rusti whispered in the darkness. Sliding into his arms, she kissed him. They were still embracing when the lights came back up. After one last kiss, she screamed into the microphone, "Thank you Payne! And thank you, Oklahoma!" Rusti King took her final bow with Payne at her side.

"Rusti, you crossed the line tonight!" Dennis was livid. "You can't say that! You can't say he wrote that damn song!"

"He did write it!" Rusti answered, then exploded. "Dennis, just shut the hell up! I asked you to get it fixed."

"I'm working on it! I've talked to Houlette about it. He's calling Branch. What else do you want me to do? Wave a magic wand? These things take time."

"Then what's the problem?"

"We're trying to keep the press out of this as long as we can. That's the problem. We want to get it fixed first, then announce it. It's a matter of timing."

"I don't give a tinker's damn about your timing or the press! I want the world to know who wrote that song!" Rusti spun away.

Payne waited until they were alone in her bus to ask, "Did I miss somethin?"

Bursting into tears, she held on to him. "Baby, please don't leave me. Please don't go."

Payne buried his head into her thick hair and whispered to her, "Just for a little while, babe. Then, never again. I swear it. Never again."

*

Rusti had done her best to fight the clock and the schedule, insisting the usual night travel be postponed until noon. But light had already fallen to the floor beneath the thick hotel curtains when Payne opened his eyes on Friday. He lay in the darkness recalling the past week, moment by moment. It was almost eight when he gently kissed her hand. "I love ya this mornin."

"What time is it?" Rusti asked, without opening her eyes.

"Time to wake up."

Payne carefully rolled over on his ribs and began to play with her hair. He waited for her to open her eyes. "Do ya want me to order coffee or breakfast?"

Rusti let out a sigh and closed her eyes again. "Payne, what am I going to do without you?"

"Finish your tour and come back to get me in Luckenbach."

"Promise you'll come back to Nashville with me on the bus?"

"Can Pardner ride on your bus?"

"He can drive it, if he wants to."

"Nah, he's too lazy for that." Payne smiled at her. "Are ya hungry?"

"Not really."

"I'll order a little somethin for ya anyway."

Rusti was still in the bathroom when the food arrived. Payne had the coffee poured and breakfast served in bed when she came out. But she only picked at her food. Leaning back, she rested against a pillow and the headboard. She closed her eyes after the first tear drop fell. Payne turned at the sound of her first sniffle.

"Babe, please don't cry. You'll get me started."

She wiped her eyes. "I'm trying."

Payne took the food tray away. When he returned to bed there was a steady stream of tears flowing down her cheeks. "Okay, I'm warnin ya. If ya don't stop cryin, I'm gonna have to give ya somethin to cry about." Payne gave her his charming smile.

"I'm trying."

"Close your eyes."

"Why?"

"Because I asked ya to. Ya trust me, don't ya?"

"I'm not sure. You've got that mischievous twinkle in those blue eyes of yours."

"Please?"

As soon as her eyes were closed Payne grabbed the small metal pitcher of maple syrup and walked to her side of the bed. He held it behind his back. "Okay, now, stick out your tongue."

Rusti giggled, but stuck her tongue out. Payne pulled down the top sheet. She retracted her tongue and opened her eyes. "What are you doing?" she asked, struggling with Payne over the sheet position.

"Nothin."

"Nothing?"

"Keep your eyes closed tight and stick your tongue back out." Payne sat on the edge of the bed and poured the maple syrup over her tongue.

"Payne!" The sticky syrup spilled down her chin and dripped to her neck. She wiped at it while Payne laughed at the expression on her face. "I'm going get you for that," she said, and made a grab for the pitcher. But he easily moved it out of her reach. Yanking the sheet away, he emptied the pitcher on her breasts. "Payne! I can't ... " But her tears and anguish had turned to hysterical laughter. She used a finger to wipe at the mess and smeared it on his nose. "I can't believe you just did that!" she screamed, catching her breath. "Okay big boy, you're going to have to clean this mess up."

Using his finger, Payne drew a heart on her with the syrup. "I was plannin on it."

*

Their mood sank faster than the elevator could count down the floors during its descent to the lobby. Payne held Rusti's hand in one hand and his bag in the other. When the elevator doors opened in the lobby, a camera flash blinded their eyes. It flashed again, and again.

"Rusti, can we have a word?"

"Will you answer some questions?"

From nowhere, Randall stepped between the lovers and the reporters. "Back off! Give them some room."

"Rusti, is Payne McCarty the new man in your life?"

"What are your plans?"

"Why isn't Payne's name on the song if he wrote it?"

"No comment," Randall answered. He extended his muscular arms, giving Payne and Rusti a head start through the lobby.

The cab driver was engrossed in the sports pages when Payne slammed the palm of his hand down on the hood of his Yellow Cab. Randall was backing out of the lobby door trying to hold the reporters at bay. "Randall, tell Dennis she'll be back in an hour," Payne yelled.

He held the door while Rusti slid into the backseat. "Airport, please," she said.

The cab driver started the meter and accelerated from beneath the Hilton's marquee, swerving to dodge the reporters. Payne caught him staring at Rusti in the rearview mirror.

"Buddy, we appreciate ya gettin us outta there, but we'd appreciate it even more if you'd watch the damn road."

Turning completely around he asked, "Are you really Rusti King?"

"Yeah, she's really Rusti King," Payne snapped at him. "Now watch the damn road."

"Yes, sir."

"I need ya to drop me at the Southwest Airlines gate, then take her back to the Hilton."

"Yes sir. Can I have an autograph?" he asked, again looking over his shoulder.

"Only if ya get her back alive."

Rusti was looking out the window when Payne patted her on the leg. "Hey, it's gonna be okay. The time will pass before we know it."

"I'll call every chance I get."

"And I'll see ya ever time I close my eyes." Payne held both of her hands with his. "Please don't forget I love ya."

"Promise me again. I want to hear you say it. Tell me you'll go back with me to Nashville."

"I promise. I'll be on your bus. I swear it."

Rusti laid her head on his shoulder. "I love you."

The cab came to a stop in the loading zone, beneath the red and gold Southwest Airlines sign. But Rusti and Payne held to each other, refusing to turn loose. The traffic cop blew his whistle at the Yellow Cab. "Move it or lose it!"

"Come on folks. I'm fixing to get a ticket here."

Payne pried her arms from around his neck. "Hey, where's that pretty smile?"

Rusti closed her eyes. She cried and shook her head. "I can't smile."

Payne lifted her chin with his hand and kissed her. There were tears in his eyes. He swallowed hard. "Me either," he managed to say and left the cab. "I love ya," he called from the curb. "See ya in Luckenbach."

The cop blew his whistle and pointed at the cab. It lurched forward and Payne was alone.

CHAPTER THIRTY-TWO

Charlie Keith had come to 16th Avenue from Ohio in June of 1983.
He carried with him a briefcase full of songs, a little cash in his back pocket, and a heart full of dreams. Three months later, his briefcase was still full of songs and his pockets were empty. His dreams of stardom had turned into a Nashville nightmare.

Charlie had talent. More than most who left it all to roll the dice on Music Row. Proficient on the piano and guitar, he could read music easier than most people could read the Sunday Comics. And his short brown hair gave him the innocent looks of a Baptist choirboy. What Charlie didn't have in 1983, were connections.

In the beginning, the quiet, stately buildings on 16th Avenue appeared as unassuming as their Southern heritage. Charlie first thought the tree-lined street looked more like a Norman Rockwell neighborhood than the power seat of country music. But the tight-knit clique had treated Charlie like a displaced refugee. Everyone but Roger Durwood. It had been the flamboyant Durwood who had befriended him just before Christmas, his first year in Nashville.

Late Friday morning, after returning from the plush office of T.R. Branch, Charlie looked at his trembling hands. He placed them firmly on top of his small wooden desk in the writer's room; somehow he had to stop shaking. His hands appeared detached, as though they belonged to someone else.

Charlie drew a breath and closed his eyes. He thought about the first time that he had met Durwood. The two-and-a-half years now seemed like a lifetime ago. It was the first time he had showcased his original music at Ruby's Bar and Grill. The small club was famous for their endless string of talented songwriters and performers who played for free on the small stage. The music was always as diverse as those who performed it. But the one common thread for all who took the stage, was the hope that someone, anyone who mattered, would hear their music.

Durwood was a regular at the club. He always sat alone, dressed in his ridiculous western suits and hat, searching the hungry young faces. He was selective and smooth. Charlie Keith had been easy prey.

Glancing at his watch, Charlie tried not to panic. It was just before noon. Some of the songwriters were beginning to pair up for lunch. But eating was the last thing on his mind. Charlie had to talk to Roger, but didn't dare use the office phones. At straight up noon, he walked alone to the closest phone booth. Charlie even checked his back, to see if he was being followed. His hands were still shaking when he deposited the quarter.

"Charlie, my man," Roger answered.

"We've got problems. Big problems. I got called on the carpet this morning. Golden Star Entertainment is asking questions about *our song*."

"Don't ya mean *your* song?"

"Rusti King seems to think the song was stolen."

"What'd ya tell him?"

"I told him I wrote it. Didn't have a clue as to what she was talking about. I stood my ground with Branch."

"Good. How'd he leave it?"

"He said that he certainly did hope so, because he had every intention of getting to the bottom of it. Roger, we need to talk about this."

"It don't sound like it's my problem. Your name's on it, not mine."

Charlie hit the side of the glass phone booth with his fist. "Roger, if I go down, I'm taking your ass with me. We need to talk!"

"Okay, just calm down. Come on by the office this evenin, after work. Look, I've been through this before. This kinda shit's real hard to prove."

Charlie walked along Grand Avenue to kill time and think. Turning down 17th Avenue, he circled the block beneath the clear sky and green trees. The June day had turned hot and he could feel sweat dripping beneath his arms. Turning again on Edgehill Avenue, he returned to Branch Publishing Company. He took a deep breath and held his head proudly. He felt slightly better. The shaking had stopped.

Charlie looked through the small window of the recording studio as he walked down the hallway. He had a session scheduled for the afternoon. He and his co-writers had two new songs to lay down. It would take the rest of the day. And that, at least, would keep his mind busy.

*

Durwood sent his receptionist home early. She had never seen Charlie. He wanted to keep it that way. If called to testify, Joyce needed to be a friendly witness. He could simply remind her that she got lots of phone calls. There would be no way she could be expected to remember all the names. He thought about firing her, just to be safe.

Durwood watched Charlie enter the door of Sure-Star Publishing through the glass wall of his office. "Lock it!" he yelled at him.

Charlie's fair complexion was flushed. He took a seat across the desk from Durwood. "Bitch of a day," he complained. Removing his glasses, he rubbed the bridge of his nose before replacing them.

Durwood opened his drawer and pulled out a bottle of vodka. He wiped out two small glasses with a Kleenex. "Drink?"

"Yeah."

Durwood poured and scooted the glass across his desk. The glass shook in Charlie's hand before he managed to take a shot. The vodka burned. He closed his eyes and shuddered as the fireball hit the bottom of his empty stomach.

"Charlie, things are never as bad as they seem. Did ya have any more conversations with T.R.?"

"No. I was in the studio all afternoon. Roger, I've got a bad feeling about this."

"Relax, I've been doin this for years. Nobody can copyright an idea. They can't even get ya for stealing lines. Words are fair game. So are the tunes as long as ya don't just copy somethin. Ya know that. Hell, I've been sendin ya the crap I get in the mail for over two years. I had somebody else before ya. I've even got a few more scattered about Nashville. I've never had a problem."

"Okay." Charlie took another shot of vodka. His hands had steadied some.

"The way I figure it, we've had ten songs published. Two were top tens. It's been good for both of us." Roger raised his glass. "Here's to our first number one hit."

Charlie sipped his vodka. He looked down at his tennis shoes. "I'm worried."

"What's the big deal?"

"I didn't change anything on that song." Charlie finished off his vodka before looking across the desk at his co-conspirator.

Durwood had leaned back in his chair. His deep-set eyes were wide open and seemed out of place on his thin, weathered face. "Surely ya changed somethin."

"I was going to." Charlie leaned forward. "I re-recorded it at my apartment. Exactly as it was written. Then, I took it to the office, as a work in progress. I was listening to it when Judy heard it. She went absolutely crazy over it. I told her it wasn't finished, that it still needed work. She said,

'bullshit,' and grabbed the cassette out of the player. The bitch played it for everybody in the damn building. What could I say?"
"Go on."
"She took it to Branch. He said the only thing wrong with it was it needed a female vocalist on the demo. He told Judy to sing it. We laid it down in less than an hour. The song was just magic."
"Shit." Roger poured another glass of vodka then slid the bottle across his desk to Charlie. "Okay, let's say somebody sent the song to Nashville. Sent it to me. I don't have it. Never heard it. Never got it. That's exactly what I told that cowboy from Texas, right before he yanked me across the desk."
"What cowboy?"
"He was a good lookin kid. Had a midget with him. Claimed he wrote it. Said he wanted what was owed him." Roger snickered. "He got it okay. Ten days in jail for attempted assault."
"Was it McArthur, or McCurley ... something like that?" Charlie asked. "I've still got the tape. I can look when I get home."
"Might have been. Hell, I don't remember. Forget it. Like I told him, things get lost in Nashville." Roger leaned across his desk. "Charlie, lose the damn tape, and all the others I've ever sent ya."
Charlie's hands had begun to shake again. He poured another drink. "What are we going to do? We need a plan, or something."
"Look dumb-ass, *you* wrote the damn song! That's the plan. Just turn it around. Your position is, somebody's tryin to rip ya off. Take the offense. Don't play defense. They can say they wrote that song all day long, but they have to prove it. Between all the attorneys for Rusti King, Golden Star Entertainment, and Branch Publishin, it'll take years to prove in court, if it ever even gets that far. Relax."
"I don't know."
"Just stick to your guns." Roger slapped the desk with his hand. "*You* wrote it! It was your best work. Your first number one hit and now somebody's tryin to rip ya off." Roger slapped the desk again and yelled at him, "Don't that just piss ya off?"
Charlie nodded his head. "Yeah. It pisses me off."
"Then act like it!"
"What if they can prove it?" Charlie asked, and sat his empty glass on the table.
"The only way that's gonna happen is if they could prove it was performed or recorded prior to ya writin it. That ain't gonna happen. Most of the shit I get in here was recorded around somebody's coffee table. The only time it gets performed is in their shower."

Taking a deep breath, Charlie closed his eyes. "I think I feel better."

Roger stood behind his desk and folded his skinny arms. "Charlie, I can't afford to have a dumb-ass workin for me. What ya did was stupid. Our deal is over. As of right now, I don't want ya callin me, ever again. We never met."

Charlie nodded and walked toward the door with his head down. "Fine by me. What about the royalties on this song?"

"There ain't gonna be no royalties. Not for a long time. They've probably already called ASCAP and BMI. They'll be puttin a hold on ever thing till this is settled. But, if and when the day comes ya do get paid ... ya still owe me fifty percent, just like always. And I'll be around to collect, so don't forget about me."

Charlie Keith walked down the narrow flight of stairs, relieved Roger Durwood was finally out of his life. Leaving the old office building, Charlie nervously glanced up and down the street. A 35-millimeter camera snapped twice from the car parked across the street, capturing both sides of his face.

CHAPTER THIRTY-THREE

Skeeter followed Red again on Friday. His routine hadn't varied in over two weeks. The only question in Skeeter's mind was how much money would be there over the Fourth of July weekend.

Skeeter thought about Payne and worried about Pardner on the way home. The dog was either depressed or sick. He'd barely moved the last three days. Skeeter chose to believe Pardner was just missing Payne. He'd seen it before.

Lisa had been packing Skeeter's things all morning. But when she heard his truck, she ran to meet him at the back door. "Baby, come look at Pardner. He sounds like he's got something caught in his throat."

Skeeter stepped around the boxes on his way to Payne's bedroom. Looking at Pardner's eyes, he shook his head. "Somethin's bad wrong. We gotta get him to the vet." After several minutes of coaxing, Pardner got to his feet. He slowly followed them to the pickup. Skeeter lowered the tailgate. But it took them both to load him.

Doc Holdens didn't look like a vet. He wore old clothes and had a wad of chewing tobacco swelling out the left side of his face. He took a look at Pardner, then ran his hands through his thinning gray hair. He shook his head and spit, missing the spittoon by a foot. After listening to Pardner's chest, he turned to Skeeter. "How old is he?"

"Hell, I don't know. He's been around since I met Payne in high school. I guess that'd be ten or twelve years."

"He's suffering. If he was my dog, I'd put him down. I can't heal old age."

Lisa burst into tears. Skeeter knelt down and petted Pardner. "Ya sure? I mean, this just came on him sudden."

"His lungs are filling and his heart's weak. I'm positive. From the size of him, I'd say he's lived a good life, till now."

"Shit," Skeeter mumbled. "Payne should be back this afternoon. I'll send him by."

"I'll be here till six, if I don't get called out of the office. I'm sorry, folks. I hate this part of my job."

*

Payne was still fighting off his depression over leaving Rusti when he walked through the backdoor. He glanced at the moving boxes before pulling the last Budweiser out of the refrigerator. "Skeeter, ya leavin me anything?" he yelled from the kitchen.

"Just takin what's mine. And half of yours." Skeeter appeared in the doorway, but without his usual grin. He held his arm out for Lisa, who slid in next to him. She looked at Payne with sad eyes.

"Damn," Payne said, observing their faces, "y'all don't look very happy for a couple fixin to get married Sunday."

"How was your trip?" Skeeter asked. He looked at the floor.

"Fine." Payne took a drink. "What's wrong?"

"How ya feelin?"

"Better. Thanks for askin. What's goin on?"

"Pardner's at Doc Holdens' place."

Payne's face fell. "What's wrong with him?"

"Doc wants ya to come by this afternoon."

"What's wrong with him?"

"Hell, I don't know. Just go by."

Payne looked at Skeeter. But he was staring at the floor again. He looked at Lisa and saw her eyes beginning to tear. The screen door slammed behind him.

*

Payne followed Doc Holdens down the hall to the back room. "He's an old dog. His age has just caught up with him. Son, I can't help him."

Pardner lay on the floor in the back room. Falling to his knees, Payne gently lifted Pardner's head. "Hey, Pardner. What's goin on here? Ya feelin bad?" Pardner's eyes were cloudy. He was struggling for breath.

"Payne, I don't think he can recognize you. His brain isn't getting much oxygen."

"Come on buddy, it's me." Payne spoke louder.

But Pardner barely moved.

"We can help him go, or you can take him home. But he's suffering."

Payne laid his head down on top of Pardner's big head without answering. Doc Holdens waited until he saw Payne nod.

*

Payne parked the Jeep next to an oak tree near the house. He walked with his head down from the shed, carrying a shovel. Grimacing from the pain in his ribs, he dug in the black, rocky soil. Skeeter walked up behind him, watching him dig the grave. "Need some help?"

"I got it," Payne answered, without stopping or turning around.

"Reckon the soil's this rocky in Tennessee and Kentucky?"

"Wouldn't know." Payne stopped digging and held his ribs. He stared into the blue sky.

"It wasn't my fault."

"Didn't say it was. Just leave me alone."

"We're playin at Heidi's this weekend. But not next, she's already ... "

"Skeeter, shut the hell up."

"Guess I'll catch ya there. Payne, I'm sorry. I know what he meant to ya."

Payne nodded his head, but didn't answer.

"I guess we'll go on and take another load to Lisa's."

Payne leaned on his shovel, his ribs were screaming with each labored breath. He said nothing.

"Jimmy Earl threatened Nova with a rehab center. Told her the next time she got that drunk he was gonna check her in. Hartman slipped about her guitar. She knows ya broke it."

Payne stared at the ground.

"Did ya have a good time with Rusti?"

"Yeah."

"Y'all still in love?"

"Skeeter, please don't talk any more."

Skeeter walked up to Payne's side. Reaching up, he put his hand on Payne's shoulder. "It'd be a big honor for me to help dig this grave."

"Can ya dig without talkin?"

"Probably not." Skeeter took the shovel from Payne. "I'm gonna miss ya. I mean ... when we all leave here."

Payne looked at Skeeter, then looked in the Jeep, at Pardner. He sank to his knees between his two best friends. Skeeter stopped shoveling and patted his buddy on his shoulder while Payne cried.

CHAPTER THIRTY-FOUR

Skeeter and Lisa had been busy for a week, planning the wedding. They had arranged for a cake, a few flowers, the Methodist preacher, Bar-B-Q, and a keg of beer from Heidi's. Skeeter had even taken a lawn mower out to Jerry's old property and knocked down some of the tall grass. But they hadn't planned on rain.

Payne left his bed and answered the phone early Sunday morning, hoping it was Rusti. It was Skeeter. "Payne, I thought ya were in charge of the damn weather. I guess it's rainin there?"

"I magine. Pourin. Gonna call it off?"

"Hell no. We're goin to plan B."

"What's plan B?"

"Don't have a clue. That's why I'm callin my best man."

"Guess we could have it here. I've got lotsa room after ya moved ever thing out. I can't believe ya cleaned out the kitchen."

"I left ya some food."

"What am I suppose to cook it with?"

"Have ya got Casey's phone number?"

"I did, unless ya packed it."

"Call her for me. See if we can have the weddin at Heidi's, in the restaurant."

"Why don't I just give ya her number, and *you* call her. I don't wanna be the one to wake her up this early on Sunday mornin. She can be a real bitch."

"You're the best man. Start earnin your keep." Skeeter laughed. "Call me back."

"Skeeter ..." Payne looked at the phone, listening to the dial tone. "Ya little shit."

Payne found Casey's number and dialed. He decided to just let it keep ringing until she gave up and answered it. She finally surrendered. "This better be good."

"Casey, this is Payne. It's rainin."

"No shit." She hung up on him.

Payne redialed. "Casey, don't hang up."
"Payne, I'm hung over and I've got company. What the hell do you want?"
"Skeeter wants to know if him and Lisa can get married in your restaurant this afternoon, since it's rainin."
"Same time?"
"Yeah, three o'clock."
"Fine." Casey hung up on him again.
Payne dialed Skeeter. "She said fine. Is there anything else I can do for ya at seven in the damn mornin?"
"Call Nova and Hartman."
"Can I wait till later, or do ya just wanna see how many people ya can make me piss-off on Sunday morning?"
"Do ya have Billy Gotzen's number?"
"Hell no. I ain't callin over there."
"Look it up for me."
"In what? Ya took the phone book."
"Okay, I'll handle them. I guess you'd better drive out to Jerry's place and catch the preacher and the lady with the flowers and cake. Send em to Heidi's."
"Can't ya just call em? I mean, as long as your wakin people up, don't stop with me."
"Yeah, okay. I'm just a little nervous. I shoulda thought of that. I'll call em."
"Is that it?"
"Yeah. I'll call ya back if I think of anything else."
Payne was almost back to bed when the phone rang again. "What!" Payne yelled into the phone.
"Well, good morning to you, too," Rusti said.
"I'm sorry. I've been on the phone to Skeeter all mornin. It's rainin here and we're havin to change the weddin plans. Still love me?"
"Hopelessly."
"I love ya, too." Payne sat on the floor. "Man, I miss ya. Where are ya?"
"Lubbock. Hometown of Buddy Holly and Mac Davis. I couldn't sleep."
"Seems to be a lotta that goin around this mornin. How'd your concert go?"
"Albuquerque was almost a sell out. Lubbock's tonight. Sales have been strong. I tried to call yesterday."
"I worked all day on Casey's deck. Just went from there to Heidi's. We played there this weekend. Sorry I missed ya. I thought about ya all day."
"How are you?"

"Fine, considerin."

"Considering what?"

"Considerin I miss ya so bad it's takin my mind off my ribs." He smiled listening to her laugh. "Skeeter moved out. It was kinda sad. Took almost ever thing. He even got the coffee pot."

"I'm sorry. But you won't need anything where you're going. You're still going with me, right?"

"Can't wait." Payne took a deep breath. "I buried Pardner ... Friday, when I got home."

"Oh, baby, I'm so sorry. What happened?"

"Old age ... I'd guess. He was almost gone when I got back. Skeeter took him to the vet. There wasn't anything he could do. We put him outta his misery." Payne moved the phone away and swallowed hard. He coughed, trying not to choke up.

"Are you okay?"

"Not really. But I'll get over it. It was a helluva Friday."

"I wish I were there to hold you. What are you going to do today?"

"The weddin's not till three. I haven't given up on goin back to bed yet. Why?"

"I was hoping you might have time to write me a love song."

"I've got time for that."

"Do I still inspire you?"

"Sometimes it just seems like I dreamed it all. Then I close my eyes and I see your face."

"It wasn't a dream. Baby, I miss you so bad."

"Me, too."

Neither spoke for a prolonged moment.

Payne finally broke the silence. "Nova was almost sober the last couple of nights. Jimmy Earl threatened her with rehab if she ever pulls another stunt like she did in Austin. I haven't told her I'm leavin."

"When are you going to tell her?"

"Maybe this afternoon, after the weddin."

"Dennis is still working on getting your name on your song."

"That's not important. Anyway, I already gave it to ya."

"Well, it's important to me. I'm giving it back to you."

"God, I miss ya."

"I miss you, too. I miss everything about you. Payne?"

"Yeah?"

"Close your eyes."

"Okay. They're shut."

"Do you really see my face?"
"Yeah. Hey, I think I'm seein more than just your face."
Both laughed. Then the phone went silent again.
"Baby, I hate this," Rusti finally spoke. "The time is passing so slow."
"Yeah."
"Can I call you tonight?"
"I'd appreciate it."
"Okay, then you go back to bed. I'll call tonight and you can tell me all about the wedding. I love you."
"I love ya too. Can't wait to talk to ya again."
Payne hung up the phone. Alone in his empty house, he bowed his head. "Lord, I know Ya haven't heard from me since I was in jail. But I ask Ya to hear me this mornin. I'm kinda feelin that same way today. Real alone. Thank Ya for Rusti. Thank Ya for the good times with Pardner. Please bless Skeeter and Lisa. Help them to have a good marriage and stay in love forever. I ask the same for me and Rusti. Thank Ya for healin my heart and blessin me with a new love in my life. I know I haven't said so, but I really do appreciate all the good things You've sent my way since the last time we talked. Amen."
Payne raised his head. His eyes came to rest on his Martin Guitar. He thought about Rusti and closed his eyes again to see her face. Then the words came ... *Ever time I see you ...*

CHAPTER THIRTY-FIVE

Charlie Keith liked Hendersonville. It was just north of Nashville, off I-65. The small suburb was convenient to work, but without the hassles of life in the city. He even liked the commute. It gave him time to think, or listen to his latest musical creation. But Friday afternoon's commute had been different. After his visit with Durwood, the drive had only given him more time to worry. Saturday had been no better.

Lying beneath the covers, Charlie opened his tired eyes. It had been another sleepless night and he welcomed the first light of Sunday morning. But his anxiety over the stolen song drove him from his bed. He was restless.

Having never married, music remained his only true love. The second bedroom of his apartment was cluttered with home studio equipment. The floor was littered with cords and wires leading from his four-track recorder to his electric keyboard, guitars, amplifiers, and drum machine. Charlie loved musical gadgets. He had them all.

Charlie had several rituals. The first, preformed each morning, was to leave his apartment for a short walk to the corner convenience store for coffee and a paper. Moisture from the warm, foggy morning collected on his glasses. He paused before entering the store and wiped them clean with his handkerchief.

"Morning, Charlie." Louise knew most of the regulars by name. She was a frail woman with short graying hair. A grandmother.

"Morning," he answered, without looking at her. He took the largest cup for his morning coffee and tore open five small packets of sugar. Another ritual. He stirred as he walked to the counter, stopping only to pick up the Sunday paper.

Charlie watched her work the register and handed her a five before glancing at the headlines. Her smile went unnoticed as Charlie took his change. "Thanks," he managed to say.

"Hang over?" she asked. "You don't seem your usual cheerful self this morning."

Charlie forced a smile toward her general direction without answering, tucked the paper under his arm, and left the store with his coffee. The cheerful

201

side of Charlie Keith had disappeared on Friday. His mood remained as gloomy as the Tennessee morning.

*

T.R. Branch lived in Brentwood, south of Nashville. By the time he entered the kitchen of his mammoth house, his coffee was ready. Just like Charlie, T.R. went for the Sunday paper. He returned from the front yard with it tucked under his arm, coffee in hand. He sat in his plush study and, just like Charlie, went first to the Entertainment Section. News and sports could wait.

It wasn't a big picture. It was near the bottom of the second page. The headline above the picture read *Rusti King Has New Man In Her Life.* T.R. liked Rusti. She had been his first choice on Charlie's song. That's why he had insisted Judy sing on the demo. The song had been an easy pitch. But the great songs usually were.

He studied the picture of the cowboy with her. He was tall. The cowboy hat exaggerated his height, but shaded his face. T.R. could only assume he was handsome. "Lucky man," T.R. spoke out loud, before reading the blurb at the bottom. *Texan, Payne McCarty, has recently been seen with Rusti King hanging on his arm. Controversy looms over her Number One Hit Song. See story page 4.*

T.R. read the article twice. News of the copyright controversy had already surfaced. "From Oklahoma of all places. Who the hell is Payne McCarty?" The article had T.R. Branch talking to himself.

*

Charlie Keith laid his paper down. His hands had begun to shake halfway through the article. Panicking, he left the table and rushed to his studio. Stepping over the wires and cords, he opened the closet and pulled out the shoebox full of tapes from Durwood. He held the tape in his hand and stared at Payne McCarty's name and Texas address. The shoebox fell from his hands, scattering the hopes and dreams accumulated by Sure-Star Publishing on his closet floor.

Charlie jumped when the phone rang. He knew better than to answer it. The answering machine, one of his favorite gadgets, recorded while Charlie listened.

"Charlie, T.R. Branch here. If you're there, pick up the phone ... Damn it, Charlie, pick up the phone!" But Charlie stood paralyzed with fear. T.R.

paused ... "Charlie, have you read the article about *your* song in the morning paper? We need to talk. Call me back at home, 2-9-8 ... 9-9-2-4. Charlie, call me."

Returning to the kitchen table, Charlie re-read the article on page four. Rusti King had blown the lid off his little secret with her announcement that Payne McCarty had written *When Love Turns Out The Light*. By tomorrow, Music Row would be reeling from their little duet in Oklahoma City.

Charlie didn't bother mixing water with his scotch. He sat at his small kitchen table staring at the picture of Payne and Rusti until the phone rang again. Screening the call, he picked up when he heard Roger Durwood's voice. "Charlie, did ya see the article?"

"Hello." The machine automatically clicked off and rewound the tape.

"Charlie, did ya ... "

"Yeah, I saw it. So has Branch. He's already left a message."

"Did ya get rid of the evidence?"

"Roger, I told you, if I went down, I was taking you with me. I've still got that tape and all the others."

"Shit."

"Now what?" Charlie rattled the ice in his glass.

"Okay, here's the deal. You confess and leave me out of it. I've got fifty grand for ya if my name don't come up."

"I could be looking at jail time, and just where did I get the tape?"

"Hell, I don't know. Say ya found it on the street. Say anything that don't sound like my name. A bright boy like you will come up with somethin. Just leave me out of it."

"Fifty now and fifty when it's over. I'm going to need money for a damn good attorney, up front. And I'm going to need traveling money when it's over."

"That's a lotta money."

"Durwood, I want the money and I want it today. The shit's going to hit the fan tomorrow."

"It's Sunday. I can't get that kinda money on Sunday."

"Bullshit. I've been paying you in cash for two years. I know you keep cash. Lots of it." Charlie removed his glasses and rubbed his eyes. "Roger, you've been reporting all that cash to the IRS, haven't you? I'd sure hate to see you get audited."

Durwood considered the threat. "Okay. Look, we can't be seen together. I know a place where we can meet. Take I-65 north. Then turn east on 174 toward White House. There's a roadside park about halfway there, on the right.

Meet me there at ten o'clock. That's just over an hour. I'll have your damn money, but I want all the tapes. And I mean all of em. Understand?"

"I'll be there."

Charlie hung up the phone and decided to duplicate Payne's tape, for insurance. Sitting at his studio desk, he listened to Payne sing the song. The meters on the tape machine bounced with the music as he listened to the emotional vocal and beautiful acoustic guitar. He labeled it, complete with the Texas address, and took a drink. "Payne McCarty," he said out loud, and lifted his glass of scotch above his head. "Here's to you buddy, and your first number one hit song."

*

Charlie drove his white two-door Toyota along I-65. He thought about his first months in Nashville as he drove. The Nashville Songwriter's Association had kept him in Music City by suggesting he talk with Jerry Hill at ASCAP. Jerry had patiently listened to his songs then personally recommended him to T.R. Branch.

The pay had been miserable. Staff writers had to pay their dues. Charlie had been forced to take a second job, working nights as a clerk at a "stop-and-rob" for a year. But the monthly royalty checks had gradually started to roll in. Life had turned bright in Nashville, until Friday.

With a number one hit, Charlie Keith had plans to go on his own. No more staff writing. He would have had enough money and recognition from the Gold Record to write his own ticket. He had even dreamed of his own publishing company. Gold Records for songwriters didn't come easy in Nashville. He wondered if Payne McCarty had a clue just how hard it was to pay the Nashville dues.

Charlie spotted Roger leaning on the trunk of his gold Cadillac Seville near the back of the roadside park. The park, obscured from the highway by trees, was deserted. Parking behind the Cadillac, he watched Roger approaching his Toyota and rolled down his window.

"Tell ya what." Roger grinned. "This ol music bidness is gettin tougher ever year."

"You got the money?"

Roger patted the left pocket of his dark blue western jacket. "Right here. Ya got the tapes?"

Charlie opened the lid of the shoebox. He held up Payne's tape. "This is the one."

"That's all of em?"

"Everything you ever sent me."

Roger reached into his left pocket and pulled out a wad of green with his left hand. Charlie reached for it, but Durwood withdrew his hand. "Tapes first."

Leaning over to the passenger's seat, Charlie replaced the tape and lid. He carefully slid a rubber band around the box. Turning back to Roger, he felt the steel barrel of a revolver press against his head. "What the hell ... Roger, you're not really serious ... "

Two shots shattered the skull of Charlie Keith. Reaching through the window, Roger retrieved the blood-splattered box of tapes. Staging a robbery, he shoved Charlie's body over and removed his watch and wallet while the young man's blood spilled into the passenger seat. He carefully wiped his fingerprints from the car. "Charlie, I told ya. You're a dumb ass."

CHAPTER THIRTY-SIX

The Texas flag, painted on the tin roof of Heidi's, was visible from over a mile away, despite the rain. Payne parked next to Skeeter's pickup at the Roadhaus, turned wedding chapel. He was half an hour early. Dressed in his newest boots, jeans, and western shirt, he jogged through the rain, guitar case in hand, dodging puddles.

Entering the restaurant, he realized that he had overdressed for the occasion. Looking at Skeeter and Lisa, a smile crossed Payne's otherwise somber face. Both were dressed in white jockey silks and black riding boots. They wore pink jockey caps with number "8", Skeeter's lucky number, on the sides.

"Payne!" they yelled simultaneously.

Setting his guitar down, Payne removed his wet hat and laid it upside down to drip-dry on the table by the door. Four small arms embraced him.

"Ever thing under control?" Payne asked.

"Is it ever?" Skeeter laughed.

"Nice outfits."

Lisa was bubbling with excitement. "Skeeter thought of it."

"No shit?"

"Payne, meet my sister, Diane."

Payne shook her hand. "Payne McCarty," he said, looking down at Diane. He guessed her to measure about five-foot in all directions. Her long pink dress tightly covered her bowling ball body before falling to her ankles. A pink carnation was stuck in her brown hair.

"It's certainly a pleasure to meet you," Diane said. She was grinning and blushing like she had just met Elvis. "I've heard an awful lot about you."

"Well, I hope some of it was good." Payne politely flashed her a smile.

"Not much good to tell about ya," Skeeter said, and slapped him on his lower back, jarring his sore ribs.

"Damn, Skeeter. Watch the ribs."

"She's my maid of honor."

"You guys shoulda told me ya were goin with pink. I'd wore somethin different."

"No problem. I brought an extra pink jockey cap for ya to wear."

"No way." Payne shook his head. "No damn way. I'm drawin the line on that one."

"You'll hurt my feelins if ya don't wear it." Skeeter managed a straight face.

"Good."

"Well, if it isn't Mr. Early Bird," Casey yelled at Payne from across the room.

"Sorry about that. That was Skeeter's fault."

"All's forgiven, with one exception." Casey kissed Payne on the cheek.

"And what would that be?"

"Falling in love with a redhead."

Payne grinned. "Couldn't be helped."

Salazar's Weddings and Catering, Inc., consisted of Maria Salazar and her gray-headed, stooped-over mother. Entering the restaurant, they took one look at the bride and groom and began laughing and spitting Spanish. The cake was a double-decker with white icing. The flowers were pink, almost matching the ridiculous jockey caps. Lisa and Diane left the group to take charge of decorating.

Hartman arrived next and assumed his post by Payne. He nodded hello to everyone without speaking a word.

"Who wants a beer?" Casey asked, leading the group to the keg. They followed her, each taking a plastic cup. Casey worked the pump and spigot like a pro, pouring without a hint of foam.

Payne pulled out his timepiece. It was ten-till-three when Pastor Robins came through the door. Skeeter introduced himself, then Lisa to the stunned Methodist preacher.

"I've done some unusual weddings," Pastor Robins said, while looking back and forth between the group surrounding the keg and the bride and groom, "but this one may top them all."

"Take a beer?" Payne asked.

"I don't usually, but I guess one won't hurt."

"Heard that before." Skeeter laughed and slapped the preacher on the back just as Ragina and Billy walked in beneath a dripping umbrella. Billy was sharply dressed in one of his expensive lawyer uniforms. But all eyes were on Ragina's cleavage, including Pastor Robins.

Ignoring the bride and groom, Ragina went straight to Payne. "What in the world happened to you?"

"He got his ass kicked in a fight," Skeeter answered.
"It was a brawl. Happened at a bar in Austin." Payne glared at Skeeter. "It wasn't a damn fight. It was a barroom brawl."
"Are you alright?"
"I'm fine. Thanks for askin."
Ragina took his hand. "I wanted to apologize for what I called you at the race track. I didn't mean that."
"Sure ya did."
"Forgive me?"
"Forgiven."
"Can I have a hug?"
Payne patted her on the back as she pressed her breasts into his chest.
"Can I have one of those?" Skeeter asked.
Ragina bent down toward Skeeter. Her short skirt hiked up and the blouse separated, exposing even more cleavage, and her lacy white bra. Pastor Robins choked on his beer.
"Who's missing?" Casey asked.
"Nova and Jimmy Earl," Payne answered.
"Figures," Casey said, in a snit.
"Jimmy Earl ain't comin," Skeeter said. "Talked to Nova this mornin. They had a little misunderstandin last night. She was already sailin with two sheets to the wind. I couldn't tell if she'd been up all night drinkin or had just started over."
"What was the misunderstandin about?" Hartman broke his silence causing everyone to stare at him.
"I don't know how to put it in front of a preacher."
Pastor Robins laughed. "Never mind me. I've heard it all before."
"She said that son-of-a ... "
"She said she'd be here." Lisa smiled at the preacher. "Let's give her a few minutes. It's just now three."

*

Nova left late for the wedding. Her eyes were puffy from a sleepless night and red, from too much tequila. She thought about Jimmy Earl during the drive. Things had changed since the incident in Austin. He had begun treating her with a calloused indifference. She had seen it before. So she wasn't too surprised last night when he slammed her front door behind him. He hadn't been that special or any different from all the others, but somehow it still hurt.

After the first one, she had stopped counting the men who had come and gone out her front door. It was a number that had disappeared long ago, in the bottom of a tequila bottle.

The first two curves on the Devil's Backbone caused Nova to swerve recklessly out of her lane on the rain slick road. Glancing at her watch, she accelerated down the short stretch of straight highway, then punched the Trans Am up the hill. Two deer flashed in front of her as she topped the hill. She hit her brakes and jerked the wheel, sending the black Pontiac into a spin. An oak tree was the last thing she saw before impact.

*

Pulling out his timepiece, Payne checked the time again then looked at Skeeter. "It's a quarter after."

"Let's go on without her." Skeeter yelled through the restaurant, "Okay, y'all. It's time to gather around the hitchin post."

A few regulars from the bar had staggered in, joining the small group of friends. The crowd gradually became quiet as Lisa and Skeeter stood facing each other, holding hands, in front of Pastor Robins. Payne strapped on his Martin guitar. The rain, beating on the old tin roof, accompanied him as he played Lisa's favorite Charly McClain song *Surround Me with Love*. After the song, Lisa looked at Payne with tears in her eyes. "Thank you. That was beautiful."

Payne nodded. "It was an honor."

Fiddling with Lisa's ring, Payne thought about Rusti while the preacher spoke of love and commitment. They were the two words he had avoided at all cost for the last five years. They were now the very words he longed to whisper in Rusti's ear.

Payne handed Skeeter the ring. Without the quick cash from the song, he wondered how he was going to get enough money together to buy one for Rusti. He wanted more for her than the simple gold band he had just handed Skeeter.

"I now pronounce you man and wife, in the name of the Father, His Son the Lord Jesus Christ, and the Holy Ghost." A loud clap of thunder sounded outside, startling the wedding party. Pastor Robins laughed. "You apparently have the Lord's seal of approval. You may now kiss your bride."

Skeeter laid a lip-lock on Lisa, knocking their pink caps to the floor. Cheers from the small crowd echoed off the walls of Heidi's Roadhaus, temporarily drowning out the sound of the rain. Payne shook Skeeter's hand. "Congratulations, ya little shit."

"Thanks. Thanks for ever thing. For bein my friend."

Payne nodded to Skeeter and hugged Lisa. "Now ya take care of my little buddy."

"I will." She smiled up at him and squeezed his hand. "I promise. And Payne ... thanks again for asking me to dance."

Payne hugged her again and winked at Diane. "I'm sure as hell glad he ain't my bother-in-law," he said, with a grin, then watched as well-wishers crowded around the newlyweds, obscuring them from view. He packed up his guitar and went for another beer.

"Sorry Nova missed this," Hartman said. He stuck his cup under the spigot while Payne drew a beer for him.

"Yep," Payne agreed. "Hartman, I'm goin on to Nashville. This deal with Nova drinkin herself to death ain't gonna get it done."

"Don't blame ya." Hartman extended his hand to Payne. "It's been a pleasure playing with ya. Maybe one of these days I'll come see ya up there in Nashville."

"Hell, I ain't goin today. We still got one more set to play on the Fourth." Payne slapped him on the shoulder. "Hey, cheer up. This is a happy day."

Hartman nodded his head. "Yeah."

"Okay folks, let's move the cake and the keg to the bar," Casey ordered. "We'll serve the food later."

After the couple cut the cake, the music on the jukebox was cranked up. Payne leaned against the bar and watched the two newlyweds dancing across the floor in their jockey silks and boots. Casey slid in next to him and hugged him lightly around the waist. "You know, Payne," she nodded at Skeeter and Lisa, "that's just about the funniest damn thing I've ever seen."

"Yep," Payne chuckled, "they make quite a pair."

"Speaking of pairs, Ragina looks like she's trying to set her claws in ol Billy Boy."

"Yeah, and she's got some claws, too."

"And then there's you." Casey smiled and shook her head. "Rusti King. Hell, I thought you were shittin me the day you came back from Houston and told me you were in love."

"I was shittin ya, at the time. Sometimes it's still hard for me to believe."

Casey laughed and rubbed Payne's back. "Well, I'd have to say she's a lucky woman. I don't care if she is a big time country music star, a good man is hard to find. And believe me, I ought to know. She's lucky to have you. I'm guessing you'll be heading to Nashville."

"Yeah. Goin back with her on her bus. After Willie's Picnic."

Casey hugged him again. "I'm going to miss looking at your handsome face, and that tight ass of yours."

Payne took a long drink of beer. "I'm gonna miss a lotta things around here. Friends are hard to come by."

Casey raised her plastic cup and toasted Payne. "Here's to tomorrow, and finishing my damn gazebo."

Payne toasted and shoved off the bar, heading for the cake. He was cramming the last bite in his mouth when Billy and Ragina flanked him.

"Still going to Nashville?" Ragina asked.

"Still goin," Payne said, through a mouthful.

"Billy, would you get me another glass of wine?"

"Certainly."

Ragina ran her hand up and down Payne's arm. "Every time it rains, I think about you. I'll never forget that weekend."

"Yeah ya will." He smiled. "Looks like you and Billy are hittin it off."

"I don't like settling for second best. Any chance you'll ever fall in love again?"

"Already have."

"With Rusti King?" She laughed.

"Yeah. That funny?"

"I'd bet money she's going to break your heart."

"You'd lose." Payne walked away.

"Call me when she does," Ragina yelled after him.

He stopped and faced her. "When your phone don't ring, that'll be me callin ya from Tennessee."

*

Accounts of Nova's accident arrived just after the mesquite smoked brisket, beans, and coleslaw, via two regulars. Payne listened to the news, then called the hospital from the phone behind the bar. After ten minutes of being transferred and placed on hold, he hung up. "Skeeter, I'm gonna head on that way."

Hartman had been pacing. "I'm goin with ya."

"Call us when y'all find somethin out," Skeeter called after them.

Payne grabbed his guitar. He tipped his hat to his old friends at Heidi's and walked into the rain. Hartman followed Payne's Jeep in his pickup to New Braunfels.

NASHVILLE GOLD

The nurse in the Emergency Room was cute. She was blonde and her blue eyes were twinkling at Payne. He turned on the charm and two phone calls later she was pleased to announce Nova's condition. She had undergone surgery for two broken legs, had sustained several lacerations, but was in stable condition, in room 128. "Looks like you've been in an accident yourself," she said, smiling at Payne.

"Happened last Saturday, in Austin. Say, ya reckon ya could take these stitches out for me, as long as I'm here?" Payne glanced at her nametag. "Rita, I'd sure appreciate it."

Moving in close, she looked at the wound. "It's healed nicely. I'll take them out, but you're going to need to be careful. I'd hate to see an ugly scar on such a handsome face."

Payne smiled at her. "Hartman, can ya wait up a few minutes?"

"I think I'll just go on."

Payne nodded to him and followed Rita into an examination room. "This may pull a little, but it shouldn't hurt." She rested one hand on his shoulder and carefully began to extract the stitches. "What's your name?"

"Payne McCarty."

"Live around here?"

"North of town a few miles."

"How'd you do this?"

"Got my ass kicked." Payne chuckled.

"What's funny about that?"

"Oh, it's just been a little runnin joke between me and my roommate."

"Is your roommate male or female?"

"He's a male."

Rita took out the last stitch and applied an antiseptic. "That wasn't too bad, was it?"

"Didn't feel a thing. Thanks. What do I owe ya?"

"It's free. Just don't mention this to anyone around here." Rita touched his face. "Payne, do you have a girlfriend or anything?"

"I've got me an ever thing."

"Figures."

"But if I didn't, I woulda been askin ya the same question." He tipped his hat to her. "Rita, thanks for your help."

When Payne entered Nova's room, Hartman was sitting on the bed holding Nova's hand. Both legs were in casts, suspended at the foot of her bed. Her arms were cut, scraped, and bruised. Her eyes were almost swollen shut. "She's drifting in and out," Hartman whispered.

Payne leaned over his shoulder. "Nova, it's Payne."

212

She moaned. Her eyes fluttered.

"Look, we're here for ya. Anything ya need. Just give us a call."

"She squeezed my hand," Hartman said.

"I'll catch up with ya tomorrow. I need to call Heidi's. Ever body's been worried about ya."

She mumbled something and Hartman bent over closer to listen. She spoke again and Hartman grinned. "She said, Casey's a bitch."

Payne laughed. "She's gonna be fine."

Hartman followed him out the door and grabbed his arm. "I'm gonna stay with her for awhile."

"Suit yourself."

"Payne, I've never been very good with words or women." He paused and looked at the floor. "I think I've been in love with Nova for awhile now. I ... I know she's got some problems, but ... "

Payne leaned against the wall and folded his arms. "Ever tell her?"

Hartman shook his head. "No."

"Well, once ya admit it to yourself, the next thing is, you've gotta admit it to her. But only if ya want it to go anywhere. Hell, it's only three words. You can say three words, can't ya?"

"Yeah."

"Then go tell her. I figure if anyone ever needed to be told, it's Nova."

CHAPTER THIRTY-SEVEN

T.R. Branch drove his emerald green Jaguar through heavy Nashville traffic on Monday morning. He half expected to be greeted by attorneys, dressed in expensive suits, inside the front door of Branch Publishing. Two men were waiting in the small lobby, but their suits were cheap.

"Mr. Branch?"

"Yes?"

"I'm Detective Lang and this is Detective Morgan." They flashed their badges. "Davidson County Sheriff's Office. We need a few minutes of your time. In private."

"Sure. No problem." T.R. stopped at the receptionist's desk and checked for messages. He ran his fingers through his thick salt and pepper colored hair. Houlette hadn't called. "Landa, hold my calls." Glancing over his shoulder, he asked, "Would you gentlemen care for some coffee?"

"Thank you. Black is fine," Lang answered.

"The same for me," Morgan answered, eyeing Landa. She caught him and cut him a vile look. Flipping her long brown hair over her shoulders, she went for coffee.

The two detectives took their seats in the plush office, across the desk from T.R., and studied the gold records hanging on his ego wall. Landa returned with two mugs of coffee and a Pepsi for Branch.

"Impressive," Morgan said, pointing at the records. After thirty years in Nashville, T.R. had more gold records than his office could hold. The long wall now only held his favorites. The others were at his house, in boxes.

T.R. wiped the top of his can off with a finger before popping the top. "So, how can I help you gentlemen?"

Lang was overweight, with balding hair and a thick tie, which lay crooked on his beer belly. "We're investigating the murder of a Charles David Keith."

"Charlie?" T.R. blinked in disbelief.

Lang looked down at his notebook. "He was found yesterday afternoon in his car. It was parked at a roadside park on Highway 174."

"Charlie?" Branch leaned forward. "I can't believe this."

Morgan folded his skinny legs and rubbed his long protruding nose. "Two shots to the left side of his head. Point blank range. No witnesses. We're starting from square one. Did Charles Keith have any enemies?"

"Not that I'm aware of."

"Anything unusual at work in the last month or so?"

T.R. leaned back and closed his eyes. "Yeah, but I can't believe it would have anything to do with murder."

"What?"

"We're in the middle of a copyright dispute over a song he wrote."

"Who's the dispute with?"

"Golden Star Entertainment. Over Rusti King's hit song."

"*When Love Turns Out The Light?*" Lang asked. He glanced at Morgan.

"That's right. I just found out about it on Friday. The story was in the Sunday paper. I called Charlie after reading the article. He didn't answer."

"You left two messages on his machine. What times did you call?"

"Eight or eighty-thirty, Sunday morning. Then again mid-afternoon."

"Did he return your calls?"

"No."

Morgan took out a Kleenex and wiped his nose. "We've gone through his apartment. He left a tape with that song title on it, lying on the Sunday paper, next to the article you mentioned. Do you know Payne McCarty?"

"No. But according to Rusti King, he's the guy who really wrote the song. It was in the paper."

"Do you know where we could find McCarty?"

"Hell, I imagine he's still in Texas with Rusti King. I damn sure would be." T.R. managed a smile. "Look, if I were you, I'd talk to the folks over at Golden Star. They probably know more about this than anyone." T.R. leaned forward. Laying his forearms on the desk, he interlocked his fingers and twiddled his thumbs. "Can you tell me anything about the tape?"

"Not yet. You might check with us later this afternoon." Lang pulled out his business card and handed it to Branch. "The tape did have McCarty's name on it. I'll tell you that much. Is there anything else you can tell us about Charlie?"

"That son-of-a-bitch." T.R. rubbed his temples. "He was single, quiet, and worked hard. He was also apparently a thief. I'm going to be looking at a lawsuit you can't believe."

"How would he have stolen it?" Lang asked, and reopened his notebook.

"Wouldn't have a clue. You need to talk to James Houlette at Golden Star. I'd guess if anybody had a trail on that song, it would be James. He's the one who called me about it Friday morning."

"Thanks for your time," Morgan said.
"And the coffee," Lang added. "We may need to visit again."
"Not a problem." T.R. saw them out and returned to his big leather chair. He folded his arms across his chest and leaned back, staring at the phone. "Charlie, Charlie, Charlie, why'd you do this to me?" He flipped through his Rolodex, stopping at Golden Star Entertainment. "Shit."

*

At three o'clock sharp T.R. Branch walked into the plush lobby of Golden Star Entertainment. Pacing, he studied the posters of Golden Star's past and present recording artists. He was eying the Rusti King poster when James Houlette appeared. Short and stocky, he was well dressed, but casual; boots, jeans, and a red Polo shirt. T.R. shook his hand and followed him into his imposing office.

"T.R., I hate like hell this happened." The president of Golden Star Entertainment sat on the couch and propped his boots on the expensive coffee table. Branch sat on the other end. "I hate it for you, for me, for everyone involved. But this is likely to get ugly. Nothing personal."

"Already has. I guess you've heard about Charlie Keith getting murdered."

"I'll tell you what I told the cops. We've been looking into this for awhile now. According to McCarty, he mailed the song to Sure-Star Publishing over a year ago. Roger Durwood's the owner. He's a sleaze bag. We knew the song started there."

"So Friday, when you called and said we *might* have a problem, you already knew we *had* a problem."

"We hired an investigator when this came up. Last week he suggested we turn up the heat at your place and see who jumped out of the pan. Obviously, we suspected Charlie had his hands dirty, since his name was on the song. Our guy got some real good pictures of Charlie going in and out of the building where Sure-Star Publishing is located. That was Friday evening." Houlette walked to his desk and handed T.R. a picture of Charlie. "I gave the rest of them to the cops."

"I can't believe he did this to me." T.R. studied the photo before tossing it on the coffee table. "I want to do what's right here." Branch left the couch and paced back and forth in front of Houlette's big desk. "James, this isn't the way I've built my business. You know that. I didn't know anything about this. Where do we go from here?"

"First, you'll need to talk to Rusti's record label. I'd guess they'll want you to cover their cost for recalling and re-printing the album. I hope you've got insurance."

"Some."

"At this point, we don't have a lot of expenses or legal in this. I'll let you out for our cost."

"No lawsuit?"

"Not from us. T.R., we all have to stick together. This business is tough enough without turning on our friends."

"I appreciate it. Very much so."

"Make your deal with the record label. We want to see this go away. Fact, we tried to buy McCarty off. Dennis Couch thought he had a deal done, but Rusti apparently has fallen in love the damn guy. She wants his name on the song. And, what she wants, we want."

"I understand completely."

"Besides the record label thing, your biggest problem is McCarty. By paying the label, you're as much as admitting it was his song. Any attorney in town would take his case. I'd say you and Sure-Star Publishing are going to get your asses sued off and I wouldn't count on much help from Roger Durwood."

"What do you know about McCarty? You said you almost had him bought off. What'd Dennis offer him?"

"Twenty grand. We were planning to get our money back from you." Houlette laughed.

"Only twenty?"

"Hell, it almost worked. Would've worked if Rusti hadn't fallen in love with the guy." Houlette threw his hands in the air. "Hell, figure the odds on all this."

T.R. sat back on the couch and crossed his legs. His foot was beating the air in four-four time. "Wonder if there's still a chance of buying him off?"

"Don't know. All I know is, Rusti wants his name on the song. That being said, my interest is clear. I think if I were you, I'd be taking my checkbook to Texas on the next flight to Austin. He's going to have all the royalties coming to him. Some cash for an honest mistake might keep you out of the courthouse."

Houlette crossed the room. "T.R., Rusti's in his corner. She's not going to let him get screwed on this. It's none of my business, but I'd offer six figures and try to cut my losses. Maybe offer a public statement of apology or something. Stroke the kid's ego."

"Ouch. That's a lot of money."

"Look, Rusti is going to be in San Angelo on Thursday. I think that's close to Austin. When Dennis calls in, I could try to set up a meeting for you.

I'll try to get McCarty there. I'd go that far for you."

"When Dennis calls, you tell him I'm on my way to Texas with money and a release. I'll be in San Angelo on Thursday. I'll call the record company this afternoon." T.R. shook hands with Houlette. "James, I won't forget your help on this."

"Neither will I." Houlette slapped T.R. on the back. "Good luck in Texas."

*

Lang and Morgan entered Sure-Star Publishing just before noon. Joyce rudely ignored them until they flashed their badges. "Detectives Lang and Morgan. We'd like to speak with Roger Durwood."

Durwood saw it all from behind his desk, through the glass wall, and met them at the door. "I'm Roger Durwood."

"Detective Morgan, Davidson County Sheriff's Department. This is Detective Lang. We need a few minutes of your time."

Durwood ushered them into his office. "Take a seat. What's all this about?"

"Charlie Keith. We're investigating his murder."

"Who's Charlie Keith?"

"We think you know exactly who Charlie Keith is. Want to start over?"

"We can if ya like." Durwood flashed a grin. "But I'm still not gonna know Charlie Keith."

Morgan pulled out the photo and laid it on the desk. "This is Charlie Keith. He's a songwriter at Branch Publishing. This photo was taken last Friday after he left your office."

Durwood studied the photo. "He didn't leave my office. I've never seen him before. Hell, there's lotsa offices in this building. Looks to me like he's outside, on the sidewalk."

"May we ask your secretary?"

"Joyce," Durwood yelled. "Come in here a minute."

Lang showed her the photo. "Recognize this man?"

Joyce held the picture and studied it. "Never seen him before."

"He's never been in this office?" Lang asked.

"I said, I've never seen him."

"Were you working Friday afternoon?"

"Yeah."

"What time did you leave?"

"About four-thirty."
"Is that early for you?"
"Yeah."
"I sent her to the post office before it closed at five." Durwood stood behind his chair. "Is there anything else?"
"Sit down," Morgan ordered.
"Shit." Durwood reluctantly took his seat. "Are y'all done with Joyce? She has work to do."
"She's excused." Lang took over. "Where were you Sunday morning?"
"At home."
"Anybody with you?"
"No. I'm not married. Unfortunately, I didn't take nobody home with me Saturday night." Durwood grinned at them.
"What time did you leave the house Sunday?"
"I don't know. I went to Poor Boy's for lunch. It was before noon. I like to try to get there before the church crowd." Durwood leaned forward. "I don't know this fella. And I don't understand why you're questionin me."
"Do you know Payne McCarty?" Morgan took a turn.
"No. Who's Payne McCarty?"
"Ever heard the song *When Love Turns Out The Light*?"
"Yeah. Who hasn't?"
"It's our understanding Payne McCarty wrote that song. Mailed it to you."
Lang finished, "You gave it to Keith. He put his name on it. And you killed Keith to shut him up."
"That's crazy. I don't have a clue as to what the hell you're talkin about. That's absurd. I don't know either one of em. Are y'all finished?"
Morgan and Lang exchanged glances. "For now," Lang said.
"But don't leave the county," Morgan threatened. "As of right now, you're a murder suspect. We'll be back."
"Wasn't plannin on goin nowhere. Do I need to call ya before I take a piss?"
"Not unless you're planning on pissing outside of Davidson County," Lang answered. "Have a nice day."
The two detectives walked down the dark, musty stairwell and entered the bright afternoon. "He did it," Lang stated.
"Yeah, but we've got nothing on him. We can't put him at the scene and we can't prove he even knew Charlie Keith."
"Not yet," Lang said, opening the door of their dark gray Dodge. "Let's go back to Keith's apartment. There's got to be something we're missing."

CHAPTER THIRTY-EIGHT

Tommy and Darla Jennings' small frame house was just off South 5th Street. Monday afternoon, Darla answered another call regarding their ad in the Abilene newspaper. The litter of golden retrievers was only four weeks old. She explained over the phone that the pups wouldn't be ready for another ten days, but they were going fast. First come, first reserved. Unsuspectingly, she gave Rusti King driving directions to their home.

The blue and yellow tour bus drove down the tree lined street and pulled up in front of their small white house, just before six. The bewildered Jennings and their two small children rushed to the front porch and watched in amazement as the bus door opened. "Honey, that's Rusti King!" Darla squealed to Tommy.

"Well, I'll be a son of a ... "

Rusti waved from the hot sidewalk. "I called about the golden retriever puppies." Randall escorted her up the steps to the porch.

"You're Rusti King!" Darla exclaimed.

"Yes, I am," she said, shaking Darla's hand.

"I'm Darla and this is my husband, Tommy. This is Becky and Michael." She placed her hands on her children's heads then patted her swollen tummy. "We're not sure who this one is yet."

Tommy, still dressed in his dirty blue work uniform, started to shake Rusti's hand, but thought better of it. He withdrew his grease stained hand. "I'm afraid my hands are still dirty from work."

Rusti looked at his hands. "My daddy was a mechanic." She extended her hand. "A little grease never hurt anybody."

Tommy nodded then shook her hand.

Rusti squatted in front of the two brown-haired kids. "Becky, it's very nice to meet you. You're just as pretty as your mother. How old are you?"

"Six."

"Michael, nice to meet you, too. I'd bet you're about twelve." She grinned.

"No I'm not. I'm just four."

"Well, you're sure a big boy for just being four. This is Randall Reynolds. He drives that big bus," she said to the two children. "Do you have some puppies?"

Becky nodded. Michael said, "Yeah."

"Could I see them?"

The kids looked at their parents. "They're in the back yard," Tommy answered.

"You'll have to excuse our house. We both work." Darla fretted.

"I'm sure it's neater than mine. Please don't apologize."

There were ten little gold balls of fluff who excitedly began stepping and tripping over each other when the backdoor opened. Barking, the two parents of the puppies approached the strangers aggressively, but obediently sat at Tommy's command.

Rusti sat on the back porch steps surrounded by the eager pups. "Darla, I know you said they weren't ready yet, but I was hoping to take one with me today. I'll take good care of him."

"You'd have to feed him baby formula while he's learning to eat solids," Tommy cautioned. "It'd take an awful lot of attention, but it could be done."

"I wouldn't ask, but I'm not coming back this way."

"Male or female?" Tommy asked.

"Male."

Tommy separated the four boys. "Take your pick."

Rusti picked each one up and looked at their precious faces. The second time around she saw a little bit of Pardner's mischievous face in one. "This one. You said a hundred and seventy-five for the males, right?"

Darla glanced at Tommy. He nodded and she looked back to Rusti. "That's what we're asking," she said, "but it would please us if we could just give him to you. We're both real big fans."

"Oh, no, but that's sweet." Rusti asked Randall, "Would you run out to the bus and get them four backstage passes?"

"Oh, my God!" Darla screeched. "Thank you!"

Tommy went to the doghouse and cut a small square from an old green army blanket with his pocketknife. "This will have his mother's scent on it. I heard a windup alarm clock works good, too. They think the ticking is their mother's heartbeat."

Rusti followed the family back through the house and squatted down on the front porch, facing the kids. "Will you come hear me sing tomorrow night?"

They nodded their heads.

Randall handed the passes and money for the puppy to Tommy. "Come to the stage door and show these," he said. "They'll let you in."

"Could we have your autograph?" Darla asked.

"Certainly." Rusti took a pen from Randall and signed each of their passes. "I'll see y'all tomorrow night then." She handed Tommy their autographed backstage passes.

A small crowd was beginning to gather along the green front yards of South 5th Street. Rusti held the tiny pup in one hand and waved to the Jennings with the other before disappearing into the tour bus.

*

Dennis was coming down the motel hall when he spied Rusti walking in, baby talking her puppy. Strong, burly Randall followed, carrying a sack full of baby formula. "Rusti, I'm really beginning to worry about you." Dennis chuckled at Randall. "You, too."

"Screw you," Randall muttered, and opened Rusti's hotel room door. He followed them in. "Where do you want this stuff?"

"Just set it down. Thanks."

"Is that it?"

Rusti nodded. "Thank you."

"I talked to Houlette this afternoon," Dennis began, after Randall had shut the door. "Seems the shit is hitting the fan in Nashville on this song thing. The guy who put his name on the song at Branch Publishing has been murdered. Roger Durwood is the suspect." Rusti sat on the floor rubbing on the big ears of the tiny pup. Dennis paced back and forth in front of her "T.R. Branch is flying into San Angelo on Thursday. He wants to meet with Payne. He's prepared to offer him a settlement in exchange for Payne agreeing not to sue his ass off." Dennis squatted next to Rusti. "Did you hear anything I just said?"

"What kind of settlement?" she asked, without looking up.

"I don't know. I'd guess big money or he wouldn't be coming to Texas."

"And his name's on the song?"

Dennis used his hand to push off the floor. He stretched his back. "The record company is standing by, ready to recall the album and re-print it with his name on the song."

Rusti stood up, still holding the puppy. "Thank you, Dennis. I knew you could do it."

"I wish I could take credit for it. You're the one who forced the issue. After Oklahoma City, it's all over the papers in Nashville. The whole story, including your love affair with Payne."

Ignoring him, Rusti dug through the sack and pulled out a small bowl and a can of baby formula. She bent down and filled the bowl with the thick milk. "Isn't he cute?" She sat the pup in front of the bowl, but he refused to drink.

"Put your finger in it and let him lick it off." Dennis squatted down and dipped his finger in the formula. The pup hesitated, then licked his finger dry.

"See, there he goes." Dennis looked up and smiled at Rusti. "You think you can put him down long enough to sing tomorrow night?"

"Dennis, I think I've just seen a whole new side of you. You don't mind holding him backstage, do you?"

"That's not in my contract." Dennis stood to leave. "You going to call Payne and get him to San Angelo?"

Sitting on the floor, Rusti picked up the pup and pressed him against her chest. "I'll call him." Jumping to her feet, she held the puppy away from her. "Damn! He just wet on me!"

CHAPTER THIRTY-NINE

Payne rolled up his extension cords Tuesday afternoon. After loading his tools in the trailer, he stood back and admired Casey's new redwood deck and gazebo with the pride of a craftsman.

During the drive to Heidi's Roadhaus, the hot wind dried the sweat off Payne's tan, muscular body. The thought of seeing Rusti again had him smiling. Just one more day and they would be together. Accompanied by the wind, Payne sang Rusti's new love song until the Jeep slid to a stop in the loose graveled parking lot. He slipped his shirt on and sprang out of the Jeep. Even his ribs felt better.

Sliding onto the barstool, Payne smiled at Casey. "All done."

"Payne, I haven't seen that big smile of yours in a long time. Does getting paid make you that happy?" She sat a cold Bud on the bar.

"It's always nice." Payne took a long drink. "Speakin of gettin paid, Rusti got my name on *When Love Turns Out The Light*."

"Are you going to get royalties?"

"Yep."

"How much do you think a number one song pays?"

"Beats me. I'm hopin it's enough to pay out my bar tab."

"I'm not waiting for that. I've already taken it out of your check." Casey handed it to him. "Twelve hundred less forty-two dollars worth of Budweiser."

"Damn. Ya gone up?"

"No. You haven't paid your tab in a month. That one you're drinking wasn't included either."

"I'm goin to San Angelo tomorrow to catch up with Rusti. I guess I'll be leavin here after next Monday." Casey nodded and watched Payne guzzle his beer. He pulled out a five and laid it on the bar. "Thanks for ever thing. Keep the change."

"Not so fast." Casey came around the bar and hugged him. "You better come to see me when you get back this way. I can be a real bitch when I get pissed off."

Payne tipped his hat to her. "I'll be back. I wouldn't piss ya off for the world."

*

Wednesday afternoon, after a short drive from Abilene, Randall pulled the bus to the rear of the San Angelo Holiday Inn. "There's Payne!" Rusti screamed in Randall's ear.

He sat on the hood of his faded red Jeep holding his guitar in his lap. Rusti hit the door button and jumped off the bus. "Hold it right there, lady," Payne ordered, and hit a "C" chord on his guitar. "I believe ya wanted a love song." He sang.

Every time I see you, I just fall to my knees.
Every time you smile, I find it hard to breathe.
I'm so in love, I can't think of anything else.

I don't care about golf anymore.
I don't care about the Super Bowl score.
I'm so in love, I can't think of anything else.
Don't you agree,
That your love's got a hold on me?
Why can't you see
I love only you, and nobody else ...
I just go crazy.
My eyes get glazy,
Cause I'm so in love with you ...
But, I'm just no good, without you loving me too.

If I sent you flowers, would you tell me you care?
If I bought a diamond, would you always be there?
I'm so in love, I can't think of anything else.

I don't care about the baseball strike.
I don't care if the bass don't bite.
I'm so in love I can't think of anything else.

Laughing and clapping, Rusti approached him. She stumbled over a few of the words in the chorus, as she sang with him.

> *Don't you agree,*
> *That your love's got a hold on me?*
> *Why can't you see*
> *I love only you, and nobody else ...*
> *I just go crazy.*
> *My eyes get glazy,*
> *Cause I'm so in love with you ...*
> *But I'm just no good without you loving me too.*
>
> *No, I'm just no good without you loving me too ...*

"I *do*! I *do* love you!" Rusti sighed and melted into his arms. "God, I've missed you," she managed to say, between kisses. "Thank you so much for my love song. It's beautiful."

Time and miles apart disappeared as the two lovers continued to kiss and hold to each other. Randall watched from his driver's seat while Dennis looked on holding the pup. "It's hopeless," Dennis said.

"Yes, sir. I could've told you that back in Ft. Worth."

"Hold the damn dog. I'll go get everybody checked in." Dennis left the bus and approached the amorous couple, who were still lost in their own private moment. Ignored, he finally cleared his throat. "Payne, nice to see you again."

Still holding Rusti under his left arm, Payne shook his hand. "Hey, Dennis. Good to see ya."

"I'm going to go get some rooms. Not that y'all would be interested in that."

Rusti lead Payne by the hand toward the bus. "Come with me. I've got a surprise for you, too." Payne followed her into the bus. "Close your eyes."

"This doesn't have anything to do with maple syrup, does it?"

"Maybe." Rusti laughed. She took the puppy from Randall and covered him with the small piece of green cloth. "Okay, now open your eyes." She pulled the small square of army blanket off the pup. "Say howdy." On cue, the puppy yelped. She handed him to Payne.

"Well, I'll be damn." Payne instinctively held him close. Looking at the pup in his arms, he managed not to cry, but the tears swelled in his eyes. "You have no idea ... how much this means to me."

"Excuse me," Randall said, leaving the driver's seat. "I think I'll go check on Dennis."

Payne lifted the puppy up to his face and was licked on the nose. "Babe, I don't know what to say." He held the small pup in his arms. "Thank you. What's his name?"

"Nash."

"Nash?"

"Yeah. I remembered you telling me about the night you and Skeeter made a toast to Kentucky roses and Nashville gold. Nash. It's short for Nashville Gold."

CHAPTER FORTY

The chartered twin engine King Air touched down Thursday, just after noon, in San Angelo, Texas. T.R. Branch left the plane carrying an overnight bag in one hand and his black briefcase in the other. Dressed in a gray short-sleeved shirt and faded jeans, T.R. Branch looked like anything but a Nashville song broker. At fifty-five, T.R. was still a handsome man. He had a thick head of graying hair, which he wore stylishly long and could easily have passed for a man in his forties.

After a short, hot cab ride, T.R. was greeted in the cool motel lobby by Dennis Couch. "Welcome to Texas, and life on the road," Dennis said.

"Hell, I paid my road dues." T.R. shook his hand. "Back before air conditioned buses. Damn, it still gets hot in Texas."

Dennis nodded in agreement. "It's good to see you again. I wish it were under different circumstances. Care to wet your whistle?"

"You bet. I could use a drink after that plane ride." T.R. glanced at his Rolex. "It's got to be five o'clock somewhere," he said, and followed Dennis into the deserted motel bar. T.R. laid down his baggage and pulled out a chair. "I figured as long as I'm here, I might as well stay the night and see the concert. Payne around?"

"Yeah. He's with Rusti. They haven't been out of the motel room since yesterday afternoon." Dennis yelled at the bartender, "Two Jack Daniel's on the rocks."

"That's got to be the luckiest man God ever let live."

"Yep. No doubt about that."

The bartender delivered the drinks to their table. T.R. handed him a fifty. "Keep them coming." He took a sip. "Houlette said you almost had him bought off for twenty grand. He can't be that stupid, can he?"

"No. He's not stupid. But I can't figure him. I was trying to get a quick deal done. In addition to the twenty grand, I promised I'd get him connected to some reputable publishers in Nashville for his other songs. Like you."

"You're kidding." T.R. laughed. "After we just stole his song?"

"Anyway, fireworks start going off between him and Rusti. He says he won't sell the song for that, but he'd *give* it to her. Said he'd take the twenty thousand. Two grand a day for every day he spent in the Nashville jail, and the promised publishing connections."

"Whoa. You lost me. How'd he end up in the Nashville pokey?"

Dennis sipped his drink. "He had a little misunderstanding with Roger Durwood back in May about his song. Ends up getting charged with assault. Durwood had him set up. Spent ten days in Davidson County."

"I like him already. I wish he'd killed the prick." T.R. leaned back. "What happened to the deal?"

"Rusti." Dennis finished off his drink and stuck two fingers in the air. "Hell, after the concert in San Antonio, she ran off with him for three days. Nothing's been the same since. She shows back up in love and demanding we get his name on the song."

"Damn."

Dennis leaned back in his chair. "I was sorry to hear about Charlie. I heard Roger Durwood is the suspect."

"Cops don't have shit on Durwood. And as far as I'm concerned, they can both rot in hell. I still can't believe all this. It's been a living nightmare for me since last Friday when Houlette called." He took another sip of Jack. "Hell, I think my wife was glad I was coming to Texas for a couple of days."

The young bartender delivered another round of drinks. Dennis raised his glass. "Here's to fine Tennessee whiskey."

T.R. drank and set his glass down. "I'd just as soon get this over with. Think he'll take less than a hundred grand? That's all I brought."

"You brought cash?"

"Hell yeah. I figure he's never seen that much money at once. I'm hoping money still talks."

"I'd start at fifty," Dennis said, and took another drink. "I'll call their room and see if he can come up for air long enough to get rich."

Two rounds of Jack Daniel's later, Payne and Rusti walked into the dimly lit bar. Branch stood from the table. "T.R. Branch." He shook Rusti's hand. "It's a pleasure."

"And it's a pleasure to meet you. I've heard about you for years. You're quite the legend in Nashville."

"Payne McCarty." Payne returned his firm handshake. "It's a pleasure, Mr. Branch."

"You kids want something to drink?" Dennis asked.

Payne glanced at Rusti. "Two Buds would work."

Dennis yelled across the bar. "Two Budweisers!" He glanced at T.R. then yelled again, "Two more Jacks!"

"Payne," Dennis began, "T.R. here is the president and founder of Branch Publishing Company in Nashville."

Payne nodded at Branch, ignoring Dennis. "Yes, sir."

"He's ... "

"Payne, I'm not one to beat around the bush," T.R. interrupted. He spoke with confidence and authority.

"Me either."

"I'd first like to apologize for what happened with your song. From the best I can tell, one of my staff writers, a guy named Charlie Keith, was in cahoots with Roger Durwood. They had a thing going. Durwood was furnishing my writer with songs he got in the mail. Son, I had no idea that was your song. I thought Charlie wrote it."

The bartender set the drinks down and stared at Rusti before Dennis shooed him off like a fly. Dennis spoke across the table to Payne. "It wasn't T.R.'s fault. He's good as gold."

T.R. took a drink. "I've already agreed to reimburse the record company for all their expenses to recall and re-print the album. That song is rightly going to have your name on it."

"What's that gonna run ya?"

"Close to a million, give or take."

Payne almost choked on his beer. "Damn."

"He's got it," Rusti said, and squeezed Payne's hand, "or he's got insurance."

"The only thing still left to fix on this deal is you. I'm prepared to offer you fifty thousand dollars, cash money. All you have to do is sign a piece of paper saying you won't sue my ass off."

"Payne," Dennis said, "you're still entitled to all the royalties to the song. This is in addition to that."

"How much ya think is comin on royalties?" Payne began peeling the label off his bottle.

T.R. spoke up. "Since there's not a publisher involved any more, I'd say anywhere from two-fifty to half-a-million. Depends on airplay and record sales. Maybe more. Publishers and writers split their end fifty-fifty. Since there's no publisher, you get the whole damn thing."

Rusti squeezed his hand again. "This is just bribe money he's talking about and it sounds pretty thin." She looked at Branch. "Do you realize what he could do to you in court?"

T.R. placed the briefcase on the table in front of Payne. "Open it."

Payne looked at the money and closed the briefcase. "That's a lotta money." He pushed it back to Branch.

"I'm laying all my cards on the table. After the record company gets done with me, I'm going to be out of insurance money. You're looking at one hundred thousand untraceable, unreportable U.S. dollars. A lawsuit could take years and who knows what would happen. I've got good attorneys." T.R. took another sip of whiskey. "If there is such a thing." Branch laid his hand on top of the briefcase. "Son, I'd just as soon see you get this money as a bunch of damn attorneys. This is my best offer."

Payne's eyes met Rusti's. "Hon, would y'all excuse us for a few minutes?" He looked at Dennis. "If ya don't mind."

"Certainly." Dennis shoved his chair back. Rusti looked at him questioningly then nodded. She gave him a quick kiss and followed Dennis to the bar.

"Let me see if I've got this straight." Payne leaned back in his chair and crossed his arms. "Ya flew all the way to Texas to give me all that cash, just so I wouldn't sue ya for somethin ya didn't do?"

"That's about the size of it."

Payne looked at the briefcase and shook his head no. He leaned closer to Branch. "Tell ya what. I'll make ya a deal. Ya loan me ten thousand dollars outta that briefcase. When I get my royalties, I promise to pay ya back. You take the rest of your money back to Nashville. I ain't gonna sue ya for somethin ya didn't do. Hell, my beef's with Roger Durwood. He's the one I'm after."

T.R. tossed back his drink and cleared his throat. "What?"

"I said, I'd pay ya back. My word's good."

"I have no doubt about that." T.R. pulled the briefcase to his lap without another word. Opening it, he counted out the money and handed Payne ten, one thousand-dollar bills. He watched with amusement as Payne pulled up the right leg of his jeans and stuck the money in his sock. "It's refreshing to meet a man of honor." T.R. ran his finger around the top of his empty drink glass. "Son, I've got to ask. What in the hell are you going to do with that ten thousand dollars?"

Payne glanced over his shoulder to the bar. "Can ya keep a secret?"

"Take it to the grave."

"I wanna buy Rusti a ring. A damn nice one. I'm gonna ask her to marry me when the time's right."

T.R. smiled at Payne and shook his hand. "Well, congratulations ... I'd have to say, in all honesty, she's a lucky woman. Payne, you're a good man."

"I'm a lucky man."

"Yeah." T.R. chuckled. "You are that, too." Leaning back in his chair, he asked, "Will you be settling in Nashville?"

"Yes, sir. Goin there after Willie Nelson's Fourth of July Picnic."

"Well, after you get settled in, I'd like to hear the rest of your music."

Payne finished off his Budweiser. "Might take awhile. I've got lotsa songs."

"I'll make time. You give me a call when you get there." T.R. handed Payne his business card before waving Dennis and Rusti back to the table. He leaned over to Payne. "People in Nashville, they don't forget things like this. The day ever comes you need a favor, anything at all, you look me up."

"Deal done?" Dennis asked, returning to the table.

Payne looked to Rusti. "There's no deal. I'm not gonna take money for an honest mistake."

"What?"

"I'm not after Mr. Branch. I'm after Roger Durwood."

Rusti kissed him on his cheek and sat down. She took his hand and patted it. "I love you."

"Hell, I love him too!" T.R. let out a loud laugh.

Dennis yelled across the bar, "Another round!" He turned to Rusti. "T.R. is staying for the concert tonight. I think I feel another duet coming on. Like y'all did in Oklahoma City. That *was* awesome."

"Hell, I'd sure like to hear him sing it." T.R. slapped Payne on the back. "I've already heard everybody in Music City sing that damn song but you."

*

Payne watched from the motel window as Rusti's bus left the parking lot. His feeble excuse to skip the sound check so he could watch after the puppy had raised her eyebrows, but she had let it slide. He checked his timepiece. It was almost three. He had less than two hours to find a ring for Rusti.

Payne drove to downtown San Angelo with Nash in his lap. Zeigler's was the first jewelry store he came across. After a sharp U-turn in the middle of Broadway, he parked the Jeep in front of the store.

"Hey! You can't bring that dog in here!" the young, sharply dressed salesman yelled from behind a display counter.

"Suit yourself." Payne tipped his hat and turned for the door.

"Hold on there, young man." Old man Zeigler stood from his desk. He was thin and wore red suspenders over his starched white shirt to hold up his baggy trousers. His shoulders were stooped from years bent over his workbench. Laying down his glasses, he pointed a long skinny finger at the salesman. "Richard, I don't care if somebody brings a one-eyed-jackass in here. A customer is a customer." Turning back to Payne, he asked, "Son, what can I show you today?"

"I'm lookin for a weddin ring. A damn nice one."

Ziegler snickered. "Damn nice is damn expensive." He unlocked the back of the showcase and pulled out a wedding set. "This is $2,995. It's a nice little ring."

Payne glanced at the diamond. "Somethin nicer."

Replacing the set, Zeigler walked to the next counter. Pulling out another ring, he handed it to Payne. "This is a real flasher. Marquis cut, excellent grade, clarity, and such."

Payne set Nash on the floor and examined the ring. He held it up to the light and watched it sparkle. "How much?"

"Let you have it for ten. Plus tax."

"I'll give seven. Cash money."

The old man shook his head. "Sorry, I can't let her go for that. Nine thousand. That's it."

"Eight."

"Eighty-five hundred."

"You pay the tax?"

Zeigler chuckled. "I'll pay the governor. You want it wrapped?"

"No sir. And ya can keep the box." Payne pulled the leg of his jeans up and took out his stash. He handed Zeigler nine, one thousand-dollar bills.

The old man eyed his salesman and turned his back before pulling out his wallet. He handed Payne five hundreds in change then stuck Payne's money in his pocket. "I just love cash deals," he whispered.

"Pleasure doin business with ya," Payne said, sticking the diamond ring into the pocket of his jeans.

Nash had been busy. A pile of puppy poop lay on the carpet next to a wet spot. "Sorry about that," Payne apologized. "If you'll get me somethin, I'll clean that up for ya."

"Wouldn't hear of it. Richard, get something and clean up that mess."

"Excuse me?"

"I said, get your ass over here and clean up that pile of dog shit!"

CHAPTER FORTY-ONE

Leaving San Angelo, the caravan of buses and trucks traveled through the night like a band of gypsies. The eighteen-wheeler, carrying the equipment, led the way down Interstate10, toward San Antonio. The buses, carrying Rusti's sleeping band members and crew, followed the truck. Dennis slept on the couch while Randall drove Rusti's bus, trailing Payne and Rusti in the faded red Jeep.

The Rusti King Tour, originally scheduled to end in San Angelo, took one final detour to Luckenbach. Rusti had planned to spend a couple of days with her parents after San Angelo, then fly home to Nashville. But that was before Willie's invitation. And before Payne.

Now, with three days off, the band and crew headed for rest and relaxation in San Antonio. But the Jeep left the Interstate on the access road. It slowed as Payne prepared to turn east on Highway 46, to New Braunfels. It was approaching three in the morning when Randall sounded the bus's loud air horn, startling Dennis. Payne waved as the bus blew past the Jeep. "I'm startin to like ol Randall," Payne said, turning the Jeep toward home. Rusti yawned and nodded. Reaching over to Rusti's lap, he scratched Nash's ears. "Babe, you okay?"

"Just tired. How much longer?"

"Half an hour or so. Almost there."

*

Payne carried his guitar and luggage inside the sweltering ranch house. Rusti carried Nash. "Well, we've sure been around the block a couple of times since I first brought ya here," Payne said. He pulled out two Buds from the refrigerator.

"I've had the time of my life since I met you." Rusti held the squirming pup in one hand and pressed the cold beer bottle against her forehead to fight the heat. She leaned back, resting against the clean kitchen counter. "Kitchen looks nice."

"Yeah, well it's a lot easier to keep without Skeeter around."

"I can imagine." Rusti smiled, but was too tired to laugh.

"We'd better take the pup outside. He'll need to pee after his nap."

"Do all dogs pee this much?" Rusti asked, following Payne outside. "I swear he pees more than he drinks." She yawned and set the pup on the grass that was already becoming damp with the morning dew.

"Do ya know why God made puppies and babies so cute?" Rusti placed her hands around Payne's neck. "No. Why's that?"

"So ya don't kill em."

Rusti laughed and gave him a quick kiss. "Ever thought about having a few of your own?"

"I think one dog is plenty." Payne grinned at her.

"I'm not talking about dogs. You know, a little blonde-headed Payne running around the house."

"Or a little redheaded Rusti?" He kissed her forehead. "Yeah, I've thought about it since fallin in love with ya. I think maybe both."

"Definitely both." She smiled and closed her eyes. "I love you."

"Enough to marry me?"

Rusti's green eyes popped open. The fatigue of the day vanished. Stepping back to read Payne's poker face, she tripped over Nash. Payne grabbed her by the arm and steadied her. "Gettin more like ol Pardner ever day. Always under foot."

"Payne, was that a question or a proposal?"

Payne dug into his pocket. "Will ya marry me?" He held the ring in the palm of his hand.

Rusti stared at the ring. It sparkled beneath the back porch light. She looked up at Payne with tears. "Yes, baby. Oh, yeah. I love you enough to marry you." Rusti threw her arms around his neck. "Yes! Yes! Yes!" she shouted into the tranquil night.

"Babe, I don't ever wanna live another day without you in it," Payne whispered. "I love ya more than anything in the world."

"And I've never been happier in my life." Rusti kissed him before releasing her hold around his neck. She held out her hand. Beneath the stars and the solitude of the warm Hill Country night, he slid the ring on her finger.

*

Payne woke up just after noon. He lay still, watching Rusti sleep. Looking at the ring on her finger, he whispered, "Thank ya, Lord," before

carefully crawling out of bed. He walked quietly around the bed until he stepped in a puppy puddle. "Shit!"
    Startled, Rusti sat up in bed. "What's wrong?"
    "Stepped in a puddle of pee."
    Rusti giggled and rubbed her face. "And just where were you sneaking off to?"
    "I was gonna make coffee."
    "I thought Skeeter took the coffee pot."
    "I bought a new one and a fryin pan. I've got bacon and eggs. Hungry?"
    Rusti looked at her ring and touched it before holding it up to the light streaming through the old stained curtains. "It gorgeous. Payne, it looks expensive. Where'd you get the money for something this beautiful?"
    "T.R. Branch loaned it to me. I'll pay him back when I start gettin my royalties."
    Rusti smiled at him. "I was very proud of you yesterday. Not just anybody would turn down a briefcase of money on principle."
    "It wasn't his fault."
    "He would have paid you anyway."
    "That wouldn't be right. Anyway, I've got you. You're all I need to make me happy."
    Rusti patted the bed. "Come here, handsome. Now that you've got a ring on my finger, just what are you planning to do with me?" She motioned for him with her finger. "It seems to me we've got some planning to do."
    "Hang on." Payne limped to the bathroom and washed off his foot before jumping back in bed. He landed lightly on top of Rusti. "That's much better. Ya feel good. Umm, real good."
    "So do you, but … " Rusti rolled him over to his side of the bed. "What kind of wedding are we going to have?"
    "I don't know." Payne shrugged his shoulders
    "Large or small?"
    "Your choice. What ever, when ever, where ever, just let me know and I'll be there."
    "I'm not going to plan this by myself. You're not getting off that easy. Tell me what you'd like."
    "As small and as soon as possible." Payne stroked her face. "If it was my choice, I'd take ya to Las Vegas. We'd go to one of those little chapels, just the two of us."
    "Really?" she took his hand and kissed it. "Why?"
    "No distractions. And it'd be just me and you. Alone."
    "No blushing bride, dressed in white? No flowers and cake?"

"Babe, I want ya to be happy. If that's what ya want, that's what you'll have. You can have the biggest damn weddin in Texas, or Tennessee, or where ever. I'm game." Payne rolled back on top of her. He pinned her hands above her head. Grinning mischievously, he asked, "Ya know, I've been wonderin. Are ya ticklish?"

"No," she answered, trying to keep a straight face. "You're trying to change the subject on me again."

"No I'm not. I already told ya what I'd do, if it was me. Now, ya tell me what ya want or I'm gonna have to tickle ya till ya do."

"I told you. I'm not ticklish."

Payne attacked her ribs with both hands. Rusti screamed and giggled. "Stop!" She gasped for air. "Please! Please stop!"

"Are ya gonna tell me or do ya want some more?"

She nodded her head. "Boots and jeans in Vegas."

"What? You're not serious. Am I gonna have to tickle ya again?"

"No! Don't you dare." Rusti put her hands on his face. "I'm serious. I say, let's do it in boots and jeans in Vegas. This weekend." She pulled his head down and kissed him. "Unless you have something better to do than marry me. We could be back by Sunday. Skeeter could watch the puppy."

"You're serious?"

"You're not trying to back out on me are you? It *was* your idea."

"Hell no. Let's go." Payne kissed her and hollered, "You're as crazy as I am."

"Scary, isn't it?"

"You're sure? Ya won't regret not havin a big weddin? How bout your folks?"

"I'm positive. And, as for my parents, after four girls, nothing surprises them anymore."

"Okay. You're on." Payne kissed her and rolled over. Reaching down, he pulled a whimpering Nash into bed with them. "As long as we're plannin things, how am I gonna get my stuff to Nashville?"

"We could put it in the equipment truck."

"What about my Jeep and my tool trailer?"

"We could pull the Jeep behind the bus. I don't know about the trailer. Hon, you're a songwriter, not a carpenter any more. You're not going to need those kinds of tools in Nashville."

"I guess I could sell em all," he said, petting Nash's big ears. "We need to go to town today anyway and check on Nova. I still gotta tell her I'm leavin. Might could get somethin for em at a pawn shop."

"And I need to buy a wedding ring for my husband. Hey," Rusti rolled to her side and ran her hand over his chest, "do you know any of the songs I do besides the one you wrote?"

"Probably a couple. Why?"

"As long as we're going to the hospital, I thought I might visit the kids. Maybe do a song or two. Would you play? It's something I like to do when I get the chance."

"You bet." Payne smiled at her. "I love ya. And I'd love to do it."

"Will you sing some of your songs?"

"Sure. Anything else?"

"I'm hungry. I'll make reservations for Vegas if you'll cook breakfast. I hear they have honeymoon suites at Caesar's Palace with heart shaped bathtubs."

Payne held Nash up, bouncing him in the air. "And mirrors on the ceilin?" The excited pup shot a stream of pee splattering on Payne's chest. "Shit!" Payne jumped out of bed holding Nash while Rusti doubled up with laughter. "Damn girl, ya shoulda named this dog Pisser Gold."

Gasping for breath, Rusti manage to say, "Well at least I got the *gold* right."

*

Nova's mood was foul. After five days in the hospital, she was oscillating between depression and fits of rage. The pain pills and sedatives were no substitute for her usual daily dosage of tequila. Following several vicious attacks on the nursing staff, the sedatives were now being administered in self-defense.

Payne received a "heads up" warning from one of the nurses, and approached her bed with caution. Her short dark hair was flat and oily. The bruises were lighter, but still evident. "Well, ya sure look like hell," Payne said, from a safe distance.

Opening her eyes, Nova stuck her middle finger in the air. "Oh goodie. You brought your guitar. Am I going to get a serenade?"

"Hell, no." Payne set his guitar down. "Remember Rusti?"

Rusti stuck her head out from behind Payne and gave a little wave. "How you feeling?"

Nova looked at Payne. "Can I smart off to her?"

"Take your best shot," Rusti answered.

Nova almost smiled. "Payne, I think I like her."

"We're engaged."

"Shit!" Nova screamed at the top of her lungs. She looked at Rusti, "I can't believe somebody cracked Payne's hard heart. Not even you. When's the big day?"

"Tomorrow. We're flyin to Vegas tonight," Payne answered.

"Shit!" Nova let out another outburst.

"Damn, Nova. Hold it down or the nurses are gonna come chargin in here."

"Bet me. Hell, they're all just hoping I'll die before their next shift anyway." Nova clapped her hands. "I can't believe it. Shit! I mean congratulations."

"Thank you," Rusti said. She moved cautiously from behind Payne into Nova's line of fire.

"So, you taking him back to Nashville with you?"

"That's what I came to tell ya." Payne sat on the edge of the bed.

"Just as well." Nova's face fell. "The deal with Jimmy Earl is shot to hell."

"Does he know you're in here?"

"He wouldn't give a shit if he knew. I told him to get his fat ass and bald head the hell out of my life last Saturday night."

"Has anybody bothered to tell him we're not playin on the Fourth?"

"Hell, no. It'd serve him right."

"Nova, that ain't right. We oughta at least warn him or somethin."

"Darlin, we were the first band. I don't think Willie is gonna give a shit if it starts at eleven or eleven-thirty. I doubt he'll even be awake."

"Do ya have Jimmy Earl's number? I'll call him."

"It's in the book. Jimmy E. Thompson."

"Payne, why don't you play in that spot?" Rusti asked. "I could ask a couple of the guys in my band to help y'all out. They'll be there anyway."

"Damn, Payne, she's smart, too."

"Yeah, she is." Payne considered it. "That might be fun. Have ya seen Hartman?"

"Bless his heart. He's almost camped out here."

"He cares a lot about ya."

"Yeah. He also said he *loved* me. Can you believe that?"

"Yeah." Payne nodded his head. "He told me that, too."

"He told you that he loved you?"

"No. He told me that he loved *you*, not me. I hope ya didn't hurt his feelins."

"I don't guess I did. He's still coming around. It's hard to tell anything about Hartman. It'd be nice if he'd talk to me when he comes by, instead of just sitting and grinning at me. That makes me nervous."

"He's just shy. Help him out some."

Nova closed her eyes. "I intend to. He's about all I've got left."

"Well, next time ya see him, tell him we're still on for the Fourth. Tell him to show up around ten. We'll meet at Rusti's bus. It's the blue and yellow one." Payne took Nova's hand. "Like ya always say, the show must go on."

"He'll like that."

Payne patted her hand. "Nova ... I guess we're gonna head on down the road."

"What? You're not going to play and sing for me?"

"Not today. Rusti's gonna do a couple songs for the kids here before we go."

Nova nodded her head and closed her eyes. "Payne, thanks for coming by. You've been a real friend. I'm going to miss you." She looked at Rusti and choked back her tears. "Take good care of my favorite songwriter."

"I will."

Payne leaned over and hugged her. "I'll miss ya, too. Hey, I'll be back. We'll see ya again."

"Promise?"

"I promise." Payne kissed her on the forehead.

"Well, don't forget you owe me a damn guitar."

"The hell I do."

"That was my fault," Rusti said. "I owe you the guitar."

"Y'all get the hell out of here." Nova forced a smile. "Go get married or something crazy."

*

It took only an introduction and a phone call from the nurse's station to obtain permission to gather the kids on the pediatric ward into the hall. Payne escorted *the* Rusti King through the hall with the charge nurse, entering every room of those children unable to get out of bed. She signed autographs and gave each child a special word of encouragement before going to the hall to start her performance.

Word had spread quickly at McKenna Memorial Hospital. The small wing was crowded with doctors, nurses and visitors. Payne stood at her side and accompanied her on his Martin guitar. The dynamic Rusti King, who had it all, tried to give some of it back to her small audience.

"I want to introduce y'all to someone very special to me." Rusti took Payne's hand after her fourth song. "This is Payne McCarty from right here in New Braunfels. He's a songwriter. And the man I'm going to marry." Payne was greeted with a few cheers and splattering of applause. "He's going to sing a couple of songs for you."

Payne strummed his guitar. "This is a song I wrote about a cowboy who lived up near Denver. He decided to take a trip down to Corpus Christi with his dog. He ... well, I guess you'll just have to listen to the song to hear what happened." Payne grinned at the kids and played *Texas Rivera*.

I heard Corpus Christi sure is pretty,
Between the ocean and the summer sun.
And I sure did need a small vacation,
And the beach sounded like a lot of fun.
So I loaded up my old pickup – truck
With my dog and everything that's dear.
I took one last look at Denver
And I threw it into high gear.

Well I stuck my truck on high center,
Just as the ocean appeared.
So I set up camp in the moonlight,
Built a fire, kicked back and had a beer.
Fell asleep and the next thing I remember
I was staring at the girl of my dreams.
She said welcome to the Texas Rivera,
This ain't no Rocky Mountain stream.

Chorus
She said welcome to the Texas Rivera.
You don't have to speak French to get along.
Well she looked like Lady Godiva,
And I wondered how a cowboy could go wrong.

We broke camp and headed toward the sunrise,
To a place she said nobody knows.
She said trust me and I'll show you a good time,
But those cowboy clothes have got to go.

NASHVILLE GOLD

> *We worked on our tans all weekend,*
> *But I got burned from my heart down to my toes,*
> *Cause I woke up Monday morning without her.*
> *She left my dog, but took my truck and my clothes.*
>
> *Now I'm a mile high, but feeling low in Denver,*
> *And I'd swear it was all a bad dream,*
> *But my girlfriend's still mad about my tan line*
> *And my dog is still looking at me mean.*
> *So if you travel to the Texas Rivera,*
> *And meet a long-haired beauty on the beach,*
> *Just remember this ol cowboy's story*
> *And save yourself a whole lot of grief.*

Rusti joined in on the chorus.

> *She said welcome to the Texas Rivera.*
> *You don't have to speak French to get along.*
> *Well she looked like Lady Godiva,*
> *And I wondered how a cowboy could go wrong.*
>
> *Now I know just how a cowboy can go wrong ...*
> *She said welcome to the Texas Rivera.*

Finishing the song to cheers and laughter, Payne gave Rusti a quick kiss. The kids laughed louder and giggled at their affection. "Here's another song I wrote. Ya might have heard it on the radio. Tell y'all what. I'm gonna let Rusti sing this one. "It's her latest number one hit."

"I think he should sing it with me," Rusti said. "What do y'all think?"

The crowd clapped. Payne winked at Rusti before they sang *When Love Turns Out The Light*. The small crowd listened intently until the final note echoed off the depressing, pale green hospital walls. Rusti waved to them. "Thank you for sharing your afternoon with us. We hope you all get well really, really fast. God bless each of you."

Payne leaned against the wall watching Rusti patiently sign autographs until a young girl approached him. She had short brown hair, big brown eyes and wore pink pajamas. Payne guessed her to be seven or eight years old. "Mr. Payne, can I have your autograph?"

"Mine? Honey, I'm not famous." Payne squatted down and looked into her hopeful eyes.

"But I bet you will be someday. Then, I'll already have it."
"You know," Rusti squatted next to them, "I think you may be right."
"What's your name?" Payne asked.
"Jeanie."
He took her paper and wrote. *Jeanie, thanks for being the very first person to ever ask for my autograph. I will never forget you. Get well fast.* Payne signed it and kissed her on the forehead. "Don't ya want Rusti's autograph, too?"
She looked up at Rusti. "No. She's not as cute as you are."

*

Payne looked over the guitars at Don's Pawn Shop while Don ran his calculator behind the counter. He pulled a black acoustic guitar off the rack, a Catalina, by Fender. After tuning it, he did a series of scales along the neck until Don yelled across the small shop. "I can go fifteen hundred for everything, including the trailer."
Payne put the guitar back. "You and me both know all that's worth more than that. Most of those tools are new. Hell, the trailer's worth that much. Two thousand and they're yours."
Rusti hid her smile, listening to Payne bargain. Don left the counter and approached them. "Can't go that much. But I'll tell you what. I'll throw in that guitar you were looking at. It's a good one and I don't have much in it. I'm asking three hundred."
"Come with a case?"
"Yeah. I'll throw in a case."
"Hard case. I don't want one of those cardboard jobs."
Don nodded. "Hard case it is."
"Fair enough."
Rusti hung on Payne's shoulder while Don counted out the fifteen hundred dollars. "There you go, cowboy."
"Gotta magic marker I could borrow a minute?"
"Sure."
Payne opened the case. On the lid, in the red felt lining, he wrote in large black letters.

NASHVILLE GOLD

To Nova,
"The show must go on!"

Yours in Music,

Payne McCarty
July 1985

CHAPTER FORTY-TWO

Friday evening, Payne drove Rusti and Nash to the Doeppenschmidt's apartment complex. It was enormous. Heat from the July day was still rising from the black asphalt as they drove through acres of parking. They searched the small numbers above the identical yellow doors for fifteen minutes before locating 197E. Payne knocked on their door with Rusti by his side and Nash on his arm.

"Payne, you're runnin thin on favors here," Skeeter said, grinning. "This better be good. Well, I'll be damn. Another Pardner." Skeeter opened the door and waved them inside. "Y'all come on in."

"He's got a ways to go on that," Payne said, following Rusti inside.

"Payne!" Lisa came bouncing in from the kitchen. "And Rusti!" Lisa gave them both a hug. "It's great to see you. Oh! He's so cute!" Payne handed Nash to Lisa. "Did you have any trouble finding us?" she asked.

"A little," Payne answered. "Skeeter, ya coulda told me there was three hundred damn *yellow* doors. We've been around this place twice."

Skeeter plopped down on the couch. "So what's the big news? Ya gotta puppy?"

"Nope." Payne put his arm around Rusti. "We're gettin married."

Lisa jumped up and down, squealing with Nash in her arms. Payne put his hand on her shoulder to calm her down. "I wouldn't get him too excited. He's got a tendency to turn his little water hose loose."

"I'll be damn." Skeeter left the couch and was hugging Rusti before Payne could turn back around. He shook Payne's hand. "Congratulations. When's the big day?"

"Tomorrow," Rusti announced. "We're going to fly to Vegas tonight and get married tomorrow." She held her hand out to show off her ring.

Lisa handed the puppy to Skeeter before jumping up and down, clapping her hands. "This is so exciting!"

"Damn, Payne," Skeeter held Rusti's hand, looking at the rock, "what'd ya do, rob a bank?"

"It's beautiful," Lisa added.

"Gotta loan against my royalties. Rusti got my name on that song and the whole damn thing straightened out."

With his hands on his hips, Skeeter squinted up at her. "Ya sure about him? I can't honestly recommend him as a roommate." He winked at Payne.

"I'm sure." Rusti hugged Payne. "Very sure."

"So, anyway, we need ya to keep the puppy," Payne said.

"Can't. No dogs allowed."

"He's not a dog, he's a puppy. Hell, we'll be back Sunday."

"Can't do it," Skeeter said, with a straight face.

"Yes, we can, too." Lisa shot Skeeter a look, just before he laughed and did a little dance.

"Had y'all goin for a sec. Will ya help me load the U-Haul Monday mornin?"

"Can't."

"Why not?"

"That's the other thing. We're still playin at Willie's Picnic, without Nova. Rusti gotta couple of guys from her band, a guitar and keyboard player, to help us out. We're gonna drop the music by on the way to the airport. We play at eleven. Need to be there by ten. Hell, it's just up the road to Fredericksburg. You can still make it to the track in plenty of time."

Skeeter scratched his chin. "I need to think about that for a minute."

"Don't hurt yourself." Payne teased him.

"Might work. If they chase me from the track, we could get lost in the crowd at Luckenbach. Okay, look. Let's load our stuff Sunday night, after the races. Then we'll drive out and spend the night with y'all."

"Hey, we could put the rest of my stuff on your truck. Ya gotta go through Tennessee to get to Kentucky anyway. Just drop it off on the way."

"And stay a few days," Rusti added. "We could all party in Nashville and celebrate everything." Rusti looked over at Payne. "What are you guys talking about? Getting chased from the track?"

"I'll explain it later. It's a long story."

"We can't go back to the ranch house after the races. Red knows where it is. We'll need to stash the U-Haul somewhere." Skeeter sat down on the couch holding the pup. "What's his name?"

"Nash," Payne answered.

"It's short for Nashville Gold," Rusti added.

"Cute." Skeeter lifted the pup's long ears in the air. "Hello, Nashville." He looked up to Payne and Rusti. "Hey, are y'all gonna sit down or what?"

"Just passin through," Payne said. "We gotta hit the road. You'll need to soak his dog food in the baby milk. He's not old enough for just dry food. I got

it all in the Jeep. Skeeter, ya get it figured out and we'll talk about ever thing Sunday evenin." Skeeter and Lisa followed them to the Jeep. Payne handed the sack of puppy supplies to Lisa. "He's not quite house broke yet. I've been puttin newspapers down for him in the kitchen."
"Does he use em?" Skeeter asked.
"Hell, no."
"Don't worry about a thing," Lisa promised. "I'll take good care of him. Y'all just enjoy yourselves."
"We appreciate everything," Rusti said, climbing into the Jeep.
"See y'all Sunday evenin. Hey," Skeeter pulled out a dollar and handed it to Payne, "play this in a slot machine for as long as it lasts. Quit at a hundred bucks."
"Feelin lucky?"
"Yeah. Real damn lucky."

*

It was 4 a.m. when Skeeter crawled out of bed. In the living room, he dressed in dark clothes and old tennis shoes. He completed his outfit with a black stocking cap then tiptoed past the sleeping pup. Entering the still night, he opened the trunk of Lisa's Pinto and transferred a five-gallon can of diesel to his pickup before driving the forty miles to Red's trailer.

Turning onto the dirt road, Skeeter killed his lights and drove under the moonlight. He slowed and looked at the trailer for any movement, then topped the hill and turned his truck around. Walking through the trees, he carefully approached the trailer from the back, carrying the can of diesel. He picked up a rock and threw it against the side of the trailer then hid behind the brush and waited. No one appeared. He threw another rock, then a third.

Crawling through the same window he had used before, he entered the vacant bedroom. He stood still while his eyes adjusted to the darkness, listening to the rapid thumping of his heart. After double-checking the house, he opened the back door and brought the can of diesel inside.

Popping off the cover to the heater, he lit a match. There, within the soft glow of the flame, was the stash and cash. Taking a paper sack from his back pocket, he unfolded it. He lit another match and stuffed the sack with Red's money, without bothering to count it. There was plenty. He lit another match and looked at the cocaine. There were two kilos of the white powder next to the pistol. The flame flickered and went out. Skeeter sat in the darkness fighting his temptation. "No more," he spoke out loud. "No damn more."

NASHVILLE GOLD

Removing the cocaine from the heater, he carried it around the house to the abandoned truck. After wiping off his fingerprints, he placed the plastic bags on the dash of the rusting pickup. Returning to the house, Skeeter left a trail of diesel through the trailer and out the backdoor. He tossed the empty can inside and smiled to himself before lighting the match.

The fire erupted as he made his way back through the trees. He listened and looked both ways before crossing the road. It was still deserted. Skeeter slowed the pickup to a crawl and watched the flames spreading through the trailer. "Hey, asshole!" Skeeter yelled out the window. "Paybacks are hell!"

Skeeter drove through the darkness to Ranch Road 306 before turning on the headlights. He stopped in Gruene just long enough to call the fire department.

*

Skeeter quietly re-entered their apartment. He flicked on the small light above the stove and opened the sack. From the darkness, Lisa held Nash in her arms watching him count the money. "How much?"

Skeeter's feet cleared the floor. "Shit! Ya scared the hell outta me."

"What have you done?"

"It's not what ya think. I can explain ever thing."

Lisa flipped on the kitchen light and sat at the table. "I'm listening."

"Baby, this is just part of the payback to Red. It's his drug money. I found his stash a few weeks ago. He's been dealin coke in the Hill Country for years. I told ya that. I told ya what he did to me."

"You stole it?"

"It's not stealin." Skeeter paced in front of the stove. "He had me almost beat to death." He waved his hands in the air. "It's a pay back. I don't consider this stealin. It's revenge."

"Skeeter, I don't like this. Why didn't you tell me about it?"

"I didn't want ya to worry."

"What if you get caught? What if Red finds out it's you?"

"He won't. I didn't leave any evidence. Hell, he can't go to the cops. I mean, what can he say? Somebody stole my drug money?"

"People always leave evidence."

"Well, if I did, it's damn sure gonna be hard to find. I burned down the whole trailer. It was just an old piece of shit. Wasn't worth haulin off. He was just usin it as a stash."

"So, the cocaine burned up with the trailer?"

248

"Not exactly."

"Skeeter, you promised me ... "

"I left it where the fire department could find it." Skeeter walked behind her and rubbed her shoulders. "I promised ya, no more. I meant it. I didn't touch it, other than to move it." Skeeter sat next to her and took her hand. "The son-of-a-bitch had it comin. Look, I was closin in on ten grand when ya scared the hell outta me and I'd just got started."

"Skeeter, this frightens me."

"Hey, it's all over now. There's nothin to be scared about. It's a done deal. Hell, I may be little, but nobody screws with the Skeeter and gets away with it."

"I just hope you *get* away with it."

"He won't suspect me. Especially after I throw that race on the Fourth. He'll be after me for that, not this. No way he'll figure me for both. Anyway, once they find the coke, Red's gonna have a whole new set of problems."

"I wish you hadn't done this."

"Stop worryin about it. Just act regular. We'll be a long way from here this time next week. This is gonna work. I promise. I've been figurin on it for a long time."

"Well ... okay, if you're sure." Lisa looked at the pile of money on the stove, then back to Skeeter. "Let's count the damn money!"

CHAPTER FORTY-THREE

Rusti pulled out the Las Vegas Yellow Pages early Saturday morning. She read the various wedding service advertisements to Payne while they lay on the round bed, beneath the mirrors.

"They all sound about the same to me," Payne said, leaning back on the pillows with his hands behind his head.

"Then let's go with the Little White Chapel. They have limo service."

Payne picked up the phone and dialed the number as she called it out. "We need to get married," he spoke into the phone. "What's your best deal?" Watching Payne, Rusti giggled as he listened to the sales pitch. He placed his hand over the phone. "Can we be ready by ten? That's an hour."

"No problem here."

"That fine. We're at Caesar's Palace. Okay. Thanks."

"They'll pick us up at the east entrance at ten. It's a white limo with their name on the side."

Payne showered and shaved then watched Rusti hustling about the room getting ready. He flipped through the channels on the TV before settling on the station explaining the various casino games. He patiently waited for her to place the finishing touches on her makeup and hair. "All set," she announced. It was five till ten.

Payne took her hand. "Miss King, you're even prettier than your pictures."

"Why, thank you. But just call me Mrs. McCarty."

Dressed in boots and jeans, they walked down the long, winding halls leading to the casino. "Which way is east?" Rusti asked.

"Hell if I know. I'm just barely sure which way's up." Payne asked a change-lady near the slots. She pointed and they were off again, winding their way through the crap tables and slot machines.

The limo was waiting. Payne waved at his own reflection in the tinted window. The electric window slid down, revealing the driver. "McCarty?"

"That's us," Payne answered.

The driver sprang from the car and high stepped it around the back to open the door for them. "You folks already have your license?"

"No. Didn't figure ya needed one in Nevada. Ever thing else seems to be legal around here."

"Most things are, but getting married without a license isn't one of them. I'll have to take you to City Hall, first."

Payne held Rusti's hand. "Nervous?"

"Not yet. How about you?"

"I'm ready, Mrs. McCarty."

"I like the sound of that." She kissed him. The driver smiled at them in the mirror. He was in his late twenties, friendly, and handsome. Dressed in his chauffeur's uniform, he looked like an out of work actor.

The limo stopped in front of City Hall. Turning around, their driver handed them a business card. "Call this number when you get your license receipt."

"You're not gonna wait?"

"No sir. It might take awhile on Saturday morning." He left the car and opened the door for them. "Through there and down the stairs." He pointed at the double glass doors. "Can't miss it. We'll be expecting your call."

Payne led Rusti through the door. The line was backed up half way up the stairs. The *Marriage Permits* sign was barely visible in the distance.

Payne removed his hat and ran his fingers through his hair. "Well, shit. Who said there wasn't a waitin period in Nevada? We're gonna be here all day."

"Got something more important to do?"

"Not a thing." Payne winked at her.

The striking pair looked out of place in the crowd of misfits and mismatched couples. Rusti whispered in his ear, "Is the circus in town or what?"

"Yeah. That and the stork. I bet half the girls in here are six months pregnant."

"Not me."

"That's a relief." Payne patted her tummy. "Let's give that a little time. We're still just gettin to know each other. Sides that, we already got more than we can handle with that little puppy."

"I wonder how many of these people have known each other less than a month?" Rusti asked, as the line moved two steps.

"I bet we got most of em on that one."

Rusti removed her sunglasses and stuck them on top of her head. "Well, I don't see many country music fans. I think it's safe."

"Yeah. This would be about the last place in the world most people would be lookin to find Rusti King."

"Shh ... not so loud."
"Hey, ya ever played Vegas?"
"Not yet."
"Ya oughta get ol Dennis on that trail. I wouldn't mind comin back here with a little time to burn."
"Speaking of Dennis, he's sure going to be surprised."
"Bet on that." Payne grinned and pulled out his timepiece. "Ten thirty."
"Where'd you get that watch?"
"My grandfather gave it to me at my dad's funeral. He was an old rancher. Had a place near San Saba. Both my granddad and grandma died within a month of each other. Couple years ago. They always swore they'd go together. Almost made it, too."
Rusti held it. "I've wondered where the cowboy in you came from. That's really special."
"Remember in Ft. Worth, your mom said it sounded to her like we needed to do a little more talkin?"
"Yeah."
Payne closed his watch and stuck it in his pocket. "Well, I figure by the time we get outta here, we're gonna both know a whole lot more about each other."

*

Rusti studied the license receipt in her hand while Payne called the number on the card. It was just after twelve-thirty. "They're on the way."
The bright sunshine and hot sidewalk greeted them. Payne looked around for a place to sit in the shade. "Well, they don't have any problems with woodpeckers around here," he said, as they took a seat on a hot bench. "Need my hat?"
"No. I think that's our ride."
"That was fast."
The Little White Chapel was trimmed in blue. Payne and Rusti walked down the short sidewalk, lined with yellow roses. Entering the chapel, they showed their license receipt to an aging woman, who appeared to be withering away along with her faded blue bridesmaid dress. She promptly handed them more forms to be completed.
They sat in the metal folding chairs that lined the foyer and did the paper work. Payne finally handed the clipboards back to her. She looked Rusti up and down and glanced back at the name. "For real?"

"For real." Rusti smiled at her. "We're trying to keep this quiet. Okay?"
"Fine by me. Would you like to look at our options for wedding pictures?"
"I don't know. I don't think so," Rusti answered for them.
"Yeah, we'll take a couple of pictures." Payne shrugged his shoulders.
"You can choose from the wedding bouquets."
"No thanks."
"She'll take the blue one." Payne smiled at Rusti.
"Your charges will be one hundred and eighty-two dollars."
Payne pulled out his money and counted it off to her. He took Rusti's hand. "All set?"
"Not so fast." The lady held her hand out, blocking the door. "There's approximately an hour wait."
"I don't see anybody but them," Payne argued, peeking into the chapel.
"They're all in the bar. It's just through that door. We'll call you over the intercom when we're ready for you."
"I guess I could use a beer."
"This is amazing," Rusti said, sliding on to the barstool.
"Two Buds," Payne ordered.
The lady behind the bar studied Rusti. "You sure look familiar. Have you been in here before?"
"No. First time."
She leaned in closer. "Believe it or not, we've got regulars. Sometimes people come back for an anniversary. I got one guy who's been married here five times."
Payne took a drink and looked at the clock on the wall. "Hard to believe."
"Where you guys from?"
"Texas," Payne answered.
"You sure look familiar," she said, but was called to the other end of the bar.
Payne took Rusti's hand. "You were sayin? What's amazin?"
"All this hassle. Getting married has suddenly become a real challenge."
"Few things good ever come easy."
"We came easy." Rusti snapped her fingers. "Just like that."

*

Four Budweisers later "McCarty and King" was announced over the intercom. "That's where I've seen you!" The bartender screamed. "You're Rusti King!"

"Time to go." Payne laid a twenty on the bar and waved to her.
The old lady in blue escorted them down the aisle. The small white chapel was filled with beautifully arranged artificial flowers. The minister was oriental, almost as tall as Skeeter. She quickly administered the vows through thick glasses and a thick accent, from memory. She politely waited until Payne had kissed his bride to ask for Rusti's autograph.

CHAPTER FORTY-FOUR

Unaware of the fire, Red drove his shiny black Corvette to Fredericksburg late Saturday morning. Just after noon, he routinely met with his jockeys at the track to discuss the day's winners and losers. Skeeter listened for any hint of agitation in Red's voice as the bookie went through each race. But he was business as usual.

Deputy William Sommers greeted Red in the stands before the races.
"Hey, hear about the fire east of Gruene last night?"
"No."
"Just off 306. Some old trailer was burned to the ground."
"Big deal."
"Yeah, well they found two kilos of cocaine at the scene."
"Really?" Red looked off and re-adjusted his wide brim straw hat. "Where bouts they find it?"
"In an old pickup, parked out front of the trailer. DEA was called in. Heard they're estimatin the street value at close to two hundred grand. Big news for Comel County."
"I'd say so." Red tried not to panic. "Whose was it?"
"Nobody knows. Not yet, anyway. It was arson though. The gas can was still inside the trailer."
"That is big news. Hey, I left somethin in the car. Be right back."

Red's head was spinning as he sat in the leather seat of his Corvette. He closed his eyes, trying to think. There was nothing to link him to the trailer. He had made sure of that. At least there wasn't, as far as the cops were concerned. The only possible connection between him and the trailer was the person, or persons, who had discovered his stash. *Musta been followed* he thought. Red took a deep breath. *Who found it?* He fired up a cigarette. *Do they know who it belongs to? Will they tell the DEA? Why didn't they take the coke along with the fifty grand? A set up? Blackmail?* The only question that didn't cross his mind was *why*. It was a payback.

Walking back to the stands, Red mentally reviewed his list of enemies. *It could be anybody* he thought. Between his drug business and running a crooked track, he realized he was going to need pen and paper to compile the list. He didn't think of Skeeter until after the first race. But the jockey was definitely a possibility.

Skeeter acted surprised when he heard the news about the fire and the mysterious cocaine. By the end of the day, rumors were flying everywhere, especially in the jockey shack. Just the thought of that much cocaine had caused the jockeys's little noses to start running. News of the DEA's involvement had forced Skeeter to hide a smile. He now had another card to play.

*

While Lisa finished packing the apartment on Sunday, Skeeter drove to New Braunfels. He searched the houses in the ritzy neighborhood overlooking Landa Park for 1005 Peach Tree. Just as he expected, Ragina's red Porsche was parked in the driveway of Billy Gotzen's white brick home.

Skeeter picked up Billy's Sunday paper and walked through the decorative iron gates while surveying a variety of plants growing in the professionally landscaped courtyard. He took a deep breath, inhaling the fresh scent of roses that lingered on the thick morning air, and rang the doorbell. He rang it repeatedly, until the sleepy attorney opened the door dressed in his robe.

"Skeeter?"

"Hey, Billy. I didn't get y'all up did I?"

"Yeah." Billy yawned. "What's the problem?"

"I need to talk to Ragina about Dial Sammy."

Billy opened the door. "Come on in. I'll get her."

Skeeter looked around the plush living room and took a seat in the large, over-stuffed leather recliner. Removing the rubber band, he opened the newspaper. *$200,000 of Cocaine Seized Locally* read the headlines.

Ragina, dressed in a long black silk robe, stopped short and laughed at the sight of little Skeeter in the big recliner, reading Billy's paper. "I could get used to this," Skeeter said, looking over the paper. "Billy," he winked at her, "would ya be so kind as to make us all some coffee?"

Ragina laughed. "Billy, that would be nice."

"Sure thing."

"What's wrong with Dial Sammy?" Ragina asked.

"Didn't say anything was wrong with him. I said I needed to visit with ya about him." Skeeter laid the paper on the coffee table, making sure the headlines were visible. "We're gonna run him tomorrow at Fredericksburg, right?"

"Hadn't we planned on it?"

"Yeah. Just makin sure. I've looked at the field in his race. There ain't a horse there that can touch him. This would be a good time to get your money back from Red. I'd bet big."

"How big?"

"Whatever ya want. I'll personally guarantee you'll win."

"Haven't I heard that before?"

"Yeah, and ya won, too."

"I lost ten grand in Seguin. Remember?"

"Did I tell ya to bet in Seguin?"

"No."

"Well, there ya go. Now I'm tellin ya to bet. Remember I told ya he would win in Fredericksburg. Tomorrow is the day to bet."

Billy returned from the kitchen and sat next to Ragina on the couch. He adjusted his robe before bending over to pick up the paper. "Whoa, two hundred thousand dollars worth of cocaine. Here?" He plopped on the couch. "That's big time."

"Probably Red's," Skeeter said.

"The bookie?" Billy looked at Skeeter.

"Hell, ever body knows Red runs the drugs around here."

"I didn't know it. I bet the DEA doesn't know it either."

"Well, shut my mouth." Skeeter slapped his hand over his mouth.

"You're serious?" Billy leaned forward and set the paper down.

"Ya didn't hear it from me." Skeeter reached down and released the handle on the recliner. "This is nice," he said, from a reclining position. "I need to get me one of these. How much did this run ya?"

"Look, I've got friends at the DEA." Billy ignored Skeeter's question and began pressing for more information about the drugs. "I used to work closely with the DEA when I was in the District Attorney's office in Austin."

"No shit?" Skeeter popped the lever again and sat up.

"Skeeter, he told you that," Ragina said. "Remember, at your wedding, when we were all sitting at the table ... "

Billy interrupted her. "What else do you know about this?"

"I'd best not say anything else. I forgot ya was connected to the law. Red's already had me beat up once."

"Red was the one who had you beat up?" Ragina sat forward. Her robe separated, flashing most of a Double-D in Skeeter's direction. "He's the one who did that to you? Why?"

"I was tryin to help your daddy," Skeeter answered her question, but his eyes were riveted to her exposed breast. Ragina followed his gaze and adjusted her robe. "Jerry didn't want nobody to know how fast Dial Sammy was. I was

257

gonna ride him and lose in a few races, then Jerry was gonna bet big and clean up. Red saw me dead wrap him durin that first time-trial and figured we was up to somethin."

"What's dead wrap?" she asked.

"Crossin the reigns above a horse's neck to slow em down."

"How did you come to your conclusion it was Red who had you assaulted?" The old District Attorney was coming out in Billy.

"That was the last thing I heard. The guy who hit me said, 'this is a little message from Red. Remember who ya work for.' The next thing I know, I'm wakin up in the damn hospital. Almost killed me."

"How do you work for Red?" Billy continued his interrogation.

"Is the coffee ready yet?" Skeeter asked.

"I'll get it," Ragina volunteered.

"Red runs the tracks." Skeeter scooted forward with his size seven boots still two inches above the carpet. "He tells the jockeys which horses are to win and which ones are to lose. That's the way he makes his money. We don't mess with Red. He used me for an example."

"This is amazing."

Ragina came back and sat the steaming cups of coffee on the table. "What if Red tells you to pull Dial Sammy tomorrow?" she asked, checking her robe.

"I figure he will. But I'm gonna let that horse run. It's my last race around here. We're packed. If he wants a piece-of-my-ass he'll have to go all the way to Kentucky to get it. I'd like to see ya get your money back. That's why I'm here."

"That's sweet."

"I'd also like to see him get burned. It'd be kinda a payback from me before I go."

"I'll make the bet," Ragina said. "I'd love to help." She nodded to Billy. "Wouldn't we?"

Billy nodded. "Definitely."

"Great." Skeeter took a sip of coffee and set it down. "Hey, thanks for the coffee. I guess I'd better get goin."

"Hang on a minute," Billy ordered. "Tell me more about the drugs."

"Ya tryin to get me killed before I get outta town? No, thanks."

"Skeeter, wait!" Billy stuck his hand out like a traffic cop. "This wouldn't have to go any further than you and me. I'll leave your name completely out of all this. I'll just give an anonymous lead to my friend at the DEA."

Skeeter took his coffee off the table and took another noisy sip. "All I know is what I've heard. I ain't actually seen nothin." He took three more loud sips before continuing. "I hear Red runs the drugs between Austin and San

Antonio. Mostly coke. He's gotta bunch of goons workin for him. He gets his stuff from a place out in the country between San Marcus and Austin, near Driftwood. It's guarded like Fort Knox. Dogs, razor-wire, guns, and shit like that. I bet your DEA buddy already knows all about that place. Look, I gotta go." He put his coffee back down. "Just leave me outta this."

"I give you my word, as an attorney."

"No, thanks. Just your word. No attorney shit. I'm allergic."

Billy shoved off the couch. "You have my word."

Skeeter crawled out of the recliner and shook Billy's hand. "Ragina, it's been real nice knowin ya. If ya ever get up to the Kentucky Derby, look us up."

"I will." Ragina bent over and hugged him. "I'm going to miss you. You've been an absolute delight in my life." Straightening up, she asked, "Is Payne still going to Nashville?"

"Yeah. Goin with Rusti."

"I still can't believe that. I told him she'd break his heart."

"I doubt it." Skeeter grinned at her. "They got married yesterday in Vegas."

"Shit!"

"Billy, thanks for the coffee. Hey, don't do nothin about Red until Ragina gets her money back, and I'm way the hell outta town. I mean, *way* the hell outta town."

*

Red showed up for the Sunday races with a beer-buzz and a nose full of cocaine. Twice, the bookie eyed Skeeter during the pre-race meeting. Skeeter's heart was racing, but he blankly returned Red's stare, without so much as a flinch. Otherwise, the day at the track proved to be pleasantly uneventful.

Skeeter pulled his pickup in next to the U-Haul. Payne was leaning against it, soaked with sweat, nursing a Bud. "You're all loaded."

"Damn, Payne. What would I do without ya?"

"I reckon you're fixin to find out. That was my very last good deed."

"Hell, I'll think of somethin before we get to Nashville."

"No doubt."

"Hey, let's get some steaks and cook out at the ranch house tonight." Skeeter slapped Payne on his lower back. "I'm buyin."

"Damn, Skeeter, watch the ribs, would ya?"

Spotting Skeeter, Lisa bolted from the apartment. She hugged him. "Everything okay at the track?"

NASHVILLE GOLD

"Couldn't be better." Skeeter looked over Lisa's shoulder at Rusti. "Well, if it ain't my favorite female country music star and her little dog, Puddles."

CHAPTER FORTY-FIVE

Blue skies greeted the Fourth of July. The four improbable friends were up early. Within minutes, the last of Payne's things were loaded into the back of Skeeter's U-Haul.

"Time to piss on the fire and call in the dogs," Skeeter said, the screen door slamming behind him. "Payne, ya gonna miss this place?"

"Nope."

"Yeah. Me, too."

Skeeter drove the U-Haul with the Pinto in tow. Lisa followed in Skeeter's truck. Rusti held Nash and rode with Payne in the Jeep, trailing the Doeppenschmidts. The caravan wound through the Hill Country to Blanco, where they stashed the U-Haul and Pinto.

By nine-thirty, the Jeep and pickup rolled into Luckenbach and were each tagged with security parking permits. The four walked along the rows of trucks and tour buses until Payne spotted Rusti's bus.

Rusti introduced Skeeter and Lisa to Dennis, then Randall. Payne draped his arm around Rusti's shoulder while she dropped the bomb on Dennis. "Payne and I got married Saturday."

Dennis was dazed. The over-weight manager shook his head back and forth in denial, before slumping to the couch. "Rusti, you can't get married!"

"That's not what they said in Las Vegas."

"You flew to Las Vegas and got married? Am I saying that right? It doesn't sound right." He continued shaking his head. "It can't be right."

"Ya got wax in your ears, or what?" Skeeter asked.

Dennis glared at Rusti. "Did your little friend just say something to me?"

Skeeter raised his voice. "I said, do ya have wax in your damn ears? Maybe ya can read sign language." Skeeter flipped him the finger.

Dennis made a move off the couch toward Skeeter, but Payne stepped between them. "Just calm down. Both of ya."

"I can't believe you've done this!" Dennis said, facing Rusti. "I don't guess you bothered having him sign a prenuptial agreement?"

"Just shut the hell up!" Rusti yelled at Dennis. "I don't need a prenuptial any damn thing with Payne. Of all people, you ought to know that!"

Dennis sat back on the couch and rubbed his temples. "I give up."

"Not before you apologize to him," Rusti demanded.

"Forget it, babe. I don't need an apology." Payne spoke through clinched teeth. "Dennis, this is the last time I'm gonna say this. The very next time ya yell at either one of us, I'm gonna kick your ass into next week." Then he raised his voice. "Did ya hear that?"

"If y'all will excuse me. I need to get off this bus."

"I hear that!" Skeeter yelled.

Randall contained his grin long enough to hit the door button. Dennis turned back at the door. "Rusti, we'll talk about this later."

"No, we won't."

Randall closed the door behind him. "Congratulations, you two."

*

Nova was wrong. Willie was awake and did give a shit what time the opening act took the stage. He was dressed in jeans and a sleeveless red, white, and blue shirt. His long red hair was pulled into a ponytail and fell from beneath the matching American flag bandana. Willie Nelson was already back stage by the time the remains of Nova-Scotia arrived.

Rusti walked along side Payne, followed by Randall and her two band members. She was dressed in a short, white leather skirt and white boots. Her shiny gold blouse sparkled beneath the sunny July morning. Most of her red hair was tucked beneath her white leather cowboy hat. She further hid her identity behind gaudy, white rimmed sunglasses. "Ya look damn good for a backup singer," Payne joked as they approached backstage.

Jimmy Earl waved them over. "Payne, where's Nova?"

"She's in the hospital with two broken legs," Hartman spoke up.

"Yeah. She traded two deer for an oak tree on the Devil's Backbone last Sunday, but we're still playin'," Payne explained. "Rusti's gonna help us out. This is Bobby Davis, her keyboard player, and this is Russell Williams, her guitarist."

Jimmy Earl shook Rusti's hand. "Good to see ya again. Gentlemen, my pleasure," he said, shaking hands with her band members. "This is Eric Jacobsen, Willie's production manager."

Payne stuck his hand out. "Payne McCarty. It's a pleasure to meet ya. This is my wife, Rusti King."

"You're married to Rusti King?" Eric shook Payne's hand and looked again at the backup singer.

Rusti removed her sunglasses. "Nice to meet you. Tell Willie I said thanks for the invitation."

Eric shook her hand. "It is you. The pleasure's all mine."

"We're going to help them out a little," Rusti said. "Don't worry about a thing. We've got it under control."

"I'm sure you do." Eric spoke to Jimmy Earl. "Well, I'm not sure what the hell's going on here, but I think I like it." He eyed the group. "I'm going to say good morning to the crowd to get things started, then I'll introduce y'all. But somebody here needs to tell me who I'm introducing."

"Singer-songwriter, Payne McCarty," Rusti said. She put her sunglasses back on and leaned into Eric's ear. "Payne's going to introduce me before the last song," she whispered. "If you see Willie around, ask him to come on up and give us a hand with it."

Eric nodded. "He's already here. I'll be sure to tell him."

"Payne, are ya gonna do that song with the line about Willie in it?" Jimmy Earl asked.

"First song."

Jimmy Earl nudged Eric. "That's the one I was tellin ya about. You're gonna love this."

Eric whistled and waved at the stage crew. "Get their stuff up there. Let's get this thing rolling!"

Two towering stacks of speakers, separated by the newly constructed raised stage, crackled with static at straight up eleven o'clock. Off stage, Jimmy Earl took a microphone. "Ladies and gentlemen, welcome to Luckenbach! Please put your hands together for the man in charge, Willie Nelson's production manager, Eric Jacobsen."

Looking over the cheering throng of fans, Eric shaded his eyes with one hand and took the microphone in the other. There were already fifty thousand people in front of the stage with a steady stream of fans continuing to file into the cow pasture. He waited for the rowdy crowd to settle down. "Good morning, Luckenbach!" The crowd roared back. "Happy birthday, America! And welcome to Willie's little picnic ... "

Payne was nervous. His eyes met Rusti's.

"You're going to do great, babe," she encouraged him. Reaching over, she unsnapped the top two snaps on his western shirt. "There. That's better."

Eric continued, "Please help me welcome to the stage, singer and songwriter, Payne McCarty!"

Walking on stage to a lukewarm round of applause, Payne strapped on his Les Paul Gibson electric guitar. He looked behind him. Skeeter gave him the thumbs up and Rusti blew him a kiss. Raising his drumsticks in the air, Skeeter clicked off *Crankin Up The Country*.

Dennis joined Eric and Jimmy Earl backstage. "When did they get married?" Jimmy Earl asked.

"Over the weekend in Vegas. She's totally out of control."

"Totally in love," Jimmy Earl said, and slapped Dennis on the shoulder.

"Hey, Eric, listen up. Here it comes." Jimmy Earl pointed to the stage in time to catch Payne's lyric ... *ya won't catch Willie wearin no glove* ...

Eric grinned. "I like that kid."

The crowd roared at the end of the song. "Thank y'all!" Payne yelled over the noise. The pre-show jitters had disappeared. "Thank y'all!" He winked at Rusti and nodded to her two band members. They were pros. "Nova-Scotia" had never sounded better.

Performing before the pasture of people, Payne played and sang each song with a passion. The spirited crowd responded enthusiastically to the new talent, roaring with appreciation. "We've gotta little rocker for ya," Payne yelled, before ending his solo portion of the set. "This is a little tune I call *Follow Your Dream*."

Rusti's guitar player began by soloing the slow intro of the song on his acoustic guitar. Payne joined on the ninth measure, taking off on his electric guitar with a fury. He sang his song with a soul full of emotion. Then, as the upbeat song came to an end, the acoustic guitar again soulfully played the last few measures. Jumping high in the air, Payne struck the last chord on his Les Paul Gibson. Timed perfectly, he landed with the band's final note. Payne took a bow on stage. On their feet, the cheering Fourth of July partygoers filled the peaceful hills of Luckenbach with a thunderous ovation.

Payne waved his hat in the air. "Thank Y'all!" he screamed into the microphone. He waited until the crowd had calmed down to speak. "I've gotta little surprise for ya." Payne motioned to Rusti. "I think ya might recognize our backup singer." Rusti pulled off her sunglasses and hat, letting her long red hair fall. She fluffed it as she approached stage front. Payne bowed to her then yelled into the microphone. "Folks, please say howdy to ... Rusti King!"

The roar was deafening. Rusti waved her hat over her head. The keyboard player took off in the gettie-up beat of Pari-mutuel Blues, playing the first four measures over and over till the crowd settled down. Skeeter shouted out the count the fifth time around and the band took off.

During the third verse, the music was drowned out by the screaming multitude of Willie Nelson fans. Payne was puzzled until he spotted Willie approaching the microphone. The legend joined them with his old beat up Martin guitar and classic vocals just in time for the final chorus.

It's got us singing, got us singing,
Got us singing those Pari-mutuel Blues ...
It's got us singing, got us singing,
Got us singing those Pari-mutuel Blues ...
Pari-mutuel Blues,
Pari-mutuel Blues,
Pari-mutuel Blues ...

The cheering crowd was on their feet. Backstage, Jimmy Earl grabbed the stage microphone. "Let's hear it for Willie Nelson! - Payne McCarty! - and his new bride, Rusti King!" Rusti threw her arms around Payne and kissed him. Their wedding announcement was postmarked ...
Luckenbach, Texas. July 4, 1985.

*

"I've gotta get to the race track." Skeeter was the first to break up the celebration in Rusti's bus. "Y'all gonna come watch?"
"Wouldn't miss it for the world," Payne answered.
"I'd like to go," Randall spoke up in his deep voice. "I'd like to see him race."
"See me win," Skeeter corrected the big man and winked at Lisa.
"I need to get back to the hospital," Hartman said, and extended his hand to Payne. "Thank ya. Today was ... well, I'll never forget it." Hartman lowered his head and mumbled, "It's been pleasure playin with ya."
Payne embraced him. "I got somethin here for Nova. Hang on." Payne pulled out the guitar, still in the case, and handed it to him. "Don't ya give this to her till she gets outta the hospital. She's liable to hit one of those nurses up side the head with it."
The group erupted with laughter. Then Payne turned serious. "Hartman, ya take care of yourself. And Nova."
Skeeter raised his beer in the air. "Here's to Nova-Scotia."

CHAPTER FORTY-SIX

Skeeter arrived late to the pre-race meeting. Red glared at him and glanced at his watch, wondering if the weekend would ever end. Saturday and Sunday had been less than stellar days for him at the track. He was running thin on cash. The banks were closed for the holiday weekend and his reserve had been stolen. He rarely indulged in cocaine, but this weekend had been different. Red had been up on the drug since Saturday. His eyes were red, his nose was raw, and the pressure in his head was on the verge of erupting. "You're late!"

"Yep," Skeeter said, taking his seat. "Sorry."

Red slapped the palm of his hand with his racing program. "We're on the second race. There's nothin special for ya in the first race."

"Got it."

"Is tits comin today?"

"Who?"

"Jerry's daughter." Red stuck his hands out in front of his chest. "Ya know, big tits."

"Last I heard she was."

"Fifth race. Pull her horse. Understand?"

"Got it."

Red stared at Skeeter. "Ya better have it."

"I said, I got it. Anything else?" Skeeter asked, returning his stare.

"I'll be lettin ya know if there's anything else." Red again slapped the program on the palm of his hand. He shook it at Skeeter before going on to the next race.

Red concluded the meeting by repeatedly slapping the rolled up racing form on his hand. "Questions?" One by one, he searched the eyes of his jockeys.

There were no questions.

Red stopped at his car long enough for another four lines of nose candy before heading to the stands. Leaning against the railing, Red's world was spinning out of control. His eyes were blurring. His heart was racing. He held onto the railing with sweaty hands and lowered his head.

"Ya feelin alright?" Deputy Sommers asked.

*

Marcus McDermott looked and dressed like an aging cowboy, not a DEA agent. Beneath his cowboy hat, his face was hard, leathered, like the vest he wore. But all eyes were on Ragina's cleavage, not the vest that hid his shoulder holster and revolver. He walked unnoticed behind the couple into the stands and took his seat by the aisle, next to Billy. They were eight rows up, directly above Red. Billy whispered to Agent McDermott, "That's him, leaning against the rail."

"I hope your source is reliable. We've been looking for a way into that compound at Driftwood for a year."

"He's reliable. There's no way he could have made all that up." Billy put his arm around Ragina. "Still feel confident enough to bet all that money?"

"Skeeter promised he'd win. I trust him." Ragina laughed. "I think."

"Me, too. I think."

"Well, well, look who's here," Ragina said.

Payne and Rusti walked up the ramp, followed by Randall. They paused while Payne eyed the stands for a good seat. "It's hot as the Fourth of July," Randall joked.

"That's real cute," Rusti said, and took Payne's hand. Dressed in jeans and a turquoise western shirt, she hid her identity beneath her Stetson straw hat and sunglasses. Payne tipped his hat to Ragina and Billy as they climbed the stairs. But he didn't bother speaking, and never broke his stride.

Ragina acknowledged them with a nod. She whispered in Billy's ear, "Did you see the size of those diamonds on their fingers?"

"No. I was looking at you."

"Good answer." She sighed and pulled his arm to her.

Randall acted like a kid at his first County Fair. He studied the racing program and all of the horses before surrendering his fifty bucks per race to Red. He was down two hundred going into Skeeter's race.

"Here's your chance to make some money," Payne told Randall. He handed him a thousand in hundreds. "Mind takin my bet, too?"

Rusti raised her eyebrows at Payne. "You're gambling on a horse race?"

"This ain't gamblin," Payne answered. He watched Randall pull out his own wad of hundreds before heading down the bleachers.

Ragina dug in her purse, beneath her daddy's pistol, for her roll of money. Descending the stairs, she stood in line, in front of Randall to place her bet.

"Do you think they'll really chase Skeeter?" Rusti asked.

"They can chase him all they want. Catchin him is gonna be a whole different deal." Payne rubbed Rusti's leg. He took off his hat and bent beneath her hat to give her a quick kiss. "I sure love ya."

"I love you, too." Rusti kissed him back. "This has been fun, but I'm ready to get back to Nashville. We could use a little rest and relaxation."

Payne replaced his hat and put his arm around her. "Darlin, we're almost home."

Randall watched when Ragina stepped up to hand Red her roll of money. "Twenty thousand on Dial Sammy."

Randall coughed.

"Girl, have mercy." Red eyed her cleavage. "That's a lotta money."

"The less you bet, the more you lose when you win."

Red laughed and wrote her bet down. "Gettin more like ya ol daddy ever day. Good luck." He handed the large wad of money to the Deputy, who counted it.

"Randall. Twenty-two hundred on number *eight*," he said, stepping up.

The bookie took the big man's money and marked number "8" on the program. "Randall, twenty-two hundred on number *eight*." Red confirmed the bet. "Y'all know somethin I don't about that horse?"

"Just betting on the jockey."

Post time was three o'clock. Dial Sammy, snorting and prancing, was the last horse led into the starting gate. Gate eight. The bell rang and the horses broke to the track. On the outside, Dial Sammy was easy to spot. Skeeter didn't take a chance on getting boxed in. Instead, he gave the black horse his reigns and let him run. Skeeter glanced over his left shoulder just before the turn, then began moving inside, toward the rail. He took the early lead entering the turn.

Through bleary, bloodshot eyes, Red watched the *eight* horse begin to pull away from the field at the top of the homestretch. Randall was yelling, jumping up and down with his fists in the air, as Dial Sammy extended his lead, headed for the wire. He bolted down the stairs to collect his money before Skeeter even crossed the finish line.

Three days of pressure exploded in Red's head. Leaning over the rail, he screamed at Skeeter over the sound of thundering hooves. "You're a dead man! Your ass is mine!" Red waved his hat in the air and pointed at Skeeter. Having gotten the attention of his goons across the track, he made throat-slashing gestures with one hand and pointed at Skeeter with his other.

Red tried to push past Randall on his way after Skeeter, but the big man didn't budge. "Going somewhere, asshole?" Randall took a firm grip on Red's arm. "You owe me forty-four hundred bucks."

Red jerked his arm free. Without a word, he peeled off the bills and slapped them down in Randall's big hand. "There!"

Out of the corner of his eye, Red saw Ragina and Billy reach the bottom of the stairs. He again tried to step around Randall. "I don't think so," Randall said. He shoved Red backwards. "Time to pay up."

Stumbling backwards, Red fell into the deputy. While his cohort was helping him regain his balance, Red pulled the gun out of Deputy Sommers' holster and pointed it at Randall. "Back off!"

"Red? What the hell are ya doin?" Sommers stood helpless as Randall put his hands in the air. Randall stepped back against the rail, giving Red plenty of room.

Skeeter hadn't bothered riding Dial Sammy back to the winner's circle for a picture. Instead, he galloped the horse toward the turn, away from the stands. Red stepped past Randall and fired the first of three shots at the runaway jockey.

Skeeter heard the first shot and the bullet whistle over his head. He looked back in time to see the flash of the second shot. Crouching on top of Dial Sammy, he slapped the riding crop across horse's rear. Dial Sammy responded, accelerating from gallop to race speed before the crop had a chance to land again.

Missing with the first two shots, Red took aim before firing the third shot. But it fell harmlessly short, landing in the soft dirt of the racetrack, behind Dial Sammy. Safely out of range, Skeeter looked back and waved good-bye to the crowd with his pink hat, but nobody was watching. With the sounds of shots fired, panic had filled the crowded bleachers. The hysterical fans were screaming and diving for cover. Marcus McDermott pulled his .45 automatic out of his shoulder hostler. "Freeze!" he yelled at Red.

Ragina, who had been crouching by the railing, was busy fumbling through her purse for her gun. Her finger was on the trigger when the gun hung on her hairbrush. She tried to jerk it loose. The .38 fired. Exiting her Paloma Picasso purse, the bullet splintered the bleachers in front of Red's expensive boots.

Red aimed at Ragina. Agent McDermott fired. The bullet shattered Red's right shoulder. He spun backwards in front of Randall, dropping the Deputy's gun. Bouncing off the railing, he slumped to his knees. Randall kicked the gun away.

Ragina was hysterical. "Oh my God! Oh my God! I shot the son-of-a-bitch! I shot him! Oh my God!" Agent Dermott bolted from the bleachers to the railing. Deputy Sommers retrieved his gun and stood over his friend. "Red, are ya outta your damn mind? What the hell ... "

"DEA!" McDermott flashed his badge. "His ass is all mine."

"Marcus shot him! Marcus shot him, not you!" Billy kept repeating to Ragina. He shook her with both hands, trying to calm her down. His words finally registered and her hysterics turned to rage.

Ragina charged Deputy Sommers. "Give me my damn money!" she demanded. She struck a pose with one hand on her hip and held her other hand out, like a teacher taking gum away from a first grader.

Skeeter had a lifetime of practice running away from tormentors. Sliding off Dial Sammy on the backstretch of the track, he crawled under the track railing and took a beeline toward the exit. Lisa saw him coming. She opened his pickup door and had the motor running before sliding over to the passenger seat.

Red's two goons took an angle toward the exit gate, trying to cut him off. The race was on. The goons ran in boots, trying to hold on to their cowboy hats. All three approached the small gate at full speed. Taking their chance, the two goons left their feet near the gate and dove through the air in an attempt to tackle the agile jockey. But Skeeter had seen it coming. Braking, his riding boots slid through the loose dirt. The two assailants sailed by in front of him. Skeeter dashed to the pickup.

Lisa was screaming at the top of her lungs when Skeeter jumped in the pickup and slid behind the wheel. Yelling, "Yea-ha," he stomped the gas and grinned at Lisa. "Goin my way, good-lookin?"

Payne had watched Skeeter's successful exit, but had also seen the two goons take off after him in a blue Ford pickup. He rushed Rusti down the steps and waved at Randall to follow.

Randall caught up to Payne and Rusti as they jogged through the parking lot. "Tough crowd," Randall said.

Skeeter raced the pickup through the back streets of Fredericksburg to the main highway, then pressed the gas pedal to the floor with his small riding boot. Lisa's nose was glued to the rear window. She spotted the blue pickup when Skeeter slowed on the highway to turn on the narrow winding Ranch Road, leading to Luckenbach. The blue truck turned after them, appearing briefly behind them on hilltops, then dropping out of sight. Distance was difficult to judge, but the blue Ford was gaining ground during the short race to Luckenbach.

Traffic slowed near the picnic to an agonizing crawl. Parked cars, and pickups lined the narrow ranch road. Late arrivals, carrying ice chests and folding chairs, littered the countryside. Skeeter was almost to the restricted parking entrance when Lisa saw the pickup top the last hill. "Here they come!" she screamed.

Skeeter turned in and flashed his permit to the two attendants. The barricade was raised. Skeeter stomped the gas, covering the two security guards in a cloud of dust.

The wooden barricade was lowered. The goons turned in after Skeeter. They laid on the horn before crashing through the white barricade, narrowly missing the two attendants. Central security was alerted by radio.

Skeeter slid the pickup to a stop by Rusti's bus. They left the truck on foot, running hand in hand in front of row after row of trucks and busses, toward backstage. Red's two goons sped past Skeeter's truck. With the small targets in their sights, they accelerated.

Looking over his shoulder, Skeeter saw them closing. He shoved Lisa to the right, between two busses and broke left. The truck followed Skeeter, bearing down, but the quick little jockey dove left at the last second. The pickup, narrowly missing Skeeter, skidded to a stop. Skeeter started to run, but stopped when he saw a small army of yellow vested security officers descending on the blue pickup.

"Hey! Did y'all see that?" Skeeter yelled. "Those son-of-a-bitches tried to run us down!" Lisa jumped into his arms, nearly knocking him over. Skeeter pried her off. He continued to shout in the direction of the seized pickup while dusting off his white jockey silks. "What the hell's wrong with you people? Can I press charges?"

Skeeter was still taunting them when the Jeep pulled up. Rusti shook her head at Payne's little buddy. "Honey, I'm afraid life in Tennessee isn't going to be this exciting."

"Hell, I sure hope not."

*

Rusti King concluded her performance at Willie's Picnic, and three months of touring, by singing *When Love Turns Out The Light*. But unlike the dramatic endings seen in the indoor concerts, the lights didn't go out at Luckenbach. The sun was beginning to set, but the persistent heat refused to relinquish its grip on Independence Day.

Exhausted, Rusti held on to Payne as they walked to the bus. Lying on the couch, she managed a smile when Payne handed her a Budweiser and a damp wash cloth. He sat next to her, petting her leg with one hand and the pup with the other. "Ya okay?"

"Just a little tired," she said, without opening her eyes.

NASHVILLE GOLD

Skeeter and Lisa banged on the bus door. Payne hit the button and the door hissed opened. They took seats on the couch, across from Rusti, their little feet dangling off the edge. "Payne, I think we've worn her out."

Rusti nodded in agreement. "I've had about all the excitement I can handle for one weekend."

Skeeter put his arm around Lisa. "Well, guys, I hate to miss Waylon and Willie, and the grand finale and all, but we're gonna skip the rest of this little party and get on up the road to Blanco."

"Seen enough fireworks for one day?" Payne asked.

"I still can't believe that son-of-a-bitch shot at me. Hell, I know he was havin a bad day, but shit." Skeeter chuckled. "Anyway, we're gonna go on over to Austin and spend the night. Get an early start in the mornin."

"We're makin a quick stop in Ft. Worth to visit with my new in-laws, but we oughta be in Nashville by the time ya get there."

"You still have my phone number?" Rusti asked.

"Yeah. I got it." Skeeter slid to his feet. "And directions. I'll call if we get lost."

Lisa hugged Payne and squatted in front of Rusti. "You okay?"

"Yeah. Nothing a little R&R won't cure."

"Well, I wouldn't count on much of that with Payne around." Skeeter winked at Rusti and headed for the bus door.

"See y'all in Tennessee," Lisa said, and they were gone.

*

Just before midnight, the concert was concluded with Willie and Waylon's famous duet about Luckenbach, Texas. One by one, the day's performers took the stage behind them and joined in the song. Payne and Rusti held hands and sang along. Then the sky exploded with orbs of red, white, and blue.

"Quite a send-off," Rusti said, waving to the hordes of cheering fans.

"It's damn sure been a Fourth to remember," Payne added. He squeezed Rusti's hand while the final ball of fire exploded over Luckenbach.

It was well after midnight when the blue and yellow tour bus left Luckenbach and made its way out of the Texas Hill Country. Beneath the *IN TOW* sign on the back of Payne's faded red Jeep, Randall had thoughtfully added *Just Married*.

EPILOGUE

Detective Morgan had drawn duty over the Fourth of July weekend. Not that it mattered. Since his divorce, he rarely had plans. Now, the only dates he kept track of were the second and last weekend of each month. That's when he got his two boys for their visitation.

Unlike most Mondays, the Davidson County Detective Division was almost deserted. It had been a quiet day. Even the felons around Nashville had taken the day off to celebrate the Fourth of July. But the murder of Charlie Keith still weighed on Morgan's mind. With the unexpected quiet time, he studied the file again. Except for a DWI in 1979, Durwood had a clean record. Not even a parking ticket.

Morgan looked at the newspaper clipping of Rusti King and Payne McCarty. He re-read the article on the stolen song. It was a long shot, but he called records. "Nancy? They got you working today, too?"

"Always."

"Say, do me a favor. See if we've got anything on a Payne McCarty. Then get on the wire to Texas. See if anything shows up down there."

"Today? I was catching up on filing."

"I'd appreciate it."

Morgan left his desk and stretched his long frame. He walked to the windows and watched a pigeon on the windowsill before going for his fifth cup of coffee. Returning to his desk, he blew the steam off the black brew. The phone rang with his first sip. "Morgan."

"Ten days for assault."

"What?"

Nancy repeated. "McCarty spent ten days, right here in Nashville, for assault."

"When?"

"May. This year."

"Who'd he assault?"

"Victim's name was a Roger Durwood. Looks like McCarty pled guilty."

"Bingo!" Morgan slammed his hand down on the desk. "Thanks, Nancy."

*

Skeeter and Lisa parked his green Chevy pickup and the orange U-Haul truck in front of Rusti's Brentwood, Tennessee estate just after noon on Thursday. Skeeter punched the talk button on the intercom at the front gate. "Payne. Ya in there?" A buzzer sounded, releasing the lock. "Guess so."

Dressed in faded cut-offs, Payne waved to them from the front porch of the gray stone house. "Well, there goes the neighborhood," he yelled. "Glad ya finally made it."

"Hell, ya didn't have to dress up for us." Skeeter slapped him on his lower back, entering the house. Following Payne, Skeeter looked up at the elegant, winding staircase before walking into the large living room. The massive stone fireplace dominated the back wall of the room. "Damn, Payne, this is way too nice for you. I bet it even has air conditionin."

"It's beautiful," Lisa added.

Payne led them through the living room into the vast, spotless white kitchen. "Y'all wanna beer?"

"I magine," Skeeter answered. Payne opened their beers and led them out the French doors to the backyard.

"Hey, guys!" Rusti waved to them from her lounge chair by the kidney shaped pool. "How was your trip?"

"Probably not as good as yours." Skeeter's eyes followed Rusti while she walked toward them adjusting her yellow bikini. "So this is how the other half lives."

"I just love your house," Lisa said.

"It feels like home for the first time." Rusti kissed Payne on the cheek. "We're so glad you're here."

"Buddy, just keepin this back yard mowed is gonna keep your ass busy," Skeeter said, viewing the tall trees and landscaped surroundings. "There's that little dog!" Skeeter squatted to pet Nash. "House broke yet?"

"Hell, no," Payne answered, and picked up the gangly pup.

"Almost." Rusti laughed.

Payne slipped on his T-shirt. "Let's go get our stuff off the truck."

"How long can we stay?"

"As long as you want," Rusti answered.

"I'll let ya know." Payne winked at Lisa.

*

Early Friday morning, Rusti rolled over in bed to answer the phone. She shook Payne. "It's for you."

"Me? I don't know anybody here."

Rusti shrugged her shoulders and handed the receiver to him.

"Yeah?"

"Payne McCarty?"

"Yeah?"

"My name is Detective Lang, with the Davidson County Sheriff's Department, here in Nashville. We'd like to visit with you about a murder investigation involving Roger Durwood."

"Roger Durwood? Hell, I didn't kill him."

Lang laughed. "No sir. Roger Durwood is still alive."

"Too bad."

"We're investigating him, as a suspect. Would it be possible for you to come by the Department? We'd like to ask you a few questions."

"When?"

"This afternoon?"

"I guess. Where is it?"

"Downtown. We're in the same building with the County Jail. I believe you know where that is."

"I do believe I do."

"Two o'clock?"

"Yeah. I'll be there." Payne handed the phone back to Rusti. "Sheriff's Department. They wanna ask me some questions about Roger Durwood."

"About what?"

"A murder investigation. I guess he graduated from stealin to murderin."

*

Skeeter rode with Payne in the Jeep to downtown Nashville. "Damn. I think it's just as hot here as it is in Texas," Skeeter complained, walking up the steps to the Sheriff's Department.

"Think it's hot outside, ya oughta sit in that damn jail for ten days." Payne opened the door for Skeeter. "Man, I'm startin to get nervous just bein in this place again."

"I'll handle it."

The large clock behind the tall counter read 2:05 when Payne asked for Detective Lang. The overweight cop came through the swinging doors at the end of the counter before the pair from Texas could get comfortable on the creaky wooden bench. "Payne McCarty?"

Payne nodded. "That'd be me."

"Detective Lang."

"Stanley Doeppenschmidt." Skeeter introduced himself. "But just call me Skeeter."

"If you wouldn't mind, come with me."

Payne and Skeeter followed him upstairs to a long narrow room containing the Detective's Division. They took their seats in front of his cluttered wood desk that looked like all the other desks lined neatly in a row against the wall, opposite the wall with windows. "This is my partner, Detective Morgan." Morgan sat on the edge of Lang's desk and crossed his thin legs. He studied the cowboys.

"Stanley Doeppenschmidt. Just call me Skeeter. That's Payne McCarty."

"Thank you for coming," Morgan said, shaking their hands.

"We believe Roger Durwood killed a man by the name of Charlie Keith," Lang began.

"Never heard of him," Skeeter answered.

Morgan took over. "He was a songwriter, employed by Branch Publishing Company."

"Never heard of it," Skeeter answered.

Payne shot Skeeter a look. "I have. I met T.R. Branch in Texas. Heard the whole story."

"I haven't." Skeeter looked at Payne and crossed his arms.

"This Charlie guy was takin songs that Durwood got in the mail and puttin his name on em. That's what happened to my song."

"Exactly," Lang interrupted them. "Charlie Keith was found, shot twice in the head, at a deserted roadside park north of Nashville."

"Payne, I can't believe ya didn't tell me this." Skeeter chuckled. "Don't much sound like suicide."

"Could you tell us about your visit with Roger Durwood?"

"We were … "

Morgan cut Skeeter off. "Mr. McCarty, would *you* tell us, please?"

"After we heard my song on the radio, we tried to call Sure-Star Publishin to find out why I didn't get a contract or somethin on the song before it was recorded. They said they had no idea what I was talkin about."

"It was that bitch secretary of his," Skeeter added. "He never got to talk to Durwood over the phone."

Payne looked at Skeeter. "I know how to talk." He looked back at Lang. "We decided to come to Nashville and pay Mr. Durwood a personal visit."

"We is me. I came with him."

"Skeeter, just shut up a minute." Payne looked up at Morgan. "Damn. So anyway, we tracked him down. The receptionist was tryin to give us the run around. Skeeter got into it with her and Durwood came outta his office to settle things down. I swear he set us up."

"She musta called the cops as soon as we went into his office," Skeeter added.

"He stalled us around until he saw the cops come in the front door, then smarted off to me. I reached over the desk and pulled him to me by his tie. The next thing I know, I'm gettin thrown to the floor and a night stick pressed against my throat."

"Mr. Doeppen ... uh, Skeeter," Lang asked, "you weren't arrested?"

"Hell, no! When Payne yells run, the Skeeter runs."

Lang leaned back in his chair from taking notes, trying to hide his smile. "Mr. McCarty ... "

Payne interrupted him. "Look, just call me Payne."

"Okay, Payne. Did you have any more contact with Roger Durwood after you were arrested?"

"No, sir. I went back to Texas. Just got back in town this week."

Morgan spoke. "It's our understanding the problem with the royalties on your song have been straightened out between you and T.R. Branch. Is that correct?"

"That's right."

"That's all he knows," Skeeter concluded.

Morgan slid off Lang's desk and stretched. "How do you feel toward Roger Durwood? After all, he did send you to jail for ten days."

"What do ya mean?"

"Don't you still have some ill feelings towards him?"

"Sure. But I've had so many good things happen to me lately, it's been kinda hard to stay mad."

"He married Rusti King," Skeeter informed the detectives.

"We heard. Congratulations."

"Thanks."

"Payne, our investigation has hit a brick wall. We know Durwood killed Charlie Keith, but we can't prove it." Lang showed them the picture of Charlie coming out of Sure-Star Publishing. "That's Charlie Keith."

Payne studied the picture and passed it to Skeeter.

"Durwood has denied knowing you or Charlie Keith," Lang said.

277

"We know what happened," Morgan continued. "Durwood killed Keith to shut him up. But we can't put him at the murder scene. We didn't find the gun. Everything we have is purely circumstantial. We need your help."

"I don't see how I could help ya." Payne shifted in the hard wood chair.

"You're the one person that could still upset Durwood's little apple cart," Lang said, and looked to Morgan who continued.

"We'd like to put a wire on you," Morgan said. "Send you into his office. Get into it with him over the song. Tell him you want money. Tell him you're going to sue his ass. Mention Charlie Keith's name. Anything to stir it up."

Lang finished, "Try to get him pissed off. Maybe he'll say something to you we can use. It's a long shot, but we're desperate."

"We'll do it!" Skeeter said, and sprang from his chair. "I bet I can get him goin. Who gets to wear the wire?"

"Skeeter, sit down and shut the hell up," Payne ordered.

"I'll wear the wire." Skeeter nodded to the detectives. "Love to do it."

"Payne, how about you? Will you help us?"

"Yeah," Payne answered. "I'd like to see him spend a little time in your Nashville hellhole."

"Great!" Lang and Morgan shared a look. "Can you guys be back here in the morning about ten? We'll put the wire on Skeeter and send you in. We'll be right out side, listening."

*

Despite the objections from Rusti and Lisa, Payne and Skeeter arrived at the Sheriff's office at ten sharp. Skeeter watched closely as they taped the wire on his hairless chest. "Man, this is just like the movies."

"Let's hope it has a happy endin," Payne muttered.

Payne's Jeep followed the unmarked car and parked outside the red brick building housing Sure-Star Publishing. "Testin, testin," Skeeter whispered. He waved at the two detectives until they signaled. "Payne, ya just let me do the talkin."

"Ya usually do."

Joyce looked over her glasses. "Not you two again."

"I need to talk to Roger Durwood," Payne started.

"I don't believe Mr. Durwood is expecting either of you."

"Am I gonna have to say somethin about your fat ass again?" Skeeter asked, and laid both hands flat on her desk.

Durwood saw them and rushed out his door to greet them. "Well, if it ain't Payne McCarty."

"Nice suit." Skeeter grinned. "What'd ya do? Steal it from Buck Owens? I really like purple on ya. Looks real good." Skeeter nudged Payne. "Don't it?"

"Payne, I've almost been expectin ya. Come on in. I do believe I owe ya an apology," Durwood said. He waved them into his office. "I'm sorry about our little misunderstandin on your first visit."

"Not as sorry as you're gonna be when he sues your ass off." Skeeter pounded his fist on Durwood's desk.

"Payne, do we have to include your little smart-ass friend in this meetin?" Payne took his seat. "He is a smart-ass. I give ya that." He spoke to Skeeter. "Would ya please sit down? I'll handle this."

Durwood leaned back in his chair and folded his arms. "What's on your mind?"

"Money. The same thing that was on my mind the last time I was here."

"Nashville's a small town. Rumor has it that you're already gettin paid royalties for your song. I don't see where I owe ya anything further."

"Screw the royalties." Payne set his jaw and leaned forward. "I'm after a piece of your ass. You're a thief, and from what I hear, a murderer. Ya owe me for my trouble and ten days in jail."

"Or what? You're gonna sue me?" Durwood laughed.

"No, I ain't gonna sue ya. I'm figurin on just kickin your ass till some money falls out."

Durwood sprang out of his chair and slammed his fists on his desk. "Now ya look here. Do ya think that just because ya married Rusti King, you've got the right to come in here and threaten me?" he yelled.

Payne lunged from his chair. His right fist connected with Durwood's nose. The blow sent him reeling backwards into his leather chair.

"Ooh," Skeeter snickered, "that had to hurt."

Durwood wiped the blood from his nose. "I'll have your ass for that," he muttered. "Expect a lawsuit. Big time."

"That's it?" Skeeter laughed. "That's all?" He looked at Payne. "Hell, Payne, I figured he'd shoot ya for that. Like he did that ol boy that helped him steal your song."

"Hell, I didn't shoot him. Thought about it though. Hey, this is a tough bidness. You boys need to learn that. That's exactly what I told Charlie. Cops got nothin on me or I wouldn't be sittin here." Durwood wiped more blood oozing from his swelling nose. He reached for his desk drawer.

Skeeter sprang to his feet. "Watch him, Payne," Skeeter ordered, moving around Durwood's desk.

"Hell, I'm just gettin a Kleenex." Skeeter relaxed, giving Roger the split second he needed to pull a black revolver out of his drawer.

"Shit!" Skeeter raised his hands in the air. "Nice *gun*," he said, praying the wire was working. "Payne I told ya he'd *shoot* ya for that. Hey, is that the same *gun* ya used on Charlie?"

"Do I look stupid?"

Lang and Morgan left the car with their weapons drawn and charged down the sidewalk and up the steps to the second floor.

"Ya don't really think I'm gonna answer that honestly. Not with a *gun* pointed at me, do ya?" Skeeter glanced at Payne.

Payne raised his hands when Durwood pointed the gun in his direction. "Keep your seat, cowboy." Durwood stood, waving the gun back and forth between the two. "Midget, you move back to your chair."

"Now look, Durwood," Payne pleaded. "We were outta line here. Ya don't need the gun. Just let us go. Ya made your point. I won't be back."

Joyce screamed when Lang and Morgan busted through the door of Sure-Star Publishing, wielding their pistols. "Gun!" Morgan yelled, and opened fire. The wall of glass shattered. From their seats Payne and Skeeter watched Durwood stagger backwards. Three shots to his chest.

"Anybody hurt?" Lang yelled, entering the office.

Skeeter stood, carefully picking off a few pieces of glass from his cowboy hat. He glanced at Payne. "We're fine, but I don't think ol Durwood's feelin worth a damn."

"Dead." Morgan announced checking for a pulse.

"Damn it, Skeeter!" Payne yelled. "I oughta shoot ya myself. Just had to keep talkin didn't ya?"

"Hell, I wasn't the one who broke his nose. You're the one that got him pissed off!"

"Hey!" Lang yelled at them. "Knock it off! You're both lucky to be alive. We didn't intend for you to push him *that* hard."

"Are we done here?" Skeeter asked. He opened his shirt and yanked off the wire.

The detectives exchanged glances and nodded at each other. "Yeah," they said simultaneously.

Closing the door behind them, Payne started in on Skeeter as they descended the musty stairwell. "We'll do it, he says. Can I wear the wire? Can I wear the wire? This is just like the movies. Shit! Skeeter, we coulda been killed."

"Damn, Payne. Just settle down. The way I see it, right now, we're both square with the world." Skeeter grinned and slapped Payne on his lower back.
"And quit slappin me on the back so damn hard!"
"Well, excuse the hell outta me." Skeeter slid into the seat. "Payne?"
"What?" he snapped.
"I got an idea on the way to Tennessee."
"Oh, shit." Payne started the Jeep. "I really don't wanna hear it," he said, and popped the clutch.
"Ya ever considered investin in racehorses? There's big money if ya win."
"I said, I don't wanna hear it."
"Okay. Never mind."
The two drove in silence down 16th Avenue. Passing by the stately buildings on Music Row, it finally hit Payne. He had made it. Payne glanced at Skeeter. His friend was looking away. Payne recalled the night in San Antonio, when they had toasted to Nashville gold and Kentucky roses. And to good friends. He hit the brakes and jerked the wheel. The faded red Jeep with Texas tags slid to a stop along the curb. "What kinda racehorses?"
"Thoroughbreds. I could train em and we could ... "

ABOUT THE AUTHOR

Born and raised in barren West Texas, Dekker Malone fell in love with the Texas Hill Country during the spring of 1972. That was the year of the big flood, the one that killed and uprooted. And the year Dekker began learning to play guitar. The year he wrote his first song.

Dekker was attending college there; one that was divided into two major ethnic groups ... cowboys (also called rednecks and kickers, short for shit-kickers) and hippies (also called longhairs, freaks, and dopers). The two diametrical groups even had their own sides in the dorm cafeteria. But Dekker, like his music, was somewhere in the middle. And that worked fine, most of the time, unless there was a food fight between the cowboys and hippies, or later in life, when he began sending his music to publishers. Then he was pelted from both sides.

In 1985, Dekker returned from West Texas to the Hill Country just long enough to marry his bride, the daughter of a racehorse trainer. The wedding was held in a bend of Lake Dunlap, beneath the shade of enormous oak and pecan trees that had somehow managed to survive the flood of '72. There was beer and Bar-B-Q.

Dekker's Hill Country bride, Rosanna, is a published author of children's literature. They live in the country, outside a sleepy West Texas town, with their children, horses, cats, and two golden retrievers.

This book may be ordered from
Booklocker.com

Correspondence for the author should be addressed to:
Dekker Malone
P.O. Box 93534
Lubbock, Texas 79493-3534

Visit the author's web site for a sneak preview of the sequel

KENTUCKY ROSES

Red Phillips was released from prison in the year 2000,
time off for good behavior.

Printed in the United States
2896